I0593694

Adelina Cohnfeldt Mrs. Lust

A Tent of Grace

By Adelina Cohnfeldt Lust

Adelina Cohnfeldt Mrs. Lust

A Tent of Grace
By Adelina Cohnfeldt Lust

ISBN/EAN: 9783337002022

Printed in Europe, USA, Canada, Australia, Japan

Cover: Foto ©Andreas Hilbeck / pixelio.de

More available books at **www.hansebooks.com**

A TENT OF GRACE

BY ADELINA COHNFELDT LUST

BOSTON AND NEW YORK
HOUGHTON, MIFFLIN AND COMPANY
The Riverside Press, Cambridge
1899

A TENT OF GRACE

CHAPTER I

"SIR, have you any kid or goat skins to sell?"

It was early November, but already wintry and cold along the beautiful Rhine. Pastor Feldern, digging up some belated geraniums in the trim parsonage garden, half turned round to look at the speaker through his silver-rimmed spectacles. It was a young girl, probably about thirteen years of age, with the angularity of hobbledehoyhood. Her faded blue print gown, evidently outgrown long ago, reached a little below her knees. She wore the peasant's wooden shoes, and an old gray shawl was pinned tightly under her chin. A long crook stick with several small pelts dangling from it swung over her right shoulder.

"If thou wilt go round to the kitchen door," said the pastor, "Babbett will tell thee."

She passed him with a curtsy, swinging her petticoats as she went. Yes, Babbett had some skins. She had saved them for some time in the old smoke-house. Now she went to bring them out for the small merchant's inspection.

"H'm," said the girl, pouting her lips disdain-

fully, as she turned over the skins the old peasant
woman spread out on the graveled walk. But
there was a covetous gleam in the downcast eyes.
She slid the stick from her shoulders, the better
to inspect her wares.

"H'm, indeed," echoed Babbett wrathfully;
"look at them, wilt thou, before thou mak'st
h'm."

"It does not need a magnifying glass to see
they are worth next to nothing. How much wilt
thou take for them?"

"If they are worth nothing, I won't cheat thee
into buying them. Come, hand them back."

"Yes, take them and put them in brine, and
thyself with them. Mayst thou wait for a pur-
chaser as long as thou hast waited for a sweet-
heart."

"Sweethearts thou mayst get in plenty, thou
Jewish jade. But none but the executioner will
ever marry thee."

"When he cuts off thy head for a foul-mouthed
old witch, I'll dance at thy funeral in a pair of
brand-new clogs."

"Wilt thou go, or shall I give thee the other
end of the broom?"

"Well, for charity's sake and to relieve thee of
them, — here's two kreutzer apiece."

"Two what? Holy Father! Be off, I tell
thee; thou and thy Jewish impudence. Dost
think I never sold skins before?"

"Honestly now, are they worth more? Look
at this — and that — and there."

"This, and that, and there? Thou hast wet the palms of thy hands and crumpled them up like parchment. They are as good and fine and perfect skins as ever were sold between the Neckar and the Rhine."

"Three kreutzer apiece, and this one thrown in. Convince thyself if it is not damaged."

The old woman spluttered with wrath. "Three pig's feet for a charm and their blood to sprinkle in thy synagogue. Thou shalt not have them, thou skinflint Jewess."

"Then keep them for a shroud, and mayst thou need it quickly," retorted the girl, as she shouldered her stick and made a great show to be off. But the skins were in the tail of her eye, and she carelessly jingled the kreutzers in her pocket. The sound decided Babbett. She was as anxious to sell as the other was to buy, and equally as anxious to get the best of the bargain. "Six kreutzer apiece and thou mayst have them," she said.

"Now if it were the price of thy friendship, I'd think it cheap and gladly give it thee. But this is business. Therefore, two kreutzer apiece. Here is the money. Take it, and do so quickly, before I repent of the bargain."

"Thou child of Sodom and Gomorrah! thou saidst three kreutzer just now."

"Did I? Oh, very well. Here are thy three kreutzer, and this skin thou must throw in."

"Throw thyself into the Rhine! Now thou shalt not have them at all. I'll sooner make a present of them to Schmul, who'll soon be passing this way."

"Alas, poor Schmul!" said the girl, in a tone of deep commiseration; "thou hast not heard, then, what has happened to him?"

Babbett dropped the skins, which she had gathered up in great anger. She was instantly devoured by curiosity.

"What has happened to him, then? Do open thy mouth and speak."

"He has broken his leg."

Babbett's jaws parted in a wide gasp as she squatted down on her skins.

"Broken!— the poor child! and he has neither father nor mother."

"Well, for that matter, neither have I. Gently, Babbett; let me draw forth the pelts."

"When did it happen? How did he come to do it? Yes, yes, here they are."

"And none the better for thy pressing. Listen thou, can I have them?"

"For three kreutzer? No. But go on; tell me how it all came about."

"He was trying to leap a fence, you understand, — this skin surely is somewhat damaged."

"Nothing is damaged but thy imagination. Go on, then, do. How long wilt thou keep me in suspense?"

"He was leaping a fence, when his boot caught on a big rusty nail, — three kreutzer and this one thrown in. Take it, or leave it. My time has been wasted too long already."

"Four kreutzer and nothing thrown in! What! Thou wilt rob me like this, thou arch jade? Here, then, take them. Now wilt thou at last tell me about Schmul?"

"Thanks, nicely, thou dear Babbett. One, two, three, four, five, six," — she slung the pelts on her stick as she counted; "here, take thy ten kreutzer; my blessing shall surely bring thee a rich percentage. Five skins at two kreutzer apiece and one thrown in. Auf Wiedersehen."

"Come back, this instant! Three kreutzer apiece, thou saidst, — three kreutzer. Thou forsworn Jewess, dost take me for a fool? And Schmul, — what of him, poor boy?"

"Schmul?" asked the girl, with an indescribably droll air of astonishment, as she shouldered her stick and carefully edged further away from the old woman; "what of him?"

"His leg, his leg!" bawled Babbett, goaded beyond endurance in her baffled curiosity.

"His one sound leg and his two sound legs send you their best compliments. When last seen — and that was early this morning — they were taking him across the Nassau frontier as fast as they could travel. You will no doubt see him soon. Remember me most prettily to him, and tell him how nicely I forestalled him."

She cleverly dodged the broom the enraged Babbett sent flying after her. The pastor, who had been an amused and edified listener, slightly inclined his head as she passed him with another respectful curtsy. Then she blithely swung herself out of the gate into the village street.

CHAPTER II

SCHOOL was just out. Like a pack of hounds at full cry the village youth came trooping down the High Street. As they saw the girl with the crook stick dangling from her shoulder, they gave a shout of recognition and immediately surrounded her.

"See there, if this is n't Jette. How do, Skinnymelink?"

"Skingirl, where hast been all this time?"

"In her own skin, of course."

"Let her alone, thou tow-headed Hans. She is a wild goat and butts like fury."

"Holy Moses, Jewess! Thou hast made a good trade somewhere. Thy stick can hardly hold all the pelts."

"Look, thou Skinnymelink, hast any marbles?"

"Hast thou?" she asked suspiciously.

"I asked if thou hadst any," persisted Hans, the tow-headed.

"First show me thine," she retorted.

"Well, here are mine." "And mine." "And mine."

She looked at the well-filled bag each boy dangled in her face. Deep into her own pocket she dived. Her hand came out empty as she said, "That thieving Schmul won all mine. But if each of you will lend me one, I 'll give it back if I come out winners."

The yokels scratched their heads under their

caps and looked foolishly at each other. Said Hans sagely, "And if thou dost not come out winners?"

"But she will," said his sister Gretel, who had a strong cast in her eye; "she 'll cheat thee out of every one."

"Perhaps I would," said Jette, "if I looked like thee, both ways at once."

The boys laughed derisively. Gretel, who was tall and strong, made a furious grab at her. But Jette, during her one year of vagabond life, had graduated in all the tricks of the most accomplished gamin, and could writhe and twist and turn like the cleverest of them.

"Go home," she said, with a mocking sweep of her hand; "go straighten thy conscience with thy vision before thou wouldst set others' straight. And now stand aside, if thou canst. We have no further use for thee."

Gretel glowered angrily upon her, but she remained, jealously watchful of her brother's interest. A ring was quickly formed. The boys put their books upon the ground. But Jette retained firm hold of her stick. It dangled from her shoulder with its suspended load, as she knelt down and knocked out the marbles one after the other, with an accuracy of aim which first astonished, then chagrined the boys. As with each dexterous shot their stock diminished, they set up a protesting howl. There were perhaps a dozen of them, ranging all the way from seven to fifteen. Big, brawny fellows some of them were, who did a man's work in the harvest field, and had all the muscle and traditional feeding capacity of the model ploughboy; broad in the girth and long of limb, as stupid, thick-headed, and numskulled as rustics remote from·travel and all intercourse with the outside world possibly could be. Fed upon superstition, local influence, and family traditions, they were ready, like their elders, to let prejudice run riot, at any and every provocation.

"Come, Jewess, thou 'rt not playing fair," said a big hulking fellow, as again her accurate shot sent the ring of marbles flying in all directions.

She jumped to her feet, flushed and disheveled, the pelts dangling from the stick, bobbing up and down in her excitement.

"What!" she screamed, "thou darest say that? Haven't I knocked out each game fair and square? Say, thou, haven't I, now?" She thumped each boy on the chest, as she went the rounds asking this question.

"I 've lost all my marbles," whined a little flaxen-haired fellow, as he prodded his knuckles in his eyes.

"So have I." "And I." "And I." "Mine are all gone, too," chorused the rest.

"I told you so," said Gretel, who now saw a way of getting her innings. "I said she 'd cheat you all out of every one."

She advanced upon Jette, who, flushed and elated, was slipping her winnings into a stout leather bag already well filled.

"Give him back his marbles," she commanded,

pointing to the little whiner. For answer the
• girl drew the mouth of the bag well together and
tightly wound round the string several times.
Then with a thud she dropped it into her pocket.

"He can win them back next time I come," she
said, balancing her stick. They were on the
outskirts of the village. On one side stretched
the dusty chaussée, down which the post-chaise
occasionally rattled on its way to Cologne, or
when guests visited the village. On the other
stretched a beautiful woods, through which a foot-
path conducted to the pastor's orchard and vegetable garden. A stream clear as crystal, one of
the numerous tributaries of the Rhine, wound in
and out among the trees lifting their bare
branches to the sky. In the spring the whole
village turned out to wash their linen in this pure
and limpid water, and the children came to bathe
in the hot days of summer. The girl turned
towards the chaussée, but Gretel struck her a
sounding blow in the face.

"Thou dost not stir from this spot until thou
givest him back his marbles," she said.

The Jewess spat in her face. "Thou cat! not
one shall he have, not one."

Then they all fell upon her. She kicked and
struggled and scratched, and every muscle in her
body worked in vigorous resistance. She made a
little run backward, doubled herself up, ducked
down, and with a sudden lurch butted the biggest
bully full in the stomach, so that he fell sprawling
upon the ground, howling with pain. She was as

fleet as a roe, and had she been willing to abandon
the miserable crook stick, she might have escaped.
But before she had fairly time to turn around, they
had seized hold of it. They caught her by her
long black braids and swung her round till she
could hear each individual hair crack. The palms
of her hands were gashed before the stick was torn
from her despairing clutch. They brought it
down upon her shoulders and limbs till it clung
there, slippery with blood. The girl she had spat
at clawed her face till the eyes shone out of a raw
and shapeless mass. They trampled upon, they
kicked her, they scattered her clothing in a thousand shreds to the wind. They seized upon the
skins, and tearing them apart with their teeth,
sent them flying after her clothing. One last
wail she gave when she saw this. Maybe the
mother's spirit hovering near her forsaken child
caught it and wafted it to the living; for while
the tiger crew bent over her with the blood instinct rampant beyond control, a lusty thud came
with a vigorous thwack upon their backs and
limbs. A howl, a startled cry, "His reverence,
the Herr Pastor," a hurried shambling of feet,
and the trees with their gaunt bare branches
crackled in the wind above the pastor, where he
knelt beside the bleeding form of the maltreated
child.

CHAPTER III

THE Frau Pastorin sat in the south window
stitching. Pure white bands they were, of finest
linen. Every thread in that precious linen had
passed through the Frau Pastorin's own soft,
dimpled hands. The flax was grown in her own
fields. She had carded and spun it in the long
winter evenings. Then she had it woven into the
finest of weaves by the village loom. Babbett,
the old peasant servant, who had accompanied her
to the parsonage from her father's rich homestead
in far-away Pomerania, washed it in the clear,
limpid woodland stream, and laid it to bleach in
the parsonage orchard, where the perfume of the
white clover refreshed the weary senses of the
traveler, as the mail coach rattled by. Whiter or
finer stitched bands than adorned the shirts of the
Herr Pastor and the Herr and Frau Pastorin's son,
Herr Friedrich Feldern, familiarly called Fritz,
now cramming for his doctor's examination at the
University of Bonn, were not to be found in the
whole Rhine province. The Frau Pastorin was
justly proud of her stock of fine white linen. Some
of it came from her great-grandmother, and but
for its pious associations, was as good for use as
when that now peacefully reposing dame had laid
it out to bleach, her own self. The Frau Pastorin's linen closet was catalogued in strict regard to
social etiquette. On the topmost shelves, as befitted
their quality, the embroidered, rosemary-perfumed

'company linen, distinguished by different colored satin ribbon, tied in neat rosettes, reposed in aristocratic exclusiveness. Then came the middling class, which was only for occasional use, distinguished by less elaborate ribbon. Finally came the every-day wear-and-tear stock, which was not ornamented at all, except for the exquisite neatness of grouping, and marked in the red linen sampler stitch, dear to the hearts of our grandmothers. Babbett's kitchen and glass towels piled up the lowest shelves, each article tabbed with a neat loop of linen tape, and marked the same as the rest. This closet, with its exquisite array of rosemary-scented linen, was the Frau Pastorin's jewel casket, the heirloom which was to descend to Fritz, as in part it had descended to her. It was the monument which every good German housewife of those times — fifty odd years ago — reared to her memory, by which her habits and housewifely qualities were judged.

As the Frau Pastorin sat complacently stitching in the resplendent afterglow of the departing sun, she was a tonic for the weary soul to look upon. Time certainly had been a-nodding since she was young. Her cheeks were as rounded, as rosy, and as smooth as a baby's. The dimple in her chin came and went with the calm placidity of her thoughts. A white mull cap, adorned with broad lilac satin ribbons, sat lightly upon her thick ash-blond hair, parted Madonna fashion in the middle, from which it rippled behind her rosy ears into broad plaits, wound around the back

of her head.   A young girl may be beautiful by
virtue of her grace, her youth, her vitality.   The
Frau Pastorin's beauty was the matronly queenli-
ness of middle age, with the frolics of young girlhood still lurking in her dimples; the gayety of
a heart which had never come into contact with
anything unclean, and a purity of habit which
shone on her brow and beamed from her well-
opened gray eyes.   The impression she made was
that of immaculate purity.   If ever in God's
world there lived a being who practiced "cleanliness next to godliness," in the very spirit of the
letter, it was the Frau Pastorin, not alone in her
own personal habits, but in all her surroundings.
Everything in the parsonage, from attic to cellar,
smelled sweet and shone resplendent with purity;
and the Frau Pastorin's mind was as clean as her
body.   Filth, whether mental or physical, was
abhorrent to her.   She held that all vice had
its stronghold in dirt.   There would be no need
of doctors or hospitals, if only every one would be
clean.   "We cannot all be princes in station or
wealth," she was wont to say, "but every one may
be a prince in cleanliness and behavior."   When
a beggar came to her door, she first gave him a
piece of soap and a towel.   When he had made
lavish use of both at the yard pump, he got his fill
of bread and meat and wine.   If the women stood
gossiping at their doors and the Frau Pastorin was
spied coming down the street, they would make a
hasty dash for their young, and immediately their
howls of protest made music in the distance, as

their faces were scrubbed and they were quickly hustled into clean pinafores. For the prevention of every ill flesh is heir to, the Frau Pastorin had but one universal remedy, — it was cleanliness.

The pleasing twilight was fast fading into dusk. The Frau Pastorin, mindful of her eyesight, folded up her work and put it into her large wicker work-basket. The broad window-sill was filled with myrtle, rosemary, and jasmine, and monthly roses. Since Fritz was grown up, and no longer in need of her motherly care, these flowers were the Frau Pastorin's children. Strong, sturdy, and healthy they were, perfuming the whole house with their fragrant blossoms. For miles around, the myrtle in the Frau Pastorin's window furnished the wedding crowns for the peasant maidens. It was considered to bring luck to the wearer. Everything that came from the parsonage savored of a benediction.

The Frau Pastorin plucked a leaf here and a leaf there, then looked out of the window into the gathering darkness. The Herr Pastor had slipped out, as was his wont, after drinking his afternoon coffee and eating his cake. He had lounged forth in his down-at-heel slippers and his "Schlafrock," with his shabby black velvet skull-cap, which he always wore in the house in cold weather, pushed back on his scant gray hairs. It was growing cold. He should have been home long ago in his warm, comfortable Stube, where a roaring fire leaped in the large Herrenhuter stove, and the fine silver sand on the snow-white floor glistened like flecks of stray moonbeams. The Herr Pastor's chess-table, with the red and black chess-men, stood just as he had left it in front of the cushioned settle in the warm ingle-nook. Surely it was more inviting within than without. The Frau Pastorin wondered what could keep him.

As she continued to peer into the darkness, she saw him staggering along, bearing a heavy burden in his arms. Another rescued sheep, she thought, with commiseration. They often tumbled down from the hill where they were browsing into the stream below. Many a four-footed patient had the Herr Pastor nursed back to health and re-stored to its owner, a rich cattle-dealer in the vil-lage, who received back his property as a matter of course. This sheep must be terribly heavy, she thought. The Herr Pastor could hardly stag-ger along. She hastily called to Babbett, and flinging her shawl across her shoulders, went to meet him. It was time. Unable to proceed fur-ther, panting, he had braced himself against a stout tree, for the houses were sparingly scattered. No one had seen him. Lights were lit and cur-tains drawn long ago. The villagers were at their Abendbrod-supper. Babbett came clatter-ing behind her mistress in her wooden shoes.

"Help thy master," said the Frau Pastorin, "quickly. He has rescued another sheep, and the weight is more than he can bear."

Babbett gave an amazed cry. "'T is a two-legged one this time," she said; "the same as you and I, mistress."

The Herr Pastor held Jette in his arms. Alone
and unassisted he had carried her from the woods.
Her hair, matted with blood, had coiled itself like
a cobra around his throat. Great streaks of blood
smeared his face and hands. He motioned Babbett to take hold of the child's limbs. He was
too exhausted to speak. The Frau Pastorin,
greatly troubled, led the way to the back entrance
into the kitchen. They laid the unconscious child
on the wooden settle. The light from the lamp
fell upon her battered face, closed eyes, and
bruised limbs.

"Holy Jesus," cried Babbett, "'t is Jette, the
skin girl."

The Frau Pastorin sickened with horror. "Is
— is she dead?" she faltered.

"She may be saved, I think, if something is
done for her, and quickly," said the Herr Pastor;
"the village youth fell upon and maltreated her.
As you see her now, I found her in the woods.
They were beating her to death. I could not
leave her there alone, and there was no one to
help me. So I carried her home the best way
I could."

While he spoke, the Frau Pastorin had been
busy tearing up strips of fine old linen. Babbett
placed a soft sponge, some towels, and a pot of
ointment on the kitchen table, taking care first to
spread papers over its immaculate surface. Then
she lugged in a big tub. She knew as well as
if her mistress had spoken what would be the first
preliminary. The huge copper boiler stood on

the stove, filled to the brim with hot water. It was always there, summer and winter, ready for use at a moment's notice.

The Frau Pastorin took down a large pair of shears. "Papachen," she said cheerfully, "do thou go and change thy linen and clothing. Thou art sadly in need of it, I assure thee. Go to the cupboard and refresh thyself. *This* sheep thou mayst leave to me."

The Herr Pastor was tall and gaunt, with something of a stoop in his angular shoulders. He bent down to kiss his wife on the forehead. Usually he kissed her on the lips. But in his present state he knew she would not have liked it. He went, and left the two women to their task.

CHAPTER IV

JETTE got over her hurts in gallant style. The Frau Pastorin's skillful treatment and her own hardy constitution battled successfully against what at first seemed to be a very hopeless case indeed. True, it would take some time before the swollen and disfigured features would resume their natural shape, or the discolored skin its usual fairness. And worst of all, the shock to her nervous system remained. The horrors she had passed through became a perpetual nightmare. Towards dawn she would start up, screaming in terror. The whole scene of murderous attack was acted over again. She fancied they had her by the

throat, and were choking her to death. It was
a very trying time indeed to the household at the
parsonage. The healthy glow in the Frau Pastorin's cheek paled to sallowness, and the stoop in
the Herr Pastor's shoulders intensified. Time
and the security of a permanent home would, they
knew, remedy this evil. The Herr Pastor, with
his head sunk on his breast, moved his chessmen
mechanically. He was thinking long and deeply.
The child was convalescing rapidly; but she refused to get up. She clung, screaming, to the
bedclothes, imploring them not to thrust her out
to be torn to pieces. The Herr Pastor pushed
the chessboard from him. The red and black
factions which had just stood pitted against each
other in fiercest hostility tumbled to the sanded
floor. The Herr Pastor had made up his mind.

He went upstairs to the whitewashed attic room.
A small stove stood in the middle of the snow-
white boards, diffusing a grateful warmth. Upon
the feather bed lay Jette. The bandages had
been removed from the raw surface of her face.
The new skin was forming nicely in patches here
and there. At one time it was feared she would
be scarred for life, the sharp nails had so cruelly
lacerated the flesh. This had been happily averted
by the Frau Pastorin's healing salves and oint-
ments. She predicted confidently that, given a
reasonable time for the swelling and discoloration
to subside, no disfigurement would mar the child's
natural appearance. If the Almighty so willed,
she might thrive in perfect health and beauty.

Jette reclined on her pillow, gently stroking Minka, the great parsonage cat, who lay on a rush-bottomed chair near the bed. Minka, who followed the Frau Pastorin all over the house like a dog, had gravely shared her duties during the girl's illness. She was left in charge when her mistress was called downstairs, or during the intervals the patient slept. As soon as she stirred, Minka tiptoed to the partially open door and meowed lustily till some one came running up. She would sit at the foot of the bed, gravely eyeing the patient, and when she moaned, sympathetically lick her feet. Minka seemed to have a proprietary right in the girl, and except for her meals, spent all her spare time in the sick-room. When the Herr Pastor entered, she jumped down, rubbed herself against his legs, and politely surrendered her seat to him. He sat down, looking at the child with his near-sighted brown eyes. His clear-cut Roman features were softened by the frame of finest gray hair, which, brushed straight from his high, broad forehead, fell behind his ears and touched his shoulders.

"Thou art better," he said, in his strong, resonant voice.

"Not well enough to get up," she said distrustfully.

"Thou wilt not get strong as long as thou liest there," he said. "See how beautifully the sun shines. And the ponds are covered with ice. Canst thou skate?"

She nodded. "I don't want to go out," she said.

"Is there no one belonging to thee who will be uneasy at thy absence?" he asked.

She shook her head. "No one. My father is dead. My stepfather turned me out of doors to get my own living. He took everything belonging to my mother and went no one knows where. All but this," she added, drawing a small bag, suspended round her neck by a ribbon, from underneath her night-jacket; "my mother gave it to me secretly on her death-bed, charging me never to part with it."

The Herr Pastor opened the small chamois bag and drew forth a seal emblazoned with a coat of arms. There was an inscription in Latin, which he could not very well decipher.

"Whose was this?" he asked.

"My father's. It came to him from his father, who got it from my great-grandfather, and so on, from one generation to the other, my mother said. My father's people were Spanish, hundreds of years ago. They were rich and powerful in their own country. Then a very wicked king and queen, who wanted them to change their religion, took all their land and riches from them and drove them from the country."

"Where did thy father live?"

She jerked her thumb over her shoulders. "Over yonder in Nassau. He was rabbi there. He died when I was eight years old. Then my mother married my stepfather. He was very different from my father. He was a very common man, a Pollack," she said disdainfully.

"Thou shouldst not scorn a man because of his country," said the pastor, who knew nothing of the prejudice the Jews have against those of their own faith born on the frontier between Germany and Poland, who are generally stigmatized by the name of "Pollack;" "the disdain of the conqueror always clings to an oppressed race. Since when is it thy mother died?"

"A year ago. I was just twelve, and getting on famously at school. My mother was hardly buried when my stepfather told me to go and take service somewhere, as I was big and strong enough to earn my own living. Then he sold the house, took everything he could lay his hands upon, and went away."

"What didst thou do?"

"There was a poor boy my mother had befriended, Schmul Itzig by name. He supported himself buying and selling small pelts. He took me into partnership. At first I was very timid and afraid. My mother had always kept me at home, and said I should go away to boarding-school, so that by the time I was grown up, I could be a governess. Schmul said it was better tramping the highway one's own master than working one's self crooked in some big family for one's board, and getting ill-treated besides. So I soon got used to it. Then I found out that Schmul cheated me, and having saved a little money, set up on my own account."

The pastor softly stroked Minka, who had perched herself upon his knee. The spirit of her

father's race, he thought, was in this child who
had so pluckily fought life's battle alone. Then
he asked, closely watching her, —

"What made the village youth ill-treat thee?"

She shuddered, clenched her teeth, and closed
her eyes. "Because I am a Jewess," she said.

The pastor shook his head. "Oh, no," he
said, "but because thou wouldst not return them
their own."

"But it was not their own, your reverence. I
had won the marbles in perfectly fair play. It
was strictly a matter of business. Friendship is
one thing, business another," she persisted, repeating the formula Schmul had taught her.

"Why should they beat thee because thou art
a Jewess?" asked the pastor.

She looked puzzled. "I don't know," she
finally said; "but this I do know, that they take
by foul means what they cannot get by fair.
There are more of them, and stronger than we
are; that is why they beat us and rob us, the
dogs! May lightning destroy them!" she added,
grating her teeth angrily.

"Didst thou hear these things in thy home?"
asked the pastor.

"Your reverence! no, indeed. My father,
bless his memory, was gentle and kind, always
studying his books. Everybody loved him.
While he was alive, my mother went about the
house singing, smiling, and laughing. She did
not laugh or sing much when she married that
Pollack," she said vindictively.

"Then you have picked up all this knowledge on the highway?" said the pastor.

"Schmul told me, your reverence. Didn't they beat his parents to death over yonder in Nassau? Yes, indeed. Some man in the village owed his father money. He would not pay it back. Schmul's father said if he would not pay, he must give up his house and cow and furniture. Then the man went around to every house in the place. At night when the Jews were asleep, they came and smashed their windows and broke in their doors. Those whose doors they could not break in, they dragged through the broken windows with reapers' hooks fastened to long ropes. Schmul saw his father dragged from his bed with a reaper's hook thrust through his chin. They took all the money they found in the house, then set fire to it. If Schmul had not fled to the woods, they would have killed him too. Next day the gendarmes came and took them all to prison. May their bones rot there! But Schmul's parents were dead. He was a homeless, outcast orphan."

The pastor still softly stroked Minka. His hand trembled. He shuddered once or twice when he looked at the excited child.

"Thou hast no one in the world belonging to thee, then, no one who would have guarded thee from such a companion?" he said.

She shook her head. "No one at all. My mother was an orphan like myself. Somewhere in the world, perhaps, some relatives of my father's may be living. But I don't know how they are called, or where they may be found. I am all alone."

"Wouldst thou not," said the pastor cheerfully, "like to be adopted into some good home, where thou couldst be taught cleanly, self-respecting habits, and grow up into a useful, happy life?"

"I would doubtless have to work till my back grew round and crooked," she said distrustfully.

"Thou wouldst be put only to such tasks as are suitable to thy age and strength," said the pastor. "We all have to work, — each in his own way. 'T is the only thing which gives a purpose to life. It is not seemly that a child of thy age should roam the highway at the mercy of everybody. A girl, especially. Ugh! Thou dost not know of the frightful dangers lying in wait for thee. Happily thou never shalt know. Thou wouldst not like to shoulder thy stick and go forth again as thou hast been doing?"

He was sorry when he had said it. She wrung her hands and moaned pitifully.

"Not that, your reverence, not that. Please, *please* do not thrust me among those wild beasts again. I am not well; indeed, I cannot get up. Oh, Minka, dear Minka, what shall I do?"

"Thou shalt stay here," said the pastor; "thou shalt have a home here, where it has long been desolate for a child's voice since my only son went away. But thou must be good and obedient. In this house no strife has ever entered. Thou must lay aside thy wild wishes, thy intemperance of speech. Docile and gentle as befits thy sex thou

must become. That is all that will be required
of thee."

"Stay here?" she said. "Stay here?" she repeated incredulously. "But thou — dear God, you
are Christians!"

"Here," said the pastor, "thou wilt grow up
without knowing of any distinction. Neither must
thou ever mention it. Thou shalt live strictly
according to the requirements of thy religion.
Trust me; I know all about it. Thou canst have
thy own pots and pans, thy own dishes. Thy own
meats thou canst buy and prepare thyself. Thou
shalt keep thy Sabbath and thy holidays. Aided
and encouraged thou wilt be in the strict dis-
charge of thy religious duties. So long as thou
respectest them thyself, thou wilt find others to
do so. Don't cry, my child. Have I refused
shelter to a stray sheep, and should I refuse it to
thee? I think," he added, with a twinkle in his
near-sighted brown eyes, "thou wilt feel like getting up now."

Downstairs he said, "The child is better, and
will soon be about again. She will remain here
for good and all. Thou wilt teach her to grow
up into a good woman, eh, Liebste? And see thou
here, Babbett, the child's nerves are terribly
shaken. Thou must have patience with her when
she assists thee in thy duties until she grows quite
strong again."

"We have everything in the house," said Babbett, with a puzzled look, "but nerves. If she
must have any of that, your reverence had better

send word with the carrier next time he starts for Cologne."

The Herr Pastor smiled. "Let it be, my good Babbett," he said good-naturedly, tapping her on the shoulder. "I don't think we will commission the carrier this time."

The Frau Pastorin said nothing. In her placid, contented life the first disturbing element had come. She felt that never again would it be as it had been before.

CHAPTER V

So Jette remained at the parsonage. And the villagers called her "Pastor's Jette." She was adopted into his household; she was part and parcel of his belongings. That was enough. Once a fortnight she went to Neustadt, six good miles from Neukirch, — as the village was called, — to the rabbi for religious instruction. Punctually at sundown every Friday evening she rested till the sun went down again the following night. She bought her own meats, killed according to the requirements of her faith, and prepared them in the vessels set apart for her own use. When the family took their meals, she sat at a little table by herself. Babbett was inclined to grumble at this, for she looked upon Jette as no better than herself. But, as the Herr Pastor demonstrated to the Frau Pastorin, the child could not acquire proper table manners in the kitchen. She came of good blood, and must be treated accordingly. She had no dowry; her whole fortune consisted in herself. The more attractive she would be when grown up, the better prospect of a good settlement she would have in life. The Frau Pastorin, who, according to the fashion of most German wives, was accustomed to let her husband act for her, readily acquiesced. She had a great deal of practical common sense, and she saw the truth of the pastor's keen perception. It was a little irksome at first to have the strange child sit diffident, shy, and silent at her own little table, but in course of time one gets reconciled to everything. The girl became quiet, tractable, and docile. No one can pass through the valley of the shadow of death without its leaving an impression even on the youngest mind. And though Jette gave no outward sign, — her nights were peaceful, her days cheerful, — the experience she had passed through was graven on her mind and on her heart like molten lead.

Jette being a perversion of Henriette, the Frau Pastorin, who thought it vulgar, scrupulously called her by her full name. The Herr Pastor, who was fond of diminutives as he was of kittens, kisses, and babies, called her Jettchen. And Babbett, who could not all at once get accustomed to regard the vagrant child in the light of respectability, called her Jette. Babbett resented the girl's intrusion into her kitchen, and was very averse to letting her help with any of her household duties. By and by, when Babbett returned

from church on a Sunday and found a hot dinner
nicely prepared, instead of having to bustle about
herself, she grew more reconciled. Jette was
kept busy from morning till night. When her
duties about the house were finished, the Frau
Pastorin taught her the sampler stitch, to knit
and to sew. In the evening she took her spinning-
wheel till it was time to go to bed. But she had
one great compensation. All day Saturday she
could read. The contents of the Herr Pastor's
bookshelves were at her disposal. There she
rioted to her heart's content. Heaven only knows
what that young brain absorbed and brooded over
the rest of the week. Kant, Schlegel, Schiller,
Heine, Goethe, Bulwer, all were mixed up in a
heterogeneous jumble. If the Herr Pastor had
known, his fine silky gray hair would have stood
on end. He thought she confined herself to the
light works of fiction which had been Fritz's own
particular property when he was her age, the
beautiful Rhine legends, works of chivalry, a careful selection of Sir Walter Scott, books of travel,
German history, simple biographies of celebrated
men and women. She saved up her kreutzers and
commissioned Müller, the carrier, with many vows
of secrecy, to buy her a pocket edition of Schiller's
poems. She knew them by heart, but she went
to bed and rose again with this precious little
volume hidden in her breast. The same carrier
brought a liberal supply of books and magazines
once a fortnight to the Herr and Frau Pastorin
from Cologne. That was always a feast day to

Jette. Such books as were thought suitable for her, she was allowed to read. Secretly she devoured them all. Once Babbett found "Ernest Maltravers" under her pillow, and suspecting something wrong, threatened to tell the Frau Pastorin. Babbett, good soul, never read anything herself, except the cards, which she punctually consulted every Friday before going to bed. In a moment of good nature, she had confided this secret to Jette, who was a great deal awestruck by this necromancing. Each Friday night of the new moon she reverentially tiptoed into Babbett's room, where, by the dim light of a tallow dip, they crouched like a pair of conspirators, breathlessly alert for the slightest noise, while they reveled in the dim mysteries of the future. Jette sat shivering at the foot of the bed, wrapped in an old quilt, while Babbett perched on a stool, the cards spread out on a little table before her. Only Minka, who had attached herself to Jette and slept on the rush-bottomed chair near her bed, was the sole witness of these secret conclaves; and Minka, of course, could not tell, and would not if she could. Babbett was perfectly well aware that the Herr and Frau Pastorin would have strongly disapproved of these proceedings. So when she threatened Jette with exposure, that young damsel spiritedly promised to retaliate; whereat complete rout and vanquish of the old peasant woman; and Jette was left in undisturbed possession of her lawless readings.

CHAPTER VI

ABOUT Christmas the Herr Studios, Fritz, the son of the house, came home for the holidays. Like sunrise in May he came, bounding with joyous life, waking the echoes of the staid old parsonage into gay song and laughter. With his student's cap set rakishly upon his thick, fair curls, his guitar slung over his shoulders, he vaulted from the post chaise at the gate, hugged father and mother, who had run out to meet him, and with an arm around each, fairly waltzed them up the graveled path into the house. The warmth of sunshine, the gay abandonment of a happy heart, the infectious joy of life, Fritz brought with him as his companions. His brown eyes — dear, beautiful eyes of velvety softness, his father's eyes without their nearsightedness — danced with fun and the intense enjoyment of existence. He thrummed his guitar, and in his sonorous, deep baritone sang love ditties to his mother. He caught her around the neck twenty times a day, rubbed his cheek — upon which the down of boyhood still lingered — against hers, stroked her white, plump hands, and admired her till she blushed like a schoolgirl. He played chess with his father, and stupefied that clever tactician with a most brilliant draw. From attic to cellar his voice reëchoed in merriment. He kicked up his heels like a colt, challenged the pastor to feats of strength, compared biceps with him, and taught

his mother the Laendler, the new waltz step. He
imitated every actor and actress he had seen, and
he did it in such a droll manner that the tears of
merriment ran down his listeners' cheeks. The
pastor lived over again his own student days when
he stood on guard opposite his son with the foils
grasped in his hand. Into the house came life,
joy, and merriment. The pastor received an
assortment of long-stemmed pipes with immense
china bowls, and the portrait of the king or old
Marshal Blücher on every one of them. For the
Frau Pastorin Fritz brought a handsome sandal-
wood box, lined with a baker's dozen of Maria
Farina, that precious perfume so dear to the
German feminine heart. Babbett, his old nurse
and playmate, was not forgotten. He came into
the kitchen with a gayly checked kerchief pinned
over his shoulders, and a cap with rainbow ribbons perched askew on his head. Fritz was only
twenty, but he was full-grown, broad-chested, and
square-shouldered like a man, as indeed he could
not help being, as everything throve into strength
and beauty under his mother's judicious care. He
surprised the old woman by coming behind her
and putting his hands over her eyes. Then he
jerked her round, and when she saw him, she
screamed, then flopped upon the kitchen chair and
doubled herself up with laughter.

"How dost thou like me?" he asked, smirking
at himself in the little glass over the table.

He took off the cap with a flourish. "'T will
become thee immensely when thou goest to church

on a Sunday," he said, dropping it lightly into her lap. The kerchief followed suit. He had wound a string of colored glass beads around his wrist, and undecidedly fingered them as he took them off. Jette came out of the poultry yard up the kitchen steps, and met the full glance of his large brown eyes straight into her own. He turned away with a shiver of repulsion.

"Who is yon hideous object?" he asked Babbett, in a low tone.

"'T is the Jewish child the mistress took into the house."

"Indeed. I saw her last night and wondered what she was doing here. 'T is a pity mamma could not have picked up something handsomer. I hate ugly people. Here, do thou give her this string of beads. 'T was a pretty girl at the Kirmess sold them to me. I would not have the memory of her rosy cheeks profaned."

He swung himself out of the kitchen. One could hear him whistling the serenade from "Don Giovanni" as he went down the passage back into the sitting-room. He did not know he left a broken heart behind. A child's heart, it is true; but children's sorrows are far more poignant than grown people's; their inexperienced vision sees no remedy beyond. Poor Jette. She had overheard every word. Fritz's sonorous voice could not easily be subdued into a whisper. She was quite recovered now except for the scabs and bruises which, with the best of care, would take some time to disappear. Jette's feelings were mostly

dormant yet. She had never known what vanity
was. Now it was aroused. She studied herself
in the glass. What she saw there made her recoil
in horror. Swollen, discolored features, greasy
with ointment, a mouth askew, eyes half closed.
She thought herself hideous, horrible beyond compare. She would never be different. She was
disfigured, an eyesore in a spot where all else
was beautiful. In all her life she had never suffered so intensely. When first she saw Fritz, she
felt she must adore him. Unseen and unnoticed,
she had laughed at his pranks and warmed her
desolate heart in the sunshine of his presence.
She had wept tears of longing when he caressed
his mother, and felt jealous when like a great
baby he put his arms around his father's neck.
The neighboring "honorationen" young Fräulein
adored him. He rode and drove with Thekla
von Hermersdorff, the Professor's daughter, whose
baronial castle was near by. Thekla was seventeen, small, dark, petite, vivacious as a Parisi-
enne, her father's only child, and heiress to all
his wealth. When Fritz should have his doctor's
diploma, he would settle in Bonn, and then there
would be a wedding. The Frau Pastorin, bridling
with pride, invariably harped upon this subject
when she showed Jette how to stitch her immaculate shirt bands. She rang the changes upon this
theme in every conceivable form of variation. It
was always clear and distinct: Fritz was to marry
an heiress, and have full scope for his extraordinary abilities. Of course it would be Thekla;

why not Thekla? They had known each other
since childhood; her father was professor at the
university. He would be of immense use to Fritz
in his future career. In course of time Fritz
would be a professor himself; his father-in-law's
influence would be of great weight. The young
couple would spend their holidays at the castle, —
how charming, how delightful, to have her dear
son and his beloved wife and their darling children
so near her. Of course there would be children,
her grandchildren, oh, dear, simple soul! She
lost herself in an endless vista of ecstatic contemplation during the stitching of those fine white
bands. Magic power those bands ought to have
had, for the thoughts which were interwoven with
them. The bands were finished to make way for
others, but the same thoughts always remained.
Happy privilege of the present, to which it is not
given to see beyond its own limited vision.

In Jette's eyes Fritz was a hero. He was the
first gentleman with whom she had come into
direct contact. The neighboring Honorationen-
gentry, upon whom she looked with awe, and
worshiped as belonging to a sphere far removed
from hers, were his associates and equals. When
Thekla von Hermersdorff rode by on her white
pony and danced gayly into the house, she stood
from afar eagerly devouring every detail of her
appearance, and longing with a desperation that
amounted to heartsickness to be like this elegant,
easy-mannered child of the world. For Thekla
had the grace and distinction of manner that all

high-bred German Fräulein have, — the hallmark
of caste and breeding. She might at least try and
pattern herself after her. She eagerly watched
the half-coquettish, wholly gracious inclination of
the head, just the least little bit sideways, the
graceful ease with which she used her hands, the
light elegance of her movements. She felt abased
to the dust by her own inferiority. No wonder
Fritz had called her hideous, if those were the
kind of people he was accustomed to as his daily
companions.

One afternoon the young people came in from
skating on the pond. There was quite a number
of them. They crowded into the sitting-room, and
unanimously demanded coffee and cake. Jette
was kept busy running backward and forward.
The best silver service had to be fetched out, the
finest china, the fragrant linen used only on rare
occasions. Everybody would have been just as
well satisfied to have their coffee in the usual
every-day fashion. But the Frau Pastorin's punc-
tiliousness would have been outraged. So when
at last the fragrant Mocha made its appearance,
it was greeted with a shout of joy. There were
hardly hands enough to wait upon everybody.
Such quantities of cake as were consumed! Again
and again Jette had to trot to the kitchen to re-
plenish the coffee-pot. Fritz, who sat next to
Thekla, demanded his fourth cup in stentorian
tones. As Jette handed it to him, her hand ever
so lightly touched his. He shivered, drew his
brows together, and looked at her with such a

feeling of repulsion that, confused and frightened, she dropped the cup and its contents plump into Fräulein von Hermersdorff's lap. The young Fräulein wore a violet velvet dress trimmed with narrow bands of sable, which had just come from the modiste at Cologne. Fritz jumped up with a smothered exclamation; the Frau Pastorin hurried to the young lady's side, full of distress. Everybody looked daggers at the girl, who, trembling and frightened, prayed the earth would open and swallow her. "Clumsy, awkward, stupid rustic," muttered everybody. If Thekla was annoyed, she did not show it. She composedly followed the Frau Pastorin to her room, and seemed more upset by her profuse apologies than the damage done to her dress.

"Go thou to the kitchen," said the Frau Pastorin sharply to Jette, who hovered near with a sponge and towel, "and do not show thyself in the sitting-room any more when the company is there, thou awkward rustic, thou."

"Do not scold her," said Thekla, cheerfully shaking out her dress; "she could not help it, I am sure."

She looked at Jette, who with difficulty kept herself from bursting into a storm of weeping. Where every one had nothing but blame for her, Thekla's goodness entirely overcame her. As Thekla took the towel from Jette's hands, the piteous appeal in Jette's deep blue eyes stirred Thekla's very soul.

"Thou couldst not help it," she said, raising

the drooping chin, as if she were consoling a child.
Then, indeed, the floodgates of the girl's grief
broke loose. The Frau Pastorin, scandalized beyond measure, bade her be silent, and wanted
to hurry her from the room. But Fräulein von
Hermersdorff gently interposed.

"Let her remain with me, I beg," she said,
"until I have made myself presentable. Pray do
not keep the others waiting on my account. I
shall be with you again in a minute."

"She is an angel," said the local doctor's wife,
when the Frau Pastorin returned, extolling the
Fräulein's goodness. "If that had happened to
me, I should feel more inclined to box the of-
fender's ears than to caress her."

"Thekla can afford to be generous," said Fräulein von Sprechnau, the old ex-court Fräulein,
who dwelt at the old Schloss up the mountain;
"the loss of a dress more or less won't make much
difference to her."

"Fräulein von Hermersdorff has cultivated her
feelings," said the pastor, with his fine smile, "as
she has her manners. Hers is the goodness of a
high-bred heart."

Meanwhile, Thekla was busy comforting Jette.
She sobbed so piteously, and shook so with the
intensity of her grief, that Thekla pulled one of
the Frau Pastorin's elaborately worsted-worked
footstools forward, put Jette upon it, and seating
herself beside her, laid the girl's head in her lap,
where her tears added their quota to the already
irretrievably ruined dress. Thekla was perfectly

silent, only passing her hand gently over the close-cropped black hair. For one of the first things the Frau Pastorin had done, when Jette was carried unconscious into the house, was to cut off the long black braids close to the scalp, which, indeed, on account of their hopelessly tangled condition, was imperatively necessary. When the sobs had grown less violent, the girl groped for Thekla's hand, and timidly pressed it to her quivering lips.

"Oh, Fräulein," she said, raising her tear-swollen eyes to the young lady's face, "I love you so."

In her young, exceptionally favored life, Thekla had received a great deal of admiration. Indeed, she demanded it as her natural heritage. But no devotion had ever touched her as this naïve love declaration. Her eyes moistened, and she blushed rosy red with gratification.

"Since when hast thou loved me," she asked gayly.

"Since the nightingale sung in the elder bush. That very night you passed by on your white pony. The Herr Baron, your father, rode by your side. You looked so sweet and gracious, and you vanished so quickly, it made me think of Schiller's ' Maedchen aus der Fremde.' "

"That is surely a flattering comparison," said the young lady, smiling; "thou seem'st to know thy Schiller very well."

"I have read all his poems," said Jette proudly.

"Hast thou no companions of thy own age?"

"I have no time for play, except on the Sabbath. I prefer to read then. Besides, whom should I play with? The girls in the village are not nice. They were worse than the boys when they fell upon and beat me. No, indeed. I cannot bear the sight of them."

"Dost thou not feel very lonely at times?"

"Yes, now. Since the Herr Doctor has come. He is always merry, and has so many companions. Ah, it must be very nice to have a father and mother."

"I have no mother," said Thekla; "I do not even remember her. I was quite young when she died. But I have never missed her. My father has brought me up. Such a dear, good papa! I don't know what would become of him, if he had not me to take care of him."

"You take care of your papa, Fräulein?"

"Yes, indeed. You smile! It is the truth. What do you suppose he would do, if I were not there to watch over him? He would never think of putting on his hat or his boots. He would mount the rostrum in his slippers. He thinks so much of his lectures all the time, he has no room for anything else. What do you suppose he did one day? He had to go out, and I was not there to put his hat on his head, place his gloves in his hands, and see that he changed his house slippers for his boots. He walked down to the university with his coat unbuttoned, no waistcoat underneath, one of my mull fichus knotted around his neck, and my lace parasol in his hand, instead of his own stick. A nice plight for a grave and revered professor to be in, eh?"

"Oh," said Jette, half choked with laughter. She clapped her hands to her mouth, for she did not want to appear impolite. But the picture Thekla had conjured up was too irresistibly comical. She burst into a hearty guffaw.

"I beg your pardon, Fräulein," she began.

"Oh, laugh," said Thekla. "I laugh, everybody laughs. It does not hurt papa. He laughs himself. For all that, he is so beloved, I really do believe if he were to mount the rostrum in his dressing-gown, the students would not even titter. They all know his absent-mindedness. That only increases their respect for him."

She rose. She had succeeded in diverting the child's grief and giving her something to think about. She felt strongly interested in her.

"When the nightingale sings again," she said, "and we return to Hermersdorff, thou must often come to visit me. Wilt thou promise to do so?"

"Fräulein — I — you wish that I should come to the grand castle, your home, — I — to see you?"

"Why not? And I shall expect you very often. Auf Wiedersehen, little one. Remember. When the nightingale sings again."

That evening, before retiring, Fritz said to his mother, "Do me one favor, liebst' Mammachen. Keep that ugly object thou hast taken into the house out of my sight when next I come home for the holidays. I cannot explain how it is, but she makes me creep with aversion. I can take no comfort in my home as long as she is about."

CHAPTER VII

So it came to pass that Jette was sent to the Wildhof, a large farm halfway between Neukirch and Neustadt, and owned by one of the Herr Pastor's parishioners, whenever the son of the house came home. For the next three years he was not troubled by either sight or sound of her. He never inquired what had become of her, and, in fact, he did not care. The present year was his last at college. He was twenty-three now, had matriculated with high honors, and held his M. D. diploma in his pocket.

It was the year '48, a most exciting time for Germany. The whole European continent was in a blaze. In Hungary, Kossuth was preaching the gospel of freedom. In Baden, the citizens had revolted. In Berlin, the people dragged their dead, butchered by the soldiery, before the king's palace, shouting, "Friedrich Wilhelm heraus." The imbecile king, crouching in terror, came out upon the balcony at midnight to look upon the dead and dying, the ghastly faces illuminated by innumerable torches. The vast square before the palace was filled with a clamoring crowd, held back only by a superior armed force from tearing him to pieces. His brother, the Prince of Prussia, who had led the attack upon the people, was obliged to flee for his life, while everybody went about singing, —

" Come thou, come thou, Prince of Prussia,
  Come thou, come thou, to Berlin,
  That we may with stones salute thee,
  And thy skin flay out of thee."

Whatever errors that same prince committed
in the rashness of youth he nobly atoned for as
king. For nowhere in the annals of German history is there a more beloved memory than that of
old Emperor William, the idol of his people, the
hero of his race. At the universities the students
revolted, and formed themselves into insurgent
bands. At Bonn, the patriot Professor Gottfried
Kinkel, the idol of his class, led his pupils into
battle. Among the most enthusiastic who gathered around his banner was Fritz — now Dr.
Friedrich Feldern — and his friend and fellow
student, a young Hungarian noble, Hans von
Czechy. It was a terribly trying time for the
family at the parsonage. Even in that remote
and peaceful region the flaming torch of insurrec-
tion reflected its lurid glare, and the din of battle
cast its echo through the peaceful valley.

In the gray dawn of a summer morning there
came a subdued knock at the parsonage door. No
one heard it; after a most troubled night all were
sound asleep. All but Minka, who rubbed her
cold nose against Jette's neck. She started and
heard the knock repeated. She cautiously tiptoed
to the casement to see who was the disturber.
A peasant stood at the door, and he made signs
for her to come down. As if by some premoni-
tion, the thought of the son of the house flashed

through her mind. She hastily dressed herself and crept down. Then she led the messenger a little distance away, that the household should not be disturbed.

"Out in the ditch," whispered the man, "in the Herr Pastor's garden lie two young men fast asleep. They are covered with blood, their uniforms are in rags, and they have the red sash of the insurgents across their shoulders. They are students, as you can tell by their caps. We are all stanch royalists here, Fräulein," he hypocritically cast down his eyes, "and the Herr Pastor's loyalty is well known. I thought I would do my duty by reporting here. The Herr Pastor will know best what to do. No one is up yet; no one has seen them."

"Go thy ways, Hans," she said, trembling all over, "and never cast one look behind thee. God bless thee for thy loyalty. Be sure, when the proper time comes, thou shalt not be forgotten." He touched his cap and went.

She watched him till he had turned the corner. Then like lightning she sped down the road. She knew well the spot the peasant had indicated. It was a ditch skirting the orchard and dividing it from the vegetable garden. In summer it was generally dry and filled with ferns and falling leaves. In the gray dawn of the morning the village looked ghostlike and silent as the grave. She kept to the middle of the road, that the sound of her flying feet might be deadened in the sand. The outskirts were reached in less than no time;

she gathered her skirts tightly around her, and like a young colt, leaped the inclosure so as to lose no time. In and out of the orderly, well-kept garden beds she dodged till she came upon the ditch. And there, as described by the peasant, lay the doctor and his companion, sound asleep.

CHAPTER VIII

JETTE had been told the reason of her banishment to the Wildhof during the doctor's vacations home. In a burst of rage Babbett had once taunted her with it. She accepted it as a matter of course. It was a relief for her to be out of range of his cold stare of dislike, the general air of repugnance he openly showed when she was around. Jette had compensations he did not dream of. At the Wildhof there were children of all ages and sizes, boys and girls, healthy, hearty, romping children. There no one showed any dislike to her. She had only such tasks to perform as she pleased; it was one long, delicious holiday. She went up to her idolized Fräulein at the castle; and when the doctor was not about, the Fräulein often stopped at the Wildhof in her afternoon drives and had coffee and delicious new bread and butter, and freshly baked cake, served to her out in the grape arbor. And afterwards they all went hunting for eggs, — could anything be more heavenly? 'T is an ill wind surely which blows no one any good.

Now, as she stood over his prostrate form, she

felt a great aversion to touching him. But he had to be awakened. Should she rouse his companion? Spite of the disorder of his dress and the grime and dust covering him, he seemed a strikingly handsome, distinguished-looking youth, of high birth and breeding. No. Her modesty would not allow her to rouse him, a perfect stranger. The doctor knew her. Although she already saw the cold stare of repulsion, when he should open his eyes, it must be done forthwith.

In the east a faint rosy flush heralded the rising of a new day. Broader and broader it grew. It slanted athwart the sleeping men's faces, and enfolded her who was bending over them in its young roseate embrace. The doctor opened his eyes as he felt himself vigorously shaken by the shoulder. He lay as if entranced.

"Glory of the Morning," he murmured.

"Arise," said Jette, "no longer must you stay here. You are in danger. I beseech you, rise."

As she spoke, the strange youth stirred. He raised himself on his elbow and gazed at her.

"Ah, heavenly vision," he said.

The roseate glow had enfolded her now all over. With a hand of fire it caressed the silky sweep of her hair and flashed its fiery glow into the intense blue of the eyes appealingly turned upon the young men.

"Herr Doctor," she urged, "you and the Herr here must lose no time in getting to the parsonage. See! already the sun is up. In another moment the village will be astir. No one must see you like this!"

They both sprang quickly to their feet. "Heavenly Father!" said the doctor, "who art thou?"

"Hasten," she urged. "I will stay here to see no one passes by." She added quickly as she still saw them linger, "The Herr Doctor has forgotten me. I am the Herr Pastor's Jette."

"Thou!" ejaculated the doctor, stupefied. She trembled, as his dislike of her flashed across her mind. She did not see his half-outstretched hand, but retreated, giving him a cold, composed look out of her dark blue eyes. He flushed scarlet, grasped his companion's arm, and quickly hurried away.

CHAPTER IX

THE Frau Pastorin came down to breakfast anxious and ill-humored. She had had a bad night. Fear and anxiety for Fritz had kept her wakeful. Neither was the Herr Pastor less anxious. But he strove to be cheerful and buoy up his wife. The Frau Pastorin sank into her accustomed seat at table, and looked around fretfully.

"Get thee down, Minka," she said; "thou hast no manners at all. I do not want thee on my lap. Get down, I tell thee."

The big tabby cat was behaving very unusually. She persistently rubbed herself against her mistress, meowed as if she would talk, and looked up at her with her round yellow eyes. Then she went over to the Herr Pastor and did the same.

"Something ails the creature," said her master,

"or she would not behave so unusually. She is telling us something. What is it, then, old girl, eh?"

"Where is Henriette," said the Frau Pastorin, looking round; "she should have brought in the breakfast long ago. Really, such negligence is unpardonable. I am fairly dying for my coffee."

She struck the bell sharply. Jette came running in, a bright spot in either cheek. Her manner was eager and alert. She tried to be subdued, but her eyes were bright and gleaming.

"Why hast thou not brought in the coffee?" said the Frau Pastorin severely; "hast thou again overslept thyself? and look at thy hair! thou hast not even brushed it; nay, but such slovenliness is shameful in a girl brought up like thee."

The girl stammered and looked confused. There were tears in her eyes, and her lips trembled.

"I — I will bring in the coffee directly," she said; "we — we have visitors to breakfast, Frau Pastorin."

"Visitors!" said the Frau Pastorin.

"Visitors," repeated the Herr Pastor; "nay, but" — He wheeled round and took hold of her arm. "Come here, Jettchen," he said; "thou knowest something."

"Herr Pastor," she said, "the Herr Doctor" —

"He is here!" shrieked the Frau Pastorin. "Fritz, Fritz!" She flew out of the room and flung herself upon her son's neck in the passage outside, crying and sobbing as if her heart would break. Beside him stood his friend, who heartily shook the Herr Pastor by the hand. The doctor kissed and caressed his mother, and led her back to the breakfast-table.

"Mammachen, lieb' Mammachen," he said, "thou must try and control thyself. It must not appear that we came unexpectedly. It might arouse suspicion."

"Suspicion," she stammered, "I do not understand " —

"We came here at dawn," said the doctor, "fresh from the battlefield. If the gendarmes found we were here, it might go hard with us. We must lie low a little while. Then all will blow over, and no further danger need be apprehended."

"Fritz," she said, "Fritz," she repeated, "hast thou taken up arms against the government?"

"In the cause of freedom and liberty," he said, "and so did my friend here, Hans von Czechy. He is a Hungarian, mamma, and the same ardor which animates Kossuth runs in his veins. We made our escape together. We thought if we once got here in safety to this remote place, we would be free from pursuit. We were overcome by fatigue, and went to sleep in the orchard, where Jettchen found us."

"And allow me to say," said Herr von Czechy, with a deep bow, "that never was awakening more agreeable."

"Jettchen, thou," said the Frau Pastorin.

"Hans from the Wildhof came to the door,"

she said, "while you were asleep. He said two
fugitive insurgents with student's caps were lying
out in the orchard. I thought of the Herr Doctor, and went to rouse them before any one should
be stirring, and brought them here."

"Thou didst this, Jettchen?" said the pastor.
He took her hand, stroked it affectionately, and
kissed her on the forehead.

"Never in my life will I scold thee again," said
the Frau Pastorin, "thou good and discreet child.
Thou hast acted like a sensible woman. Thou art
sure no one saw thee?"

"It was too early for any one to be stirring,"
interrupted the doctor; "make thy mind quite
easy, mamma. It was just sunrise when we were
safely housed."

"And I'll be bound the sun never rose on any
one in sorrier plight," exclaimed the young Magyar noble, laughing; "luckily we have had time
to make ourselves presentable. Holy Father! but
we were in a fine state."

"What has become of your uniforms?" asked
the Herr Pastor anxiously. "They must be put
out of sight immediately. Nothing must remain
which could throw the slightest suspicion upon
you."

"They are burnt," said Babbett, who just entered with the breakfast equipage. "That Jette,
I must say she has wit at times. When she came
to me and told me the Herr Doctor and his friend,
the Herr Baron, were here," she bobbed a curtsy to
the young Magyar, "and what a plight they were

in, I made a fire in the old smoke-house, took everything they cast off, even to their shirts, and burnt it. There is nothing but ashes left to tell the tale," she added complacently.

That was a joyous meal, that breakfast. Babbett had wrung the necks of a few unsuspecting pullets, and had prepared them as none but she knew how. The young men sniffed the delicious incense of the food and polished off the very bones. Such a meal they had not tasted for many a day. They were both ravenous. The Frau Pastorin's eyes glistened with pleasure as she saw one appetizing dish after the other disappear. Jette whisked in and out, attending upon their wants. She had had time to run upstairs and smooth her hair and tidy herself up a bit. She wore her dress according to the graceful fashion of the times, cut low in the neck, with short, ruffled elbow sleeves. Her white throat rose like a column of polished marble from the pink mull drapery of the fichu, and her ivory arms, rounded and full like a young divinity's, most exquisitely tapering at the wrists, twinkled in and out of the coffee-cups. Each time she presented a dish to Herr von Czechy, his fiery black eyes spoke their language of adoration, while he thanked her as if she had been a duchess. Like a rare flower suddenly bursting into bloom, delighting and astonishing the beholder, she grew in loveliness under the fiery warmth of the Magyar's glances. The doctor, while volubly talking to his father and mother between big mouthfuls and gulps of scald-

ing hot coffee, watched her furtively as if stunned.
Had this magnificent creature evolved from the
stupid, repulsive, greasy object he had looked
upon with aversion three years ago? Was it possible in nature to produce such results? In truth,
the change had been so gradual that her daily
associates hardly noticed it. Those who, like
him, had not seen her develop from a lanky, over-
grown child into sweetest girlhood, found it hard
to reconcile one with the other. She listened as
they related their adventures. Her heart swelled
with pride that she had been fortunate enough to
be of some service to two such heroes as she evidently took them to be.

"We fought behind the barricades at Baden,"
said the doctor, "until the soldiery beat us back.
It was no use holding out against such overpower-
ing numbers. Our class had banded together.
Hans commanded us. He fought like a lion. But
we were only a handful against a whole regiment.
Some of us were slain. Some wounded. But no
one was captured. We retreated shouting, 'Liberty and equality.' Then every one had to look
out for himself."

"And didst thou never think of father and
mother, thou hot head?" said the Frau Pastorin
reprovingly.

"We made our way to Cologne," said Hans
von Czechy, "the best way we could. We were
in hourly danger of being taken. Then Fritz
suggested that if we could manage to find our way
as far as this, we would be safe from all pursuit.

We marched all night, and arrived at the outskirts of the village just before dawn. We did not wish to startle you with a too sudden appearance. Fatigue overpowered us, and we slept until the Fräulein, like a guardian spirit, appeared and led us to safety, peace, and " —

"Home," interrupted the doctor, looking at him with an immense glance out of his brown eyes.

"Thou hast placed thyself in fearful jeopardy," said the Frau Pastorin, "and endangered thy parents besides. Was it wise of thee, my son, to do this?"

"It was well done," said the Herr Pastor, walking up and down with his hands in his pockets. "Be silent, Liebste. No harm will come of it. It was just what I should have done, had I been in thy place," he said, pausing before his son and placing his hand upon his shoulder.

"Blessed are the fathers," said the doctor, "who reprove their sons in this wise."

CHAPTER X

"Thou codfish," said Hans von Czechy, as soon as he and his friend were alone, "how comes it thou never told'st me of this heavenly maid? A sly, selfish rascal thou art! Our whole class would have turned out to do her homage."

The doctor made a grimace. "Then it is just as well thou wert left in ignorance so long. Fancy those wild, rakish fellows thrumming their guitars

under her window in the still hours of the night
and caterwauling over each other, 'Ich liebe
Dich.' "

"One has n't codfish blood in one's veins as
thou hast," said Hans. "Wilt thou answer my
question?"

"Being a codfish," said the doctor coolly, "is
a great advantage in this world of scatter-brains.
It preserves one from all sorts of follies."

"I would sooner let my heart rend me," retorted
Hans, "than allow it to be ruled by such an infernally cool head as thine. At all events, one
lives. Ugh! fancy going through life with reason
constantly padlocking every blissful heart-throb
of love and passion."

"And its agony," said the doctor. "Thy heart
is frittered away in such small portions, one bit
here, another one there; thou hast not thought
of that."

"Hallo!" said Hans; he wheeled round and
looked at the doctor. A fine smile crossed his
lips. "Nature," said he, "has a fine rod in pickle
for thee. I shall hear of thee when I am far away
in my home on the banks of the Danube. Thou
scoffer! thy turn will come some day. 'T will go
hard with thee, my sly Fritz. Like an avalanche
't will overtake thee, crushing thy cool wits under
its might."

"Have I ever," said the doctor, carefully knocking the ashes from his cigar, "given thee cause for
thy present rhapsody?"

"Thou art so infernally sly," said Hans. "What

shouldst thou know of love's agony, if thou couldst not gauge its bliss?"

He whistled softly, plucked a leaf from the trailing vine covering the arbor in which they were seated, then said again, "Who is this divine maid?"

"She is an orphan without money, home, or friends, whom my parents adopted into the household three years ago. I did not remember her existence until she made herself known," said the doctor.

"If I had not been present when she did so," said Hans, "I should be tempted to doubt thy word. I am bewildered how this can be. How couldst thou avoid seeing her, if she was a member of thy home, when thou camest here to spend thy holidays?"

"Thou wilt make me lose patience! Was she not a child then, a perfect child? Who thinks of noticing children?"

"Bah! thou art not telling me the truth. I shall ask her myself."

"I will wring thy neck if thou dost," said the doctor furiously.

Hans burst out laughing. "Cher Fritz," he said caressingly, "get thee down on the stool of confession. Out with the truth, however painful it may be."

"Thou canst badger one to death," said the doctor. "Wilt thou believe me if I tell thee that, with the exception of her first coming, I have not set eyes on her for three years?"

"Thou dear Heaven! If she was here, thou must have seen her."

The doctor intently studied his cigar. "She was not here," he said, " whenever I came home."

The young Magyar burst out laughing. "Thy mother was wise," he said. "Such a temptation might have been too much even for thy cool head. Fräulein von Hermersdorff would have had good cause to be jealous."

"Look thou to thy own account," retorted the doctor. "I fear it is as much as thou canst straighten out. Why shouldst thou drag in the professor's daughter? I am not betrothed to her as thou art to the Countess Irma."

This made Hans wince. He fingered a gold chain he wore round his neck, as if it were something which should act as a wholesome curb to his wandering fancy. And so in truth it did. Attached to it was a miniature of the young countess, to whom his prudent father had betrothed him before he let him depart for the university. She was the daughter and only child of a neighboring noble. Their estates adjoined. At her father's death all his riches would go to her. It was an eminently proper match. The Countess Irma was a blonde, sweet-tempered girl of fourteen, contentedly eating bread and jam in the schoolroom, when the betrothal took place. She was now grown up, and perfectly satisfied to be married as soon as her lover should return home. During his four years' absence Hans's fancy had often wandered. But it had never been anything more

serious than fancy. He made love to pretty shop-
girls and coquettish Kellnerinnen; sent flowers and
bonbons to the professors' daughters; thrummed
accompaniments on his guitar in their drawing-
rooms to his amorous love-ditties, and danced the
Czardas with a fire and vim which carried all
female hearts by storm. The fair maidens adored
him, for he was in the flower of his youth, like
the doctor, just twenty-three, not so stalwart and
powerfully built, but with a chest like a Hercules,
biceps like steel, tall, with black eyes and hair,
ivory white teeth, which twinkled most provokingly
between full red lips shaded by a black mustache.
He had all the passionate ardor of his race, and was
the gracefullest dancer along the Rhine. Adroit
with the foils, he was also a skilled and scientific
swordsman. He had fought the regulation number
of duels, and bore his scars as proudly as any other
hero. His features were delicately handsome, of
the true aristocratic type, chastened and refined
through a long line of noble ancestry. With his
superabundance of fiery ardor, he was calculated
to carry havoc into the feminine camp. Many
there were who had surrendered to him; innumerable were the scrapes he had got out of and fallen
into again. But the little miniature around his
neck was his talisman which preserved him from
serious harm. He would fall back upon it as his
consolation, after a peculiarly severe rebuff from
some fair one. In sentimental moments he would
draw it forth and gaze upon the innocent childish
features, like a devout Catholic upon one of his

saints. Once he fought a duel to the death with
a fellow student, who had audaciously snatched
the picture from his hand and kissed it. Now the
child was grown into the woman, and he was going
home to marry her. The wedding trousseau was
already under way; there were to be grand festivities at Castle Czechy, one of the finest baronial
piles on the beautiful, fascinating Danube. And
the doctor was to go with him, and be best man,
for they two were bosom friends. It was just as
well they should leave the country as soon as ex-
pedient. They had taken too active a part in the
uprising against the government to escape being
sought for long. And yet — those student days
had been beautiful. The fullness of life they had
indeed given him. Never again would they return,
those golden, free, careless hours, when the wine
of existence was alluringly placed to the lips and
quaffed in deep, heartfelt, satisfying draughts.
"Die shoenen Tage von Aranjuez sind zu Ende,"
he quoted, with a half sight of regret. He turned
to the doctor.

"Tell me," he said, "if thou canst, why does
the beautiful Fräulein sit apart from us at table?
She seems as high-bred and well-mannered as any
of our patrician demoiselles."

"Thy words," said the doctor, "imply a reproach to my parents they are far from deserving.
It is by their sanction she sits apart, not because
it is their will. I can give thee the explanation
in a word. She is a Jewess."

Like the radiance of the sun suddenly obscured

at the full tide of noon, fell the countenance of the young noble. He seemed both astonished and crestfallen. "A Jewess," he faltered, "here — in thy father's house?"

"Even so. She sits apart by her own wish, for fear of her food being contaminated."

"'T is the most inconceivable thing heard of," said the Magyar; "and thy parents encourage her in this?"

"'T is part and parcel of her creed. My father sees to it that she keeps all the requirements of her religion most scrupulously. She is probably more exact in their performance than if brought up in the midst of her own people. To her 't is all quite sacred."

"But fancy her isolation! to be with you and not of you. To feel herself something apart, of a different race, people, persuasion — has thy father acted wisely in this?"

"Thou judgest my father," said the doctor, "as a very different man from what he is. In his estimation the better life beyond is our common goal. No matter by what road we travel to attain it, so long as we go about the right way to reach it. Thou as the Catholic, I as the Protestant, she as the Jewess. In this house Jettchen has never been made to feel any different from the rest. She has grown up in it quite naturally, — as part and parcel of her surroundings."

"Wait," said the Magyar, "till the time comes for her to marry. Then she will realize the evils of her position."

"She will marry one of her own faith, of course," said the doctor.

"If she does," said Hans, "she will feel like a bird in a strange nest. But hush. Here she comes. Maria! How beautiful she is."

CHAPTER XI

JETTE and the Frau Pastorin came down the graveled walk, followed by Minka. The blonde-haired, pink-cheeked, stately matron was the most desirable foil one could have wished for the young creature just budding into the most exquisite womanhood. Her wavy black hair, glossy as finest satin, rippled and curled and caressed and coquetted around a face of the purest oval; the chin, in which a dimple slyly peeped forth, perched rather saucily forward. Her mouth was adorable, the upper lip short and curved, the lower pouting and most beautifully moulded. The nose was delicately aquiline, and sweeping, long black eyebrows contrasted with nobly shaped eyes of the most intense blue. "Stiefmuetterchen Augen," the Herr Baron called them. In truth, the darkest purple of the pansy could only be likened to the color of Jette's eyes. And those eyes, how shy, how innocent, how wistful in expression when lifted to one's own. And yet how full of fun, of sweetest merriment and laughter, hiding itself demurely under the upward curled fringe of thickest black lashes. The brow, wide and somewhat high, gave its stamp of nobility to her features, with their dazzling purity of complexion. Her hair, which had grown again in luxuriant profusion, was the crowning glory of this beautiful being, a fit frame for such a picture. Like the Frau Pastorin's, it was parted in the middle, from where it undulated to the nape of the neck, and coiled in silky masses around a most shapely head. Two long curls fell behind either ear, and contrasted with the snowy neck they adorned. Her manner was one of harmonious repose. She held prisoner the eye, and fascinated the understanding.

Afternoon coffee was to be served in the arbor. There were to be strawberries, of which the doctor was very fond. Jette carried a basket of twisted bamboo in which to gather them. As she came up the path, swinging her basket in innocent gayety of heart, Hans von Czechy looked at her with redoubled interest, not untinged with melancholy. This beautiful being, so strangely situated, so isolated and apart, would she ever wake up to the true bitterness of her position? Some day, he felt certain. Ay, some day!

"Surely, dearest Fräulein, you will permit me," he said, with a bow, such as only this fascinating rascal knew how to make. He took the basket, which she blushingly yielded to him. Minka stood undecided, alternately looking at the Frau Pastorin, then at the retreating girl, with the young baron at her side. Then she elevated her long brush and scampered after them. Their merry jests and laughter reached the ears of the

Frau Pastorin and her son, as the former stooped
over her rosebushes.

"Minka has turned traitor, mamma," he said;
"art thou not jealous?"

"It is wonderful how she has attached herself
to Henriette," said the Frau Pastorin, cutting a
rose here and there; "thou hast no idea how she
pines for the girl during her banishment to the
Wildhof."

The doctor winced. He savagely kicked a pebble out of his path. It flew high up in the air
and alighted near the strawberry-bed.

"Fritz," said his mother hurriedly, "will — will
it be necessary to send Henriette away again?
Thou camest so unexpectedly — thou seest there
was no time to" —

"Father in heaven," interrupted the doctor,
"how one's sins find one out!" He was scarlet;
his eyes blazed. "Dear mamma," he said, "thou
knowest I shall not stay here long. 'T would
hardly be worth while, would it, to *banish* her
again?" He emphasized the word vindictively.
"Let me assure thee that neither now nor at any
other time will it be necessary to send her away
on my account."

"Oh," said the Frau Pastorin, relieved, "I was
afraid thou hadst not overcome thy aversion to
her."

"Aus Kinder werden Leute," he said oracu-
larly; "she has changed somewhat from then."

"Yes, indeed!" said the Frau Pastorin. "Thou
sawest her first under very unfavorable circum-

stances. Papa says her own mother would not have known her. Before then she was a very likely looking child."

"She kept the promise of her childhood, then," said the doctor.

"She has developed beyond my expectations," said the Frau Pastorin. She spoke with as much professional pride as a gardener of a cherished plant or flower. " 'T is a lucky thing for her, as it is the only dowry she will have. 'T will enable her to get settled in life the better and quicker."

"Mamma," he said suddenly, "has — has she ever been told why she was sent to the Wildhof?"

"Babbett told her," said the Frau Pastorin. "Papa was angry with Babbett, and scolded her roundly for doing so. But she was always glad to go. 'T was a joyous holiday for her. They were very fond of her at the Wildhof, and quite spoilt her by letting her do as she pleased."

The doctor bit his blonde mustache. His eyes glistened with a suspicious moisture.

"Thank God for that," he said; "she is not at all like any one I have ever seen, and yet she reminds me so strongly of some one. If I could only nail my elusive fancy! It plagues me to death."

"I can help thee out," she said cheerfully. "In her manner and gestures she is just like Thekla."

He gave her a great glance. "Good Heavens!" he said, "thou art right. She is Thekla over again, even to the manner she inclines her head."

" 'T is easily explained. She has been with

Thekla a great deal when thou wert not up there. Thou rememberest that afternoon, three years ago, when thou and thy friends came in from skating, and she threw the cup of coffee over Thekla's dress? Thou surely must remember it, since it was that very day thou didst beg of me not to let thee see or hear her any more? Thekla took to her then, and begged of me to send her up to the castle whenever she could be spared. 'T was a lucky thing for Henriette, I assure thee. For all she knows of graciousness, attractiveness, and breeding, she owes to Thekla."

"How much better women are than men," said the doctor. He lifted his mother's hand to his lips. "Dear Thekla," he murmured.

His mother's eyes sparkled. "There is no one like her," she said. "Fritz," she urged, "before thou goest away, ought not matters to be settled between you? She is twenty now; thou wilt be gone some time " —

"No, no," he interrupted hastily; "'t would not be at all fair to her. I shall be gone three or four years at least. Thekla must be left perfectly free. She will have chosen some one long before I come back."

"Thekla will never marry," said his mother positively; "had she wanted to do so, she need not have waited till she is twenty. She loves thee, Fritz. She will never marry any one else."

He turned away impatiently. His eyes were strained towards the strawberry-bed, from which sounds of gleeful mirth and laughter came.

"I should think," he said severely, "those strawberries ought to be picked by this time. Are we never going to have coffee?"

"I will call Henriette," said the Frau Pastorin, startled at his tone; "it shall be here directly."

"Mamma," he said abruptly, "why should Jettchen sit apart, now she is grown up? You and papa are used to seeing her so. But from strangers it arouses comment. 'T will surely not contaminate her meats to eat them at the same table with us."

So it came to pass that from that day Jette sat apart no more.

CHAPTER XII

"Ach so hold und so traut," sung Jette, as she squatted among the beans and cabbages, pulling up weeds and exterminating slugs. It had rained the night before; and as it was her duty to keep the large kitchen-garden just outside the village outskirts in perfect order, she had put on her sunbonnet and started out to investigate. The sun was hot, but she worked on industriously. The garden had been neglected of late; she had been obliged to help Babbett all day long. The sudden invasion of the quiet parsonage, where everything moved with clockwork regularity, by two young men effervescing with a superabundance of animal spirits, who played all sorts of pranks on each other and everybody else, was not calculated to

speed any one in his work. Of course Jette enjoyed it; every one did. In another week or two,
at most, they would have to leave. Then all this
heavenly time would come to an end. For they
were golden days to Jette, — days in which time
seemed to stand still in one long, mirthful holiday.
Then fate gave her all of happiness it had to give.
It was not stingy about it. With full, lavish
hands it crowded into her young life all the sunshine it had ever known. In its benignant rays she
unfolded like a gorgeous flower, so that there was
no pain mixed with the delight of beholding her.
Jette was now in her seventeenth year, but the
delicious fragrance of innocent childhood hovered
about her still. When she raised her deep violet
eyes, with their veil of long, sweeping lashes,
straight as truth, to one's face, the fearlessness
which knows nothing of evil and suspects still less
spoke out of them still. The enticing dew of the
early morning was upon this blossom yet, and woe
to the hand which sacrilegiously should be lifted
to brush it hence.

"Mother Mary," said the Magyar to his friend,
"how beautiful she is! Codfish! how canst thou
behold her day after day, each succeeding one
more ravishing than the last, and not lose thy
head completely?"

"Thy father showed his wisdom," said the
doctor, "in tying both thy hands before thou
wentest; otherwise Heaven knows what folly thou
wouldst be capable of."

Hans rumpled his lavish black curls in anger.

"''T was not wisely done," he said; "'t was cruel, tyrannical in the extreme. My consent was not even asked. 'T was all done as a matter of business."

"As all matters of this kind are done," said the doctor.

The young baron stared at him fiercely. "Wait thou," he said; "I will take my innings out of thee one day. 'T will go hard with thee, I tell thee: far harder than with me. The barricades girding thy cold, phlegmatic breast will be stormed without warning. Then there will be an earthquake. Vesuvius, with all its hell-fires let loose, will be nothing to it. 'T will be grand, but it will consume thee to ashes."

"Why dost thou rave at me," said the doctor, "because thou fanciest one maiden, and art betrothed to another? Be easy! 'T is an accident which has happened to thee more than once."

"I will never survive this," groaned Hans; "this time, I tell thee, 't is serious. She haunts me, this angel maid, wherever I go. Waking or sleeping, I dream of her. She is there with her eyes soft and velvety as the heart of love. I have no peace anywhere."

"H'm!" said the doctor attentively, scanning his face, which flushed and glowed with the vehemence of his words, "thou hast the fever seriously this time. Give me thy pulse to feel."

"I will strangle thee," said Hans savagely, "if thou mockest me into the bargain. I have half a mind" —

"As a good Catholic," said the doctor, "thou oughtest to know that open confession is good for the soul. Go on. Unburden thyself."

"I have half a mind to run away with her."

The doctor laughed. "She would not go with thee," he said.

"She would not, eh? Not if I told her of my passion and the life that awaited her?"

"What life?" said the doctor. He wheeled round suddenly. "Thou forgettest," he said, "that she is a Jewess. She would no more forego the religion of her fathers than thou wouldst thy own. 'T is an abyss, an unbridgeable chasm, which, aside from all other considerations, divides you. Speak no more of such folly. 'T is unworthy of thy manhood."

"What did thy father mean," said Hans moodily, "in bringing her up in such fashion? Some time or other she will have to be settled in life. What will become of her then?"

"My father," said the doctor, "believes in the inalienable sacredness of the rights of the individual. This girl was born a Jewess; she had to remain a Jewess. 'T was his duty to see she grew up no half-hearted one. As to her future, thou needest not puzzle thyself. She will marry, as most maidens do. Thou wilt own she will not lack for suitors, dowerless as she is, if the fame of her beauty once gets abroad. Only it will have to be some one of her own faith."

"I do not believe it," said the Magyar; "she has not grown up among them; she will feel out of place. Thy father may have acted conscientiously in bringing her up as he did. Whether it was wisely done remains to be seen."

Meanwhile, Jette was pulling up weeds, raking and hoeing as if her life depended on it. Her dear garden was beginning to look like itself again. When the Frau Pastorin came to inspect it, or Babbett fetched her daily supply of vegetables, there would be no scolding or fault-finding. She wanted to be back before supper, in time to change her dress, to set the table, and help Babbett with the dishes. And as she worked, she sang one song after the other, those she had heard the doctor and Herr von Czechy sing, the latest languishing love ballads of the incomparable Jenny Lind, who was then in the zenith of her fame. For in addition to the lavish gifts nature had already so bountifully bestowed upon Jette, she possessed a glorious contralto voice, magnificent chest notes, deep and vibrating as the full tones of an organ; sweet, sonorous, and pure, full of a thrilling sympathy which came straight from the heart. In the limited opportunities she had, Fräulein von Hermersdorff had taught her how to manage her voice, and to accompany herself on the guitar. Added to this she had a quick, unerring ear, which enabled her to repeat accurately everything she heard. The pastor's eyes would glisten with pleasurable emotion when she went about her tasks, yodling like a Tyrolean till she challenged the echoes from every nook and cranny of the quiet old place. Verily she was the sunshine of the house.

As for the fiftieth time she sung, "Marta, Marta Du entschwandest," she almost jumped with surprise, when a clear, fine tenor fell in with the strain, mingling with the tones of her voice as if it had found a fitting mate. In another moment Hans von Czechy vaulted over the high paling, and laughingly lifted her to her feet.

"Talk of the angels," he said; "I was just wishing with all my heart and soul you were out here with me under the trees, and I had my guitar with me. Then your beautiful voice rose upon the air. 'T was my fairy guide to just where I wanted to be. May all my wishes in life be as satisfactorily fulfilled."

She laughed in pure sympathy with his delighted mood. "'T is so lonely here," she said, "one could sing all day long without being heard. I always sing when I work. I don't know why, but it is so."

"Song and laughter," he said; "if I had my will, they should be your life companions. Nothing rough should ever breathe upon, much less touch you. Surely if any one was destined for happiness, it is you."

She blushed, then said, "I thought you miles away. Have you not been up to Hermersdorff? I fancied you and the Herr Doctor started hours ago to see if the young Fräulein had returned from her visit to Silesia."

"Aha," he said slyly, "that's my secret."

Again she had to laugh. His merriment was so contagious. Really one could not be angry with him. He sat down under a large sycamore-tree, whose ample branches afforded a grateful shade on the hottest day. He took her hand and made her sit down beside him. A brook, widened by last night's copious rains into quite a little stream, lapped its tiny wavelets at their feet. The scent of mignonette, sweet lavender, and wild marjoram perfumed the balmy air. High up in the sycamore-tree a lark was bursting its little throat with its pæan of praise. The soft summer breeze lifted the thick, luxurious curls from the Magyar's brow. His dark face kindled, as with distended chest he drew his breath in deep, delighted draughts. His eyes roved over the undulating valley, where in the far distance the blue Rhine beckoned like a beacon of hope.

"What a quaint place this is," he said, "tucked snugly away among these hills like a child in its cot. One could almost fancy the footprints of time had never strayed here; that it was always so, and always will be, — an Eden, where no hateful strife or contending passions ever can come."

Jette thought of the time when, in the road just outside of the garden inclosure, she was all but beaten to death. The recollection made her shudder, as it always did. It was thus it continually obtruded itself in her happiest moments.

"There are human beings here," she said, "and wherever they are, there is human nature."

Hans peered under her sunbonnet. "Take that disfiguring thing off," he commanded. "What horrible aged sarcasm out of such a young, lovely mouth!"

Meekly she took off her bonnet. Somewhat troubled she seemed that her words should have made such an impression on him. She had said them in all innocence just as she thought. In her confusion she stooped to pick up a pebble at her feet. Her book fell out of her pocket, her beloved Schiller, without which she never rose or went to bed. His attentive eyes saw it. He hastily forestalled her in picking it up. Feeling herself very guilty, she tried to seize the much-bethumbed treasure, but Hans retained firm hold of it.

"Is it from this," he said, "you imbibe such ideas? Ah, but then it shall quickly be destroyed."

"Give it me back," she implored; "the Frau Pastorin would be so angry if she knew."

"Schiller's poems," he ejaculated, in astonishment. "There is no harm here. Why should the Frau Pastorin be angry?"

"She might think I was wasting my time," said the girl, very much relieved. "When I stoop down to do much weeding, my limbs get very cramped. Sometimes I take a little rest here under this tree. There is no harm in reading a little then, is there?"

She said it half timidly, half coaxingly, as if afraid he might disagree with her. It moved him so strongly, he could hardly refrain from kissing the mouth which knew how to plead so sweetly.

"There is no harm in your reading while you rest," he said quite seriously; "why should the Frau Pastorin object?"

"She might think I ought to have my knitting in my pocket instead of my book, and so I could, of course. But then my fingers are too stiff to hold the needles after weeding so long."

How sordid it all seemed. How he longed to take her in his arms, kiss her, and love her, as mother nature had so evidently intended she should be kissed and loved, — this, her pet child. The melancholy which always shared the delight he had in looking at her overcame him now, when he reflected that this humdrum, obscure life might be her portion, — married to some horrible under-bred fellow, who saw in her only a desirable, good-wearing housekeeper. What would his father say if he returned to his distant Hungarian home with this beautiful, sweet young creature hanging on his arm. His hot Magyar blood rushed to his head; involuntarily his arm stole towards her. She was humming a plaintive little tune, lacing and interlacing her fingers in perfect contentment of mind.

"What is that you are singing?" he asked. He did not expect an answer. He wanted to hear the sound of his own voice.

"'Tis a little Jewish hymn," she said. "Is it not quaint and grand? It is only sung on the high holidays that come once a year."

His madness was over. He, the Catholic, she, the Jewess — 'twas an abyss he was about to hurl himself into. And yet — the pity of it. Involuntarily he took her hand, and smoothed and patted it as if he wanted to console her.

"Nay," he said, "did I ever see such a beautiful hand! so slim and perfectly formed, the fingers arched and tapering at the top, nails rosy as cupid's bow and shaped like the heart of a hind. 'T is the hand of a goddess. 'T is the most beautiful hand in the world. Why do you not wear gloves to protect them? See; they are all burnt red from the sun."

She looked at her hands in astonishment, not unmixed with gratified vanity. No one had ever told her they were beautiful. Hands were made to work with, and not to spare themselves at that.

"Gloves to work in!" she said; "I have none to spare for that."

"You shall have all mine," he said. "They will be just the right thing. It is quite what you want. Long and loose, to move your hands in freely."

"No, no," she said, "I could not think of that. But if you have any old ones — those that are past darning, I shall be glad " —

"I have heaps of them," he said. He was fibbing, but it was no sin to impose on her childish credulity. He had a whole box full he had never used. The doctor was also well provided, he knew. He inly resolved to make a raid on them. He would not spare him one pair. She should have every one of them. It gave him unalloyed pleasure that even in so trivial a matter he could provide for her. He kissed the hands he had praised, and put the rosy finger - tips into his mouth.

"Which finger do you like best?" he asked.

"This one," she said, indicating the third finger of the left hand.

For a moment he was staggered. Was she, after all, a consummate coquette? But her hand lay within his quite passive. Her blue eyes looked at him seriously.

"Why?" he asked.

"Because my mother used to put my fingers into her mouth, as you did just now. No one has ever done so. I had quite forgotten it till you reminded me. This finger she would always pretend to bite, and laugh at my terror."

"Is that the only reason?"

"Surely, yes. How could there be any other?"

She did not know, then, that it really was the ring finger. He had great ado to restrain himself from kissing her, he was so charmed with her simplicity.

"See here," he said, drawing a wide, flat hoop of dull black from his little finger; "this circlet, unpretentious as it is, bears invaluable recollections for me. With it are entwined the dearest, sweetest memories of my youth and childhood. 'T is an antique which has been in my family for generations, and has descended from father to son. Will you wear it on this finger, — this one you like the best, — and sometimes think of me when I am far away?"

"It does not require any reminder," she said, smiling through her gathering tears, "to make me do that. But I will wear it gladly, as something treasured by yourself; and I will never part with it as long as I live."

It really was so small and looked so insignificant, with the funny hieroglyphics engraved all over it, she had no hesitation about accepting it. Yet when he placed it on her finger, it showed in sharp contrast against her white hand. She fell to admiring it immensely, and turned it round and round.

"'T is the first ring I have ever had," she said. "I had no idea it would look so pretty."

"I will return," he said, strongly moved, "and replace it with another." Then he thought of the Countess Irma, and gave a great gulp.

The girl beside him felt her heart thump like a sledge-hammer. She jumped up, startled and confused.

"Heavens! It is time to go home, and my garden is not half finished. I shall be finely scolded."

"That you never shall be. Come, I will help you. In two minutes all will be done."

Laughing like children, they began such a fierce onslaught on the weeds that in a very short time hardly one remained. Then Hans, who had stripped off his coat, got the rake, and made a neat pile of them, and threw them into the wheelbarrow, ready to be carted away. He enlivened his work with so many droll sallies that Jette's laughter rang out incessantly, to which the song of the birds lent a joyous accompaniment.

"You have not yet told me," she said, "how you came here."

"I gave the Herr Doctor the slip. While he was toiling up the mountain to Hermersdorff, imagining me trudging behind him, I dodged through the woods and came here. Bah! 'T is his business to find out whether the Fräulein has returned. He is more interested in her than I am."

"Do you think," said Jette quite anxiously, "that Fräulein Thekla likes him?"

"Likes him?" he repeated. "Dear child, as many separate hairs as the doctor grows on his mossy scalp, so many separate times does Fräulein von Hermersdorff worship him, each time more fervently than the other."

Jette drew a deep breath. "I am sure he must be very fond of her also," she said, as if half to herself.

"The doctor! Oh, he's a codfish! I fancy he likes her well enough according to his fashion. If nothing else, his vanity must be touched, as any man's is bound to be, when a pretty woman shows undisguisedly how she adores him."

"He is a very disagreeable, repellant man," said Jette severely, "and not at all worthy to be loved by such a lovely young lady as Fräulein von Hermersdorff. I am sorry she could not bestow her affection on some one more amiable than he."

"What a severe arraignment!" said Hans, not ill pleased she should be so hard upon his friend; "so you do not like the doctor?"

She threw up her lips disdainfully.

"Oh," she said indifferently, "I dare say he is

quite attractive to some people. I hope he will stay away so long I shall have forgotten all about him. I never want to meet again any one I dislike half as much."

She picked up her basket and her sunbonnet. "Now," she said, "you see that cherry-tree yonder, in the orchard? No, not that one, but the one a little to the left, loaded down with the big oxheart cherries? You may climb it and fill my basket. Then we will go home."

"Where is my coat?" said Hans, looking around. They both looked and searched, but no coat was to be seen.

"Never mind," said Hans, laughing; "we will return like those ideal harvesters one sees in pictures, — you in your sunbonnet, carrying the cherries, and I in my shirt-sleeves, with the rake over my shoulder."

Jette, who was greatly distressed, and could not account for the loss of the coat, still spied earnestly around. Then she gave a little cry. "Look," she said, pointing towards the orchard.

There dangled the coat, suspended from the topmost branch of the cherry-tree.

"Who has done this?" exclaimed the young Baron von Czechy.

Then they both ran towards the tree, and there sat the doctor, high up near the coat, grinning down upon them through the ripe fruit and green leaves.

"What do you think of my scarecrow?" he said.

"So it was thou, thou rascal?" cried Hans, laughing; "throw me down my coat, please."

"Thou wilt have to ransom it first," said the doctor.

"Willingly. What dost thou claim?"

"That Jettchen shall climb up and get it."

"I certainly will, with pleasure," she cried, turning rosy red.

"Fräulein Jettchen, you! Never will I permit it. Surely you cannot climb that tree," cried Hans angrily; "let the coat stay where it is."

"If thou hadst seen," said the doctor, "what I saw the other day, thou wouldst not be quite so alarmed. H'm! It lent an extra zest to the cherries, I assure thee."

"Stand off, Herr von Czechy," said Jette. "I will get your coat." She put her foot on the tree, and swung herself up with an ease and agility which scarcely caused a flutter of her petticoats. Hans saw her face glowing among the leaves, then his coat alighted at his feet.

"Well done," said the doctor; "now downward, march!"

"Herr Doctor," said Jette, "the limb is giving way. It is not strong enough to hold us both."

"I am waiting for you to go down," said the doctor.

"Then we shall both break our necks," she said. She held on to the topmost branch. Her body swayed to and fro. She met the doctor's eyes coldly.

"Will you go down!" he commanded sternly.

"I will fling myself down," she said. "Your parents shall not see you crippled, perhaps killed, on my account."

"Stop!" he cried. He slid down as if whipped by the Furies. Prone upon his face he fell, pulling his friend down with him.

It seemed an eternity before they heard her laughing voice close beside them. "Now we will go home."

"Maria!" said Hans; "what a fright you gave us! Are you really unhurt?"

The doctor walked up to the tree. The limb on which she had stood lay upon the ground. It was snapped in two.

"I must fill my basket," she said.

"Come away," said Hans, with a shudder. "When I think of your narrow escape, I shall never be able to bear the sight of cherries again."

He took her empty basket, and turned to go. The doctor lingered a moment behind. He hastily broke off a small twig of the broken branch, and slipped it into his pocket.

CHAPTER XIII

WHEN Hans von Czechy threw open his casement early the next morning, he heard Minka purring on the path below. Wherever Minka was, Jette was never far off. He hurriedly splashed the cold water over himself, dressed, and went down to join her. Jette had charge of the poultry yard, and she was there, feeding her feathered friends. The chickens surrounded her, squabbling and fighting for the biggest share, just as if they were human. She held a little switch in her hand to drive back a big, quarrelsome old gobbler.

"Now, Patriarch," she said, " make way for the rest of thy tribe. Thou hast gobbled enough for six. Thy crop is so full thou art fit to choke. Still thou art not satisfied. There thou stemmest thy broad shoulders and plumest thyself, till none can approach within an ell of thee. Greedy, thou! Thou canst do no more than satisfy thyself. Back — back, I tell thee! Approach, my children, approach! do not be afraid of him. There is a mightier power than he, which will see that you get your rightful share. For shame, Patriarch! thou posest as a philanthropist, and wouldst devour the whole."

She put some corn between her lips. At this, as at a signal, a swarm of pigeons fluttered down upon her. Wherever they could find a place they perched. Upon her head, her arms, her shoulders, all bending eagerly downward, and up, to take the food from her lips. They swarmed over Minka, who sat immovable, and let them ferret out some stray grains which were scattered among her fur. The big tabby seemed to enjoy it immensely. She blinked her eyes, and purred as benevolently as if she and the pigeons were of the same family. Suddenly she gave a great bound, which scattered them right and left. A great black cat, with gleaming green eyes, had slunk

near, stealthy as a fox. In a moment Minka was
upon her. Then there arose an uproar of snarls
and hisses, a digging of claws, which made even
the Patriarch forget his greed and his dignity,
and with the rest of his tribe beat a safe retreat.
Like all fierce encounters, it was short and decisive. A great deal of fur was left on the ground;
but it was not Minka's. She returned to her
former place, blinking her eyes as if nothing had
happened, licking her fore-paws with a great look
of disgust. She wanted to purge herself from the
unclean attack of the enemy. The chickens returned, the pigeons came back. All was as it had
been before.

"That was Gret's cat," said Jette to Hans, who
had enjoyed the encounter hugely. "She comes
here every day, trying to kill our pigeons. Nasty
creature! See how she goes limping over that
fence. She can hardly drag herself along. I
should think she would stay away, when she knows
she gets so unmercifully mauled each time. But
she always comes back. Some day our Minka
will kill her."

"Does she treat all interlopers that way?"
asked Hans.

"Oh, no. The others never attempt to inter-
fere with Minka. They have a great respect for
her. They know how strong and vigilant she is.
But this nasty creature will not keep away. She
is as spiteful as her mistress. Do you know, I
think that animals partake of the characteristics
of their owners? Again and again she will return

to the attack. She is as pertinacious as she is
vicious. Then, too, she is a born thief. She is
always prowling around our meat safe. One day
she will get her proper deserts. Then both Minka
and I will be glad."

She stroked and kissed her favorite pigeons,
cooed to them, reassuringly scattered another
handful of grain, and leaving Minka in charge,
went to cut some roses for the breakfast-table.
Hans walked beside her, singing the Kossuth
March. He carried his stick like a bâton, with
which he beat time with fiery energy. His shoulders swayed gracefully in even rhythm. Everything Hans did was done with the lightness and
ease which comes from early and constant associa-
tion with high-bred people. He was so happy this
radiant morning, he might have known Fate had
a rod in pickle for him. The wicked rascal, with
a great show of assisting her, ran innumerable
thorns into his fingers, which, of course, she had to
pull out. He paraded his sufferings with so much
ludicrousness while she prodded the needle into
his flesh that, convulsed with laughter, she made
him scream out more than once in real earnest.
Meantime, he looked into her eyes far oftener
than was just to the Countess Irma, whose future
happiness came very near trembling in the balance.
Then the measured tones of the doctor's voice fell
upon their ears.

"There are letters awaiting thee, Hans," he
said, — "important documents from home. The
carrier has just brought them from thy bankers at
Cologne."

The Magyar's swarthy face flushed darkly. "Cannot I be left one minute alone!" he said pettishly. He glared at his friend as if he would gladly annihilate him, and, bowing to Jette, strode towards the house.

She had picked up her scissors, and bent her blushing face assiduously over the roses. With all her heart and soul she was wishing that horrible doctor would go. But no. He remained. And she knew that he was looking at her. What made him stay? Was he going to reprimand her for wasting her time?

"Jettchen," he said.

She started in sheer surprise. Like his father, he always called her Jettchen. But he did not use the familiar "thou," as the rest of the family did. He had always been distant and formal, scrupulously polite, as he might have been to an outside acquaintance. Now there was a tone in his voice which came straight from the heart. She stared at him in astonishment.

"See here," he said, drawing a small volume from his pocket; "I took this just now from the kitchen table when I went to look for you. Babbett said she had found it under your pillow. Do you think my mother would be pleased to find you reading Heine?"

It was worse than she thought. That treacherous Babbett! Wait! She should be paid out for this.

She looked at him with frightened eyes. "I have read worse books than that," she stammered confusedly.

"Oh, indeed! Does my mother know that also?"

"You have not told the Frau Pastorin?" she said, in agony.

"Make yourself easy. I am not a tale-bearing schoolboy." She looked at him gratefully. "No. Perhaps I 'm not quite as bad as you think. I have not told her — yet."

At the emphasis he put upon the last word, she started again in alarm. She folded her hands like a child beseeching pardon.

"What shall I do?" she said; "please do not tell her. I will do anything in the world for you, if you will not." She saw his eyes twinkle and the corners of his mouth twitch under his long, blonde mustache. "I don't care if you do," she burst out inconsequently.

"Oh, yes, you do," he said; "you do care a great deal. You are frightened to death. I can just tell to a beat how rapidly your pulses are galloping. Your heart is frozen with terror. You are agonized to think that all your charming contraband reading will come to an end. And the lecture you will get. Brrr! Mammachen *can* lecture, you know, when she is wound up for it."

The spiteful creature! There he stood with his six-foot odd inches, shoulders like an athlete, and chest like a Greek god, and mocked her with his aggravating brown eyes! He dwindled to the most contemptible proportions in her estimation.

"That is true," she said, shivering. "My Heaven!" she cried, bouncing round so furiously he involuntarily took a step backward, "what do you want of me, then?"

"Tell me what you have read of Heine," he said, with sparkling eyes, "and I won't tell."

"I won't," she said, pouting her lips. It was a trick she had, and a dangerously enticing one. She opened her eyes very wide. "I have read him all," she said, with great complacency.

He laughed till the hills reëchoed. "Buy my silence," he said. His fair face bent very near her own. She could feel his breath caressing her neck. With a gesture of repugnance she drew back. He flushed vividly.

"Give me one of those rosebuds," he said. "No, not that one, this one just opening its first shy leaves to the kisses of the sun."

"You are easily satisfied," she said gayly; "of course you shall have it."

"Put it to your lips," he said.

"And brush the dew off? No, no, 't were a sin to do that. Here, take it — take it — with all its native fragrance moist upon it."

The doctor took it silently. He looked at the rosebud. He looked at her.

"Here is your book," he said.

She took it gladly, and hid it under the roses in her basket. Then they both went in to breakfast. The doctor's rosebud had disappeared.

CHAPTER XIV

Babbett had just placed the silver coffee service upon the table. But no one paid any attention to it. A lively discussion was going on between the Herr Pastor, the Frau Pastorin, and Hans von Czechy. The young baron's face was flushed. He was walking up and down, in strong agitation, rumpling his black curls as he went.

"'T is all over," he said forlornly, when his friend came in; "brother-heart, we have to pack up and be going."

"Is that why you are all so wrought up?" inquired the doctor.

"Fritz," said the Frau Pastorin, "how canst thou talk with so much levity? Is it not enough to wring our hearts to see thee and thy friend go hence? But that is not what we are discussing. There is a large sum of money awaiting the Herr Baron's disposal at his banker's at Cologne. How is he to get it?"

"Fetch it," said the doctor laconically.

"Thou forgettest, my son," said his father, "that you are both secluded here. 'T will never do to show yourselves in your accustomed haunts. 'T is just as well this urgent summons has come to the Herr Baron. Freiherr von Czechy, his father, is alarmed, and justly so. You are both of you far safer away for the present. But the Herr Baron needs the money for his journey. Some accredited person must go and fetch it."

"Papa cannot go," said the Frau Pastorin; "it would arouse comment. Equally so if I went. Yet it must be some one perfectly reliable. Now who is there whom we can trust with this delicate mission?"

Jette, who had arranged her bouquet on the table, said timidly, —

"I will go."

"Thou, Henriette!" exclaimed the Frau Pastorin.

"You, Fräulein Jettchen!" repeated Hans.

"You, Jettchen!" echoed the doctor.

They all stared at her, as at some new revelation. The pastor said nothing, but passed his thin, white hand over his slightly bald crown.

She blushed furiously, but said with courage, "I will go, if you think I can do it."

"But, child," said the Frau Pastorin, "thou hast never been away from home. How wilt thou find thy way alone in a strange city?"

"I will never allow it," said Hans.

"'T is not to be thought of," said the doctor.

"'T is an errand which requires a great deal of circumspection and secrecy," said the pastor; "one careless word might lead to discovery and ruin. 'T will be necessary to depart with the greatest caution, and to come back the same way. Thou canst talk freely enough to Herr Goldman, the banker, for he knows everything. But to any outsider 't would be productive of the greatest danger. Added to this, thou wilt have to spend the night alone among strange surroundings. Dost think thou canst do this?"

"Yes," she said, with sparkling eyes; "and keep my own counsel besides. I am not afraid. I will do it gladly."

"I think thou wilt," said the pastor kindly; "thou needest not spend the night among strangers. I will give thee the address of an old friend, who will take good care of thee. Only, not a word to any one."

But Hans and the doctor broke into a torrent of protests. 'T was not to be thought of. No, no! She was far too young to send on such an errand alone. What! were they, men, to sit at home, and let a young and lovely girl — Here the Frau Pastorin signed Jette to leave the room.

"A young and lovely girl," exploded Hans, "beautiful enough to attract the eye of the most casual observer, to run Heaven knows into what danger! No, no! Sooner than that, let matters take their course."

"Herr Baron," said the pastor calmly, "Jettchen is a child, — courageous and guileless as one. She has the wit and circumspection of a woman. There is no one I would sooner trust."

So, then, it was settled. Jette was called in to breakfast, and the matter fully arranged. She was to meet the mail coach a mile or two from the village, and so go on to Cologne, which she would reach early in the evening. She was to proceed direct to the house of the pastor's friend, and after spending the night there, visit the banking-house of Goldman & Son early the following morning. Then, having transacted her business, she was to return the next day by the regular coach. The most minute instructions were given her about the care of the money and her credentials.

"Thou wilt take care of thyself, Liebchen," whispered Hans tenderly, when she was ready to depart.

"Of course," she laughed; "no one will eat me." She went, full of happy exuberance of spirits.

CHAPTER XV

IN the early fifties, the house of Goldman & Son stood high among the foremost and most powerful banking-houses in Europe. The shabby, old-fashioned brick pile in the Hochstrasse seemed to shake hands with its neighbor across the narrow, dirty street. There was an air of mysterious importance about this musty pile, where the destinies of many powerful personages were arranged as on a chess-board. It struck a chill to the heart of the little country girl as she mounted the steps, worn with innumerable footprints of time. Her courage almost failed her when she entered the large square counting-room, where several clerks bent over their desks, too busy to see who entered. Her voice stuck in her throat, as for the second time she repeated her request to see Herr Goldman. A small, dark man, with a shaven lip and strongly marked aquiline features, looked up. He stared at her in a manner which was not calculated to restore her confidence.

"Herr Goldman? Which one? The elder Herr Goldman or the younger?"

Her confusion increased. She did not know, she said desperately. She wanted to see the Herr Banquier.

Ah, indeed! Well, then, she must state her errand. It was not usual for either of the bankers to see strangers unless they sent in their name, and distinctly stated their business.

By this time at least twelve pairs of eyes were focused on her, as if she were a camera, and they all had to stare unblinkingly to get photographed. Twelve pairs of eyes, all young, all dark, and brimming over with mischief and self-assurance.

"It must be Herr Julius Goldman the young Fräulein wishes to see," said one young clerk, with a discreet smile. "Doubtless the Fräulein is a relative?"

Brilliant idea! Of course! What a splendid fellow! She could have hugged him for it. She wondered why he winked at the rest, and why those twelve dark, aquiline-featured countenances should simultaneously blossom out into exactly the same length and breadth of a grin.

"To be sure," she said eagerly; "yes, indeed. A relative, of course." She could have laughed in the excess of her relief.

"Some one whom he has not seen for a long time?" asked the same young man.

She nodded vivaciously. The young imps

looked at each other, and again that grin popped out, — if possible, broader than before.

"I beg you will be seated, honored Fräulein. I go to announce you to Herr Julius Goldman."

In passing, he said something to his neighbor, who snickered audibly. In a moment he was back, and motioned her to follow. Immensely relieved, yet her heart palpitating violently, she followed him across a dark, narrow, uncarpeted passage, at the end of which was a massive oaken door. This door he opened noiselessly, as noiselessly placed a chair for her, said, "The gracious lady, Herr Julius Goldman," in a deferential, muffled voice, and quickly disappeared.

At the farther end of the square, dingy room, before a ponderous desk, sat a squat, broad-shouldered man. His back was turned towards her; but the strong light from the large uncurtained window fell full upon his red hair, of that peculiarly flaming, repulsive color which instinctively inspires one with distrust. It was sleek and brittle, and cut very close to the scalp; but unfortunately, little as there was, there was too much of it, carefully brushed and combed as it was, so that each hair seemed to be in its right place. Either he was too engrossed to notice her, or he had not heard the low voice of the clerk as he announced her. The young girl grew hot and cold by turns as the interminable scratching of the pen continued. After a while it was energetically flung aside, Herr Goldman said, "So," and slightly moved in his chair. The girl's heart

thumped wildly; now at last he would turn round
and see her. But no. The banker stemmed his
elbows on his desk, and meditated, while he nervously bit his finger-nails. She sat so mute she
scarcely dared breathe. What should she do?
Should she cough? Walk boldly up to him and
say, "Here, you man, your business doubtless is
very important to you, but mine is equally so to
me. I may be very small and insignificant compared to your mightiness. But I have a trust to
perform; it is getting near dinner-time; I am
hungry; I want to look at the shops before I go
home. What! No matter how great and powerful you are, you can't eat me. So there, you
horrid, unmannerly creature. I 'm going to pull
the cobwebs from your mind by kicking over this
stool or yourself, I don't care which."

She had just pulled the papers with which she
was intrusted from her bosom, desperate enough
to carry out her resolve, when suddenly Herr
Goldman, as if in answer to some invisible query,
said very decidedly, "Quatch," pushed the ledger
from him, and turned round. The rays of the
noonday sun fell subdued through the grimy window panes. Like a loving benediction they en-
circled the young girl where she stood, in her
light delaine summer dress, her large leghorn hat
pushed from her brow, her cheeks flushed, the
deep violet of her eyes almost black with excitement. The banker grasped hold of the back of
his chair, and stared at her as if she had descended from the skies, and he momentarily ex-

pected to see her vanish. His confusion gave her confidence. She was as "ready to go off as a popgun," now, as Babbett would have expressed it. Advancing fearlessly, she made a sweet little curtsy, the grace of which was partly acquired and all the rest her own, placed the papers in his hands, and waited. One rapid glance he gave at them, then he looked back at her. In fact, he preferred to look at her.

"What must you think of me?" he stammered; "but this is unheard of. How long have you been here, gracious Fräulein?"

"Quite long enough to feel hungry," she said demurely.

"Heavens! Fräulein, you — I will ring — everything in the town shall be at your disposal — the finest — the best" —

He caught sight of her quizzical face and twitching lips. No, she could hold out no longer. The relief to her feelings after her long wait, coupled with his consternation at her ridiculous answer, was so great, if it had cost her her life, she would have had to laugh. She burst into such a ringing peal as surely the grim old building had never heard. The ghosts of gone and departed generations of Goldmans must have been scandalized at such unheard-of levity. For Jette's merriment came straight from the heart, — it had the true, spontaneous ring of contagious mirth; not your smothered, snickering ghost of a ladylike laugh. Like a joyous peal of bells it rang out, pure, resonant, and full, gladdening the spirit, and

bringing an answering refrain from the lips of
the most pessimistic.

The banker's face flushed dusky red. Then he
fell in with her laughter. Indeed, how could he
help it? Who would not join in mirth at once
so gladsome and sweet? The fresh, pure breezes
of her native hills she brought with her, rarifying
the atmosphere of this musty old place.

"Really," she said, "I am ashamed of my bad
manners. I beg your pardon a thousand times.
I have not been here so very long, I dare say.
Only when one is in a strange place, and waiting "—

"Yes, yes," he interrupted eagerly, "that is
just what I want to know. I heard no one announce you. Some one came in and said, 'A lady
wants to see you, — a relation.' I have so many
relations — good Heavens! they pester my life out.
To tell you the truth — I thought it was my grandmother!"

"Oh!" she said. She tried to look very sympathetic. Then the idea of being his grandmother
overcame her so completely, she had to laugh
again. And so had he.

"You see," he said, in high good humor, "how
it is. A man has no peace anywhere. If they
cannot catch me at home, they are always sure
of finding me here. My grandmamma — well!
she is an estimable old lady, — oh, very, — but she
plagues the life out of me. I say it without any
disrespect to her. It is always, 'Julius, thou
shouldst not do this. Julius, thou must stop

that.' She thinks I am still a little boy, to order around at her pleasure. To her I have never grown up. She means well, of course; but one can kill one with good intentions."

He threw out his white, slightly freckled hands, in graceful gesticulation. When he rose, she noticed he had a club foot. He was quite a young man yet, perhaps twenty-eight, but already showed signs of baldness. Herr Goldman had the dissipated appearance of the finished blasé man of the world. He had the fair, freckled complexion of the red-head, prominent dark eyes, with a gold ring around the iris, set very near each other, bristling red eyebrows, a bull neck, fat, puffy cheeks, and a rotund, squat figure. His features were of a decidedly Oriental cast, large, firm, and strongly animal from the high massive forehead to the wide, thick lips. His chin was dimpled like a woman's, and somewhat softened the cold sensuality of his face. His dress was careful to elegance, and spite of his deformity, he moved with the ease and nonchalance of a well-bred, cultivated man.

He referred to the papers in his hand. "The Herr Baron," he said, "is stopping at the parsonage, which is your home also, I think, Fräulein?"

"Yes," she said. "The Herr Pastor told me I could talk quite unreservedly to you. But I think he explains everything in his letter."

"Quite explicitly. And so you are Fräulein — Fräulein" —

"Jettchen." She smiled.

"Ah! the baron is fortunate to have found such
a haven of refuge.   But pardon — I do not think
I quite caught your name?"

"Everybody calls me Jettchen," she said, "except the Frau Pastorin. She calls me by my full
name.   To the villagers I am Jette."

He shuddered theatrically.   "What a profana-
tion!   What impudent familiarity!   Not to show
you the respect of calling you by your last name!"

She stared.   She had quite forgotten she was
entitled to any.   There never had seemed any
occasion to use it.

"Oh," she said, "they all have known me so
long.   It would seem strange to myself to be
called Fräulein Cajena."

She said it with mock dignity.   Then she had
to laugh.   It sounded so odd to her.

"Ah!" he exclaimed delightedly, "I thought
so.   You *are* one of our people."

"I am a Jewess," she said.

He looked at her with tender interest.   "I was
in doubt at first; you have none of the signs whatever.   But there is an indefinite something which
speaks to the blood, I suppose.   How delightful!
And so you have grown up in perfect seclusion,
hidden away from all the world like a rare treasure."

He looked at her with glowing insistence.   He
passed his plump, white, exceedingly well-kept
hands one over the other, as if he were caressing
something.   When he talked to her, as she was
accustomed to, and laughed when she laughed,

she felt perfectly at ease. But now a feeling of repulsion stirred her.

"The Herr and Frau Pastorin have brought me up," she said. "I am an orphan, and had no home. I owe everything to them."

She pulled herself up with a great shock. Here she was, wasting her time, talking to this stranger as if he were an old acquaintance. Nice, prudent behavior, truly, in a well-brought up young girl! What would the Frau Pastorin say, if only she knew?

"Sir," she said timidly, "if — if you would not mind " —

"Oh," he said reassuringly, "everything is all right. Herr von Czechy's draft shall be honored in a twinkling. There are a few little formalities to be gone through first. Pardon me just for one moment."

He read her like a book. He knew she was vexed and frightened. But he had no intention of letting her go. He sat down at his desk, and this is what he wrote: —

DEAR MAMMA, — A bird of paradise has just alighted on my hand. Come and help me tame it.   JULIUS.

He addressed and sealed this. Then he sharply rung a bell.

"This is to be taken to its address," he commanded, "as quickly as the messenger's legs can carry him. Go — fly! Stay!" he called out sud-

denly, as the obsequious young clerk, who had
entered with a deep bow, was about to disappear;
"which of you blockheads announced the young
Fräulein?"

The young fellow looked as if he wished himself elsewhere. "Sir," he stammered — "Herr
Goldman — it was I — I thought" —

"Thought, thought! What didst thou think?
— if such an ass as thou has any thought at all in
that clot of mud he calls his brain!" exclaimed
the banker furiously.

With a swift gesture Jette raised her hands.
Her face was flushed scarlet. The banker understood her embarrassment.

"Go," he said, in such suddenly mild tones that
the trembling young man almost fell over himself
in his surprise. He scampered back to the outer
office, telling his colleagues, who were all dying
of curiosity, that they would catch it finely. The
young chief was in a Donnerwetter of a humor.
A nice mistake they had made, truly! This was
none of his gallant amours. The young lady they
had treated with such disrespect was really a bona
fide relative. If they didn't believe him, just
see. He held out the missive addressed to Madame Goldman, the banker's mother. Then there
was consternation truly among the young Herren
in the large outer office of the banking-firm of
Goldman & Son. They looked at each other in
the deepest anguish of mind and remorse of soul.

"It was thou, Kohn, who commenced it," said
one young fellow reproachfully to the one who

had first spoken to Jette; "thou always hast such wicked thoughts. Thou wouldst think evil of thy own shadow."

"I!" retorted Kohn indignantly; "well, I must say but that is grand! Thou donkey, thou! Did not the whole lot of you, thy asinine self included, stare at the young Fräulein, and whisper, as if you had never seen anything else but asses like yourselves?"

"That is right," said his fellow clerk scornfully; "always place the blame where it does not belong."

"She probably is some relation from the country," suggested another.

"Bah! she is not a bit like a country pomegranate. Anyway, the young chief is going to distribute it again right and left. We had better not have eyes or ears for anything but what strictly concerns ourselves."

When, presently, Madame Goldman's carriage dashed up to the curb, she found twelve backs bending themselves almost double in obsequious greeting, and twelve pairs of eyes furtively watching her rustling silks into her son's office.

CHAPTER XVI

JETTE explained to Herr Goldman that the young clerk was in no way to blame for announcing her as a relative. Some one had suggested the idea, and as she had been told it was exceed-

ingly difficult to gain access to the private office
without stating one's business, she had gladly
availed herself of it.   Herr Goldman half closed
his prominent dark eyes, smiled, and ejaculated
softly, "A relative — ay, why not?   How charming, how perfectly charming!"   But he was careful not to pay her any more compliments, and to
put her perfectly at her ease, spoke to her as he
had at first, in the half-familiar, confident manner
one uses towards a child.   So in a very short time
he had her whole history at his finger-tips, — her
life at the parsonage, how she came there, her
daily duties, her whole routine of life.   He was
very insistent to find out how long since it was
the doctor and his friend had come.   His brow
darkened when he heard that it was fully three
weeks.

"What folly!" he muttered.   He looked at her
strangely.   That two attractive young men, high-
bred and cultivated, and a heavenly creature like
this should have been constantly in each other's
society so long —   H'm!   It was high time there
should be an end to it.

His mother entered, in high displeasure.

"Julius — it really is inconceivable — what mad
freak of thine is this now?"

Madame Goldman was short, dumpy, and pudgy,
with somewhat masculine features, but a strong
individuality of her own.   She was dressed entirely in black, rich, heavy silks, of the kind which
"stand alone."   She was dark, very Oriental-look-
ing, and grande dame down to her fine Parisian

boots. A Viennese by birth, she had all the culture, vivacity, and ease of bearing which distinguish those Parisians of the Danube, and also their fascinating little peculiarities of speech. She was the chum and confidante of her son, and had helped him out of scrapes more times than she ever had boxed his ears. He was her only child, and she had been his constant companion ever since he outgrew a nurse's care. He smiled, and enjoyed the surprise he had in store for her.

"Dear mamma," he said, "how kind of you to come so quickly. See the young Fräulein. She is a stranger to our city, and recommended to our best care. Let me present you to my mother, Fräulein Cajena."

Madame Goldman bowed somewhat distantly, but with the easy grace of a thoroughly accomplished woman of the world. She looked at the young girl with a great deal of interest, and far more curiosity. Jette dropped her prettiest curtsy, somewhat awed by the great lady's grand appearance. The banker's mother smiled. "Very unsophisticated," she thought, "but, dear Heaven, how lovely!" She followed her son to the window, where they carried on a very animated conversation in French. Mother and son spoke the language like natives. Not in teutonized, halting phrases, but the purest, most scholarly Parisian, with here and there a gesture and a shrug, as if they had spent all their lives in the city by the Seine. Occasionally the grand lady gave a side glance at the young girl, sitting expectantly in

her chair, and she would ejaculate softly, "Est-ce
que possible!" She nodded her head several
times, seemed somewhat astonished, but not wholly
displeased. The truth is, her son was making a
proposition to her, which, if she had not been his
best friend, he never would have dared to submit
to her. During his three years' absence in Paris
and one year in Vienna, he had confided all his
mad escapades to her. And let me tell you that
they were neither few in number nor tame in experience. She would storm, scold, and reprimand,
but through it all he was always sure of her
counsel and stanch loyalty. Madame Goldman
adored young people, and was idolized by them.
Only sixteen years older than her son, she was
both mother and companion to him. At the age
of fifteen she was married to her cousin, who was
just double her age. The union had been one
of financial policy, to combine the house of Goldman and her father's in a mutual interest. When
she married, she took all her dolls with her, and
found as much pleasure in dressing and undressing
them as if they were still the only claimants on
her affection. The first two or three years of her
married life were far from happy. When her
husband came home at night, weary with the
day's close mental application, he found the liv-
ing-rooms deserted. The servants did not know
where their mistress was, and the whole big house
had to be searched, till she was found in the attic,
playing with her dolls. In the mean time the
dinner had grown cold, the cook was out of temper,

—everybody did exactly as he or she pleased. When her child was born, she came near to dying. A nurse was provided. It was thought natural, under the circumstances, she should not take any notice of him; but things did not mend when she recovered. She looked at the unsightly, deformed little object with profound astonishment. He took after the red-headed, prominent-eyed branch of the Goldman family. She did not like this at all. If he had been more like herself, she might more readily have taken to him. She left him to his nurse, a robust, strapping peasant woman, from whose bounteous breasts this young hope of an opulent race greedily drew health and substance. Fortunate for him it was that the nurse was both conscientious and kind. While the mother returned to her dolls and her music, of which she was passionately fond, the child grew up under the nurse's care. When her services were no longer required in nourishing him, she still stayed on. This continued until he was three years old. Then he sickened, and the doctor said it was scarlet fever of a virulent type. The house was hushed, the most eminent professors were summoned posthaste in consultation. The mother tiptoed into the nursery and looked at the child, tossing in his little crib, moaning in delirium, and clutching the dry, parched throat. What passed within her then, only herself and her God knew. Like a tidal wave, the mother-instinct leapt into life, so that she reeled and almost fell with the magnitude of the revelation. She swept aside the

nurse, and from that hour took her station beside
her child by right divine.   Her husband and relatives implored her not to expose herself to the
disease; she had never had it; she was so young.
Why, the nurse, of whom he was so fond, and
who had done mother's duty by him since he was
born, was far more competent to take care of him
than she, who had never had any experience at all
in nursing.   She said nothing, but gave them one
long look, which silenced and overawed them,
shut herself up with her sick child and admitted
none but the doctors, and for nine frightful nights
and days matched her strength, her cleverness,
and her devotion against the fierce destroyer, and
smote him hip and thigh.   Not till then did she
consent to take a sorely needed rest; for not once
during all that time of watching had she removed
her clothing.   When the child was fully recovered, she sent the jealous, wrathful nurse — who
from a servant had fancied herself mistress —
back to her native village, loaded with presents
and every conceivable token of generosity.   But
she would have no more of her, and took her
child, who clung to her with idolizing affection, to
the Bavarian Alps, where both grew so hardy and
strong that everybody was astonished when they
returned home.   The dolls were swept into a big
cedar chest, and consigned to a corner in the attic.
There they awaited their resurrection in the coming of a new and more appreciative generation.
But the chest gathered cobwebs, the dolls got
moth-eaten; for those for whom they waited never

came. Poor, disappointed dollies! poor, disappointed mistress! The six girls and six boys, who were to join in the sports of their elder brother, patter up and down the grand staircase with their little feet, and fill the big empty house with their gleeful shouts and laughter, never came. And as each year went by, with its longed-for hope unfulfilled, the mistress of all this wealth and grandeur often looked in the glass, and saw only the shadows of her forlorn hopes mocking her. This one child remained to her, and it was all she had. When at night she kissed him, it was for all the six brothers and sisters she fancied she had defrauded him of. She thought the Lord had punished her for not appreciating the blessing he had sent her at first. She bowed her head in submission, but she suffered cruelly. It drew mother and son in bonds of the closest union, especially as the father had become a perfect business machine. His son was his heir; beyond that he had very little in common with him. So the rich, envied woman went her lonely way, and busied herself with outside interests, and tried to fill the big void in her heart by making the poor happy. She wanted her son to marry, and to marry well. The sole heir of the powerful house of Goldman could have his pick and choice among the richest and prettiest heiresses of Europe. She would dandle his children on her knee. Thou dear God! how she would love them! They should be her compensation; the dolls should have their new companions yet. But here he was already eight-

and-twenty, and showed no more inclination to marry than when he was in his teens. Several very desirable alliances had been proposed to him, — desirable even from the Goldman point of view, — but he had scouted every one, until both she and his father were on the point of losing patience.

She looked at the lovely creature, whose history he was relating in a few rapid words, as if she had fallen from the skies. Her son had had fancies before, serious ones, she had feared at times, but there was a glow on his face, a flash in his eye, which told her his time had come. He did not, of course, tell her this. But he scarcely would have proposed she should take this heavenly messenger under her protection during the rest of her stay, if he had not some other and very serious motive in the background. The girl was lovely, undeniably so. She was of the same faith as themselves, though brought up under peculiar circumstances. But this only added to the interest every one must feel in her. H'm! It might have been worse. Suppose he had fallen in love, as she so often had feared, with some one of another faith? He was so advanced in his·views, so very headstrong,— besides, he was quite old enough to be master of his own actions. If he wanted to marry a poor girl, he was quite rich enough to indulge in the luxury. He would have to settle that matter with his father. Madame Goldman turned towards Jette.

"Dear child," she said, in that caressing manner she always adopted towards young people, "my son has told me everything, and why you are here. Now that your business is finished, you must give the rest of the 'day to me. But first let us go home and have luncheon."

"You are too good — too kind," stammered Jette, terribly confused. "I — I hope you do not take seriously what I said to Herr Goldman."

The banker's face beamed. "You told me you were hungry," he said.

"And you took me for your grandmother," she retorted. Then they all three looked at each other, and burst into peals of laughter. And so, in gay good humor, they passed out by a private door, and were driven to the banker's palatial home. And the twelve young Herren in the outer office rushed pell-mell to the window to look after the retreating carriage, looked at each other, shook their black, curly polls, and said wisely and sagely, "That is going to be a marriage."

CHAPTER XVII

MADAME GOLDMAN was charmed and fascinated with her young visitor. She only regretted her stay could be of such short duration. She proposed to Jette to send a trusty messenger to Neukirch with the money and papers she was to bring, and beg for a holiday. To this Jette, in a fever of trepidation, would not consent. She was highly honored and delighted by the great lady's kindness and condescension, as indeed she had every

reason to be. But her mission was to her a sacred
one. The Herr Pastor had charged her to perform it. She had succeeded far better than she
had expected. Proud and elated, she would not
think of dividing her duty with any one else, however trustworthy. Timidly, but firmly, she reminded Madame Goldman of the secrecy of her
errand. There were other motives, besides, which
made her anxious to return. She knew that in
a very few days the doctor and his guest would
depart. For the former she did not care; for the
latter she cared a great deal. She wanted to see
the last of him, to bid him good-by and God-
speed. They had been such good friends, never,
never would she forget this summer which he had
made so delightful to her. Jette had never known
the companionship of a brother, that close inti-
macy and sympathetic familiarity which unites
two beings born of the same mother in the sweetest, purest bonds of friendship. From the beginning of the world, God intended it so; and from
the beginning of the world, man, fulfilling so little
of what was expected of him, has been false to his
trust. But Jette, having been brought up religiously, and believing in the sacredness of the Ten
Commandments, besides steeping her young soul
in all sorts of miscellaneous reading, which caused
no end of a muddle in her young brain, had
formed a very exalted ideal of what a brother
should be. In her healthy, vigorous life there was
not much time left for romancing. But she was
more alone than was good for her; she never took

counsel with companions of her own age, because she had none. So in her fervent, hero-worshiping mind she created her own idols, and prostrated herself before them. This, of course, gave her a very charming individuality. Blasé people of the world refreshed themselves with her original sayings, and forgot their scornful pessimism in her fervent trust in all that to them was most untrustworthy. Jette was by no means in love with Hans von Czechy. Never for one moment in her life had she thought of such a thing. Her intellect was cultivated beyond her years, but it had left the faculties of her heart all asleep. She thought of the young baron as a brother, and that is how she worshiped him.

Madame Goldman resolved, if she could not see as much of her guest now as she wanted to, she would see a great deal of her in the future. Then there was crowded in the few hours remaining to her so much of sight-seeing, and pleasure, and shopping, as Jette had no idea could be accomplished in a week. The great Cathedral was visited, of course. As they passed down the aisle, a woman who had been kneeling in silent worship arose, and liberally sprinkled herself with holy water. There was quite a shower of small sprays, some of which struck Jette in the face. She shrank as if she had received a blow, and from her slim height looked down at Madame Goldman in a half-frightened manner. The great lady smiled, and in a whisper jocularly remarked that now she supposed she must consider herself christened.

"Do you think so — oh, is it true?" faltered the girl.

"Dear child," said the elder lady seriously, "how can you be so simple? As if it mattered if a whole shower of the water was poured over you. It cannot affect your convictions."

But Jette's disquietude was not quite allayed till the carriage drew up before one of the large shops. In the plenitude of her purse and the goodness of her heart, Madame Goldman wanted to shower presents upon the young girl. But the latter felt a very comfortable conviction that the Frau Pastorin would have considered it very ill-bred of her to accept. Besides, her wants were so few and simple she did not know what to do with the things.

"Please, no," she said; "some other time — when I come again — when you have known me longer, and consider me more worthy of your kindness."

"But is there nothing — nothing you will take from me as a little keepsake even?" asked Madame Goldman.

"If you would not mind, there is a bottle of Maria Farina — no, no, not that big one — the little one — I had intended to get it myself — the Frau Pastorin — she is so fond of it " —

"Well, there surely must be something else?"

"As we passed up the aisle I saw a nice warm hood — I think Babbett would be pleased — you see, she is getting old — she knits them herself, but they are not near as handsome as that one.

In the winter, when it is cold, you have no idea
how one's ears freeze — she could wear that one
to church — Oh, thank you. How good you are!"

"Now I am sure there is something else."

"No," she said reflectively, "unless it is that
beautiful handkerchief over there. The Herr
Pastor would feel quite grand wearing it on a
Sunday. But I suppose it costs a lot of money.
Oh, are you really going to buy it? Well — now
— I don't see how you can be so generous to me."

"Now you must pick out something for yourself. Indeed, I insist upon it."

"Oh, but look at the lot of money you have
already spent. No, no. I could not think of it.
Besides, I have all I want."

She would not allow the obsequious shopman to
carry the precious parcel to the carriage, but took
it herself, all in a flutter of delight at the treasures it contained. Everybody looked after her,
and smiled in sympathy with her happiness.
Then they drove to a famous Conditorei, where
all the wealth, and fashion, and beauty of the town
assembled of an afternoon to drink café glacé
or eat ices. The windows were wide open, they
could see the steamboats with their joyous occu-
pants plying up and down the glistening blue
Rhine. A military band was playing Strauss's
last new waltz, with its intoxicating rhythm, —
playing as only a trained German band can play.
There was a babel of subdued voices and soft,
musical laughter. What happiness! Really the
world was beautiful!

And there, too, was Herr Goldman. He had been obliged to leave them right after luncheon, but he knew very well where and at what hour to find them. For the last twenty minutes his eyes had been fixed hungrily upon that door. With a beaming smile he beckoned to them as they entered. The best table, in the breeziest spot and commanding the finest outlook, he had already reserved, to which the waiter, all smiles and bows, conducted them. Then for the first time in her life Jette ate ices. Ye Heavens! did ever again in all her life anything taste quite like this? The first delicious tickling of the palate is very much like first love, — the same blissful sensations never return. And then the pastry — light, flimsy things, with just weight enough to contain the most delicious fillings, which surely the gods on Olympus themselves must have made. The banker watched her with the greatest amusement. In her wholesome, healthy life Jette had not been spoilt with dainties. It was such a new and wholly delightful experience to her that I am sorry to say she gave way to it more than was good for her. It was the banker's fault, wicked rascal. When he saw how much the girl enjoyed this novel treat, he gave such lavish orders to the waiter as made even that experienced functionary stare. Madame Goldman looked at her son over her glass of café glacé, and frowned.

"She will have indigestion," she said, most severely, in French.

"She does n't know what it is," he answered,

hugely delighted to see another ice disappear.
"What! with those eyes so clear you can see
right through them, and that superb complexion
beside which ours looks like tallow? Ask her.
I will wager she won't know what you mean."

Which in very truth it proved to be. Indigestion! She laughed. She had never heard of
such a thing. It was a word as foreign to her
vocabulary as nerves was to Babbett's. Herr
Goldman strolled away for a moment, and had
a big bag filled with the choicest confectionery
the place contained. Then he selected a handsome satin-lined box, had it piled to the top with
bonbons, and directed the whole to be securely and
nicely packed and taken to the carriage. He intended she should be well supplied on her journey
on the morrow, and that at the same time it was
his forethought which had so generously provided
for her. She should be grateful to him, the little
angel. Après? One would see.

As he stumped back, in and out among the little
tables, he was stared at with more than usual interest. A party of officers, haughty, overbearing
fellows, who usually contented themselves with carelessly nodding to him, stopped him with effusion.

"Goldman Liebster, tell us who is that divine
Backfisch who came in with your mother? A
stranger, eh?"

Herr Goldman's vanity was flattered. To be
thus familiarly addressed by the arrogant, proud
Baron von Z—— in the presence of all fashiona-
ble Cologne was indeed no small social distinction.

"To the city — yes," he said in his smooth manner; "but not by any means to us."

"Donnerwetter! where have you hidden her all the time? She is simply heavenly beautiful. After rending our hearts by a glimpse of her, do you intend to put her back under lock and key?"

"You must ask my mother," he said, laughing. "The young Fräulein is under her special care."

"Heavens! I wish she would allow me to share it," sighed a beardless young lieutenant.

"You had better ask her," suggested Herr Goldman, the gold rings in his eyes gleaming like fire.

"Ask Beelzebub and all his dragons. How can one approach her, guarded like that? Not once has she glanced this way, though I have sighed " —

"Enough to inflate this room, and float us all over the Rhine," interrupted von Z——.

"Cold-hearted creature," moaned the young lieutenant.

"No wonder," laughed a gay young subaltern, "if she fortifies her system with nothing but ices."

"Don't disquiet yourselves, gentlemen," said Herr Goldman; "the young Fräulein is going back to school."

"Going back to school?" chorused the young officers. "No, indeed; we won't allow that. We will lie in wait for the post-chaise, and make the postilions surrender."

"She belongs to your people, eh?" inquired von Z—— hesitatingly.

Herr Goldman bowed. "She belongs to my people," he said, measured and coldly. There was hauteur as well as triumph in his voice. He went back to his table, assisted his mother with her lace shawl, piloted Jette, with a smiling air of proprietorship, in the wake of Madame Goldman, and drove off with them in the serene knowledge that he was the most envied man in the town that day.

CHAPTER XVIII

THAT was a blissful day for Jette. So many events were crowded into it, they might well have been distributed over the whole year. She had accomplished her errand successfully, she had made new friends, who treated her like a spoilt child, and had given her a glimpse of that great world, into which she glided as easily and naturally as if she had always belonged to it. The drive along the public promenade — should she ever forget it! The band had played as band surely never played before. Such waltzes — oh, how could people lounge around without seizing hold of each other and keeping time to such ravishing music! She, for her part, could not keep still. It was with difficulty she preserved the proper decorum in the carriage. People looked at her, smiled, and looked again and again. Indeed, who could help it? Her flushed cheeks, her beaming eyes, the thrill of ecstasy which half parted her lips, showing just the edges of her

glistening, perfect teeth, — could eyes behold a
more absorbing vision of health, happiness, and
beauty? And then her sweet, gracious youth,
the air of perfect innocence and purity, which
surrounded her like a benediction from on high,
and made the boldest roué involuntarily subdue
his gaze, — surely, if she received much, she gave
as much in return. The banker and his mother
constantly exchanged glances as they watched her.
They smiled in sympathy with her joy, and echoed
her gleeful laugh for the same reason. If ever
there was a proud man in Cologne, it surely was
Herr Goldman. He enjoyed the notice they attracted, the looks of envy directed towards himself, the distinction of being bowed to by people
of the most exclusive set, who at best had only
nodded carelessly to him before. Baron von Z——
and his brother officers passed and repassed. They
sighed, looked, and languished. But not the
slightest glance did they obtain. Jette was far
too much absorbed in her own enjoyment to take
heed of anybody. She would have been seized
with the greatest consternation, if any one had
drawn her attention to the notice she was exciting.
All her pleasure would have been spoilt. This
utter unconsciousness pleased Herr Goldman and
his mother more than all else. The banker felt
that he was avenged for many a slight and covert
sneer von Z—— and his confrères had bestowed
upon the "Jew."

At dinner Jette met Goldman, senior. She
looked down upon a small, thin, wiry old gentle-

man, dressed in very shabby, rusty, black clothes.
The skirts of his swallow-tailed coat almost
touched his heels, the lapels were covered with
snuff, and his skinny little chin quite disappeared
in an enormously high collar and a black satin
stock, all frayed at the edges. He was very bald-
headed, and his eyes — prominent and dark, with
gold rings in them like his son's — had a sharp,
comprehensive look, which took in a great deal
at a single glance. His great financial schemes
absorbed all his time and attention, with one great
exception, — his wife. Her he worshiped and
doted upon, and was jealous of the great affection
she bestowed upon their son. If she kissed the
latter, she had to kiss him also, or he would be
sulky for a month. The fine clothes and jewels
and gimcracks he disdained for himself, he lavished in profusion upon her. She had the most
thoroughbred horses and the finest appointed carriage in the whole Rhine province. She could
spend money as profusely as she pleased upon her
charities, — for charity and the name of Goldman
were synonymous, — her entertainments, her hob-
bies. During the hot summer months she went
to Ems and Wiesbaden, and no more ardent ad-
mirer trotted in her train than this snuffy, shabby,
little old gentleman. His love for his old clothes
was the only point of contention between them.
He clung to them as long as she would let him.
When finally she used the utmost finesse to sub-
stitute a new suit, he was ill-humored and out of
gear until it commenced to look as shabby as the

old one. At first he flatly refused to give them up, and to his intense delight and her consternation, he recovered them, and triumphantly put them on again. After that, she always had them burnt. This caused no end of dismay, for as it happened, rigidly as the pockets always were searched, a valuable memorandum, secreted in a receptacle known only to himself, had been overlooked. So they came to an amicable understanding that he was to receive notice whenever he was required to put on new clothing. The poor old gentleman used to quake weeks beforehand, for so well was he used to the different expressions in his wife's face that he could always tell whenever she meditated one of her raids upon his old clothes. At night, when he went to bed, she had her own maid brush them, while he kept a jealous watch on her. But his trousers he positively refused to give up. These he secreted so cleverly that the most diligent search could never discover them. In the morning, before she was awake, he would with great secrecy and caution draw them from their hiding-place. At stated times during the week she laid out his clean linen, had the bath prepared, conducted him to the door, and shut him in. Her manner to him was as maternal as if he had been a pet child, instead of being fifteen years her senior. When she stooped over to kiss him, and brushed the few wisps of hair from his high forehead, very broad at the temples, the faded rings in his eyes would sparkle, and his sallow skin flush like a schoolgirl's. During the

twenty-nine years of their married life, he had
never once gone away without kissing her and
doing the same when he returned. When first
he had brought her home a mere child·from the
schoolroom, and she had shut herself up in the
attic to play with her dolls to avoid meeting him,
he had been a patient and fatherly protector to
her. Thus had she grown into his life to be both
child and wife to him. He never missed a daughter, because she was all to him. So had it been
from the first, and so would it be to the last.

Jette's awe and trepidation at meeting the great
senior of the famous banking-house vanished
when she saw him. Being all in ignorance that
people of immense means may indulge with impu-
nity peculiarities a poor man would not dare
dream of, and acquire an envied reputation for
individuality besides, she was amazed at the
contrast between himself and his surroundings.
Every detail spoke, not alone of the most lavish
wealth, but also of the most unerring and cultivated taste. Had she not been accustomed to the
grandeur of Hermersdorff, she would have been
overwhelmed at the evidences of luxury displayed
everywhere. All the appointments at table were
of the most costly crystal and solid silver. There
was quite a large party, all poor relatives of the
Goldmans and inmates of their hospitable mansion. There was Hanne, an elderly spinster, who
took all housekeeping cares off Madame Goldman's hands. She was a second or third cousin;
somewhat shrewish, but very capable, and ruled

the large staff of servants with an unsparing
hand.   Then there was a very old gentleman, an
uncle of Madame Goldman's from the maternal
side, who took snuff with a trembling hand, spilled
his soup over his napkin, and undertook on any
and every occasion the rôle of cicerone in the
Goldman mansion.   There were two or three
young gentlemen employed in the bank, receiving
their financial training there.   They did full justice to the lavish and excellent dinner, stared a
great deal at Jette, and blushed furiously when
the younger Goldman glared at them reprovingly.
The conversation during dinner was chiefly carried on between father and son, occasionally joined
in with vivacity by Madame Goldman.   It was
an unintelligible jargon to Jette, who was quite
bewildered at the fickleness of a thing they called
the "boerse," which seemed to gyrate with the
unreliableness of a shipwrecked balloon in a mad
upward or downward course.   She felt embarrassed and constrained, and was glad when at
last, to her great relief, dinner was over.   Hanne
and the young gentlemen disappeared, and the
rest went into the adjoining drawing-room.   Here
she was pounced upon by Uncle Emanuel, who,
leaning on his stick, his little old head shaking
with palsy, conducted her from one art treasure
to another, challenging her admiration, and stating
with the accuracy of a guide-book the different
value of each.

"Here, look at this group by Rubens. Is it
not ' famos ' ? Perhaps you don't know he was

a great painter, — one of the greatest the world
has produced. He was a Hollander. My nephew
paid ten thousand thalers for it. Fancy, paying
such an enormous sum for a single picture. He
got it a dead bargain. It is easily worth three
times as much. Just think of it, — three times
as much!" bawled Uncle Emanuel, in his thin,
cracked voice, his shaking little head cocked to
one side, flourishing his stick in ecstasy. "And
here's a vase of Parian marble, right in front of
you on this pedestal. Look at its exquisite work-
manship. It came from Pompeii, — Pompeii, you
know, an ancient town in Italy, which was buried
by an earthquake almost two thousand years ago.
What did you say? Hey? That you have read
all about it? Well, of course I didn't know you
were so learned. I tell you that cost a lot of
money. Ach! I tell you it would make you rich,
if you had it. But it's easily worth a great
deal more than we paid for it. There is nothing
like making a good bargain. Have you looked at
it enough? Ay, admire it, do. In all your life,
maybe, you will never see anything like it again.
Do you notice this little picture? Well, that
little oil painting, not much bigger than my hand,
— have you any idea what a fabulous sum it is
worth? It is by one of the great Florentine
masters, and represents a great poet, Tante — no,
Dante, I think they call him. See the laurel
wreath around his brow" —

"Yes," interrupted Jette unguardedly, "but
this is not the original. That is in one of the
famous galleries in Italy."

"What!" screamed the old man; "not the
original! After all the money we paid for it!
Ach, indeed! How comes it that you set yourself
up for a judge?"

Jette was frightened to death at the fury she
had invoked, and the taunting sarcasm of the old
man's voice. Goldman fils, who had no patience
with his great-uncle's vulgarity, but who was
eagerly watching to see what impression the dis-
play of wealth would make upon this unsophisticated country girl, now sauntered up as if unawares. For him, all the pictures that ever were
painted had not as much interest as the one presented by the decrepit, bent old man, trembling
on the verge of the grave, and the blooming, radiant vision of youth, shrinking away from him. It
gave him immense pleasure when she turned to
him, with every sign of welcome relief. But the
old man still scowled at her in high displeasure.

"Dost know," he said, with an angry sneer,
"that this young Fräulein possesses most wonderful knowledge? She has just told me that our
pictures, which cost more money than she ever
saw, or ever will see in all her life, which people
from afar come to see and admire, are what she
is kindly pleased to call copies. Copies!" he
added with angry emphasis, glaring as if he would
gladly annihilate her.

"Don't mind Uncle Emanuel," said Herr Goldman cheerfully. "'T is his way, but he means no
harm. You see he is old and infirm," he added,
with a shrug. He took the old man by the arm,

and led him to his own particular chair, where he sat glowering, thumping his stick angrily upon the carpet, and repeating at intervals with a great deal of vicious energy, "Copies! ach, copies, indeed!" Then he laid his head against the swelling upholstery, and in another moment snored peacefully.

"What I did say," said Jette, as Herr Goldman rejoined her, "was that the original of this Dante was in Italy. I had no idea Herr Emanuel would be so incensed. I am sure I would sooner have bitten out my tongue."

"That would have been a terrible punishment for so small an offense, which after all is no offense at all," he said laughingly. "You are quite right, Fräulein, in regard to the picture. But where, may I ask, did you obtain your knowledge?"

"Up at the castle at Hermersdorff they have many beautiful pictures. Fräulein Thekla showed me them all, and told me their history. She has been abroad with the Herr Baron, her father. At every place they visited she bought a great many things. They are very beautiful and interesting. She has engravings of the most famous pictures in the foreign galleries. So when I saw this head of Dante, I remembered having seen it in Fräulein Thekla's portfolio of the gallery in Florence. She told me who painted it, that it was the only authentic picture of the poet, and how highly it was prized by the authorities."

"Fräulein von Hermersdorff," he said attentively; "do you mean the daughter of the famous professor?"

"Yes," she said; "the castle is within easy distance of Neukirch. The Herr Professor spends part of the holidays there. It is a beautiful place."

"And you know them? Indeed, Fräulein Cajona, you are to be congratulated upon possessing such friends."

He said it with far greater respect and deference than he had shown before. It was plain to see she had acquired vastly more importance in his eyes.

"Everything I know the Fräulein has taught me," said Jette, with emotion. She added reverently, as if saying a prayer, "God bless her."

She went over to Madame Goldman, who was playing soft, pathetic music. She always played thus after dinner, while her husband lay on the sofa, and with a red silk handkerchief over his face, snored peacefully and contentedly. Madame Goldman, like most Viennese women of the highest culture, was a trained musician. It was not alone her perfect technique, but her wonderful understanding and feeling. There was life and heart in everything she played, whether it was Beethoven or Strauss. Perfect mistress of harmony, she played with a grace and skill which made her completely dominate the piano, and would have made her famous and rich, had she been compelled to earn her living. Like all good players, she was intensely, passionately fond of music, and could call up any emotion she pleased.

As Jette came up, she suddenly broke into the entrancing strains of the waltz king, Strauss, of whom it was said he could make the halt, the lame, and the decrepit dance. It was the same music the band had played on the public promenade that afternoon. Jette, who, if anything, was born to dance, who could never keep her feet still at the sound of the most cracked old fiddle, was fairly carried away. But, indeed, it must have been a codfish who could have listened to such entrancing strains, played by such a spirited master hand, without sending the feet flying. Before she knew it, she had caught Madame Goldman's fat pug, who lay lazily blinking at her from the depths of a luxurious armchair, and was off with him around the room. If ever the young banker cursed his deformity, it was when he saw Jette dance. And she had no other partner than the struggling, yawping little beastie, who, having overcome his first astonishment, vented his outraged dignity in a succession of angry snarls. Madame Goldman, seeing him sitting there, his hands in his pockets, and that moody expression on his face, struck a few skillful chords, and stopped.

"Oh, my poor Mops," she said, as she took the angry pug from the breathless girl's arms; "what outrage have they done thee? Yes, scold her, scold her!" she said, laughing, as the highly insulted little beast turned upon his late partner, and lustily barked at her.

"*Oh*, what divine music!" said the girl; "it

will haunt me all the summer. How I wish I could learn it on the guitar."

"Do you play the guitar?" asked Madame Goldman.

"Oh, no; only just enough to accompany myself to a few simple songs."

"You sing," said Madame Goldman, with animation; "I thought you had a singing voice. How lovely! Contralto, is it not? Yes, I thought so. Here we all have voices like cawing rooks. As for Julius, he has not an atom of an ear. He would insist upon joining a singing society. One conductor died of consumption, the second ran away, and the third hanged himself. Ah, here is Julius with the guitar. Sit there — there where I can see you, Liebchen. Now sing."

If Madame Goldman loved to play, Jette loved to sing. The little training Thekla had given her amounted to a great deal with a voice like hers. At first diffident and shy, she soon gained confidence, and let her pure young voice soar over the vast expanse of the drawing-room. It flooded the house from attic to cellar. The servants came out into the hall to listen. She sung an impassioned love song, a great favorite of Thekla's: —

> "Ask the roses if I love thee,
>   Ask the roses, thou heavenly maid."

She was voicing the sentiments of the banker's own heart. As he sat and watched her, entranced, he felt that it was irrevocably gone out of his keeping forever.

"You have a splendid voice," said Madame Goldman. "Heavens! with some cultivation and a great deal of practice, what could not be made of it! Let me tell you, liebe Kleine, that some years hence you will sing that passionate song with a vastly different expression."

She herself accompanied her to her room, and embraced her in farewell. Madame Goldman was a late riser, and the early post-chaise would have borne the young girl hence long before she herself would be stirring.

"Has your visit been pleasant, little one?" she asked caressingly. "Oh, but you need not answer. Your eyes express enough. Here is a letter for the Herr Pastor you must give him. It is my wish you should soon come again. Will you?"

"Oh, how good you are! Indeed, indeed, I will, if the Frau Pastorin will let me. But I cannot come till the summer is over. There is the garden to take care of, harvesting at which I must help, and — indeed, I could not be spared. But in the winter — I think it could be managed then. Perhaps I can bring my spinning-wheel and knitting," she added anxiously.

The great lady laughed and patted her cheeks. She took the brooch she wore at her throat, and fastened it in the girl's white lace fichu.

"Thou wouldst not let me buy anything for thee," she said, lapsing into the familiar thee and thou; "now thou must wear this, and never forget me till thou comest again."

"No, no," said Jette, overcome at such a magnificent present; "no, no, indeed, I dare not take it. What shall I do with such a valuable thing as that? 'T is far too grand for me."

But Madame Goldman only laughed again. "My dear! I have so much of the trash lying around; 't is a relief to get rid of some of it. Dear little one! Auf Wiedersehen! we shall soon meet again."

CHAPTER XVIII

WHAT rejoicing there was when Jette returned home. She came early the following night. The villagers were all abed; there were no prying eyes to see her. How strange the familiar living-room looked, with its sanded floor, even after so short an absence. When she handed the package of important papers to Hans, his eyes glistened, and he kissed the gracious hand which gave it, with all looking on. The Herr Pastor patted her under the chin and pinched her blushing cheek, declaring she was the most famously discreet little girl in the whole Rhine province. Of course she had to refresh herself with coffee, which Babbett brought in presently, and though supper was over long ago, they all sat around the table, each taking a cup to keep her company.

"Out there in the passage," said Babbett, poking her head in again, "are quite a lot of packages. I suppose you have forgotten all about them, Jette?"

Of course she was dying, poor old thing, to know what they contained. The everlastingly feminine heart, God bless it, knows full well that one does n't go to town without indulging in some sort of shopping, even if it be on the minutest, most limited scale.

"My presents!" exclaimed Jette, darting into the hall, from which she emerged with her arms full, Babbett carrying the rest. The Herr Pastor's eyes moistened when, with a great deal of pride and a timid blush, she gave him the much-prized handkerchief. The Frau Pastorin smiled with pleasure to find she was remembered, and Babbett went fairly wild over the lovely warm hood. She went up and put her withered lips to the girl's soft, blooming cheek.

"Thou art a good one," she said, in her direct, honest manner; "nay, indeed thou hast a good heart. But, dear Heaven, Jette! These things cost a lot of money. Where didst thou get it from? Hast thou bought nothing for thyself? And what is in this large box?"

"I have n't any idea," she said; "Herr Goldman put it in the post-chaise with a lot of delicious confectionery after I had taken my seat."

"Herr Goldman," cried Hans von Czechy and the doctor simultaneously.

"Yes, indeed," she said; "was n't it kind of him? He and Hanne, the housekeeper, took me to the booking-office, early as it was, and never left me till the post-chaise started. A footman followed with these things. I told Herr Goldman there must be some mistake, but he only laughed, and said a fairy had sent them overnight. He reminded me about the confectionery, or I should have sat down on it. Oh, it was delicious. I am afraid I have eaten every bit of it."

While she ran on in her happy, unconcerned manner, the rest looked at each other in amazement.

"Which of the bankers did you see?" asked the Magyar, with a lowering brow.

"Oh, I saw both of them — the younger one at first, of course — Herr Julius Goldman, at the bank, who was very gracious, I assure you. The old gentleman I met at the house — Thou dear Heaven! I never would have taken him for a rich banker. Oh, look, look! Did ever any one see anything so extravagant? Bonbons! this whole immense thing full, and what a beautiful box! lined with pink satin, embroidered all over in gold. Actually! I never, never, even in my dreams, saw anything half so magnificent. I really must run out to the kitchen and show it to Babbett."

"She has seen that red-headed satyr," said the Magyar furiously, in an undertone to the doctor; "of course he has fallen in love with her — maledictions on him!"

Out into the passage the pastor was calling, "Come back, chatter-pate. Now sit down like a sensible girl, and tell us everything that has befallen thee since thou leftest home." So she gave a detailed account of everything that had

happened. And as she ran on, perfectly unconscious of the sensation she created, Hans von
Czechy looked at the doctor, and the doctor looked
at him. She had tears in her eyes, when she
spoke of Madame Goldman's graciousness. Then
she dived into her pocket, and handed the Herr
Pastor the letter intrusted to her care.

"Here is the lovely brooch she gave me," she
said, taking it from among the folds of her bodice.
"I put it there for safe keeping, for I did not
dare wear it, for fear of losing it. Isn't it magnificent! a great deal too grand for me, I am sure.
Will you please take care of it, Frau Pastorin,
until I am grown up? or perhaps — perhaps you
wouldn't mind wearing it yourself. It is far
more suitable for you than for me."

The Frau Pastorin took it, with a smile and
a beaming eye. "Certainly I will take care of
it for thee," she said. "I will wrap it in some
fine wadding, and put it away in a box under
safe lock and key. Thou wilt be very glad and
very proud to wear it when thou art old enough to
appreciate such things."

"Now thou must go to bed," said the Herr
Pastor; "it is very late, and thou must be very
tired. There are a great many things to be attended to during the short time that remains
before our guests leave us. Go and take some
necessary rest."

"Fräulein Jettchen," said Hans, "I shall never
forget the great service you have done for me.
In my heart and my memory it will live forever.

If ever the time should come, you shall learn that the von Czechys know how to be grateful."

He looked at her with a meaning in his impassioned eyes which brought the blood to her neck and face.

"No, no," she said confusedly, "I only did as the Herr Pastor told me." With a hasty goodnight she ran up to her room.

CHAPTER XIX

The next morning Fräulein von Hermersdorff drove up. She had returned from Silesia the night before, and lost no time in running up to the parsonage. It was easy to see how she regretted her absence during the doctor's and his friend's stay. She knew Hans very well, and insisted upon showing him some hospitality, though both he and his friend were really on the eve of departure.

"How sorry I am!" she said; "really, papa will be inconsolable. To think that once in a hundred years, perhaps, I go away from home, and then it must just happen when one would most wish one had remained."

"Most gracious Fräulein," said Hans, kissing the pretty plump hand she extended to him, "you have no idea what a lucky escape you have had. We have run wild here, so to speak, and most devoutly thankful our dear entertainers must be to get rid of us."

"'T is a most wholesome disturbance, then," she said gayly; "one could easily put up with it for a lifetime. We know each other too well, dear baron, that you should waste pretty speeches on me. Now I have a plan. To-morrow you must give up to me absolutely. We will have a picnic, a right merry old-fashioned one. You must all come. 'T is no use to shake your heads and look at each other. What I will, I will; you know that of old."

Really, she was irresistible. She knew how to dominate people; from her cradle upwards she had done nothing else. Thekla was twenty now, but save a more pronounced dignity of bearing and added distinction in manner and appearance, she was the same petite, sparkling, vivacious, dark sprite of three years ago. Her "cultivated heart," as the pastor called it, shone out of her happy dark eyes. She was so easy and unconventional in all she did or said that one quite forgot the heiress and the position she occupied in the world, though none knew more perfectly than herself how to crush presumption or officiousness. No wonder the Frau Pastorin was anxious for her son to marry her. He would gain at one bound what it is given to very few, even under the most favorable circumstances, to acquire in a lifetime: honor, riches, a most enviable place in society, and above and best of all, a charming, most desirable companion for life. Truly, an enviable lot for any man, when even most exceptionally favored of the gods. The Frau Pastorin desired above all things

that Fritz should settle his fate definitely before he
went.   It was patent to all eyes that Thekla loved
him.   They had grown up as children together,
and had hardly had a joy or grief apart.   If Fritz
had any sense, he would speak now.   He would
be gone at least three years; he could not expect
a girl like the heiress of Hermersdorff to wait for
him forever.   Ah, what a joyful wedding there
would then be on his return!   How gladly the
Frau Pastorin would bear this long parting, which
otherwise she felt would almost break her heart!
Three years is a long time, — yes, indeed, quite
an eternity for those who have to fold their hands
and watch and wait through it all.   And then
there are so many temptations for a young man,
especially on the continent in gay Vienna, where
Fritz will study most of the time.   Though he is
not a lady's man, — no, indeed; in fact, he is
quite unimpressionable, his ideals are so high;
heart and soul he is wrapped up in his profession.
He is going to accomplish great things, — oh,
very, and come back a professor, maybe.   She
dare wager he has not once thought of a woman.
That is quite right, of course; he has been too
much engaged in earnest study to fritter away
his time in idle gallantries.   It has so long been
tacitly understood that as soon as he had made
a position for himself he would marry Thekla;
really, he must speak now.   She must find an
opportunity to leave them together.

"Indeed," said Thekla, "this last day of all we
must make up for everything.   We will spend

the whole day in the open. You remember that lovely glade near the old Schloss, Herr Doctor, where we once lost ourselves as children?"

Since they were both grown up, her modesty would not allow her to treat him in the old familiar manner. She always called him Herr Doctor now.

"Oh, yes, indeed," he said, smiling; "we fancied we were another pair of babes in the wood, and waited patiently for the birds to cover us with the traditional leaves. But as they were too stupid, or too much engrossed with their own affairs, we decided to gather them ourselves. I rather think you were quite disappointed we were rescued before nightfall."

She blushed and laughed. "It is a heavenly place," she said; "just the spot for a picnic. We will pack hampers and send the servants in advance. Our old Trudel shall bring his fiddle. I will send word to everybody on my way back. It will be charming. Something of a surprise, of course. That will make it all the merrier. I can fancy their faces when they will hear of it. They will grumble and say, ' Just like Thekla.' All the same, they will come. No one shall be left out. The old Fräulein von Sprechnau, the doctor's wife, the attorney's daughter, — if I did not ask them, they would feel sore about it. There will be a lovely moon at night. We will dance on the green. Oh, everybody must come."

The Frau Pastorin was delighted. She would

have preferred to have Fritz all to herself, this last day of his stay. But the opportunity was too propitious. She wondered if there was not some design in it. Certainly, if so, she would speed it with all her heart.

"We will all come," she said, "and, as you say, spend a long, happy day together. Ah, I see Henriette in the garden. I must go and tell her."

"I thought Jettchen was at the Wildhof," said Thekla. Involuntarily, she glanced at the doctor. His face was crimson. He turned his back to the window and said quietly, "She will not be banished again on my account."

"I will go and bring Fräulein Jettchen to you," said Hans, with alacrity; "she will be delighted to hear you are returned."

He vaulted lightly through the open window, and yodled as gayly as the most light-hearted Swiss mountaineer. The doctor turned round again.

"Dear child," said the Frau Pastorin, "you know absolutely nothing, then, of all the exciting events which have happened here of late? Then I will leave it to Fritz to tell you. I must run into the kitchen to speak to Babbett."

But the doctor made a very distrait narrator. His glance continually wandered to the garden, from where the sound of joyous voices and laughter floated upward. Hans and Jettchen were there, of course. The tall lilac bush, in which the nightingale sang to her mate at night, hid

them from view. Thekla's gayety of expression
became sober and thoughtful, as she noticed the
doctor's wandering glances.

"Shall we not go and join them?" she said.
"It is so much pleasanter out among the flowers.
Herr von Czechy seems to have forgotten his intention to tell Jettchen. Do you not think she
has changed very much?"

"I scarcely remember her from the first," he
said; "though who would not improve under such
able tutelage as yours?"

But she did not smile in return. When they
reached the truants, Hans was bending over Jette,
trying to extract a thorn from her finger. His
head, with its abundance of curly black hair, was
very near her own. She was moaning in a sort
of inarticulate manner, very much like a dumb
animal in pain. The doctor made a hasty stride
forward.

"What is this?" he said.

"Now," said the Magyar, astonished, "thou
needest not knock me over in thy professional
zeal. After all, I must yield the patient to thee.
'T is an ugly, long thorn, and so deeply imbedded
in the delicate flesh thou wilt have to use one of
the pretty baubles thou carriest around with thee
to get it out."

As he reluctantly made way, Jette saw Thekla.
She snatched away the hand the doctor had just
taken, and flew towards her.

"Dear, dear Fräulein, you here? But this is a
delightful surprise! When did you come?"

"Dear Jettchen," she said, "dear child. But when wilt thou stop growing? Already thou lookest down upon me. Did not Herr von Czechy tell thee I was here? He went out to fetch thee."

"He never told me a word," said Jette plaintively.

Hans looked guilty, but he laughed. "You gave me no time," he said. "I had just opened my mouth to speed the words when you ran the thorn into your finger. Then, of course, the words lost themselves. I think you are very ungrateful, Fräulein. I have broken my nails trying to pull the ugly thing out. My very teeth are blunt."

"So you used your teeth, too," said the doctor dryly. "That doubtless is the reason we heard you both laugh so. You have been here at least half an hour. Has the thorn been in so long?"

"How he has kept count of the time!" thought Thekla. She watched him as he took hold of the wounded hand. Though brave enough in all other things, Jette could not bear physical pain. She shuddered and cowered before it in nameless terror. The Herr Pastor said it would always be so. It was the result of that terrible time, but for which she might never have crossed the parsonage threshold.

"Nay," said the doctor, looking at her; "how can any one make so much ado about such a trifle! Steady now, one moment. I will have it out in a trice."

"It hurts," she said. "It hurts," she repeated, looking at him, her lips quivering, her eyes full of tears.

"I will not hurt you, Jettchen," he said. Ah, the tone in which he said it! An icy chill struck Fräulein von Hermersdorff's heart. She stooped down hastily to pick a spray of mignonette. He drew a little leather case from his pocket, and selected a small instrument. Jette shrieked, and hid her hand in the folds of her dress.

"Give me your hand," he said. It was the physician now who spoke. Slowly, with her eyes fixed on his, she drew it forth.

"You must not tremble so," he said; "this way I can do nothing." He flung his arm around her, held the hand in his firm clasp, and in a trice, swiftly and dexterously, he had the thorn out. The blood gushed forth and spattered itself over his fingers.

"There," he said, smiling, "that did not hurt badly, eh? Run into the house and bathe the hand. I will bind it up presently. To-morrow it will be all right again."

The Frau Pastorin now came up. "You will stay to dinner?" she said to Thekla.

"No, no," she said hastily; "I have so much to do yet. Indeed, indeed, you are very kind, and I should be delighted to accept. But papa is waiting for me, — besides, if our little feast is to come off to-morrow, 't is surely high time I let everybody know."

They all accompanied Thekla to the gate, and

saw her drive off. Jette came running out with her hand in a napkin. But contrary to Thekla's usual custom, she did not turn round to smile and wave her hand. The Frau Pastorin looked at her son.

"Fräulein von Hermersdorff did not seem in her usual good spirits," she said; "Fritz! has anything happened?"

"Anything happened!" he repeated in amazement; "why, what should happen, mamma?"

Then he had not spoken. A longing came over her to box his ears. Such obtuseness was criminal. But patience! He surely would declare himself on the morrow. Yes, of course. That was it. In restored good humor she went in with the rest to dinner.

CHAPTER XX

IF ever a fair vision dawned on the charmed beholders' gaze, it surely was Jette on the following morning. True child of the joyous Rhineland, she delighted in music, dancing, or anything that promised exhilaration to the spirits. She was going to dance to-day — really, what would life be without it? For her part, she would be content with just a crust, provided she could keep step to some joyous rhythm. She felt as if she had danced into life, and some time when she had grown very, very old, she would dance out of it. So when all were ready, she came down in her

white muslin dress, modestly draped with a lace
frilled fichu, the ruffled elbow sleeves revealing
the arms partially covered with white silk mittens,
low-cut shoes, fastened with a big buckle in the
middle, and the large white leghorn hat with the
ox-eyed marguerites, which had so charmed Herr
Goldman, shading the sweet, lovable face.   She
was so joyfully excited, her eyes sparkled in such
happy anticipation, and her cheeks had such an
enticing bloom that Hans gazed and gazed, as if
he could never feast his eyes enough.   The Frau
Pastorin examined her critically, and thought she
would do.   The Herr Pastor beamed through his
spectacles, lifted her chin with his forefinger, —
his invariable custom when pleased, — and declared with an astonishment which positively was
quite naïve that "really, it almost looked as if
Jettchen was growing up."   The doctor placed
himself opposite her in the Jagdwagen, or hunt-
break, Thekla had sent, and took hold of her hand
to see if it was really quite healed.   Hans groaned,
and wished he was in the "codfish's" place.   He
would not have let go of that beloved hand for
the rest of the drive.

Everybody was already on the grounds when
they arrived.   And the way every one went about
enjoying himself was worthy of the occasion and
the surroundings.   It was indeed, as Thekla had
said, an ideal spot.   Moss-like turf, noiseless
and soft as a velvet carpet, wherever one stepped;
wild flowers of all imaginable colors; immense
trees, whose interlacing branches formed a natural

canopy overhead; below, the shimmering Rhine, beckoning a gracious invitation to its placid bosom. The joyous orchestra of the birds accompanied the merry strains Trudel played on his fiddle. Jette danced, it made no difference who asked her. She danced with the old retired Major von B——, and told him breathlessly it was perfectly charming how young old people could be. She danced with his grand-nephew, a lad about her own age, who devoted himself to her so assiduously that it prevented her from noticing what otherwise could not have escaped her observation. The local doctor's wife and the attorney's daughter were whispering all the time, and directing the most malevolent glances towards her. As chance would have it, they were her vis-à-vis in the same quadrille. They elevated their noses in a very haughty manner indeed, looked over her head when chasséeing to each other, and in the ladies' chain drew away their hands in such an ostentatiously insulting manner that, astonished and confused, Jette entirely lost her presence of mind. She knew how to dance well enough, — every Rhineländer knows that by instinct. But she had attended the village classes, where an itinerant dancing-master taught every winter. With the groschen the Frau Pastorin put in the big balls of knitting yarn to stimulate her industry, she had paid for her lessons. She looked forward to them all the year round, and shivered many a cold night in her room, burning the candle ends while the rest of the household slept the sleep of the unsuspecting, a book on the little deal table before her, while the needles flew in and out, fast and furious, to get at the coveted coin at the bottom of the slowly diminishing ball of wool. If she lacked the elegance and finish of the more polished town circles, she certainly danced with all possible natural grace, and an enthusiastic enjoyment which made one smile. The behavior of her vis-à-vis took her entirely by surprise. She wondered if she had unintentionally done or said anything to make them act so strangely. When the dance was over, her partner left her to fetch something. For a moment she stood alone, with her two enemies beside her. She thought it would be only good manners to apologize for the confusion she had caused in the quadrille.

"I am sorry," she said timidly, "I danced so badly. I don't know what made me forget the different figures."

The doctor's wife, whose back was towards her, looked over her shoulder, and surveyed her with a long, haughty stare of astonishment. Jette felt as if boiling hot water was running down her spine, as this glance first took in her head, then slowly, with impressive scorn, ended at her feet. Then the lady, fully and ostentatiously, as if she could not sufficiently emphasize her contempt, turned round once more. But now Hans was dancing; a wide circle had been formed. Trudel had struck up the Czardas. Before he had grown so old that his wandering footsteps craved a permanent rest, and anchored him safely at Hermersdorff, he had traveled in many lands. He had seen the Hungarians at their native dance, and now he played with a fire and animation which fairly brought the impressionable Hans to his feet. At first he danced in even, measured rhythm, then faster, ever faster, — the fiddle fairly cracked itself in passionate rejoicing. Jette, watching him with sparkling eyes, forgot momentarily her trouble, and in the excess of her transports, clapped her hands, and laughed aloud.

"What does the Jewess know about dancing?" said the attorney's daughter to her companion scornfully. "Is not her behavior that of an uncouth rustic? What business has she in this distinguished company, any way?"

"'T is an insult to us all," said the doctor's wife, carefully drawing her skirts away from any possible contact with the girl who stood beside her. "She ought to be sent to her native ghetto, where she belongs. The impudent chit! to dare to speak to me, as if I were of her own kind. 'T is easy to see she picked up her dancing in the Wirthshaus of a Sunday afternoon, prancing around with Jackel and Peter, and all the rest of them, the impudent Jewess."

The blood rushed in a torrent to the young girl's head. She thought surely it must gush out of her mouth and eyes. Then she turned icy cold. She glanced around her. Hans was still dancing. Everybody was looking on, absorbed in their delight and interest. One glance she turned full and composedly on the two women. It was

so large, so grand in its dignity, that their own
fell involuntarily. Then she slowly turned and
left the grounds.

CHAPTER XXI

TWILIGHT was descending soft and fair. Its
holy radiance gave a benediction to the parting
day. The fairy colors of the afterglow still lingered in the sky. It was the hour of calm, of
rest, and of peace, soothing the troubled spirit
into the contemplation of higher and nobler things
beyond. The gate of the parsonage garden clicked.
Babbett, who had just come out of the poultry
yard, feeding Jette's doves and chickens, looked
up. Minka, who had accompanied her, gave an
expressive purr. Then she darted towards the
newcomer, who took her up and cuddled her to
her breast. It was Jette. Not as she had gone
forth in the morning, radiant and gay. Her
white dress hung bedraggled and torn around
her. The large straw hat was pushed from her
sunburnt face. She limped as if footsore. Her
aspect was one of thorough fatigue and weariness.

"Jesus Maria!" cried Babbett; "what has happened? How comes it thou arrivest in such fashion, and alone?"

The girl did not answer. The muscles of her
face worked. She gulped as if trying to swallow
something choking her.

"Wilt thou speak, then?" said Babbett wrath-

fully; "the rest — where are they — why hast
thou left them?"

"Thou needest not worry about them," said the
girl. She had limped to a bench at the back of
the house, and flung off her hat. Now she gave
a long sigh of relief. Minka rubbed her whiskers
against her. Her fur was shedding, and the
girl's neck was covered with it.

"The animal knows thou art in trouble," said
Babbett. At this Jette burst out crying. She
sobbed so that the bench on which she sat shook
with the weight of her grief. Babbett seated herself beside her, and laid her hard, work-worn hand
on the girl's arm. She was of a hardy peasant
race, not given to sentiment or any demonstration
of feeling; but she had a heart in her bosom, and
though at first she had strongly resented Jette's
coming into the family, the succeeding years had
accustomed her to look upon her as quite one of
themselves. She was growing old, and the girl
was a great help to her. If the toothache plagued
her in the cold winter nights, Jette would not allow
her to get up in the morning, but blithely and
cheerfully did her tasks for her, brought her a
cup of steaming hot coffee, tripped up and down
the steep stairs innumerable times for warm appli-
cations, and generally took care of her in the
loving, matter-of-fact manner in which life went
on at the parsonage. In the cold weather she did
all of the out-of-door work for her, knitted her
warm mittens and hoods, and gave her shawl an
extra twist so she should look nice and presentable

when she went to hear the Herr Pastor preach on a Sunday. She grumbled and scolded as usual, and showed no outward sign of appreciation. But she was as fiercely loyal to the girl as to the family in which she had lived almost all her life, and would strongly have resented any harm offered to her.

Jette sobbed on as if her heart was broken. She was so thoroughly a child yet! The consideration and loving regard lavished upon her lately made her the more susceptible to slights of any kind. She was learning the inevitable lesson which two thirds of us experience, that the fairest prospects in the morning are blighted before night.

"Now, now," said Babbett; "I should think thou wouldst have done by now. Look at thy slippers. They hardly hold together by the straps. Hast thou walked all the way, then?"

"Yes," said the girl, "every step. In the broiling hot sun, too. At times I thought I should die; but I did not care. Oh, how glad I am to be home again."

"H'm!" said Babbett, "that must have been a fine walk all the way down the mountain, with no shade whatever, and the sun right in thy face. 'T is six good leagues, if 't is a rod. Do the rest know thou art come?"

"I cannot tell. I left them all there quite happy. Perhaps they will not find out I am gone till 't is time to go home. I would be so glad."

"But what happened, then, to make thee run away?"

"I will tell thee presently. How my feet ache! Surely they must be full of holes; I feel as if I could never walk any more."

Babbett stooped down and pulled off what remained of the slippers. "They may as well be flung away," she said, "and thy stockings, too. Everything thou hast on is ruined."

"'T was my dancing-school dress," said the girl, full of grief, "my slippers and all. The Frau Pastorin will never buy me another. I fear she will be very angry."

The old woman nodded her head. "What thou hast to do now," she said, "is to go up to thy room and take off these rags before she sees thee. I will bring thee some warm water to bathe thy feet. Thou 'lt be all well as soon as thou hast composed thyself."

It was quite the old Jette who sat at the sitting-room window half an hour after. She had put on her blue gingham dress, newly brushed and coiled the glossy black hair, and, but for a slight pallor of fatigue quite unusual to the blooming young face, looked as if nothing out of the way had happened. The lamp on the big centre table burnt low. Her eyes ached a little, and she felt too tired to do anything but to sit still. A horse came dashing down the village street, as if it had been hard ridden. Its flanks were covered with foam. The man in the saddle swung himself down, and eagerly ran up the graveled walk to the house. He had seen the quiet figure at the open window, sitting in the half dusk. In

another moment, hot and breathless, he was in
the room.

"Thank God," he said, "you are home!" It
was the doctor. He drew a chair forward, and
sat down deep in the shadow, where he could see
the light fall on her face. She was softly stroking Minka, who lay full length in her lap. Her
head leaned in languid repose against the red-
cushioned back of the chair. With the unusual
pallor in her face, heightening the effect of her
black hair, she had certainly never looked more
heavenly fair. He folded his arms across his
chest, and looked at her so long it would have
embarrassed her, had she not been so tired.

"When did you reach home?" he asked.

"A little over an hour ago, I think. 'T was
just after sundown."

"And walked all the way, I suppose?"

"Yes, truly." She was too indolent to speak
much. She did not even wonder why he was there.

"What made you do it? We have been terribly anxious about you. Some one suggested you
had fallen into the Rhine and drowned. Every
one searched for you. I took the major's horse
and came home. I knew I should find you here."

"What have I done?" she said, wringing her
hands. "I never intended to leave you in anxiety.
I was sure you would know." The tears were in
her eyes again, ready to fall. She looked at him
piteously. He strode over to the lamp and set it
flaring high.

"Come here," he said peremptorily.

He spoke in the same tone he had used when he pulled the thorn from her finger. She hated to get up, but she knew she would have to obey. When she came and stood in front of him, with head hanging down, he put his hand under her chin, and gently raised it. She did not want to look at him, but she felt herself compelled to. Her blue eyes gazed into his brown ones, and she could not withdraw them. He read all he wanted to, and a great deal more. Quietly he turned the lamp down again.

"You certainly," he said cheerfully, "have the best of it here. See, the moon is rising above the firs. How peaceful and still all seems! When I am very tired, — as you are now, Jettchen, — I will come back here to rest."

"You will never be tired from the same cause as I am now," she said; "people will all be kind to you."

"Humph!" he said. So that was it? Some one had been unkind to her. "Don't you think," he said, "that a scene like this impresses itself on a man's heart, and recalls itself as an oasis when he is far away from home? I shall be gone some years, you know. Where will you be when I come back?"

"Why, here, of course," she said. She opened her eyes wide, and laughed. "Where else should I be?"

"At Madame Goldman's, perhaps."

"Will the Frau Pastorin let me visit her?" she said eagerly; "oh, how delightful!"

"Do you like Herr Goldman?" asked the doctor brusquely.

"Herr Goldman! Why, I never thought of him. He is so quiet one hardly ever notices him."

"I mean the son, the young banker."

"He was good and kind to me," she said, "but I do not like him nearly as well as his mother. I feel as if I had known her all my life."

"Then you would not go where you were not received with open arms," he said.

"No," she said, with a fierceness which was the aftermath of the day's experience, "I would not. I will not obtrude myself where I am not welcomed. If any smile at me, I will smile back at them. If they offer me their hand in friendship, I will give them mine in return. Why should we scowl and fume at one another? Surely the world is wide enough for each to go his separate way."

"How comes it," said the doctor, "that you are such a philosopher? Mature views like these are seldom entertained by one of your years. I am afraid they smack somewhat of the bookshelf."

She turned very red, and cast a half-frightened, half-stealthy look towards the Herr Pastor's library. The doctor saw it, and laughed.

"Caught again," he said; "last time it was Heine, now it is half a dozen musty old prosers, tangled up finely in that young brain of yours. Nay, but you are a veritable book-gobbler. Such contraband reading may be very hurtful for you."

"It has taught me a great deal," she said defiantly.

"H'm! You are not capable of judging of that. Older heads like mine may see a great deal of harm in it."

She pouted in her inimitably enticing fashion, and tossed her head. "You are not so very old," she said.

"It is very nice of you to think so," he said seriously; "I feel as old as a patriarch."

She flashed her eyes wide open, as she had a trick of doing, and looked at him quite compassionately. Then she saw the twinkle in his eye, and laughed.

"I am glad you are joking," she said; "indeed, I felt very sorry for you. Only people who have trouble feel old."

"Were you sorry for me, Jettchen?" he said.

She looked up, startled at his tone and the sudden fire in his usually half-veiled eyes. She recoiled as if stung by a whip.

"Look here," he said, quickly lapsing into his usual half-bantering tone, "I have discovered so many secrets of yours I feel quite guilty in concealing them longer. What prevents me from going to my mother, and warning her that you are on the high road to perdition?"

"Because of the manhood within you," she said. She arched her neck like a thoroughbred, and looked at him with the full glory of her eyes. "Truly, it would be a fine thing for you to turn telltale, when you know perfectly well that anything you wished me to keep secret, not ten thousand horses should tear from me."

"I know it," he said. "Thou art as mettlesome as a war steed." Occasionally he lapsed into the familiar thee and thou. "But being a man, you see, with all a man's selfishness and ingratitude, some sort of a bribe is due to me."

"What shall I give you?" she said. "I have very little. Nothing at all, I am sure, that you would value."

"That depends," he said, "the different ways we look at it. You could give me something I would prize very highly, and you would never miss at all."

"Yes?" she asked anxiously; "then tell me. If you *must* have something not to carry tales to your mother," she added disdainfully.

"Will you give me a kiss,— just one little one?" he said. His eyes were almost veiled as he looked at her.

"A kiss!" she ejaculated; "a kiss!" she repeated, in consternation. She looked as if she would sooner have expected the skies to fall. She threw back her head, and laughed. "Why, that is nothing," she said. "You shall have it, if that is all you want."

"Oh!" he exclaimed. He flushed darkly. He hesitated. "Do you value your kisses so little?" he said.

"Now you are joking," she said. "What can there be in a kiss to make so much fuss about? Except my mother, I never kissed anybody in my life."

He leaned over so suddenly, she was quite taken unawares. Before she knew it, his long, blonde mustache had swept across her cheek. Soft, fiery lips were pressed upon her own. With a gesture of anger and dislike, she swiftly drew back, and passed her handkerchief across her mouth.

"I don't like that," she said; "I don't like that!" she repeated furiously, stamping her foot. She looked daggers at him, and there were tears in her eyes.

"What is there in a kiss to make so much fuss over?" he mocked, with aggravating triumph. His face was radiant, and he laughed when she still persistently drew the handkerchief across her lips. "You can't wipe it away," he said; "it will stay there forever."

She threw down the handkerchief in disgust. "I will never kiss anybody again in my life," she said, with a wry face.

"But you never kissed me. 'Twas I who kissed you."

"I don't care," she said angrily; "'tis all the same."

"Oh, no," he said, "there is a vast difference. But I am glad that after this you will not hold your kisses so cheap."

"Never in my life will I allow any one to kiss me again," she repeated vehemently.

"That is right," he said cheerfully; "by all means adhere to it. When I come back, I shall ask you."

"When you come back," she said loftily, "I

shall be grown up. I shall then have forgotten
all about it."

"Then I will recall it to your memory," he
said; "till then you must never allow any one to
replace it with another."

"One must like people," she said scornfully,
"to want to kiss them. I am sure I shall never
care enough for anybody to do that."

"Not even me?" he asked.

"You!" she exclaimed. "How can any one like
a person by whom one is detested? Dear Lord!
Did you not say I was hideous? Did not the
Frau Pastorin have to send me away to the Wildhof, so you should not be offended at the sight of
me? I—I beg your pardon," she stammered
confusedly, struck by his changed face; "I did
not mean to be rude. I dare say I did not look
very nice just then. I was so disfigured, it makes
me shudder to recall it."

The doctor made a hasty step forward. Then
he stopped.

"Don't you think that people may change?"
he asked softly.

"I don't care whether you have changed or
not," she said, with that sudden transition of
mood which made one never sure of her. "You
quite broke my heart that time. If I had known
you were going to kiss me like that, I never would
have let you."

She ran out, slamming the door after her. The
doctor stared, whistled softly, and with a smile
curling the corners of his mouth, walked to the
window. Just then the others drove up.

CHAPTER XXII

THE Frau Pastorin was very angry. Such
conduct in a chit of a girl had never been heard
of. To run off from a merry-making, leaving
every one in the greatest doubt and consternation
concerning her! 'T was the last day, too, of the
Herr Baron's and Fritz's stay — to spoil everything in such inconsiderate fashion! Under the
circumstances, it was doubly reprehensible. Jette
was summoned from the poultry yard, where she
had gone to see if her pets were safely housed for
the night. She came in, pale, in somewhat of a
trepidation, but perfectly calm.

"'T is a relief to find thee safely home," said
the Frau Pastorin severely. "No, never mind!
Thou needest not help me off with my mantle.
What made thee run off in such unseemly fashion,
without leaving word with anybody?"

"Oh, but I did," said Jette; "I asked the
Fräulein von Sprechnau's footman, who was just
then repacking the hamper, to tell you that I had
gone home."

"But he never told any of us a word," cried
the Frau Pastorin; "he surely must have seen the
distress we were in."

"Why should he not have given thy message,
Jettchen?" asked the Herr Pastor. He looked
at her steadily. Whenever he did so, she knew
the full truth would have to be told.

"I cannot imagine any reason," she said, "except his insolence. When I asked him to deliver my message, he said he would, if I gave him a kiss for a Trinkgeld."

"What!" ejaculated the Magyar fiercely; "but you should have come to me, Fräulein. I would have pulled the wretch's skin over his ears."

The doctor fingered the tips of his mustache nervously. "These canaille," he said, "take their cue from their betters. Some one must have been very impertinent to you, Jettchen."

"I did not think he was in earnest," she said, evading a direct reply; "as he saw me go, I was sure he would tell the Frau Pastorin."

"But you have not told us the reason why you left," said the Herr Pastor.

"You were all enjoying yourselves," she said. "I did not want to spoil your pleasure. It was just when Herr von Czechy was dancing. The Frau Doctorin and Fräulein Schmidt, the attorney's daughter, stood close beside me. They spoke about me in a very insulting manner. If they had spoken to me direct, I would not have cared so much; but this talking at me gave me no excuse to answer. I turned and left a company where I saw I was not wanted."

"Thou dear Heaven! but what could they say about thee?" cried the Frau Pastorin, in great agitation.

She kept her eyes on the floor for a moment. If she had looked at any one, she knew she must have burst into tears. The Herr Pastor would not have liked that. She knew that under all circumstances he wanted her to show self-control.

"They said I had no business there," she said finally; "that I was a Jewess, and had no right to obtrude myself into such distinguished company. They would not touch my hand in the quadrille." She asked, with a gesture both proud and pathetic, "Is there any need to say any more?"

"Now may the thunder crash!" cried the Frau Pastorin, in high anger. "They, distinguished company, indeed! Why, the doctor's wife is a butcher's daughter from Gelsbach" —

"Cattle-dealer, Mammachen," interrupted the Herr Pastor mildly.

"Ah, bah! where's the difference? Cattle-dealer or butcher, 'tis all the same. And as for Fräulein Schmidt — thou dear Heaven! Her grandfather trundled a wheelbarrow on her grandmother's farm, and when her first husband died, she married him. 'Twas nothing but spite, the rancorous old maid! that made her speak thus," exclaimed the Frau Pastorin contemptuously.

"Then you are not angry with me for leaving?" said Jette timidly.

"Yes, I am, — very," said the Frau Pastorin energetically; "thou shouldst have come to me, above all things, and not minded what those two persons said. A butcher's daughter and a peasant laborer's grand-daughter to carry matters with so high a hand, forsooth! Wait till I see them again. But I will rub it into them!"

"Thou must not be so susceptible," said the pastor to Jette reprovingly; "as thou growest older and mixest more with the world, thou wilt find that envy, hate, malice, will find the weak spot in thy armor, and mercilessly take advantage of it. One has only to prick human nature to find how little humanity there lies beneath."

"Can I help being a Jewess?" she asked. "Why should they scorn me because of it?"

"Thy religion," said the pastor, in his resonant voice, which reached far and wide when he was greatly in earnest, "concerns no one but thee. 'T is something alone between thee and thy God. 'T is not a thing to cavil at, or to cast aside because of the sneers of others. As well might'st thou pluck out an eye, or hew a limb from thy body. 'T is part and parcel of thyself, as much as the blood which goes to nourish thy heart; nay, more so, because 't is the spiritual part of thee, that which never dies, — thy passport to the Almighty One, who knows of all thy doings. 'T is a thing of ancestry, of heredity, of circumstances. 'T was born with thee, and will abide with thee till death. 'T is thy sacred, inalienable right, with which the other has naught to do. Thou wert born a Jewess, and wilt die a Jewess, and being such, thou art naught else but thyself. Let those look to it who would cast it up to thee. Thou canst no more undo it than curse the mother who bore thee for bearing thee so. And being so, thou must rest content in the consciousness of thy birthright, which so long as thou actest to the utmost of thy convictions surely gives thee the advantage over those who would look down upon thee. As the reputation of the community depends upon the behavior of the individual, so the individual has often the sins of the community to shoulder. Bear thyself always that no blame can attach to thee, so wilt thou best disarm criticism, which, after all, depends as much upon the individual as education and environment."

In the doctor's room, Hans was wrestling with straps and portmanteaus long after everybody had gone to bed.

"Lie there," he said, giving the last bag a vicious kick; "thou and I are going to flee from temptation to-morrow."

"Dost thou include me in thy amiable rhapsody?" asked the doctor, yawning.

"Holy Maria! thou! thou cold-blooded cynic! Tell me," he burst out angrily, "is it wise of thy father to make such a martyr of that girl? 'T would all be very fine and quite proper among her own people. But, dear Heaven! she has a heart, I suppose, like the rest of us, and one day she will find it out. What will she do, then?"

"Give it to Herr Goldman, of course."

"I would like to fling thee out of the window. Scoffer! Oh, only wait! One of these days I will crow over thee. Fritz! dost thou not see how wretched her life must be, if she fall in love with some one not of her own persuasion?"

The doctor was leaning far over the window sill. The moon was rapidly on the wane. But

for the feeble light of the solitary candle, the
room was in semi-darkness. A dove occasionally
stirred and cooed drowsily. The scent of the
mignonette and jasmine floated in at the window.
The earth exhaled the peculiar dampness charac-
teristic of the midnight hour. Out on the tall lilac
bush the nightingale had just begun her plaintive
fluting. The doctor listened for a moment; then
he turned his back to the window.

"If the man have a man's heart in his bosom,"
he said, "he will not let anything stand in his
way, but marry her."

"He may be ten thousand times willing to
marry her, but she will never marry him."

"Ah," said the doctor out of the gloom.

"Ah and oh as much as thou pleasest. How
canst thou expect it, with such ideas inculcated
in her young mind? She will sacrifice her heart
to her religion, depend upon it."

"Thou art as cheerful as an owl, with thy
impossible contingencies. Depend upon it, they
will never arise. She is so young yet,— hardly sixteen. Herr Goldman will come and propose for
her. She 'will marry him — out goes your romance."

"Perhaps it is the best she can do," said Hans
moodily; "yet — I would have wished her a better
fate. Besides, I hardly think thy father will give
her in marriage yet."

"No?" said the doctor; he was still listening
to the nightingale.

"I heard him say the other day that a woman

ought never to marry until she is twenty; and that if it rested with him, none ever should."

"Exceptional cases require exceptional treatment," said the doctor; "depend upon it, the first news we shall receive will be of her engagement."

"Bah," said Hans pettishly; "thou hast neither heart nor understanding, else thou wouldst not talk so."

"Hark," said the doctor; "listen to the nightingale. How ravishing her song! Ah! there comes her mate. Oh, their raptures! Brr! Let me shut the window. The night has grown cold."

CHAPTER XXIII

"DOST thou grieve I am going away? Dost thou really grieve, Liebchen?"

The Magyar and Jette were standing in the embrasure of the window. The sobs of the Frau Pastorin came from the next room, where she stood, clinging to her son. The "extra post," with its postilion outriders, had just dashed up to the door. Babbett was busy bestowing traveling-bags in the smallest possible space. Everything was ready for the young men's departure. Jette really could not restrain her tears. The genial, merry Hans, with his boyish pranks and superabundance of fun, had endeared himself to everybody. Within the walls of the parsonage his memory would endure as long as its inmates lived.

His gay, hearty laugh, the graceful turn of his shoulders when he kept time to the Kossuth March, his tall, willowy figure, and his flashing black eyes, reflecting his sunny, noble disposition in their clear depths, — who would ever forget them? It was no wonder Jette felt as if the sun was going out of her life. With the exaggerated grief of youth, she thought it never would shine any more. She knew that Hans was fond of her. How fond, it was just as well she did not know. She had twined herself around his heartstrings. He was sure that never, never would he forget her. Some such memory haunts most of us. It forms a sacred shrine in the innermost recesses of the heart, where the penetrating gaze of even the nearest and dearest never reaches. Touched by her tears, and carried away by his own emotion, Hans raised the sweet face, and kissed her on the brow.

"I will return," he said, deeply moved; "be true to me, thou darling sweet one."

She slipped a cigar case, elaborately embroidered in violet and silver, into his hands.

"I sat up nights to finish it," she sobbed. "Carrier Mueller took it to Cologne to have it mounted. It is all I can give you. You have been so kind to me, — you have given me so much pleasure. I hope you will use it as a little keepsake."

Hans took it, and kissed it. "Thou dear one," he said, "thou sweet, good, unspoiled one. I will wear thy little gift, and each time I draw it forth,

thy sweet face shall rise up before me. And when
it gets shabby from overmuch use, it shall remain
the most treasured of all my possessions still."
And that he really felt what he said, and never
changed, the subsequent years proved. For in
the magnificent castle of Czechy, one of the most
palatial possessions on the banks of the blue Danube, in the study of the master, is a costly wrought
silver stand with priceless crystal globe. And
under it, worn with long use, the shabby little
case reposes, a sacred relic, — doubly sacred by
reason of what happened afterwards.

The guard swung his horn for the dozenth time.
"Die Post im Walde," rung out clear and shrill,
as a last urging. "Schier dreizig Jahre bist Du
alt, hast manchen Sturm erlebt," sung Hans.
The doctor came out of the adjoining room, his
mother clinging to his hand, his father's arm
around his neck. The Frau Pastorin's eyelids
were red, and she sobbed as if her heart would
break.

"Ah, bah!" cried Hans; "'t is not thus we must
part, with tears and sobs to speed us. No, indeed
not. Joyous as our next greeting shall it be.
Thou, Fritz! whistle, as was thy wont while we
were at Bonn. Attention!"

He bounded into the middle of the room, flung
the chairs right and left, and began to dance.
Ye gods, how he did dance! The old house shook,
and at one time it seemed as if the roof must
topple over them. The madder he danced, the
madder the doctor whistled. At first every one

caught his breath in consternation. Then they
smiled, they beamed, they clapped their hands.
The fever of the Czardas was upon them. When
at length he stopped for sheer want of breath, he
made a rush for his top coat and hat, and bounded
into the post-chaise before the rest could follow.
Jette came up, a tear in one eye, a laugh in the
other. "Thou 'lt remain true," whispered Hans.
The doctor sprang in beside him. The girl looked
at Fritz as if undecided; then she quickly placed
something in his hand. "Because you have been
good to me," she murmured. His hand closed
softly over the small, embroidered letter portfolio.
His eyes roamed over her from head to foot, with
a long, lingering gaze. His mother kissed him
convulsively. She put her arms around Hans
von Czechy's neck in a last embrace. The Herr
Pastor held a hand of each. Babbett stood at
the chaise door, ready to slam it to when they
should be off. She fingered the liberal Trinkgeld
the young men had given her with one hand, the
other held a corner of her apron to her eyes.
Minka looked on from the gate, with big, solemn
eyes. The guard swung his horn, the postilions
lashed their horses. "Adieu," "Lebewohl," "Nein,
nein, auf Wiedersehen," resounded from all sides.
One more glimpse of the travelers leaning far out
of either coach window, a frantic waving of hand-
kerchiefs, a cloud of dust, — they were gone.

CHAPTER XXIV

WHEN all the cleaning and scouring consequent upon the guests' departure was done, the parsonage settled into its humdrum routine again. It was then everybody began to realize what a frightful void was left. Each time the Frau Pastorin looked up from her sewing, she fancied she must see her son and the young Magyar come up the graveled walk, arm in arm, their heads close together, laughing over some nonsense, — so near of a height together, the one so fair, the other so dark, graceful, muscular, and strong, — so good in every way to look at. Her clear eyes would cloud with tears, — it was some time before she was able to look at her sewing again. The Herr Pastor, coming in from his parochial duties, glanced around the silent, empty room, hung up his hat, and went over and kissed her in his hearty fashion.

"'T is what we must expect, Liebste," he said; "the young birds leave the nest in course of time. At all events, thou and I are left. And right merry old sweethearts we will be, eh?"

"I shall be more reconciled," she sobbed, "after I get the first news. And I suppose before Fritz comes back, Henriette will be gone, too."

"Softly, softly, softly," said the Herr Pastor; "not so fast, Kind. Give her time first to wear out the shoes of her childhood. 'T will be a good four or five years yet, I promise thee."

"She is very tall for her age," said the Frau Pastorin; "really, the day of the picnic she looked to me quite womanly. Everybody was surprised when I told them how very young she was."

"'T is a disadvantage, certainly," said the Herr Pastor, "to be so forward in growing when one is but a child. Things are expected of one without regard to circumstances."

"Thou hast not forgotten Madame Goldman's letter?" said the Frau Pastorin. "Suppose the contingency were to arise."

"It may not arise," he said composedly; "let us put it to the proof first."

And it was not long in coming.

Jette had gone to the village on a little errand for the Frau Pastorin. For the first two or three days after the young men had left, she grieved violently and persistently. Her eyelids were red with weeping, and often in the midst of her work she would catch her breath with a great sob.

"'T is calf love," said Babbett complacently; "for a little while it hurts, like cutting a tooth, or jamming one's finger. But 't will not last long. When the tooth is safely through, and the finger bound up, we laugh and dance more gayly than ever. 'T is good for thy infant feelings to get schooled this way. Thou 'lt not be so susceptible next time."

But Jette refused to be comforted. She thought her grief was going to last forever. All the sunshine had gone out of her life, leaving it dreary and colorless as an arid waste. She continually

talked about Hans von Czechy, and speculated
at what part of his journey he must be now. It
was Herr von Czechy here, Herr von Czechy
there. The doctor she never mentioned. Nevertheless, she slept very soundly at night, and the
fourth morning came down singing a blithe little
song. A week after, she was quite her old self
again, read on the sly as usual, industriously
weeded her garden, and slid down the banisters,
if she was in a hurry to get down. Once or twice
she went up to Hermersdorff. Thekla was as kind
and gracious as ever, but a certain something in
her manner struck a chill to the girl's heart. She
was going abroad with her father. The professor
had often wished to visit Athens to make some
historical researches there. Now he had obtained
a long leave of absence. They were going to
travel leisurely, and visit most foreign cities by
the way. Berlin, Paris, Vienna, Buda-Pesth, —
yes, indeed, they were going to take their own
time about it. When Fräulein von Hermersdorff
told the Frau Pastorin, she could have hugged
her. Dear, clever girl! She was going to meet .
Fritz abroad; now at last he would declare himself, — they would come back engaged. Her rosy
visions mounted heaven high again.

So Jette attributed the certain indefinable something in Fräulein von Hermersdorff's manner to
her busy preparations for her departure. There
was so much to see to, — yes, of course that was
it. How could people be smiling and smirking
when they didn't know where their heads stood

for work? But she went to Hermersdorff no more. Her proud little heart was more sensitive than her reason. She found consolation in her books, and went out into the glad sunshine. As she had said, the world was wide; she could go her own way without rubbing elbows with others.

As she walked up the village street, a child's pitiful wail struck upon her ear. It was one of the sounds she could never listen to without keen distress. She turned her head, and there at the open window stood Gret, whose spiteful, squint-eyed face she never could see without remembering with a shudder the time when she had led the attack which came near ending in murder. Gret, or Gretel, as she was generally called, was married now, and had an angel child. No one could account how Gret came by her. It was one of those strange phenomena with which Nature, in one of her capricious moods, likes to perplex mankind. Gret, with her hair and complexion the same uniform straw color, the detestable cast in her pale eyes, pig-mouthed and flat-nosed, was as ugly a creature as one would wish to avoid meeting. She was notorious for miles around as the most evil-tongued, malicious, slandering gossip that ever incumbered a community. Everybody was polite to her, for everybody feared her. One was never safe to utter the most indifferent opinion in her presence. Her lying tongue would pounce upon it, and twist, turn, and distort it to her own malicious purpose. She had caused friends to become enemies, and occasioned more ill feeling and heartburning than any dozen persons put together. If any one wanted some disagreeable news conveyed to some one else, they had only to tell Gręt, under promise of the strictest secrecy. Before another hour had elapsed, it was proclaimed hydra-tongued from the marketplace. Her household was left to take care of itself, in her devouring greed for gossip. At the parsonage she was detested, and the Frau Pastorin never allowed her to come further than the kitchen threshold. She would come occasionally to make a great outcry about the manner Peter, her black cat, had been mauled by Minka. Ostensibly, this was her purpose. In reality, it was to find out what was going on, for she did not care a kreutzer for Peter's mauling. The last time she had come to the parsonage door was during the doctor's and the young Baron von Czechy's visit. Babbett had then told her plainly that if she ever showed herself on a similar errand, she would expedite her departure with the other end of the broom. Her husband, a thick-skulled, good-natured, well-to-do yokel, who had been entrapped into the marriage by the most fabulous promises of a fat dowry, and after the wedding got roundly laughed at for his credulity, let her do mainly as she pleased. He was afraid of her lashing tongue, and providing he had food set before him three times a day and a made bed to sleep in, was stolidly indifferent to the neglected condition of his house. His pretty little girl baby was his perpetual wonder and delight. The good looks he and his wife had between them could never be made a reproach to either. He was pretty much the same complexion as herself, a stupid, colorless clod, entirely influenced and ruled by her. What had the pretty, blue-eyed, golden-haired baby, with its delicate, lily face, to do with such parents? It cried and cried, as if it longed to go to where it rightfully belonged. It took kindly to the father, but would draw no nourishment from the mother's breast. The wise old women wagged their heads, and prophesied the baby would never live. But it did, and throve into the bargain, much to the loutish father's delight.

It happened that one day, when the baby was six months old, Jette passed the house, and she smiled at the little creature in its mother's arms, on the house-step, and cooed in her soft, caressing way, as she did to her pet doves. The baby looked at her with its large, mournful blue eyes, cried as if its heart would break, and stretched out its arms to her. There was no help for it, she had to take it, and the little creature crowed and laughed for the first time in its life, and clung to her as if it would never let her go. Since then it cried incessantly for her, and no one could pacify it but Jette. The Frau Pastorin would not allow her to go to Gret's house, so whenever the baby became too fretful, it was brought to the parsonage, where it was left by the hour together. The big mahogany cradle in which the Frau Pastorin had put her dolls to sleep, and which had accompanied her, among her other effects, from her Pomeranian home, was fetched down from the garret, the soft down ticking newly covered, and Lieschen put into it when she went to sleep. The dolls were gone long ago, but the baby fitted the cradle, with plenty of room to spare. Now when Lieschen's pitiful wail struck upon Jette's ear, she could not do otherwise than take her, though the Frau Pastorin had cautioned her never to stop to speak with Gret on any pretense whatever.

"Yes, take the brat," said Gret peevishly; "surely thou hast bewitched her. All day long she does nothing but howl after thee."

Gret had never ceased to address the girl by the familiar thee and thou, though she was growing up, and people naturally conceded her the respect which belonged to her. After the manner of her class, Gret assumed that the more effrontery she displayed, the more surely did she put herself on a footing of equality. For all the foolish coddling they gave the girl at the parsonage, Gret declared, she for one was not going to forget she was a waif picked up from the highway, who came from the dear Lord only knew, a beggar strumpet of a Jewess, who for airs and graces did not know where her head stood, beholden to charity for the very chemise she wore on her back. Oh, indeed! If she had forgotten it, and everybody else had forgotten it, Gret was not going to; but she would rub it into her at each and every opportunity, never fear!

Jette took the child from the skinny arms of

the mother into her own divinely rounded ones.
With her young, innocent eyes she smiled into the
baby ones, pursed up her rosy mouth, and cooed
so sweetly and softly that the child crowed with
rapture.

"Now let any one listen to that!" said Gret
discontentedly; "not once in all the time does she
do that with me. What is it that ails the brat?
Am I not her mother, her own natural mother, and
thou a perfect stranger? Yet she seems happier
with thee."

"Oh, no," said Jette; "'t is just the change,
that is all. If you would go out with her, —
out beyond the village, where there is nothing
but sunshine and green trees and flowers, and the
birds sing so heavenly, — I think Lieschen would
feel happier."

"I dare say," said Gret, with lofty contempt.
"A gadabout like thee, who lives on other people's bounty, and cares not from whence it comes,
can easily do that. But I have my household to
look after, a husband to care for, who comes home
hungry to his meals, — fine advice that is thou
givest me, to go lazying about all day long. As if
one had nothing else to do but listen to the birds
singing! Truly, a fine thing!"

She laughed jeeringly, and looked the girl all
over. "Well, I must say," she resumed, "they
trick thee out finely at the parsonage. A clean
dress as often as you please, and each time 't is a
different color. I dare say the young baron who
stayed there gave thee a handsome Trinkgeld.

Perhaps thou didst put an extra polish on his boots. I heard that thou and Babbett quarreled who should clean them. Thou art a sly one, thou art, and knowest a good place when thou hast got it. I only wonder that old hag Babbett stands it. Perhaps thou thinkest to step into her shoes when she is too old to work any more. 'T would be a fine thing for thee, truly. If I were thee, I would insist upon some wages then. Surely they can't think to have thy services for nothing all the time. Thou wilt have to earn money, otherwise what will become of thee? No one will marry a poor girl who has not a chemise to her back. Look at me. I am already married, and not so very much older as thou, either."

Jette rose. She gently laid the sleeping Lieschen in her cradle. All the time she had been singing softly, and the baby, with a rapturous smile, had gradually closed her eyes. She bent over the cradle, and gave the child a long, pitying gaze. The look was still on her face when she turned to the mother.

"When Lieschen cries," she said, "bring her to the parsonage. Thou mayest safely leave her there, and go about thy business."

She held her head very high as she went, vowing never, *never* to disobey the Frau Pastorin again. Gret's squint eyes were set, and her mouth agape in astonishment. Then she clenched her hands in fury. "The insolent strumpet!" she gasped; "to speak to me as if I were dirt beneath her feet. ' Thou mayest safely leave her, and go

about thy business,' indeed! With what an air
she said it! and the tone of her voice! quite the
lady of quality, I declare! The beggar. Well,
this is delicious news. 'T will make everybody
roar, I am sure." She stole out, leaving her
sleeping child alone.

Jette went on her errand for the Frau Pastorin.
It was already well on in the afternoon when she
neared the parsonage gate. Babbett beckoned
her from the kitchen window. The old peasant
woman seemed quite excited.

"Go in," she whispered, "just as thou art.
Thou 'lt do very well. Some one there is in there
who will be glad to see thee."

Jette's heart gave a great bound. The blood
rushed in a wave to her head. Was it — could it
be — but no. How absurd! He was on his way
home — probably had reached there by now. And
yet — She hastily smoothed down her dress and
went to the sitting-room. She heard voices within
in animated conversation. Softly opening the
door, she went in. Some one rose, and eagerly
came forward to greet her. It was Herr Goldman.

CHAPTER XXV

"I HAVE said it," said the pastor, "and I stand
by it. The girl is a mere child. 'T would be a
grievous sin to expect her to take the duties and
responsibilities of wifehood upon her. Why, she
has not done growing yet. Give her body time

to develop, and her judgment to ripen. Then with God's help and such enlightenment as time and circumstances shall give her, she will most probably not say you nay."

"Most dear and reverend sir," said Herr Goldman, "do I not entirely submit myself into your hands? Only permit me to point out to your superior wisdom and understanding that ideas differ as to length of time. When you urge upon me the necessity of waiting three years " —

"Four," interrupted the pastor.

"As I understand," said the exasperated suitor, "the Fräulein is close upon her seventeenth year. When you mentioned you would not allow her to marry under twenty " —

"Dear Herr Banquier," genially said the pastor, "you forget that Jettchen is no city Fräulein. She is very young for her age. Her somewhat isolated life has probably had something to do with it. At Fasching (Carnival time) she will be seventeen. We are now upon the close of the summer. You will understand I was correct when I stipulated that four years from now would be far more appropriate for renewing your suit."

"We will not split hairs, Herr Banquier," said the Frau Pastorin; "'t is a great honor you have done both us and the girl. If in three years from now you are of the same mind " —

"Four," said the obstinate pastor.

"Now, now, now," said the Frau Pastorin, "one need not be so particular about a few months when one's whole future is involved. Indeed,

Herr Banquier, I repeat, I consider it a great honor for the girl, and the rarest piece of good fortune for one in her position, besides."

"All of which does not help me," said the banker, "if you give me no better encouragement. With all due respect to your superior judgment, Herr Pastor, and yours, Frau Pastorin, can you tell me of any suitor who would be willing to wait upon mere indefinite promises?"

The Frau Pastorin looked at the Herr Pastor. Her eyes beamed meaningly. Certainly the banker was justified in what he said. 'Twould be a grievous sin and shame to let such a goldfish slip through one's fingers. Penniless girls were not pelted with such chances every day, even though he *did* have red hair and a club foot. It was a romance, one of those improbable things one read about, but which rarely, if ever, happened in real life.

"We would not be so unjust to you, Herr Banquier," she said, "or to the girl, either. Your proposal, magnificent and generous as it is, has taken us completely by surprise. We have never thought of Henriette in regard to marriage. She is so young yet" —

"My mother was married when she was a year younger," said the banker. "She was the Fräulein's age when I was born."

"Very likely," said the pastor quietly. He shuddered inwardly. "Before I decide upon the girl's future, she must have a voice in the matter. For that she is not competent yet. If I judge her rightly, the mere idea of marriage will be abhorrent to her. She has never heard of it in relation to herself. Give her time to accustom herself to the idea."

"And you expect me to be satisfied with this?" said the banker.

"Nothing of the kind," said the pastor. "I beg of you, if these conditions do not suit you, to take your own course. I take it you are really in love " —

"I am," said Herr Goldman, "really and truly. Would I be here otherwise? I loved her from the first moment I saw her."

The Frau Pastorin was delighted. The Herr Pastor also was touched.

"Believe me," he said gently, "I am acting in your best interests. 'T would not be at all for your happiness were I rash enough to grant your request. Surely you are old enough to know that."

"You may be right, reverend sir," said Herr Goldman obstinately, "but at the present moment I fail to see it. All I know is, I love her, and I want her. Thou dear Heaven! She would have a life like a queen. Do you not think she would be grateful? Bah! At all events, I am old enough to know that. She would love me, of course she would. Where, then, is the necessity of waiting?"

"Jacob waited longer for Rachel than that," said the pastor.

"Jacob," said the banker contemptuously, "was a pauper. Do you think he waited for pleasure,

or as a test to his own patience? He had to earn
the wherewithal first to satisfy that old skinflint
Laban of his ability to support her. Really, I
fail to see how in the present instance the comparison holds good."

The pastor winced. To call the revered biblical patriarch a pauper hurt him as much as if
some one had personally affronted him.

"Love leaves its impression," said the banker,
"upon a young, untouched heart. In most cases it
comes only after marriage. Look at my mother.
She was too young to be consulted. Yet I defy
the world over to point out a happier union."

"Jettchen has been brought up differently,"
said the pastor; "she is accustomed to think and
act for herself. She has very strong likes and
dislikes. Yet she is obedient and tractable."

"Let me ask her, then," said Herr Goldman
eagerly; "support my suit, and let me put the
engagement ring on her finger. 'T will help her
to accustom herself to the idea that at some time
not very far distant she will be mine. Dear
Heaven! Was ever suitor content with so little?
I will wait till she is nineteen " —

The Herr Pastor was about to interpose, but
the Frau Pastorin said quickly and cordially, "Of
course, of course. I for my part shall make no
further objections, then, neither do I think will
my husband." She looked at the banker meaningly, as much as to say, "I shall take very good
care he does n't."

"Well," said Herr Goldman, with a sigh, "'t is

a great disappointment to me, and 't will be more so to my mother. She longs to see me settled in life."

"The Herr Banquier, your father"—hazarded the pastor.

Herr Goldman laughed. "Whatever pleases mamma pleases papa also," he said; "the most ardent wish of both my parents is to see me married."

"All parents wish that," said the Frau Pastorin, "as soon as their children are grown up." She thought of her own son, and her hopes rose high. Fritz married to the heiress of Hermersdorff, and Henriette married to this rich man, — surely she was a happy woman. Could matters turn out more luckily?

"In the mean time," she said, "Henriette shall visit Madame Goldman next Carnival. 'T will give her an opportunity to get thoroughly well acquainted with her future surroundings. Oh, yes. Time will pass quickly enough. Aha! here comes Henriette."

CHAPTER XXVI

FOR a moment Jette turned cold with disappointment, as Herr Goldman stumped forward to meet her. It was unfortunate for his suit he should have come at a time when her heart was entirely filled with the bright image of Hans von Czechy. The contrast of his squat, bull-necked

figure, his deformed limb, and fiery red hair, to
the tall, handsome Hans, whose every movement
was personified grace, whose joyous dark face and
enchanting smile haunted her wherever she went,
almost made her heart stand still. A feeling of
repulsion — of loathing — suddenly came over her.
She saw the gleam of his dark, gold-ringed eyes
fixed upon her, — a look with which no one had
ever gazed at her before. She stood still and
helpless, while he took her hand and bowed over
it, uttering the smoothest, most chivalrous phrases
in his easy, man-of-the-world fashion. He thought
her more shy than when first he met her, but,
oh, so enchantingly, so divinely fair, so just what
he most wished for and desired in a wife, that
he almost died of chagrin and disappointment to
think she should be withheld from him yet. Coffee was brought in, and the guest urged to stay
to supper, to which he only too gladly acceded.
What mattered to him the surroundings, — he
had eyes only for her. And she — an undefinable
horror, a dread, took possession of her. Why
was she placed next to him at table? Why did
he look at her with glances of fire? Why were
the Herr Pastor and the Frau Pastorin so complaisant to him? Thou dear Heaven! Why was
he there at all? The coffee scalded her throat,
the morsel almost choked her. She was not allowed to carry out the dishes, as she usually did,
but Babbett was called in, and for a wonder she
did it right willingly, smirking and throwing
looks of the strangest significance at the girl.

What *did* it all mean? She went to the window,
from where she could see the sky all purple and
yellow, a magnificent panorama of colors, for the
sun was going down. In a moment Herr Goldman was beside her.

"'T is so different from our narrow streets," he
said, smiling; "one has no chance to see the sun
set across one's neighbor's tall housetops. I am
afraid you will miss it when you come to us,
Fräulein."

Her lips moved in astonishment, but she uttered
no sound.

"Has not the Frau Pastorin told you?" he
asked genially; "'t is settled you are to pay us
a long visit next Carnival. 'T is great fun, I assure you. Do you not think you will enjoy it?"

"I have heard a great deal of the pleasures of
that time," she said timidly. "Am I really to go?"

"You are to come to us," he said, with emphasis. He came a little nearer. She shuddered
when she felt this.

"You are glad, are you not?" he asked caressingly. She murmured some indistinct reply. "My
mother will be so pleased to have you with her,"
he went on. "You like my mother, do you not?"

"Yes," she said faintly.

"You will try to like me a little also, will you
not?" he said still more caressingly. "I will do
anything in the world to make you happy. I will
be so good to you, — no one in the world could be
better."

Oh, what did he mean? If only he would not

come so near. And the Herr Pastor and the Frau
Pastorin, — did they know he was talking to her
in such intimate fashion? But when she looked
around, the Frau Pastorin nodded to her quite
gayly, and stepped from the open window to the
path beneath, and the Herr Pastor followed her,
with watering-pot and a large pair of shears.
She was dumfounded. It was, then, with their
sanction he spoke to her thus, — she felt hot and
cold by turns. She liked Herr Goldman well
enough at a distance, especially if he gave her
bonbons and delicious ices. She had gloated over
her Schiller and her Heine all the more rapturously, because she had done so by stealth. The
sad fate of the lovers in "Kabal und Liebe" had
racked her very soul, and she clenched her fists
in furious hatred of the detestable Wurm who
encompassed their ruin. Now, when the banker's
head edged near her own, it flashed across her
that his appearance coincided exactly with that
of the hated secretary. The red hair, the prominent eyes, the powerful, undersized figure, — she
drew back with a feeling of horror and aversion.
Then that unfortunate club foot, — to her dis-
torted fancy it seemed like the veritable hoof of
Satan. The poor banker! Most unfortunate was
it for him that this foolish, inexperienced little
heart, fed by a romantic fancy, bore at that moment the warm impress of her favorite hero. Oh,
it would be some one like that who would one day
come to woo her, not this horrid, deformed man,
who, with his world-worn, blasé physique, appeared

quite old and detestable to her. He was rich
and powerful, she was poor — she knew that very
well. But what does an inexperienced girl of
sixteen care for that? At that time the whole
world seems at her feet.

"Fräulein Jettchen," said the banker, — "for I
may call you so, eh?" —

"Yes, yes," she said hurriedly, "I much prefer
it. I — I — it seems so odd to be called by my
surname. No one has ever done so."

"No, of course not," he said indulgently; "you
have hardly been out of your immediate family
circle. How you will enjoy getting a glimpse of
the outside world! You like to go out among
people, and amuse yourself, do you not?"

"Yes, if they are nice to me," she said, thinking of the unfortunate picnic.

"Of course every one will be nice to you.
How could they help it? When you come to us,
you will be more than loved. My mother loves
you — I love you" —

"Oh," she said. She wanted to run away from
this awful man, whose red hair was singeing her
soul. Her hand hung limp and powerless at her
side. It happened to be the right one. She was
so much taller than he that he easily observed it.

"What a beautiful hand," he said. Only a
short time ago some one else had told her the
same thing. Then, for the first time in her life,
she had heard it. Some one — yes. She thrilled
and blushed when she remembered. Had he not
said he would return?

"A beautiful hand," resumed Herr Goldman, "and quite without adornment. In that it is most noticeable for its perfection. If it have any adornment at all, it should at least be something worthy of it."

He put his hand into his pocket, and drew out a small morocco case. The Herr Pastor and the Frau Pastorin, who, for all their being outside, had kept a wary eye on the pair, now stepped back into the room.

Herr Goldman snapped back the lid. A cry of delight came from Jette, who, with heaving breast and eyes that matched the sparkle of the gem resting on its white satin bed, gazed, and gazed her heart out.

"Oh, everlastingly feminine!" murmured the pastor.

"'T is a pretty bauble, eh?" said the banker carelessly. But his face shone. "Not this hand, Fräulein, the other one — the left one — the one nearest your heart."

"Not — not — for me?" she gasped.

"For whom, then? Have I not said I love you? Do not the Herr Pastor and the Frau Pastorin favor my suit? Some day — not so very long — when you are quite grown up — I am to come and marry you. And you will try and love me a little in return, will you not?"

She shivered, and could not say a word. Her eyes were fixed upon the stone, glittering like the eye of a basilisk. Not now did she desire it; not for worlds would she be fettered with that

serpent-like thing. Her left hand clenched itself
in the folds of her dress. But he, all unwitting
of her thoughts, gently raised it, and held it in
his own. Then the dull black circlet met his
view.

"Why," he stammered, "the Fräulein already
wears a ring."

"What nonsense," said the Frau Pastorin, very
much offended; "that funny little black thing!
Doubtless thou boughtest it at the Kirmess, eh,
Henriette?"

She looked at the girl, who turned scarlet. She
put her hand over the little circlet, as if it were
something sacred and she wanted to shield it from
profane looks.

"One does not buy antiques at a Kirmess,"
said the banker harshly; "that ring has another
history to tell."

The Herr Pastor looked at Jette. She understood it very well. "Herr von Czechy gave it to
me," she said, looking back at him with her clear
eyes. "One day out in the garden he gave it to
me as a keepsake, and told me it had been in his
family a long time. I have worn it ever since."

"So," said Herr Goldman, with jealous fury;
"I wonder what his countess, whom he has gone
home to marry, would say to this. Perhaps she,
too, distributed rings as keepsakes during the
time he was away and engaged to her."

If he had only known! From that moment the
passive aversion in her breast flared up into most
active loathing. How she abhorred him! His

club foot, his flaming red hair, those prominent
gold-ringed eyes, — it was a tout ensemble which
typified everything that was most repulsive to
her. The room swam around her. This was her
first knowledge of man's perfidy. Her heart was
not touched; but her faith was gone. "Be true
to me," he had said; "I will return." And all
this time he was engaged to another. Of course
she knew he never could be anything else but a
dear friend, a sweet, sacred memory. But he had
lied to her, — the idol was broken. And with
what brutality the truth had come home to her!
Could she ever like the man who with his coarse
fist had destroyed one of her most cherished ideals?
Never would she allow him to replace the plain
little band with his gaudy sparkling gem; what
mattered? she loved it still for the dear, beautiful past. She put her hand behind her, child
fashion, and burst into tears.

"Make him go away," she said. "I — I will
not wear his ring. At least — not yet. Please,
please give me time to get used to it." She ran
out of the room, and they could hear her sob all
the way up the stairs. And thus ended Herr
Goldman's first attempt at wooing.

CHAPTER XXVII

WHEN Carnival came, Jette, as was agreed
upon, went to Cologne to pay her promised visit
to Madame Goldman. She was seventeen now,

and getting accustomed to the idea that in the time to come she was to wed the banker. The Frau Pastorin preached it to her, the Herr Pastor seemed to regard it as settled, and Babbett constantly sang pæans in his praise. That a great, rich man should be so foolishly in love with a mere chit like Jette, — 't was inconceivable. Why, she had hardly commenced to wear long frocks, — she had no family, no dowry, — the very chemise to her back he would have to give her. To be sure, she had grown up into a right trim maid; but thou dear Heaven! that was no reason why a man with more riches than he could count in a lifetime should make a complete fool of himself over her. 'T was enough to make one feel like shaking him, only to see him look at her. And she, the foolish little chit, — she had no more appreciation of the wonderful unheard-of good luck that had befallen her than if she were the veriest idiot that ever was born. Why did not some one speak the plain, unvarnished truth to her, and pound the sense into her she so sadly needed! There was the Herr Pastor and the Frau Pastorin — dear Heaven! they took everything as a matter of course — as if the girl were a princess, and entitled to all the splendor and magnificence awaiting her, instead of a beggar maid picked up from the highway.

"See here, thou she-donkey," said the irate Babbett; "hast no sense at all, then? Dost think rich bankers grow on trees like cherries, to be shaken down and assorted at will? Nix, da!

With thy ten fingers and thy ten toes to boot,
shouldst thou snatch at such a chance. 'T is
seemly and maidenly in thee to pretend a little
diffidence. No one would find fault with thee for
that. 'T is a clever stimulant to a lover's eagerness, and enhances thy own value besides. But
thou carriest the thing too far. The most patient
man — Lord save the mark — the most persistent,
I mean — will not stand it. See thou to it thou
dost not weary him out. Dost think such another
chance will ever offer itself again to thee?"

Jette listened in silence, with wide-open, wor-
ried eyes. Her whole world was changed since
this hateful man had dropped into it. She did .
not like him; the more she saw of him, the deeper
her aversion to him grew. When he looked at
her, she felt herself sicken all over, — it was as if
some one had deadly insulted her. The clasp of
his hand felt cold and clammy to her shrinking
touch. She had to clench her teeth not to shriek
out with horror whenever he came close to her.
The Frau Pastorin scolded her, and called it
childish absurdity. "Thou 'lt grow out of it," she
said cheerfully; "the years bring wisdom." But
in her inmost heart Jette felt she never would.
Between the intervals of the flying visits the banker
paid during the winter, she had tried to school
herself into the possibility of some regard for him.
Surely, if ever lover merited it, he did. So delicate as he was in his generous munificence, the
parsonage could hardly contain all his presents.
Not the most fastidious could have found fault

with him, and the Frau Pastorin was very fastidious indeed; of the old-fashioned, severe kind,
who would have thought it a disgrace and humilia-
tion for a girl not formally engaged to accept any
but the most perishable gifts. He came loaded
each time, but it was always something the whole
family could enjoy. Flowers in the depth of winter, which fairly made one's heart expand with
rapture; roses, as if picked fresh out of the garden; camellias, with their cold, waxen bloom; violets, which could make a sick person well only
to look at; mignonette, the darlings of the Frau
Pastorin's heart. The house looked like a con-
servatory; never since the Herr Pastor's vener-
able grandfather built it had it contained luxuries
such as these. And the beautiful satin-lined
boxes of bonbons he brought, veritable coffers they
were for size, — nay, was it not a shame to spend
such an amount of money in such perishable trifles?
The bottom shelf in the linen-press had to be
emptied of its contents to make way for the huge
bottles of Maria Farina; there was so much one
could have bathed in it and never missed any, had
one chosen. But Jette never chose to. Had the
flowers and the distilled waters come from any one
else, she would have been beside herself with
rapture. The beautiful, innocent things came in
for the same aversion she felt for their donor.

"I don't like him," she would repeat, always
with the same terrified persistence. It was all
she had to say now to Babbett's remonstrances.

"Nobody expects thee to fall down and worship

him," said the old peasant woman angrily;
"'t would not at all be seemly in a well-brought-up
maid. Though how thou canst refrain from putting thy arms around his neck and thanking him
for such lovely gifts is more than I can understand. May the gnats sting me if I can make
thee out. One would think thou 'd dance and
leap and sing for very joy."

"I wish he had never set eyes on me," said the
girl, with tears in her eyes.

"Have a care," said Babbett solemnly, "lest
the Lord punish thee for thy wicked ingratitude.
I suppose thou never once considerest how wonderfully He has done by thee. Thou mayst read
of such things in thy romances, but let me assure
thee that not once in a million years do they occur
in real life. Suppose anything were to happen
to the Herr Pastor or the Frau Pastorin, where
couldst thou go? What would become of thee?
Thou couldst do nothing but go to service, and
that, thou knowest very well, thou 'rt not fit for.
Perhaps, as thou growest older, young men may
come and admire thee. They may even go to the
length of loving thee, for thou art likely to be
a right trim maid; so much I 'll not deny thee.
But I, who know something of their wiles, know
exactly what they 'll do. They 'll go as they have
come, wiping their mouths with the good cheer
they have consumed, jest and laugh, nay, most
likely put all sorts of foolish ideas into thy silly
head. But they 'll not marry thee. For thou
hast no dowry, therefore what avails thee all the

rest! Years of heart-breaking suspense thou wilt pass, till thy little bit of good looks will be faded and worn, and everybody will laugh in scorn at the old maid. Then thou 'lt be fine and sorry, eh?"

She looked at Babbett in helpless consternation. What wisdom there seemed in her words! Was it really true? Was marriage the only haven in which she could find a refuge from the dreary future otherwise awaiting her? The helpless orientalism in her nature made her shrink with terror from the picture.

"If only he were not so repulsive," she murmured.

"Thou wantest too much for thy money," said the old woman scathingly. "If there were not an ' if ' and a ' but ' in the case, thou art scarcely the one to have such a piece of good luck flung at thee. The Herr is in love with thy foolish face. There 's no accounting for taste, surely. 'T is as likely to fall on a dunghill as on a rose-bed. What he lacks in good looks himself, he seeks to atone for in a wife. Wouldst rather have a man grin and smirk at his own donkey face in the glass than have eyes to spare for thee? For all thou floutest him, there are plenty as comely as thyself, with bags of money to boot, who would stretch their ten fingers to get him. If thou art wise, thou 'lt hook him fast, when thou goest up to see his mother. Life's May comes but once. That little bit of a face of thine is all thou hast got. Make the most of it while thou canst."

"''T is all he cares for in me," she said resentfully:

The old woman stemmed her hands on her hips. "Now let anybody hear that!" she said explosively; "with what folly art thou stuffed full now? What else dost thou expect him to care for, then? Thou art spoiled, puffed up with thoughts which ought never to have found an abiding-place in thy brain. That comes of thy godless reading, I trow. I told the Herr Doctor once, and I was sure he would tell the Frau Pastorin, but nothing ever came of it."

"Ay, well I remember it," said the girl vindictively. "Thou gavest him the book thou found'st under my pillow. But he did not tell his mother, as thou wert sure he would do. There is more good in him than I suspected."

"In my native town," said Babbett, "I knew of a case just like thine. The girl flouted her lover, and kept him in torment for years. Then she sickened of the smallpox. When she arose, she was a sight to look at. Glad enough she would have been then to have married him. But he would have none of her. He went and married a girl with a fair, fresh face, and left the other one to everlasting sorrow."

"Yes," said Jette meditatively, "that is the way Herr Goldman cares for me."

"She only got what she deserved," said Babbett; "'t would serve thee right the same way. What! hast thou no pride, no ambition? Think how everybody in the village would burst with

envy. Already they are saying, 'Nay, the luck
of that Jette! Was ever the like heard of! Comes
a rich, fine, powerful gentleman from Cologne, a
Herr who can ride extra post every day of his
life if he wants to, and asks to marry that snip
of a girl.' If only thou hadst seen Gret the
other day. Last time the Herr Banquier was
here, she came to the kitchen door. She had
Lieschen in her arms, and the brat was howling
as usual. She asked for thee, but I told her thou
wert making thyself agreeable in the best room,
as thou hadst every right to do. Such a face as
she made. Thou wouldst have sworn she was
twin sister to Black Peter, her ugly cat, whom
everlasting perdition seize, — the same wicked,
green squint eyes, the same devilish grin, showing
the protruding teeth between. Nay, I fancied I
saw her mop of tow bristle on her head with envious spite. A nice trollop, truly, she is to come
spying around here. I warrant thee I sent her
back with her mouth full."

Jette's eyes glistened. A great satisfaction filled
her heart. Really, it would be a fine triumph
over Gret and her ilk if she were to drive away in
a luxurious traveling carriage, with outriders in
livery, and come back a great lady to visit her
former home as often as she pleased.

"The Herr Pastor would not consent yet," she
murmured.

"What," said Babbett, eagerly catching at her
meaning, "the marriage, thou meanest? Surely
he will, and only too gladly. If only thou wilt,

he will quickly enough. Go to Cologne and show thyself sensible. Take from thy finger that silly black thing the Herr Baron gave thee. To be sure he gave me a handsome Trinkgeld, like the nobleman he is, every inch of him. A golden louis d'or it was. But then, the Herr Banquier gives me the same each time he comes. I warrant thee I have eight at least to keep the first one company. Beauties they are, I tell thee, and right merrily they chink in my stocking. But I have thy interest at heart. I know thou 'lt not forget me when thou art the banker's wife. And only think how thou couldst repay the Herr Pastor and the Frau Pastorin for all they have done for thee."

"That is true," said Jette, whose eyes sparkled.

"Thou couldst buy them each a chair of solid gold," said Babbett; "kings and queens can't have better than that. 'T would be showing thy gratitude in a proper manner, eh? and cushions embroidered in gold and silver thou couldst have made for the seat and back. Some kind of upholstery I suppose they will need, otherwise they might be uncomfortable to sit on. And hark thee! Every night while thou art away, I 'll look in the cards to make sure thou hast taken to heart that which I have taken so much pains to admonish thee with."

CHAPTER XXVIII

THE Frau Pastorin was not much behind Babbett in her counsel, when Jette was ready to start on her journey. To be sure, she was not so diffuse, neither did she go into as many details. But what she said in her plain, practical manner was quite to the point. She did not think Herr Goldman an Adonis, or quite the person for a young, romantic girl to fall in love with. But he had what worldly-wise people value far more highly, — the wherewithal to insure his wife a future free from all care. A life of luxury, of honor and ease, awaited the one who should be sensible enough to take advantage of the lucky chance. The poor would rise up and call her blessed. As Jette had the Jewish compassionate heart, and knew what poverty was from her early recollections, this reasoning did not fail to make its due impression on her. The Herr Pastor said nothing. With his forefinger and thumb he raised her pretty chin, gave one of his beaming, heartfelt looks into her eyes, and told her to enjoy herself. One could see how very fond and very proud he was of her.

So when Jette arrived at Cologne, at the close of a crisp, cold February day, she was quite disposed to be as gracious as possible to Herr Goldman, bearing in mind all the good advice she had received. He met her at the coach office, and Hanne was with him. A glow of happiness spread over his face when he caught sight of the tall, slim beauty, as the old post-chaise rumbled into the yard! Of course, he had been cooling his heels and warming his expectations for hours before the stage was due. He almost fell over himself as he rushed forward to assist her to alight, jealously pushing away the gallant guard, who, having unceremoniously bundled out a pudgy widow, smilingly extended his hand to the merry-eyed, happy girl. She sprang to the ground, light as a fawn, saying between little gasps of cold, "Oh, I am so glad, I could kiss everybody." Then she blushed, caught hold of Hanne's arm, and ran with her to the warm, luxurious carriage standing outside. Herr Goldman smiled as if he saw heaven open, thrust his hand into his pocket, and flung a Trinkgeld to the guard which made that worthy's eyes start from his head. "Now, but that one must be quite fearfully in love," he soliloquized, looking alternately at the gold piece in his hand and the flying form of the banker, as he hastened to follow the housekeeper and her young charge into the carriage. So solicitous he was about her comfort! Did she have her feet well ensconced in the fur bag? Hanne, stoop down and see, and make quite, *quite* sure the dear, sweet Fräulein has drawn it properly around her. Surely, her lovely, tiny feetlets must be perished with the long, cold journey. Allow him, — he really *must* draw the rich sable he had brought for her comfort a little more snugly around her shoulders. And the fur rug over her knees — was it sufficient — now,

really?   Young ladies were so careless, they presumed so much upon their hearty youth and vigor
— suppose she caught cold — heavens! he did not
dare think of such a misfortune.   Had she been
well looked after on her journey? and so on, until
Hanne felt as if she must box his ears, and Jette
exhausted herself with reassuring him.   He was
so happy, surely the gathering twilight caught an
afterglow from the reflection of his radiant face.
That happy, ecstatic drive, — should he ever forget it, with that fair, heavenly face opposite to
him!   As for Jette, she felt that it was very good
to have all this warmth and luxury instead of
the cold, cheerless post-chaise; the exhortations
she had received at home still abode with her; she
strove very hard not to let the repulsion born of
his presence dominate her this time.   And when
she found herself in the arms of Madame Goldman, the warmth of whose genial motherly embrace opened the depths of her heart, her eyes
moistened, and the happiness of being so welcomed was without alloy.   As she stood under the
brilliantly lit chandelier in the magnificent drawing-room, Madame Goldman looked at her with
beaming admiration.

"She grows more beautiful all the time," she
thought; "what a heavenly creature!   So divinely
made, with such gracious understanding!   One
can forgive Julius's foolish raptures when one
sees her.   Nay, I am quite in love with her myself."

"Draw off thy gloves, Liebchen," she said,

"and let me chafe thy hands. Are they not cold?"

"Not one bit," said Jette gayly; "Herr Goldman made me tuck them under the big fur skin. He was quite tyrannical, I assure you. I was too much afraid to disobey him."

The banker, who was stumping to and fro with his hands in his pockets, devouring her with big, greedy looks, beamed all over.

"'T was for your own good, though, you obeyed me, was it not?" he said as caressingly as if he wished his tones were honey.

She pouted so enchantingly that then and there he would have bartered his fortune only to kiss her.

"I had to, whether I wanted to or not," she said. Then, feeling her ingratitude, she said with infinite sweetness, "Of course you knew best."

"Ah," he exclaimed in rapture, "if only you would always think so! If only you would come to see how all my striving is solely for your comfort and to please you. I do not ask anything but a kind word, a loving look in return. Try while you are here to think of me as a little nearer to you. You shall step on roses all the days of your life. I will pierce my flesh to pull out the thorns so they shall not touch you."

Now, she discovered with dismay that, in spite of her schooling, the old horror clutched her whenever he became impassioned, or came near her. It was stronger than all her endeavors; it engulfed her like an avalanche under which she

knew she must perish. The rosy bloom withered
in her young cheek to ghastly pallor; she clenched
her teeth to restrain their frozen chatter. One
hand she put to her eyes, to shield them from the
telltale light.

"It blinds me," she said.

The banker furiously rung the bell, and commanded the agitated footman, who hurriedly answered, to lower the lights.

"You have only to breathe a wish," he said,
"and it shall be obeyed."

"If thou wouldst only restrain thyself," said
his mother, when Jette had gone to her room to
make herself presentable for dinner; "there is too
much passion in thy wooing; thou continually
forgettest her youth and innocence. Instead of
pleasing, thou frightenest her. Thou hast only
had dealings with wily, experienced women of
the world. In this wise thou 'lt never gain her
regard."

Herr Goldman kicked a costly embroidered
hassock out of his way, and angrily rumpled his
hair.

"Thou, too," he said, "turnest against me.
Dost think I do not know the difference between
her fresh innocence and a strumpet of a coquette?
'T is that which beguiles, befools me. There is
a majesty about her which abases me to the dust.
There is something in her air, her manner, the
way she looks at one, which stirs feeling to its pro-
foundest depths. I tell thee, when a man of my
age thinks so, 't is serious. 'T is then his life's

happiness or misery hangs in the balance. Oh,
I tell thee, if she does not relent, she will make
a madman of me."

"Scorn her," said his mother ; "flout her.
Show her thou art a man, and hast to be won
from thy superior height. Wrap thyself in thy
power; coquet with others; let her come to the
knowledge that they appreciate and value thee.
Treat her with condescension; be supercilious;
ignore her. So shalt thou win her, not by bending thy neck to the yoke."

"I know all that and more," groaned the
banker; "I am an ass, a fool, an idiot, where
she is concerned. I have no more control over
my feelings than the callowest hobbledehoy when
near her. There all worldly wisdom fails. I
would be willing she should give me blows with
one hand, providing she caressed me with the
other."

"So speaks a slave," said his mother, with
scorn, "not a man with an appreciation of the
manhood within him. Thou gettest this disposition from thy father, who, being a man in all
other affairs of life, is slavish in his affections.
Would to Heaven I could dispossess thee of thy
spirit, and lend thee mine awhile. We have only
to *will* to gain that which we strive for the most."

Just then Jette came in, her blue cashmere
dress clothing her like the purple of majesty, a
cluster of pink roses stuck in her bosom. As she
had developed in grace and beauty, the air of
pride and nobility which had distinguished her

already as a child had developed also. She looked like a young queen at whose gracious smile warriors were ready to bend the knee. Madame Goldman and the infatuated banker could not take their eyes off her.

"Look," she said, strutting up and down under the chandelier: "this is my first long dress, my first *really* long dress. Do you see? It has a train. A train! just think. I hardly know how to walk in it. All the same, it looks pretty. When I tried it on, I could not contain myself for pride and joy. I ran all the way home to let them see it. The dressmaker was furious. She said I came near spoiling it. Do you think I manage the train properly? Those dear, beautiful looking-glasses! One can see one's whole length in them. Oh, I think it is lovely."

Mother and son laughed at her innocent childish vanity. It was so delightfully novel. Madame Goldman had never indulged in the fripperies of young girlhood. Amid all the splendors of her surroundings, her youth had passed unheeded and alone. Sadly she thought of the early doll-playing time, when she had shut herself up in the attic, terrified because of the duties and responsibilities thrust upon her. Alone in her magnificent mansion, she had never known the sweet communion of young companionship; for as a married woman she belonged to the matrons, who would have none of her, and the young of her own age were busy with their schoolbooks. In solitude she had developed a strong individuality of character, which, without personal beauty, made her a most fascinating and much-sought-after woman, the idol alike of both husband and son, the shining light of the society she adorned, the judicious benefactor of the poor, and the providence of the needy too proud to beg. But youth with its fripperies and foibles, its vanities and its failings, its careless gayety and pulsing joy of life, she had never known. It made her sad when she saw this young girl in her innocent conceit pucker her smooth brow over the serious question whether her first train sat well on her or not.

"Thou peacock," she said, "hast thou admired thyself enough? Never, I vow, have these mirrors seen such a piece of vanity."

"Do you think I am vain?" said Jette anxiously. She blushed, and turned away from the reflection of herself. "Nay, I would not have that said of me for the world. 'T is such a pleasure to see one's whole length in the glass. I had no idea my dress looked so nice." She patted it complacently, and cast glances at herself from the tail of her eye. "'T is only since I have gone to the dressmaker I have dared to see how I look. She insisted I should judge for myself how my things fitted me. Before then I did not dare do so. Of all heinous sins, the Frau Pastorin considers vanity the worst. Babbett used to tell me that if ever I was caught looking in the glass while the clock struck the hour, I should be turned into stone. Of course I have n't believed that for

a long time.   All the same, it used to make me
afraid."

"Then thou hast never admired thyself before,
eh?" said Madame Goldman.   The banker sat
in a fauteuil, with his hands in his pockets.   Her
chatter was sweeter to him than the most divine
music.

She opened her eyes very wide.   "Admire myself, — why should I do that?   'T would be very
foolish, I should think.   One likes to see if one's
hair is smooth or one's dress sits properly.   If I
am especially anxious to know, I run down to the
brook in our orchard.   There I can see myself
full length.   My glass is so small, — about so
big."   She held up the length of her finger.

"And didst thou look in the brook long?"
asked Madame Goldman.

"Of course," she said complacently, "I looked
as long as I pleased, for there was no one to chide
me.   Sometimes, if I thought I looked more than
usually nice, I would take out my knitting so as
not to appear lazy, and look in the brook all the
time."

She was somewhat confused at the hearty fit of
laughter in which both mother and son joined.

"Where didst thou get thy pretty roses?"
asked Madame Goldman.

"From the bouquet on my dressing-table.
Herr Goldman, I want so much to thank you.
Of course it was you who put it there."

"How do you know?" he said, all in a tremor
of delight.

"Because," she said positively, "no one but you would have thought of it."

"Don't you think," said his mother, "so much forethought ought to be rewarded?"

"Yes," she said somewhat uneasily, "I will give him a pretty rosebud."

"Thou canst give him something far more precious," said Madame Goldman, "without depriving thyself of thy bud."

"I will take the rosebud gladly," said the banker eagerly, seeing her turn pale again; "only you must finish your gracious deed, and fasten it in the buttonhole of my coat."

He stumped towards her as she pretended to select a flower with great care. She was by a head and shoulders taller than he, so she had to look down upon him as she tried to fasten the flower. They were just opposite one of the great mirrors. As they stood side by side, he looked at their reflection just as she happened to raise her eyes. The flower dropped from her hand and fell at his feet leaf by leaf. The footman flung aside the heavy draperies and announced that dinner was served.

CHAPTER XXIX

IN the dining-room Jette made her curtsy to Goldman senior and Uncle Emanuel. She felt instinctively that both disliked her. The elder banker did not at all look with favor upon his

son's suit. He believed in the good old-fashioned
Oriental custom, where parents selected suitable
husbands or wives for their children, without any
reference to individual tastes. He ridiculed the
idea of personal sentiment, taking it for granted
that each adjusted himself to the other after marriage. It had been so with him and with everybody else he knew. But his son had disappointed
him in more ways than one. He had led a fast,
dissipated life ever since he was barely grown up.
With this the old gentleman would not have found
so much fault. Early partner in the bank, with
unlimited means at his command, it was but natural
that many temptations should be placed in his way.
Though for the matter of that, the old gentleman
argued that he had been young once himself, but
had never indulged in such spendthrift proclivities.
Temperate and frugal by nature, he was the soul
of simplicity. While his son drove thoroughbred
horses a king might have envied, the old gentleman
walked to and fro from the bank in his thin, low-
cut buckled shoes. His wife had her brougham,
her landau, and her pair of smart ponies, but let
the weather be never so bad, not once did he avail
himself of either unless she insisted upon it.
When compelled to go away on business, he invariably traveled third class, and wrangled over
the fare of a droschke until he tired out the
driver. His son spent more on choice cigars and
flowers in one day than the father's entire hotel
bill amounted to. But the presents he would
bring home to his wife were costly enough to

make a queen envious. He wanted nothing for
himself, all his hopes were centred in his son.
And here he was, close upon thirty, and not
married yet. Every suitable opportunity he had
flouted, and now he was running after a pauper
of a girl whom they would be ashamed to intro-
duce into the family. The old gentleman distrusted Jette; he distrusted her loyalty to the
faith of her fathers; he distrusted the manner in
which she had been brought up. She showed it
plainly enough. She was so different from the
girls brought up and surrounded by the influences
of their faith. What attracted his son was a
grave source of apprehension to him. Julius had
gone over heart and soul to the radicals; he was
an ardent adherent of the famous Dr. Geiger,
who, as the pioneer and champion of the reform
movement, ran the gauntlet of the most bitter
enmity of the old orthodox set to which the old
gentleman belonged. He saw the thin edge of
the wedge which was destined, as he imagined,
to make apostates in heart, if not in deed, of the
glorious old religion. He did not see the dawn
of a new and more tolerant era, he only saw the
dismemberment of the faith. The infusion of
new blood, lest it should starve of its own anæ-
mic condition, he regarded as a blasphemy. The
exigencies of the times were naught to him. He
wanted the old faith to remain intact; innovations
or modifications had no concern with religion, but
stank of the devil. He considered himself privileged that he was born a Jew. He would not

slink through the slime of obsequiousness as if apologizing for what he was. He knew himself to be a power among his own people, and like a sovereign he stood his ground against the mighty onsweeping tide which he foresaw neither he nor those after him would be strong enough to stem. He was proud of the old faith, proud of its ancient traditions, proud of its dead and past glories, proud of its preëminence when all others were in their swaddling-clothes, proud of the parent stem from which the world's history had sprung, proud of its sufferings, its humiliations, and its shame. Not one iota of concession would he make, flinging away the solid kernel to retain the frail husk. He was glad he would not be among the living should this ever come to pass. At dawn when he arose, he flung his thalis around his shoulders, strapped the sacred scroll upon his wrists and brow, and lifted his eyes and his voice in heartfelt worship to the Lord God of Israel, who had so miraculously delivered his own from the bondage of Egypt. The same bondage existed still, though it was in another form. No truckling and bowing to those who had scourged them with the whip of oppression and opprobrium for ages; 'twas for them to hold out the hand of fellowship and amity, if at last a new era should dawn and make the world what it was intended to be, a gift from the Almighty Creator, His garden, in which all should dwell alike in peace and harmony, until it pleased Him in his own good time to call the wanderer home.

"Hear, O Israel; the Lord thy God is One Eternal, Everlasting Being," he prayed aloud, his lean frame quivering with impassioned fervor, exalted reverence in his bowed attitude and voice. His piety was heartfelt and sincere. He was not ungrateful to the Creator of all things, this shabby, snuffy old financier. He had no ideals, no superstitions. His religion was a living fact to him, its forms and ceremonies a necessary expression. It was the giant rock against which, let contention dash itself never so wildly, he rested in perfect security. "Hear, O Israel; the Lord thy God is One Eternal, Everlasting Being." It was a grand, inspiring rhythm, which would make music in his heart when that Lord God summoned him to eternal sleep, and would be the trumpet refrain which, with its stirring notes, would rouse him. He devoutly believed in the restoration of the glories of Jerusalem, not as mortals interpret it, but as the Almighty in his own divine power will bring it about, and that, when all other dynasties shall have had their day and lie crumbling in the dust, Judah, of all other nations, will rear its head, and, like another phœnix, arise from its ashes with more than olden-time splendor, to reign preëminently and alone. "For the heart of the Jew never dies," he said. He stood in the synagogue on fast days, clad in his shroud, his feet never stirring from the spot, his voice never ceasing to uplift itself in lamentation and prayer from sunrise to sundown. His beseechings were not alone for himself or his; they took in

every one of his people. Close to stinginess in
his own personal expenses, he was lavishly generous to his family, and munificent in his charities
to the poor. Of him it might truly be said that
his right hand knew not what his left hand did.
Unswervingly just, upright, and scrupulously honest, his word was his bond with all creeds and
nations.

Goldman fils regarded his father's religious
aspirations with tolerant contempt. He looked
upon them as relics of the past and calculated to
foster prejudice. He went even further than the
most progressive of the progressive party. Creed
and religion were synonymous terms with him.
It was entirely a matter of circumstance over
which no one had any control. The faith which
consoles, the spirituality which ennobles and re-
fines, makes one suffer and endure, had no place
in his calculations. The forms and ceremonies
which were the darlings of his father's heart he
regarded as remnants of old-time superstitions.
No doubt they were right and proper when first
practiced. In those obsolete times it was necessary to have a visible religion in order to be duly
impressed. It was necessary to *see* as well as to
feel. The traditions which his father venerated
were no more to him than the ancient traditions
of Greece and Rome. Both had had their day.
Both had fallen to make way for others, which
in their turn would fall. It was an inevitable
law of nature, and would be so to the end of
time. He had ideals, but no spirituality. He

was generous, but ostentatious. Whenever he gave, he liked it to be well known. In his business transactions he was daring to the verge of imprudence, but he took good care never to overstep it. The name and fame of Goldman were very dear to him. Proud, vain, and passionate, scheming and insatiably ambitious, his aspirations soared far higher than his father dreamed of. He aimed at the distinction of being somebody in the great world; to break down the barriers which all his wealth could not storm. To this end he had steadily refused to consider the most advantageous matches submitted to his consideration. He did not want a wife whose Oriental appearance would give offense to the society he sought, and would debar him from crossing its threshold. But with Jette he knew he could storm the citadel and conquer it in triumph. Who knows? He might be received at court — he would be created a baron — Baron and Baroness von Goldman — delightful sound! He rolled the names over his tongue with epicurean enjoyment. He saw even further than this. Once let him have a sure footing, and then the world should talk of him. Backed by such wealth as he possessed, his prestige in the financial world, his shrewd wit to seize hold of the right opportunity and make the most of it, he might climb to any height he chose. "The great and powerful Goldman," that is what people should call him. Not once did it occur to him to utilize his opportunities to benefit those of his own race. He wanted to soar alone, and from his lofty eminence look down with contempt upon less fortunate ones.

As is common with such natures, he had indulged his passions, but his heart had never been touched. To his credit let it be said that he really and truly loved the beautiful girl he was eager to make his wife. That she would help him to accomplish his social ambitions greatly enhanced her value in his mind. As she developed in grace and beauty, and he caught occasional glimpses of her well-trained intellect, there entered into his feeling for her what he had never felt for any woman save his mother before — respect. He had the real Oriental contempt for women, whom he looked upon as an inevitably necessary part of creation in order to minister to man's comfort alone. Secure in the feeling of his own worth, he never dreamed that her avoidance of him arose from personal dislike. Like the rest, he attributed it to girlish diffidence. If the Pastor had not been such a country bumpkin in his obstinately starched views, he argued, and had disposed of the girl as was customary among the people he knew, she would have been his wife long ago. What did a young girl know of what was best for her? What business had she with views of her own? A husband was selected for her by her guardians, a short courtship followed, and they were married. The rest adjusted itself as naturally and as nicely as any one could wish.

Therefore, sore as he felt about it, he tried to gird his soul with patience. Secretly, both he

and his mother agreed that they would make the
most of the present opportunity to gain Jette's
consent. Then the Pastor would have to give his
also, and this wearisome probation would end.
So Jette, all unsuspicious, went about and enjoyed
herself. She wrote home twice a week, as she had
been told to do. Rapturous accounts they were
of festivities she attended. She had been to her
first ball, a real ball, where there were crowds of
beautifully dressed people, and the flash of jewels
had blinded one's eyesight like the lightning, — a
floor, slippery enough to trip one up had one not
been guided by a strong arm, but, oh, so perfectly
delightful to glide over to the strains of Strauss's
ravishing music. And it was played by a band
of skilled musicians; it was even better than the
one which played on the promenade every afternoon. And she had looked nice, — at least everybody told her so. Her white muslin had been the
simplest dress in the room, but Madame Goldman
quite approved of it, saying it was the most appropriate thing for a young girl to wear. But
the maid had looped it here and there with such
beautiful pink ribbons, and her flowers had been
the handsomest in the room; really, she was satisfied she looked as well as anybody. And she had
danced, — her card was full before she had fairly
entered the room. She had danced a big hole in
her white satin slipper, right clear through the
stocking. It had taken her a whole morning to
darn it neatly.

Madame Goldman was as much sought after

as the most spoilt beauty. At forty-five she was younger than she had been at twenty. Her card filled up rapidly from the moment she entered a ball-room. She was as light of foot as a ballet dancer, spite of her short stout, figure. While her snuffy old husband slept at home, there was hardly a ball of any importance she did not attend with Julius. Only since he was grown up had she commenced to live; and at middle age she enjoyed what in her youth she had missed.

"Liebchen," she said to Jette, who had danced opposite to her in the quadrille, "'t is time we went home. See, there is Julius beckoning. Hast thou enjoyed thy first ball? Hardly have I caught a glimpse of thee all night. Thou oughtest to have heard all the pretty things that were said to me about thee. Nay, thou need'st not blush. We all know what such sayings amount to. Nevertheless, 't is nice to hear them, eh? Now thou must not pout. By the time we are home, dawn will be streaking the sky. Console thyself. Plenty more dances will follow. But thou must learn to take them temperately. I cannot afford to have thee return home pale and wan. It would be a poor inducement for thy next visit."

After all, it was quite well on in the gray of the morning before they were allowed to depart. Jette accompanied Madame Goldman to her boudoir, where the fire burned merrily in the handsome porcelain stove, and the maid stood ready with freshly brewed coffee. She flung off her

wrap with a sigh of appreciation at the luxury of
such a home-coming. After all, it was a very
desirable thing to be rich. Seated opposite her
hostess, in a deep fauteuil, she rattled on over
the night's events. She was too excited to think
of sleep. Madame Goldman was waiting for her
son to come in and kiss her. He never retired
to rest, no matter how late, without doing so.
She sent the maid to bed, and took off her jewels.
As she put them into the satin-lined trays in the
large casket, Jette leaned over and touched them
with delight.

"You don't mind," she said timidly; "nay, I
want to touch them just to see if their fire does
not burn one. How magnificent you looked in
them to-night! No queen could look finer."

"Marry Julius," said his mother; "he will
give thee even finer than these."

She gave a little gasp. "I would marry him
to-morrow," she said, "if only he were you."

"Thou silly one," said Madame Goldman, "he
is far better as he is. Me thou wouldst not find
so easy to deal with. Thou canst wind him
around thy finger with one kind word or look."

Madame Goldman set the casket on a hassock,
and standing in front of the girl, clasped a neck-
lace around her throat. She took out Jette's mod-
est earrings, and hung drops like liquid fire in
their stead. She clasped the jewels around the
girls' arms, drew them on her fingers, and fastened
them in her hair. Tray after tray Madame Goldman emptied of their dazzling contents. A girdle

was suspended around Jette's waist, the withered flowers were taken from her bosom and jewels placed in their stead. With a dexterous movement Madame Goldman turned the girl around so that she faced the great cheval glass.

"Look at thyself," Madame Goldman said.

At first Jette was almost too dazzled to see. Then her breath almost forsook her. She gazed and gazed, all articulation smothered in its birth. Like one solid, immense blaze of light she appeared, too dazzling almost for eyes to look upon. Could one look like that? Was it really in one's power to be so beautiful? The gems flashed back from every part of her body, — there really were women, then, fortunate enough to possess such things! Her breast heaved, her eyes sparkled. She was almost suffocated with delight. If the people at home could see her thus, — nay, did it not surpass anything she had ever read in fairy tales?

From the other end of the room Madame Goldman dragged another casket. It was much larger than the first, and quite heavy, to judge with how much difficulty she lifted it. She unlocked it, and flung back the lid, drew forth its glittering contents, and flung them in a heap on the rug. Such treasures — it surpassed one's wildest dreams. In an ecstasy of delight the girl threw herself down beside them, and let the glittering mass run from one hand into the other, as children do with the shells they pick up on the seashore.

"All these shall be thine," said Madame Goldman, "if thou wilt but consent to marry Julius. Nay, and as many more as will cover thee from head to foot."

The girl laughed delightedly. She babbled as if intoxicated. Herr Goldman entered the room. He stopped short as one dumfounded. His mother beckoned to him, and took his hand.

"She consents," she said, in her rich, musical voice. "Liebchen, let me bless thee."

Like one awakening from a nightmare, the girl sprung to her feet. With hasty, feverish fingers she unclasped the gems and laid them back in the casket. "They are very precious," she stammered, "but I — I do not want them."

The banker savagely kicked over the casket, so that its contents rolled over on the rug. Then he angrily stumped from the room.

CHAPTER XXX

JETTE enjoyed herself royally during the Carnival. For the time being, every one was satisfied to wear a cap and bells, and give himself up to the hilarious pleasure of being a fool. In the club to which Herr Goldman belonged, it was decided that the public parade that year should eclipse all previous ones in originality and splendor. There were special sittings to which ladies were admitted, at all of which Jette was the happiest fool of all. Madame Goldman took her everywhere. In the girl's superabundance of youthful spirits and happy gayety of heart she herself became a girl again. They went to hear the incomparable Lind, at that time in the zenith of her fame. Jette's admiration and enthusiasm were so great, she could hardly restrain herself from jumping over the footlights, and falling in mute adoration at the songstress' feet. They went visiting, and received visits. With all her equipoise of mind, she could not but feel flattered at the distinction with which everybody treated her. But that which made the most impression on her was the widespread missions of charity on which she accompanied Madame Goldman. To have it in one's power to bring relief to the needy, clothe the naked, cure the sick, and provide homes for the helpless, — surely, that was divine. Like a harbinger of good tidings, Madame Goldman was welcomed everywhere. With a benediction she entered, and with a benediction she left. And it was all done so unostentatiously, with so much tact. Like one of themselves the banker's wife listened to their complaints, their stories of adversity. Nothing of the great lady there was to chill their sympathies or check confidences. The rich woman was just human, nothing more or less. Her sound common sense was not obstructed by sentiment. Did a case present itself where she could not suggest a remedy, it was left to her husband to dispose of satisfactorily. This dark, short, pudgy woman, with her strong face and polished manner, was the tower of strength against which numberless bruised reeds leaned and looked

up to with veneration and confidence. And all
this could be done with the power of money. Oh,
no, not always, either, unless one had the spirit
and determination to use it as a sacred trust, as
the Lord God had intended it. Money could just
as well be used for destructive purposes, — one
had not to turn to books to know that. It was
the every-day history of the world. But money
used in the right way, as Madame Goldman used
it, — what a power! It was almost like being
divine one's self. And she herself was so poor,
— she possessed nothing, — never would she know
the bliss of relieving the wants of others, saying,
"Here thou! Thou hast a right to live as well
as I, and take thy rightful share of the earth's
inheritance, in which the Lord God willed all
should have their portion according to their
work." Never, unless — She shook herself and
set her teeth together. Not yet could she accustom herself to the idea of wedding the banker.
There was time yet — two years. The Herr Pastor had said she should not marry until she was
quite grown up.

And so she put off the inevitable day, and went
on taking the goods of life so lavishly provided
for her. Madame Goldman, watching her curi-
ously, knew very well what passed in her mind.
She lived this new life of ease and luxury as if
she had never known any other. Would she be
satisfied to return to her customary duties, the
stagnant monotony of a rural life?

"Passover comes late this year," said Madame

Goldman one evening, as they sat in her luxurious boudoir. Jette's embroidery frame rested idly in her lap. It was too dark to work and too early for the lamps to be lit; just the hour for tender reverie or mutual confidences. The fire in the porcelain stove glowed like the eye of a cyclops. The paintings on the walls, the swelling upholstery of richest satin, the numerous trifles of ornament and bricabrac, valuable additions to a connoisseur's collection, looked doubly rich and fanciful in the half light. The girl settled back in the luxurious armchair, and clasped her hands above her head.

"Yes," she said, "the blossoms will already gather on the old cherry-tree at home, and the lilacs commence to bud in my garden. They will both have to be pruned this year."

"I wish thou couldst prolong thy visit and spend the holidays in our midst," said the elder lady.

"Oh, no, I could not," said Jette, in genuine trepidation. "Easter comes about the same time. There is so much to do then at home. The whole house is turned upside down, from attic to cellar. Everything is made sweet and fresh for another year. Babbett could never do it alone. Indeed, I must be there to help her."

"How canst thou think of returning to such drudgery after the life thou hast led here?" exclaimed Madame Goldman.

Jette opened her eyes very wide. "We all have to work," she said. "The Herr Pastor says work is the salt of life."

"Occupation, yes," said Madame Goldman; "but drudgery of the coarsest kind, — such as the poorest charwoman can do far more creditably than thou for a few groschen a day, — they surely could hire some one in thy stead."

"'T is not to be thought of," said Jette quickly. "I know how to arrange all the things, and to put them back in their right place. No stranger could do that. Besides, the Herr Doctor's education cost a great deal. To be sure, it was paid out of the interest which had accumulated from the Frau Pastorin's dowry. But it is all gone now, and the principal must not be touched. Part of it will have to be used to start the Herr Doctor in his practice when he returns. Though at the rate he is making progress, I do not think he will need it."

"What manner of a man is thy doctor?" asked Madame Goldman.

"*My* doctor?" echoed Jette, with emphasis. She pouted her lips scornfully. "He is no doctor of mine. He is proud and bumptious, and thinks a great deal of himself. All the same, he is very clever."

"Is he most like his father, or mother?" asked Madame Goldman.

"H'm! Very much like both, I should think. I have seen so very little of him, I am hardly able to judge. He is very tall and strong, and blonde like his mother, but he has his father's dark eyes, and the same way of making one obey. Only he is a good deal more masterful than the Herr

Pastor. He is even more distant in his manner than the Frau Pastorin. Although I have seen him quite cordial at times."

"I think I know thy doctor very well," said Madame Goldman reflectively; "tall, deep-chested, blonde-haired, fair-skinned, dark-eyed, with a proper pride in his manhood, and some professional hauteur. H'm! Quite the hero of romance for foolish girls to fall in love with."

"Fräulein von Hermersdorff is not foolish," said Jette, "and she is in love with him. He was always very gracious to her. They will marry as soon as the doctor has established himself. 'T is all settled, I assure you. The Frau Pastorin speaks of it constantly."

"They are betrothed, then?" asked Madame Goldman.

"In the letter I had from home yesterday," said Jette, "the Frau Pastorin mentions she thinks they will be very soon. Fräulein von Hermersdorff is now in Vienna with the Herr Professor, her father. She, too, wrote to the Frau Pastorin. They are all so proud of the wonderful cures the Herr Doctor has performed. He saved an Austrian archduchess from blindness after she had been given up by the cleverest doctors. That was truly great, was it not?"

"He must be making a great name for himself," said Madame Goldman.

"Apparently he is. I am so glad for the Herr Pastor and the Frau Pastorin. They are so happy, so proud. He will be a famous man yet.

Truly, it is a great thing to have one's children turn out well."

Madame Goldman laughed outright. "What dost thou know about it?" she said.

"Now," said Jette, with a blush, "I was only quoting what the Frau Pastorin said in her letter."

The junior banker entered the room. Of late he had been in a carping and morose humor, which intensified, if possible, the aversion Jette felt towards him. He spoilt her gayety of spirits, and saddened and depressed her. He made her feel vaguely as if she had done him some grievous wrong, for which she could never sufficiently atone. All that was worst in her nature he seemed to have the capacity to draw forth. She fairly bristled with antagonism and stubborn opposition whenever he looked at her. He was the blot on her fair horizon, the bitter pill among the sweets of her existence. Herr Goldman had not been very amiable of late. All his life he had got what he asked for. Where there was resistance he had known how to overcome it. Now for the first time since he was born there was something he could not get. Jette's stubborn coyness made him mad. The more she tried to avoid him, the more ardently he pursued her. He could not understand it at all. His mood became intolerable. He was jealous of the dog she caressed, the canary she chirped to, the tippet around her throat, the glove on her hand. He would have been satisfied with very little at first, but that little she did not seem inclined to give. He was

restless and irritable away from her, and yet most
miserable when near her.

This evening he appeared to be in a more cheerful mood. "Sitting in the dark and romancing?"
he said gayly.

"Ring for lights," said his mother.

"Not for worlds, mamma. This suits me very
well. Did I interrupt any sweet confidences?"
He hoped, under cover of the darkness, to take
Jette's hand. Perhaps she would let him. Surely
the hour had softened her mood.

"We were talking," said Madame Goldman,
"of doctors. The romance belongs elsewhere, not
here."

"Phew," he said, "I smell the cadavers already."

"'T is the noblest profession in the world," said
Jette.

"Supplemented by right noble bills," he said.

"Doctors can't live by pride of profession
alone," she said, "no more than can other people.
The art of healing seems to me divine. To restore the child to the stricken mother, to save
the breadwinner to his helpless family, to bring
relief to the pain-racked limbs, and hope to the
despairing heart, — it is a noble mission which
makes a man seem twice so. It is just the lifework I would have chosen, were it customary for
my sex to do so."

"Your lifework," he said, "is to break hearts,
not to mend them."

"Let me assure you," she said, with assumed

seriousness, "that the art of mending is a very laborious and intricate one. Unless one can do it creditably, one had better let it alone. One would not bungle even at mending." She gravely surveyed her left forefinger, on whose delicate tip the mark of the needle could plainly be seen.

"Thou speakest," said Madame Goldman, "as if thou hadst a good knowledge of thy subject."

"I have served my apprenticeship," said Jette ruefully.

"How nice!" said Madame Goldman maliciously; "I will bring out all my fine mending while thou art here."

"No, no," said Jette gayly; "I get all the plain fare I want at home. When I go visiting, I want a more delicate diet."

She had risen, for she had felt Herr Goldman come dangerously near. In the darkness, with the glowing firelight to enhance the deep shadows, she looked very slim and tall against the pudgy Madame Goldman standing beside her.

"So thou comest to me for thy sweetmeats?" said the elder woman softly. Gently, with a mother's touch, she caressed the shapely hand lying passively within her own. "Thou shalt have them," she said, — "enough to surfeit thee. Only thou must show thyself somewhat sensible and a little yielding. How can such a beautiful creature as thou be so hard-hearted?"

"I — I do not mean to be," stammered the girl.

"All the same, thou art," said Madame Goldman. "Look at Esther Baruch. She is as happy
as the day is long, and has seen her betrothed
only twice. It is the way with our maidens.
Their parents choose, and they are satisfied. In
that they show their wisdom, for they insure their
children's future as far as lies within their power.
Thou must not keep Julius dangling in uncer-
tainty any longer. It is neither fair to thee nor
to him. Before thou leavest here, thou must reach
some definite decision. Wilt thou promise to
do so?"

"Yes, yes," said the girl hurriedly. She closed
her eyes with a shudder, as she felt a pair of hot
lips press her hand. Then she escaped to her
room.

CHAPTER XXXI

"THE beautiful days of Aranjuez are at an
end," declaimed Jette wistfully, just as on a
former occasion Herr von Czechy had done. She
was standing at the window of the great drawing-
room, waiting for her hostess, with whom she was
to go shopping. A few days more, and this life
of luxury, of ease, and of splendor would come
to an end. There would be a busy time at the
parsonage on her return; the annual invasion of
the broom and scrubbing-brush was at hand.
For two weeks chaos would reign. Everything
movable the house contained would be dragged,

flung, or bundled out of doors. The most hidden
recess, nook, or cranny would be mercilessly exposed to the light. Beginning in the attic and
ending in the cellar, the invading forces would
continue their victorious march, before which spi-
ders or anything of the like ilk would fly in dismay, or get ruthlessly exterminated. During
this period of upheaval it would be hard to find
two more disconsolate creatures than the good
pastor and Minka. They faithfully kept each
other company, and shared their misery as they
did their scant rations. The pastor, with his
chess-table in one hand and his box of chess-men
in the other, would wander from one dismantled
room to another in search of some place of refuge,
followed by Minka, with depressed tail and drooping whiskers. Each night the pastor lay down,
he thought joyfully, "Thank God there is one
more day off the calendar," until law and order
was restored again, and probably Minka did the
same. Certain it is, when all the uproar was
done, and the house looked like itself again, glistening in its new dress of cleanliness and purity,
Minka stepped from room to room, her bushy
gray tail once more stiff and erect, her big yellow
eyes gleaming like topaz, rubbing herself against
every member of the household alternately, while
she purred with delight. "Dear Minka, she
knows everything that is going on," thought the
girl, and a little touch of homesickness crept into
her heart. She thought of her poultry yard, the
canaries in the Frau Pastorin's south window,

who pecked their sweets from her lips, her pet pigeons, her garden, where she must soon begin to hoe and dig and sow. It was all very grand and beautiful here, but — the other was home.

Madame Goldman was heard coming down the stairs in her rustling silks and rich sables. Jette went into the wide vestibule to meet her.

"Thou lookest thoughtful, liebe Kleine," said the elder woman, as they entered the carriage and drove away.

"The beautiful days of Aranjuez are at an end," repeated Jette, smiling.

"Surely, 't is thy own fault," said Madame Goldman. "Why should they ever end at all? 'T is only for thyself to decide."

"Yes," said the girl dreamily. She absently played with the heavy silk tassels of Madame Goldman's muff. "If only he were you and you were he," she burst out vehemently.

"I am not so sure of that at all," said Madame Goldman, who knew very well what she meant; "thou mightst not find me near so well to get on with. He is far too complaisant, with no head at all on his shoulders, where thou art concerned. That is what I always tell Julius. He is over-indulgent; he spoils thee utterly. Suppose thou wearest out his patience, and he marries some one else?"

"Would to heaven he would!" she aspirated fervently.

"Heyday! What is that?"

"Then you would not withdraw from me your

friendship. I love you; I love you," she said, in
tones of honeyed endearment, fondling and kissing
Madame Goldman's hand.

"Why cannot I be angry with thee, thou tyrant
and dove both?" said Madame Goldman, in trembling accents. She flung back her sable cloak
and put her arm around the girl's neck. "Stay
with me," she urged; "be my daughter indeed,
as thou hast twined thyself around my heart.
Never queen was more adored than thou wilt be
in the midst of us. Make him — make us all
happy."

In that moment Jette's fate hung trembling in
the balance. Against the pleadings of the man
she detested she could hold her own, but not
against those of the mother whom she sincerely
loved. Now her heart was touched. Deeply
moved, she was about to answer, when suddenly
the carriage came to an abrupt stop. Somebody
grasped the reins and forced the horses back, who
reared and plunged madly. Jette let down the
window nearest her to see what was going on.

They had come upon a band of penitents, who
were wending their way to the cathedral. Monks
barefooted, with shorn heads, were swinging cen-
sors, and holding the host aloft. It was near the
noon hour, in the busiest part of the town, but
everybody had stopped and doffed their caps to let
the pilgrims go by. There was plenty of time
for the carriage to pass down the side street as
Ephraim, the coachman, had intended, but the
crowd, ill-natured as they always were at that

time of year towards the Jews, surlily refused to make way for him.

"Back, thou accursed Jew," said a big, brawny, hulking driver of a brewer's dray. It was he who had caught hold of the horses' reins. The spirited animals became almost maddened as the hubbub of the priests' chant and the cloud of incense from the swinging censers increased.

"Art of the breed, too?" he said, giving the off horse a vicious kick. "Chokest at the blessed fumes of the holy incense, eh?"

"Let me go," panted Ephraim; "otherwise something terrible will happen."

"Ay, indeed. The currying of thy ill-smelling Jewish hide and those that are with thee. Accursed hound, thou! Stay where thou art until the holy procession has passed."

The coachman was from the borders of Poland, where outrages and persecutions against those of his faith were frequent pretenses for popular malice and greed of plunder. He was dark, almost like an Ethiopian, but Jette saw him turn pale to the lips. The populace were cursing and jeering at the plunging horses, who were madly tugging at the reins.

"Call upon thy God to check them, since thou canst not do it, accursed son of Abraham, thou!" jeered a wrinkled old crone.

Jette looked at Madame Goldman. She was very pale, and sat quite rigid. A shudder convulsed her limbs when any of the vile epithets struck her ear. The girl flung off her mantle,

and opening the carriage door, sprung lightly
to the ground. So much of majesty and nobility there was in her youthful mien that no one
thought of uttering a protest when she walked
to the horses' heads. Her slim, white hands
touched the brawny fist of the drayman as with
the sweetest, most gracious "Allow me," she took
hold of the reins, causing him to drop his hand
and shamefacedly step aside. "Keep a firm hold,"
he said to Ephraim. Her look, piercing and commanding, said, "Keep a cool head," and he understood her. Patting the horses' sides, speaking
soothing words as she had heard Hans of the
Wildhof do, she made a way for the carriage to
proceed, walking on in front, with an uplifting
of her bonny blue eyes, a charming smile, and a
sweetly gracious, "Bitte, bitte;" and the populace
quickly parted either side, holding their breath
lest the restive horses' hoofs should strike her.
It was high time, for just as they reached the
opposite curb, the procession was upon them.

"Drive slowly at first," she uttered hurriedly
to Ephraim, "then make what speed you can to
the bank. I shall be there almost as soon as you
are."

With a heartfelt sigh of relief she saw the
carriage disappear in the distance. She stopped
when the host was carried by and the people
prostrated themselves. Then she walked slowly
on till she reached a side street. Once out of
sight, she quickened her steps, and soon reached
the bank, which fortunately was not far off. She

almost danced into the office of the senior partner, so glad was she to see the carriage standing at the door. Ephraim took off his hat and bowed most profoundly. All the radiance of Queen Esther was nothing compared to that with which she shone in his eyes.

"What a beautiful day," she said, as she entered. "I have quite enjoyed my walk."

There had been some anxiety on her account. Madame Goldman sat in the big office chair. There were traces of tears on her cheeks. Her husband and son were with her. Jette was greeted with tender effusion.

"They did not attempt to do anything to thee?" asked Madame Goldman anxiously.

"To me? Indeed, no. They stared and made way, but uttered no word. I made all the haste I could to get here. Have I been long?"

"Thou art a famous girl," said the elder Goldman. He kissed her heartily, and left a great deal of snuff on her fichu. In his heart he vowed to give a goodly sum in her name to the poor of the synagogue next Sabbath's worship. Goldman junior, his sound foot on the rung of a chair, beamed all over with pride and joy. His looks said as plain as anything, "What did I tell you? She is quite a heroine."

Madame Goldman pulled the girl down beside her.

"Wert thou not a little afraid?" she asked.

"I had you to think of," said the girl naïvely; "alone, I might have been."

CHAPTER XXXII

A FEW days after, Jette went home. There was sorrow in the household of the Goldmans. Her youthful, high spirits and simple graciousness had endeared her to all. The lowest scullion in the kitchen would miss her. She had often gone down to watch the cook prepare some delicious dainty which had appeared at table, and which she thought they would like at home. "When I see a thing done," she said, "I can easily do it. It is of no use to tell me. I can never get it right from that." Madame Goldman missed her terribly. She would gladly have given a considerable portion of her wealth sooner than part with her. The house seemed dead after she was gone. The good lady looked forward with impatience to the time when this bright, lovely, joyous creature should be her daughter indeed, as she already was in her affections. Before she went, Herr Goldman had extracted a promise from her to marry him at the end of two years, when she would be nineteen. She had been sorely beset, and felt that against so many forces combined that were brought to bear upon her she was not strong enough to hold her own. She saw there was no escape from his detested presence in any other way. Alone with this persistent, ardent suitor in Madame Goldman's boudoir, trembling with fright and apprehension lest he should presume upon a caress, she gave a desperate assent, subject, of course, to the Herr Pastor's approval. But she would not allow him to put the betrothal ring upon her finger. Spite of his importunities and entreaties, she remained steadfast in that. Not until the last inevitable moment would she allow a visible sign of the fetters her cowardice was weaving around her. During the two years which must elapse before the formal betrothal, everything was to remain as at present. Only, necessarily, she would feel herself bound to him. Besides, there was not much use in making promises. The Herr Pastor had stipulated that her consent should not be considered until she was of a fit age to marry. This was her grand refuge. Behind this she intrenched herself. It was a shallow subterfuge, and she hated herself for using it. And the banker, knowing perfectly well how useless it was appealing against the Herr Pastor's decision, ground his teeth in impotent fury. However, he had to be satisfied. What could one do with a girl upon whom all the practical advantages of luxury and wealth made no impression, — who could not be won by the gewgaws which win the hearts of most women; perfectly satisfied, nay, happy, to return to a life of rustic, humdrum obscurity; to trudge on foot when she could ride in a carriage; to perform menial household duties when footmen might be at her command? But patience. It was the unsophisticatedness of youth. Two years would do much to mould her character and to ripen her judgment. So, though what she granted him was very little, with that little he had to be content.

If she had only had a mother, some one of her
own sex, having her interest at heart, wise and
experienced in the world's ways! If she only had
some one to confide in! That was the burden and
cry of her heart. The Frau Pastorin, with all
her kindness, was not sympathetic. The proud,
wealthy, old Pomeranian peasant stock she came
of looked with disfavor upon any ebullition of
sentiment. What was right was right, what was
wrong was wrong. It was given to man's own
good judgment to choose which way to go. If he
went the wrong way, all the worse for him. One
was as easy as the other. With all the impulses
of her own heart Jette had been alone. Sympathy she had never demanded, because there was
no one to give it to her. All her little joys and
all her little sorrows she had hugged to herself.
She was fond of the Frau Pastorin, but she was
afraid of her; the Herr Pastor she loved and
revered, but she stood in awe of him. There was
always that formal, distant little boundary line
she was too diffident to cross. Hans von Czechy
was the only one she had come into contact with
in whose presence she felt her heart expand.
Him she could have told everything. That was
the bond which drew her to him, which made his
memory sacred to her. True, there was Madame
Goldman. Gladly would she have gone to her
and poured out her whole heart. But could she
tell the mother of the loathing with which the son
inspired her, — could she tell her that his person-
ality was hateful to the girl she hoped to see that

son's wife? Could she wring the mother's heart in its most susceptible spot, — the love for the son whom she adored? Sooner would she rend her own heart and keep silence.

Who would understand her? No one. The world envied and flattered her. The Herr Pastor only waited till she was old enough to give his consent. Since she had in a measure identified herself with her suitor's family, her own was tacitly looked upon. The Frau Pastorin regarded everything as settled. Babbett called her a fool, whom fate had to bang on the head in order to make her realize her extraordinary good luck. Besides, was it not her duty to marry? Already she was a great expense to the family. It had cost quite a little sum to fit her out suitably for her visit. She was so tall, it took a good many ells to make her a dress. Did not all girls marry? Was it not the whole aim of their existence? What else could she do? Become an old maid? Brrr! Horrible! to be laughed at, made a jest of, to fill the stray nooks and empty niches of creation, — it was anything but an enviable prospect. It was imperative upon her to marry. She had to have a place in the world, — things would not go on like this forever.

So she took refuge in the grace yet allowed her. Herr Goldman came as often as the Herr Pastor thought permissible, each time more ardent and hopeful than the last. And she — The old horror grew upon her. It was no use, — she could not shake it off. Reason, argument, judgment, all were powerless against it. What would become of all this? She shuddered, but dared not think. So the time drew dangerously near.

It was towards the close of an oppressive day in July. In the orchard the half-ripe fruit hung parched and drooping on the boughs. The air was ominously still with the portend of disaster. Not a leaf stirred. The clouds hung heavy and sullen, like molten lead. From the pastures came the low bellowing of the kine. The hills, gray and indistinguishable in the gathering vapor, loomed weird and menacing in the distance. There was that vague uneasiness in the air with which all great forces of nature infect the spirit. Jette took off her large straw hat, and scrutinizingly looked around.

"Thou and I must run, Minka," she said to the big tabby. "The storm is gathering, and presently will be upon us in unfettered fury."

She drew off the large, loose gloves she always wore since Hans von Czechy had chided her for not taking proper pride in her hands, took off her apron, and turned homeward. Between intervals of reading she had worked a little at the vegetable beds. It was too hot to do anything continuously. Minka had gone with her, as she invariably did of late. Since Jette's return from her visit to the Goldmans, two years ago, the cat had attached herself almost solely to her young mistress. She followed her about everywhere.

The Frau Pastorin was standing at the window when Jette turned in at the parsonage gate. The

color in her cheeks was heightened, her eyes looked
expectant and bright.

"I am glad thou hast come," she said to the
girl; "the storm may descend at any moment.
Dost thou not feel very warm? What fearful
heat! I feel as if my palate were withered."

"I will go and make you some lemonade," said
Jette.

"Wait till papa comes. I have been anxiously
looking for him. I have had a letter."

"So?" said Jette, with interest. She knew there
was but one person in the world whose letter could
excite her so. "What does the Herr Doctor say?
He is well, I hope?"

"'T is not right I should tell thee," said the
Frau Pastorin, "before papa hears it. I had
hoped thou wouldst meet him and bring him with
thee. Only think! Fritz is coming home."

Jette laughed. "Dear Frau Pastorin, what
good news! Will you not be glad to embrace
him again? After three long years of absence —
why, you will hardly know him."

The Frau Pastorin's eyes glistened. "His
papa — he will be delighted. I can hardly wait
till he comes in. He has missed him fully as
much as I have. To be sure, Fritz had to go.
He had to gain a name and experience. Now he
has both. Now he can establish himself."

"Was not the Herr Doctor to stay away another year?"

"So we thought. But that little trouble with
the government, — when he joined the rebel stu-

dents with the young Baron von Czechy, — thou
knowest is settled long ago. Not once has he
granted himself a holiday since he went to Vienna.
He has studied and worked as young men seldom
do. To be sure, he had a most powerful incen-
tive."

She passed her plump hands over her shining
bands of hair. Here and there a gray thread had
crept in. Anxiety for her son had brought them,
not the smooth, eventless years.

"He has made a name for himself," she said,
"such as many an older head might be proud of.
He has both fame and substance now. They will
offer him a professorship at Bonn. He will marry
Thekla. Ah! I shall see all my fondest dreams
realized."

"How I rejoice!" said Jette.

"'T is fortunate he comes now," said the Frau
Pastorin; "he can have a thorough rest before
all the bustle and preparation for thy wedding.
His eyes are inflamed, he writes, from overwork
and study. He must have complete quiet and
rest. Dear boy! dearest child! where else should
he go but to his mother to get completely nursed
back to health?"

"Certainly," said Jette. She spoke with an
effort. The allusion to the ultimate settling of
her fate made her flesh creep. "Here comes the
Herr Pastor," she said. The Frau Pastorin flew
to meet him.

CHAPTER XXXIII

THAT night the storm fiend went abroad, and
right merrily did he ride his steed. It was so
suffocatingly hot no one could sleep. Trees were
uprooted, toppling over with a deafening crash.
The wrathful thunder shook the houses to their
very foundations. Great gusts of rain beat fiercely
against the casements. Jette sat at the window,
veiling her eyes from the blinding lightning.
She felt a fierce exultation in the storm. She
wanted to run out, to let herself be tossed in its
savage embrace. She wanted to mingle her
shrieks with the roars of the storm king. The
blood raced madly in her veins. She thought of
the ride of the Valkyrie, and fancied she heard
the mad galloping of their steeds in the howling
of the wind. A storm of this kind always affected
her singularly. The fierce warring of the ele-
ments found an echo in her heart. Oh, to toss
off the load that oppressed her, to rive the chains
her passive cowardice had forged around her; to
be free once more, without the haunting dread
that all too quickly her fate was closing in around
her! Towards morning the storm had spent itself.
Slowly, as if in growling protest, the reverberating
thunder withdrew among the distant hills. A
deliciously cool fragrance filled the air. She flung
up her window, eagerly welcoming the delightful
change. Then she fell asleep.

It was later than usual when she arose. It

was so with everybody. After the terrors of the
storm, it was well to sleep. Everybody went
abroad to view the havoc that had been wrought
over night. Ruin and desolation in plenty there
was. The Frau Pastorin's blooming garden lay
a dreary waste. Here and there a rosebush, solitary and forlorn, reared its ragged branches,
mourning at the general destruction. Her pretty
bed of pansies, in which every variety from the
velvety purple black — to which Hans von Czechy
had likened Jette's eyes — to the softest, lightest
blue flourished, was entirely wiped out. Ruin
pointed its gaunt finger everywhere.

It was a memorable storm. Long years elapsed
before the villagers ceased to speak of it. The
superstitious said afterwards it had been a fore-
runner of what happened later. It was just as
well no one possessed the gift of prophecy. Besides, the prophet is never heeded.

The air blew soft and invigorating from the
Rhine. The birds chirped merrily, busily engaged in rebuilding their destroyed homes. One
could sniff the bracing atmosphere with distended
lungs and inflated nostrils. The sun smiled in
subdued radiance. Surely everything has its compensation. Hope and activity resumed their sway
in the human breast. One could repair, rebuild,
restore. Things were not so bad, after all. In
fact, they might have been a great deal worse.
After each had summed up his own loss, he found
consolation in that his neighbor had suffered more
than himself.

With some forebodings and a good deal of
trepidation, Jette went forth to reconnoitre. On
the shattered wall opposite the kitchen door hung
a meat safe, the sides and door of perforated wire.
It was stout and strong, and had steadily opposed
the wear and tear of time. "Shier dreissig Jahre
bist du alt, hast manchen Sturm erlebt," Jette
often laughingly said. Babbett was always careful to lock it at night. She kept her larder well
replenished, and she prided herself upon having
never yet been taken unawares, no matter how unexpected the guests, or how many they numbered.
Of late, especially, the safe was more than usually
well stocked. Substantial solids lined its stout
shelves. People might come, and people might
go: Babbett's larder was prepared for all contingencies.

A startled cry from Jette brought her to the
spot. She raised her hands in horror. The door
swung lamely on its broken hinges. The goodly
contents were partly gnawed, and all scattered
around in direst confusion. Some of them lay on
the ground, some dragged to a distance, and
broken dishes topping all. On the broad middle
shelf lay Minka. Her fur bristled like spikes,
her yellow eyes gleamed viciously. She looked
disreputable and wicked, as unkempt and neglected as the most dissipated night prowler.

"Thou wretched beast!" shrieked Babbett;
"'t is thou who hast wrought all this. Woe, woe,
woe! My lovely tongue, my delicious shoulder,
stuffed just to suit, and fit for the palate of a

king! Would I had gorged myself like a porcu-
pine and died of repletion! Thou conscienceless,
marauding thief, thou! Mayest thou never have
anything more to feed on than the memory of thy
misbegotten deeds! Oh, woe, woe, woe, woe!"

Her loud lamentations brought out the rest of
the family. "What is the matter here?" asked
the Pastor. His rapid glance took in the situa-
tion. "The storm must have done this," he said.

"Does the storm gnaw and leave marks of its
teeth?" cried the incensed Babbett; "see here,
your reverence. 'T is all that is left of my beautiful buttock, as juicy and tender a bit of beef as
ever made mouth water. Look at my tongue,
pink as a baby's cheek, cut but a short time from
the animal's jaws. 'T was toothsome enough for
an epicure. Here is my ham, as fine a thing as
ever sow was made to yield; smoked to perfection, as indeed I have good reason to know.
There lies what is left of all. And there lies the
evil-doer."

"How," said the Pastor; "Minka — thou?"

"Who else?" said Babbett. "There she lies,
heavy with the weight of her ill-gotten spoils.
May she die of repletion, the wicked, yellow-eyed
monster."

"The door must have blown open," observed the
Frau Pastorin, "and Minka sought shelter within.
Being hungry, she could not withstand the temp-
tation."

"It merits punishment, nevertheless," answered
the Herr Pastor. "Come here, Minka," he said
sternly.

She had lain very quiet, with lowered eyes and head depressed, as if she knew very well the extent of her transgressions. Now when the Herr Pastor called her, she still made no effort to move.

"Art obstinate as well as treacherous?" inquired the Herr Pastor. He lifted her off the shelf, and gave her several smart slaps. "Have I fed thee" (slap) "and cherished thee" (slap) "and boasted of thy faith and loyalty" (slap) "and vaunted thee over all thy kind" (slap), "only to discover the nature of the beast in thee uppermost?" (slap.) "There, go thy ways, and know thyself to be in disgrace" (slap, slap).

But Minka did not run off. She looked piteously from one to the other. She rubbed herself against Jette and meowed.

"Minka is telling us something," urged Jette; "and see! she is too weak to stand."

"Too gorged, thou meanest," screamed the enraged Babbett. She took hold of her, and sent her sprawling away. Then they saw that where Minka had stood, there was blood.

"What is this?" exclaimed the Herr Pastor.

Jette hastily put her head inside the safe. "Look in there," she said.

Among the débris of broken food and crockery the fur lay thick like sand, with here and there a clot of blood. "And look here," cried Jette; "the rain has washed away the traces of blood, but in places it glistens on the pebbles. See here, and there, and here — Oh, what is this?"

A clump of fur literally torn off the body lay at her feet. It was black as coal, with specks of blood upon it. Minka came and stood over it, snarling, her eyes flaming with venom. She seemed unable to stand upright, but steadied herself painfully against the wall.

Like lightning sped from the sky Jette flew to the dovecote. The storm had wrenched off the fastenings of the door, the pigeons sat with depressed heads on the roof of the smokehouse. Now they flew to meet her, pecking at her hair and neck, all but one white dove. He sat with lowered crest and glazed eyes.

"Where is thy mate?" wailed Jette. "Where is my pretty Giselle?" A cry from the Frau Pastorin made her turn swiftly. There was her pretty Giselle, her white pet dove, stark and dead. And there, a rod further, lay Black Peter mauled to death, with Minka standing over him, her eyes glittering in ferocious victory.

CHAPTER XXXIV

"THAT must have been a great battle," said the Herr Pastor. With his own hands he had carried Minka home, cut away the fur from her wounds, and washed and dressed them. His remorse was so great for having misjudged her that he could hardly bear her out of his sight. He praised her and petted her, and she blinked her eyes and purred in delighted satisfaction.

"'T is plain enough," he continued. "Black Peter was prowling around as usual, and when the storm blew the door of the safe open, he made a raid on our larder. There our Minka found him, — see how she understands, that good, brave old girl, — and a fierce fight ensued. Thou madest the thief beat a retreat, eh, my plucky old girl, and lay thyself down to guard thy master's property. Then thou heardest the fluttering among the pigeons, and hied thee to the dovecote just in time to avenge the death of Jettchen's pet dove. Ay, but thou art a famous creature!"

"If only her hurts won't prove fatal," said the Frau Pastorin anxiously.

"Do not fret thee, Mammachen; 't were too great a pity for her to die. She will get over them bravely."

"What is to be done with Black Peter?" asked Babbett; "if Gret finds our Minka has killed him, she will make no end of an outcry. Were it not better to put him out of sight? She will believe he perished in the storm."

"By no means," said the pastor; "our Minka conquered him in fair fight, and that must content her. I will have no deceit, tacit or otherwise."

"'T is all very fine," said Babbett, when Jette carried out the breakfast things; "his reverence does n't know Gret as we do. She will try and poison our Minka, and she is wicked enough to succeed. Just thou stay here, and keep thy eyes and ears shut. What I am going to do now is no concern of thine."

She went to the tool-shed, from whence soon she emerged with spade and shovel. Jette knew very well she was going to dig a deep hole into which presently Black Peter would be flung. It would have been some satisfaction to her could she have assisted. The cruel death of her pet dove rankled sorely in her heart.

With that both she and Babbett thought the matter ended. But not quite. A few days later, when the balmiest sun shone on newly rejoicing hearts, there was a terrible outcry. It came from the neighboring pasture, into which only a little while since Minka had strayed. She was getting over her hurts bravely, and would not be kept indoors. All day long she prowled around, seemingly vexed and ill at ease. Now Gret came flying up the path, panting, and in a fine fume.

"Come out here!" she shrieked. "Come out, all of you! I want to know who has done this shameful thing."

Babbett, who sat on the shaded bench just outside the kitchen door, shelling peas, turned quite pale. Jette was in the arbor not far off, finishing some fine piece of embroidery for the Frau Pastorin. She came up with stern displeasure.

"Thou wilt rouse the Herr Pastor and the Frau Pastorin from their afternoon nap," she said. "Cease thy outcries, or go away at once."

But Gret was not to be silenced when her temper was up.

"I don't care a kreutzer!" she cried furiously. "What! are honest people to be cheated out of their own while thou puttest on airs and graces, as if thou didst not know? Only wait! The whole village shall hear of it."

"Thou grandmother of the devil," said Babbett, "come out with what thou hast to say."

"Come over yonder, then," she said, "and I will show ye." They went with her to the pasture. It was there Black Peter was buried. But how on earth had she found it out?

The reason was very plain. That terrible Minka! So that had been the cause of her uneasiness. She had prowled, and sought, and given herself no peace until she had discovered where her slain enemy lay. Her sharp claws had dug and scratched until finally she had come upon him. And there she stood, with bristling hide and elevated tail, ferociously jubilant over her victory.

Lieschen was with her mother. She was drooping and waxen, like a delicate azalea, but she persisted in living, spite of all the headshakings and predictions of the old crones. The little three-year-old was afraid of the big cat, who, in truth, looked quite formidable enough to inspire grown people with terror.

"Come away, mammie," she lisped.

Gret angrily wrenched her slight little arm.

"Be quiet, thou brat," she said furiously, "else I'll throw thee into the hole, and the beast of a cat shall devour thee."

Lieschen shrieked with horror and fright. Jette raised her in her arm, sheltering the little golden head in her breast.

"Thou spawn of the evil one!" said the enraged Babbett. She did not care now, and was determined to have it out. In fact, it was a relief to the simple old soul to have all discovered. It had lain heavy on her heart, and she felt quite guilty at times. "How such an one as thou," she said, "came to have a child like that poor little innocent, 't is the Lord's business to understand. What wert thou prowling around here for, anyhow? The devil, thy master, must have sent thee."

"Aha!" vaunted Gret, with malicious triumph, "no web is spun so fine but the sun one day on it will shine. So ye thought to conceal your misdoings from me, did ye? Death-dealers ye are, and ye know it. Ye have killed my cat, my poor Peter, my faithful Peter, boo-hoo-hoo! My g-g-good Peter! Must I see thee lie there stark dead and cold?"

"Thou art foolish, Gret," said Jette; "the night of the storm our Minka found him stealing our meats and killing our pigeons. They fought, and she killed him."

"A likely story," blustered Gret between her sobs.

"Hush thy howling!" said Babbett fiercely; "thou didst no more care for him than the veriest stranger. 'T is only thy wanton love for mischief that urges thee to this outcry. Thou used to kick him out in all weathers, and ventedst thy ill humor on him, — just as thou dost on this poor child, — and refused him food and drink. A thief and marauder was he. That is what thou madest of him."

"How," shrieked Gret, "ye call me thief and marauder?"

"Nay, I said not that. All the same, I would not give this," she snapped her fingers, "for the difference between ye. He stole meats, — thou filchest people's characters. Wherever thy slanderous tongue finds a hearing, there is a putting together of heads and hissings like unto the serpent's. Thou fattenest on gossip like a capon, and devourest thyself for curiosity about thy neighbors' affairs. Go home, sweep thy neglected house, braid thy unkempt hair, darn thy man's torn hose, and put thy prying nose into the souppot, instead of meddling with what does not concern thee."

"Thou needest not think," jeered Gret, "because thou belongest to the pastor's family, thou canst take his office upon thyself. What I know, I know. I am not quite so simple that thou canst make me believe that an X stands for a U. The whole village shall know how Black Peter came by his death, and how ye sought to hide it. And as for that accursed witch in the guise of a cat, I'll treat her the same as my poor Peter was treated."

She advanced threateningly towards Minka, who, snarling like a catamount, with dangerously gleaming eyes, crouched back, as if for a spring.

"Do not touch her," cried Jette, in terror; "she will fasten upon thee, and tear thy eyes out."

"Bah! I am not afraid of her," said Gret, but she prudently drew back. "What a beast!" she said; "sure she is the fiend incarnate himself. She actually seems to grow double her size as one looks at her."

"Thou thinkest so because thy eyes are set crosswise in thy head," said Babbett maliciously; "on thy life, do thou never meddle with her. The creature does not like thee, and in that she shows her wisdom."

Gret angrily snatched Lieschen from Jette's arms. "I'll be even with ye yet," she said.

"Leave Lieschen with me," pleaded Jette. The poor little thing! She was so fond of her beautiful young protectress. No wonder. What had such a child in common with such a mother?

"That ye may kill her like ye did Black Peter?" taunted Gret, with clenched teeth. She turned and went.

"I wish," said Babbett, looking after her, "that she was in the same hole with her cat. Of the two, she surely is the most evil."

"One could almost pity her," said Jette, "for being such an ignorant, maliciously conditioned creature. All the same, 't was not nice of thee to say what thou didst just now."

"I know her better, than thou," said Babbett, as they walked back to the house; "all her life she has been so. She is a firebrand from Sodom and Gomorrah. She is in the cards all the time. Again and again have I tossed them aside, vowing never to look at them any more. Then, whenever the need to see what is going to happen overcomes me, there she turns up with her squint eyes and leering, wicked mouth."

"What a clever card to assume such a true likeness," smiled Jette.

"Ah, thou! jeer thou and laugh. Perhaps 't would be as well for thee if thou wouldst take some little heed in time."

"Thou good Babbett! I did not mean to offend thee. 'T is a long time since thou hast laid the cards for me. To-day is Friday, eh? 'T is an auspicious day to have one's fortune told."

"Nay," said Babbett, "I have done with them. 'T is too much aggravation of mind and spirit to work out their meaning. One would rather see what one wants to see. When everything works contrary, 't is best not to know it. What is that big thing in front of our house? Jesus Maria! As I live,' t is the post-chaise. While we were wrangling over yonder, the Herr Doctor has come."

CHAPTER XXXV

FROM the arbor at the other side of the house came pleasantly excited voices. It was there the family chiefly gathered during the hot summer months. All the meals were served there. The Herr Pastor's chess-table and easy leather chair stood against the wall, as well as the Frau Pastorin's sewing-table and large old-fashioned workbasket. A spreading vine completely covered the

open trellis-work, through which here and there
gleamed bunches of purple grapes. Every autumn
there was a rich harvest from this vine, where the
luxurious, gleaming fruit clustered so thickly as
to form a perfect roof overhead. Tubs of oleander
stood at either side of the entrance, around which
the straggling tendrils were draped and festooned
quite artistically, so as to leave sufficient light
within. It looked cosy, home-like, and inviting,
with the low-cushioned ottoman in one corner, the
white-painted, rush-bottomed chairs and round
table in the centre, spread with a gay red cloth
that looked well against the background of dark
green leaves. One could see the green fields
spreading far down the undulating valley, with
the gently dipping hills beyond, on which the
sheep were browsing. Now and then a tiny silver
thread, winding in and out like a string of pearls
in the fair locks of beauty, flashed upon the vision.
It was the purling forest brook, which at that distance widened into a stream, where it hastened,
dreamily murmuring, to join the blue Rhine. One
could sit here and muse, and steep one's soul in
ineffable peace and serenity of mind, and rejoice
in the pure joy of living, with never a discord in
the harmonious hymn of nature. It was home,
such as God from the first intended all homes
should be.

No wonder, with this picture in his mind, the
doctor had come back to rest. During those three
years of absence he had worked harder than had
many before him. However, there was this gratify-

ing thing to be said, — he had achieved something.
Position and renown, such as no man of his age
in the profession had ever acquired in so short
a time, was cordially accorded him. Nature had
been his loyal helpmate. Without his stalwart,
splendid physique and robust health, which had
never been abused by excesses, he would have
dropped by the wayside as many a less fortunately
gifted one would have done. With a great task
set before him, he had steadily kept this in view,
ignoring temptation with an iron will, keeping
well in the race till the home stretch was reached.
His fame as oculist spread far and wide; the
most difficult and delicate operations were confided
to his skill. The most tempting inducements
were held out to keep him in Vienna. But over-
study and over-exertion had at last their usual
effect on even his Herculean frame. Repeated
summons to stop came rudely knocking to warn
him, each one more importunate than the other.
One morning Vienna woke up to find its honored
and beloved Dr. Feldern, with his valise in one
hand, the other extended in farewell, ready to
depart. We beg pardon, — Dr. *von* Feldern. In
grateful recognition for the successful operation
on the eyes of a near relative of the throne,
Dr. Feldern had been invested with a high order,
which raised him into the ranks of the nobility.
He was entitled now to prefix a "von" before
his name. Gay, coquettish Vienna pouted that
it could find no inducement sufficiently strong to
detain its popular guest. It shook him heartily

by the hand, and lisped a siren "Auf Wiedersehen." Then it dried its eyes, and after the
manner of coquettes, was on with the new love
before the old one was fairly off.

Gay, fascinating, alluring Vienna! "Auf Wiedersehen?" Well, hardly. Leaning back in the
post-chaise, "erster klasse," Herr Dr. Friedrich
von Feldern was perfectly clear on that point.
In his mind one fixed purpose was firmly rooted.
Years ago it had spread out its first timid feelers,
striking deeper and firmer as time went on. Like
a beacon light it had gleamed during the long,
dreary interval of absence and restless activity,
drawing him nearer, ever nearer. And now he
had come home.

Babbett hurried into her kitchen to prepare
such savory dishes as she knew from past experience the son of the house relished most. Sub-
lime in the confidence of her own skill, no thought
of a probably spoiled palate troubled her. Good
old Babbett! She would have taken up the skim-
mer and ladle with a born Vatel, confident in the
victory of her own prowess. Jette went up to
her room to see if her white muslin dress retained
its spotless purity. She scrutinized herself in the
glass and smiled. She always smiled when she
looked at herself. It was in pure sympathy with
her own loveliness. The rippling masses of her
glossy black hair were in perfect order. Near the
centre of the immaculate white parting a fugitive
lock strayed caressingly. It looked so pretty she
decided not to coax it back. The two long curls

behind either ear she twined afresh around her forefinger, tightened the thick coil of hair above the nape of her neck, and put on her lace-frilled fichu. The doctor's arrival left her quite indifferent. But then, it was only natural one should want to look one's best; one's own self-esteem as well as the honor of the house demanded it.

"Thou," said Babbett, when she entered the kitchen, "make what haste thou canst with the coffee, and take it out to them. How lucky I made a cake this morning. Surely the Herr Doctor requires refreshment after his long, tedious journey. Confidences there have been exchanged enough for the present. Thou wilt take the best silver coffee service, of course. Here is a dish of raspberries the Herr Doctor dearly loves, and there is the cream. Haste thee now, and be not squeamish about interrupting."

Hurriedly Jette ran out, and cut the stems of a handful of roses. There were not many left over from the recent storm. These were buds which had come out since, but very sweet and fragrant they looked, with their half-open leaves unfolding to the sun. She lined the pink china bowl with fresh green leaves, and gently piled the berries on top. When her tray, spread with a snowy cloth, was ready, the slender-stemmed vase with the flowers in the midst, the berries topped here and there with a gleaming bluebell, the whole surrounded with the fine old silver, Babbett surveyed it with some pride.

"I must say," she uttered, "everything thou

dost seems to have a gift of its own. Anybody
might have arranged it exactly like that, still it
would not look the same. The Herr Doctor may
be spoilt with grandeur, but nowhere could he
have things sweeter or more appetizing. Here is
the cake. Now bestir thyself. They will be sniff-
ing the aroma of the coffee and wondering it does
not come. Is that tray not overheavy for thee?"

"Heavy?" Jette laughed, as she caught it up
in her hands; "I could lift thee with it, and not
find it heavy."

As she came near the arbor, the happy, animated talk ceased. The Herr Pastor sat one side
of the round centre table, his long-stemmed pipe
unlit, his black skull-cap pushed back on his scant
gray hairs. His soft, faded cheek was flushed, his
beautiful soft brown eyes sparkled as they hung
on his son's face. The Frau Pastorin sat at the
other side of the table, her hand clasping that of
her son. The tears she had shed on his arrival
still lingered on her cheek; she looked quite exhausted with the intensity of her emotions. For
the first time in her life — and probably the last
— Jette saw that her cap was askew. Her heart
must indeed have been stirred, if she could have
abandoned herself so entirely to her feelings.

The doctor sat at the head of the table between
father and mother. He wore a green shade over
his eyes, so that only the lower part of his face
was visible. His long, blonde mustache, the tips
of which he had always worn slightly curled upward, had developed into profuse luxuriance. It

was of a bright gold color, silky, and exceedingly
well kept.   His mouth was completely hidden
by it, leaving just a glimpse of the beautifully
curved, soft underlip.   But the exposed chin
showed massive firmness and strength, an obsti-
nacy of purpose unconquerable as death.   Here
spoke the *will* of the *man*, the determination that
what he undertook to do he would do with all his
might and strength, ignoring all obstacles, true to
his resolve, like a hero to his colors.   One liked
him for this immensity of will-power, and submitted meekly to his superiority of strength.   His
whole physique inspired one with confidence and
trust.   His deep, broad chest had widened, his
entire appearance was that of strong, aggressive,
self-reliant manhood.   As Jette set down the tray,
and he rose to greet her, he towered fully a head
and shoulders above her, so that tall as she was,
she appeared to herself small and insignificant
beside him.

"Is this Jettchen — Fräulein Jettchen? " he
said.

His tone was singularly soft and low for his
full, deep voice.   It vibrated like the strings of
a harp in the wind.   Like a flash their last interview darted across Jette's mind.   The night before his departure, when he had found her safely
home after she had run away from the picnic, and
he had talked to her as she had never in her
wildest dreams expected him to speak, and he
had kissed her — Bah! what folly was this! She
laid her hand in his firm, warm clasp, and it

seemed as if an electric shock rooted her to the spot. If he had chosen to retain her hand for a year, she could not have withdrawn it. Helpless, bewildered, intensely angry with herself, she looked up at his towering height, and saw the smile deepen around his lips. Slowly and lingeringly, like an inward caress, he released her hand. She instantly busied herself in arranging the table. A fright and confusion she had never experienced in her life made her hands tremble and her whole frame quiver. Worlds she would have given to see his eyes. Underneath the odious shade he could watch her perfectly. What made him smile in that exasperating manner, and sit as if entranced? He had always had a strange effect on her; if he only looked at her, she felt as if every pore in her body bristled with aggressiveness. But why? It was only because she had never felt at her ease with him that made her awkward, self-conscious, and self-constrained in his presence. Donkey! Was it not about time to outgrow this feeling and appear perfectly self-possessed? To behave like a stupid rustic, — truly, a fine idea he must have of her.

But the Frau Pastorin, who knew nothing of all this, laughed. "Thou need'st not be formal with our Henriette," she said, "though she is grown up and quite a woman now. No matter what changes may take place soon, with us she will always be the same, eh?" She nodded at her son, and laughed slyly, as she patted the girl's hand.

A spasm contracted Jette's heart, as it always did whenever the most covert allusion was made to her marriage. The silver coffee-pot she poised in her hand clinked against the cup she was about to fill. With a wild, piteous gaze she glanced at the doctor. She knew he was regarding her. Did he know? Had his parents told him?

"Thou speakest in riddles, dear mamma," said the doctor; "what is it thou meanest by ' changes ' ? "

"As if thou didst not know," laughed his mother; "have I not told thee everything in my letters? "

For an instant he was silent. Then he said very deliberately, "Am I to congratulate? "

"Now, now, now," deprecated the Herr Pastor, "there is no hurry, no hurry at all. Wait till the suitor comes, then 't will be time enough to decide."

"Matters are decided! " ejaculated the Frau Pastorin sharply. "Thou dear Heaven! I think the banker has behaved exemplary enough. Thou surely canst find no further excuse to put him off. Let the wedding take place, say I, as quickly as possible. 'T will be a great comfort to me when all is settled."

"I don't see much comfort in giving up Jett-chen," ventured the Herr Pastor, "just as she has grown almost indispensable to us."

"Nay," said the Frau Pastorin, "I 'll not deny we shall miss her extremely. But we cannot let our comfort stand in the way when such a chance presents itself for settling her in life. Marry she will have to, sooner or later. We have to accustom ourselves to the idea, that is all."

"And Jettchen," hazarded the doctor, "is she satisfied?"

She could feel him looking at her, and a great fright seized her. Now — now, if the opportunity came, and she might perhaps speak out, — but the Frau Pastorin interrupted sharply.

"How thou talkest, Fritz. What is a penniless girl to do, but to be glad, and happy, and thankful at the chance of becoming a rich man's wife. 'T is one in a million. But men are all alike. Thou speakest just like thy father, as if she had but to choose and be satisfied."

"We will not spoil Fritz's home-coming with any such debates," cried the Herr Pastor cheerily. "Thou art a dear, famous girl, Jettchen, to have anticipated the wants of my languishing palate. Come, another cup. No one can brew coffee like thee. A little more cream, please. Thou, Fritz, hast thou tasted anything more famous in thy much-vaunted Vienna?"

"I will tell thee," answered the doctor grimly, "whenever it may please Jettchen to serve me."

"Thou dear Heaven! Henriette — nay, girl, what ails thee? Art dreaming, or bereft of sense? Thou shouldst have served him first, as he needs it the most. And now I suppose what is left is cold," cried the Frau Pastorin, highly exasperated.

"I will run and make some more," exclaimed the girl, in real distress. "How could I be so forgetful? I beg your pardon, Herr Doctor, a thousand times." She seized the coffee-pot, and was about to rush off, but he lifted his hand, which bespoke so much power.

"You will stay," he said, "and pour out what is left. I do not care for scalding-hot coffee in such weather. I shall enjoy immensely what you will give me."

She handed him his cup, and their hands met. Tremblingly she withdrew hers, and set the cake and fruit before him. All this she did with such gracious humility as if she could not make up enough for her neglect.

"It is very warm," she murmured, fanning herself with her handkerchief. She went to the entrance of the arbor, and breathed deeply. "If you do not want me any more" — she began hesitatingly.

"But we do," said the doctor. "I want more coffee, and you must serve me with more raspberries. I have not tasted any like these since I left home."

"Thou wert ever fond of them," observed his mother, hugely enjoying his relish for home food once more.

"Now, Jettchen," he said, "since you have served me, I will wait upon you. I see you are not inclined to join us. Here is your cup, and here is a piece of cake. Will you please sit down?"

She blushed, and was angry with herself for doing so. The pastor gently pulled her down on a chair beside him. Since the prospect of losing her, she had grown very dear to him.

"Big as thou art, Fritz," he remarked fondly, "thou actest the spoiled child still. Thou hadst ever a way of making people do as thou pleased."

"Thou hast not told us about Herr von Czechy," said the Frau Pastorin.

Jette looked up eagerly. "Hans," said the doctor, "is very happy. A trifle more dignified, perhaps, as becomes the magnate of large estates. But the same impulsive, hot-headed, open-hearted fellow. He completely dominates his wife. It is both comical and touching to see how she idolizes him. They have two lovely twin children. The boy was born first, and is called Henri. The girl's name is Henriette."

Jette uttered a cry of delight. "That is in compliment to thee," said the Frau Pastorin.

"Yes," replied the doctor, "he is very loyal, and will never forget the service Jettchen did him. What say you of looking them up on your wedding trip, Jettchen? They would give you a right royal welcome, I assure you."

"How cruel he is," thought the girl, with a sickening fear. The Frau Pastorin nodded her head, well pleased. She always encouraged allusions to the wedding. It was as if with that she wanted to banish some misgivings of her own.

Babbett came out to tell the Herr Pastor a peasant wanted to see him about his sick cow. At the same time she wanted to gratify her very pardonable eagerness to greet the Herr Doctor. She had rocked his cradle when he was born, and darned his little torn pinafores when he was in dread of punishment from mamma, and dragged him to the pump when he had rolled in the mud, and consoled him when he was put in a corner with his face to the wall, and surreptitiously conveyed goodies to him when banished from table. She was old, work-worn, and wrinkled now, and he had grown up into as perfect manhood as ever was seen between the Neckar and the Rhine. He was the Herr Doctor now; proper respect had to be maintained. But in her heart he was always Fritzchen, the flaxen-haired baby she had petted and spoiled and spanked.

Of course she was greeted with effusion. That doctor was a rascal, and knew exactly where the feminine heart is most vulnerable, be it with queen or peasant. A little affection goes a great way with either. Exactly as of old, he put his arm around the dried-up little body's neck, and saluted her with a smack that could be heard in the next pasture. The dear old thing blushed, and quivered all over with delight.

"Nay, but what a man thou hast grown," she said, looking up at him with tremendous respect. "I — I beg pardon, you, I mean," she corrected herself hastily.

He laughed, took her up as if she had been a shuttlecock, lifted her high in the air, then set her down as gently as if she were made of porcelain. The rest laughed, but Babbett was very much ruffled.

"It did not need that to convince me how strong you are," she said; "in future I 'll take very good care not to come near you."

He tapped her affectionately on the shoulder. "Thou," he said, "thou 'lt open thy eyes when I 'll show thee what I have brought thee."

She smirked, all her good humor restored to think he had not forgotten her. The Frau Pastorin went back with her to the kitchen to consult about the state of the larder. The Herr Pastor had already gone to his study to see the peasant who had the sick cow. Jette and the doctor were left alone.

For a moment there was silence. Mechanically the girl commenced to collect the scattered plates and cups, and heaped them on the tray. The arbor was not very large, so she had to edge her way between the chairs, and came quite close to him. He laid his hand upon hers.

"You have not yet asked me how I am," he said.

Heavens! Was that his voice? Was it possible that it could thrill and vibrate and modulate with such divine, caressing softness? Like a bandage that is gradually removed from eyes allowed for the first time to see, she began to grope, dimly, hesitatingly at a possibility which convulsed her with terror. Trembling in every limb, she tried to withdraw her hand. But he held it firmly in his strong, warm clasp. That clasp which embraced her wrist also, which noted every beat of her wildly leaping pulse.

"When friends meet after a long absence," continued he, "have they nothing to say to each other but the cold formalities of the outside world?"

"Friends," she said faintly. She looked up at him. He raised the disfiguring shade, and flung it on the table. She saw his eyes, those beautiful, soft brown, radiant orbs, looking into her own. She could not move, he held her enthralled, drawing forth her soul, absorbing it forever. Her lips were slightly parted, as if breath were suspended; only the quivering of the nostrils gave signs of life. It was as if a whirlpool of fire clutched her and she went down, down, in the eddying current. The torch flung into her breast kindled into fiercest exulting life, and would never, never be quenched any more.

The gravel on the path outside crunched under a heavy step. He caught up the green shade, and readjusted it over his eyes. She staggered back, flung her hands up before her face, and fled from the spot.

CHAPTER XXXVI

A GREAT change had come over Jette. The merry snatches of song which roused the echoes of the parsonage were heard no more. The joyous elasticity of her step became languid and subdued. There were shadows around her eyes when she came down of a morning; the rose in her cheek was transformed into a pale lily. More stately she seemed to have become, and there was a majesty in the way she held her head and looked at one which took away a good deal from her girlishness, but gave the added charm of the woman. She was very little in the house, but found a constant excuse for being out of doors.

"If you will come and look at my garden," she said to the Frau Pastorin, "you will see that a great deal of work is needed yet before it looks like itself again. Babbett can manage in the house very well without me. I must get everything in proper condition again."

"Thou art good and dutiful," said the Frau Pastorin, "and wouldst not leave anything to reflect on thy neatness before thou goest, eh? 'T is the way I would like thee to be, dear child. 'T is creditable to the way thou hast been brought up, and surely thy husband will bless me for it."

Jette shuddered as if the ague clutched her. Minka came up, purring, rubbing herself affectionately against the girl's dress.

"No, thou canst not come," she said pettishly; "thou art forever following me as if I were a mouse, and thou wert only waiting to gobble me up. Go thy ways, thou treacherous thing."

"Now," said the Frau Pastorin, opening her eyes very wide, "how comest thou to such foolish talk? The creature fairly dotes on thee, and thou knowest it. Art thou not well?"

The girl's lips quivered. She stooped down, caught the big tabby in her arms, and bent over to caress her. The tears had welled up into her eyes, and she wanted to hide them.

"I have a little headache," she muttered.

"Thou!" ejaculated the Frau Pastorin. Her astonishment grew and grew. It was the first time in her life the hearty, healthy girl complained of such a thing. "Nay," she said gravely, "that needs attending to. I shall ask Fritz to catechize thee, for 't is best to take heed in time. Now I come to look at thee, thou dost not seem the same as usual. Thou shouldst appear thy very best now for the honor of the bridegroom's coming. Go to thy garden, but do not exert thyself. Remember it will have to do without thee very soon."

She went to join her husband and son, who sat on the shaded bench, smoking and enjoying the delicious morning air, while Jette went to fetch her large shade hat and gloves.

"Something has come over her," said the Frau Pastorin suddenly. The Herr Pastor and the doctor looked up, startled.

"I mean Henriette. Just now she complained of headache. 'T is extraordinary. 'T is unheard of."

"Bah," said the pastor, with equanimity, "young girls are privileged to put forward excuses of that kind."

"'T was not an excuse," said the Frau Pastorin; "she is not spoilt that way. Dost thou not find Henriette much changed, Fritz?"

"She has grown up," said the doctor, "exactly into what I fancied she would."

The doctor certainly had a great advantage over others. In wearing the shade over his eyes, one could see very little of his face. Therefore, when sometimes — as now — his words and tone were at variance with each other, he left his listeners greatly in doubt as to what he really meant. Several days had now elapsed since his arrival, and he declared himself already greatly benefited, but his eyes still had to be protected, and would for some time to come.

"She is," said the pastor, "like one of Solomon's songs,— all myrrh and sweet-smelling things and frankincense. She has a majesty of mien which well might have become the Biblical queens of old. I grudge her to the man she is to marry. Much rather would I see her led to the altar by one more akin to herself. 'T is grotesque to see them together."

"Every advantage has its disadvantage," replied the Frau Pastorin; "with him she will have a life like a queen. 'T was extremely lucky for her matters shaped themselves this way. Thou knowest very well what the poor men of her faith are. Her comeliness would weigh very lightly against her want of dowry, I assure thee. 'T would have been her greatest drawback. Her womanhood would have been dragged into the dust by degrading drudgery and irksome surroundings. I warrant thee, 't would be far more grotesque to see her brought down thus, living her foolish mother's life over again, than a trifling discrepancy in appearance."

"Mamma," asked the doctor suddenly, "hast thou ever asked her if she cares for him?"

"How thou talkest, Fritz! Of course she cares for him. How can she help it? How could any girl help caring for a man who has perfectly exhausted himself in devotion? Has he not waited patiently for three long years? Have not his family received her with every mark of approbation? Has she not seen sufficiently during her visits there the splendor and luxury of the life awaiting her? My only wonder is that she did not clamor to return."

"Thy logic seems very well sustained," smiled the pastor, stroking her hand softly; "but confess thou didst not reason this way when we were married."

"Confess," she said affectionately, taking him by the ears, "that thou art an old donkey. Ever and always thou forgettest how exceptionally she is placed."

"That is true," answered the pastor, with a sigh. "Since I have seen her blossom into most gracious girlhood, I have often wished her faith did not separate her from us. 'T would have simplified matters so much. 'T is most likely she looks forward with some trepidation to the coming of the banker. That may account for her sober mood."

"If 't is as mamma thinks," remarked the doctor, "a concern of her health, it concerns me also. As guardian of the family's well-being, 't is my special privilege to find out. I shall seek her, and she shall come out with the truth, never fear."

"I told her I would tell thee," replied the Frau Pastorin; "do thou question her, Fritz. I would that now of all times she should look her best. Thou 'lt find her in the garden adjoining the orchard. And listen, thou. Do not let her work in the sun. What matters now? The garden will have another care-taker soon."

CHAPTER XXXVII

As if he had not known where to find her; as
if he had forgotten all her favorite haunts and
nooks, and where she would most likely fly for
refuge; as if he had not hungered and watched
for this opportunity to catch her alone, the first
she had given him since his home-coming, in the
arbor where they had stood eye to eye, heart revealed to heart at last.   As he vaulted lightly over
the fence inclosing the orchard from the dusty
chaussée, he saw the drooping boughs of the old
sycamore under whose spreading branches he knew
she sat, with the purling brook babbling its secret
at her feet.   She had often idly wondered what
the brook could have so much to murmur about,
repeating the same story over and over again.
Now she knew.   She listened with eyes staring
wide in the distance, her pale, hopeless face more
wondrously fair against the frame of lustrous
black hair than it had ever seemed to him with
the bloom of joyous, unthinking youth upon it.
The great cat lay near her, stretched full length in
the sun, her gleaming topaz eyes occasionally blinking at her young mistress.   The doctor's footfall
made no sound on the springy turf, and he was upon
her before she fairly knew it.   The rosy dawn of
consciousness kissed her face and throat, and made
her thrill all over.   He sat down on the broad stone
beside her, necessarily very close, for the seat was
hardly wide enough to hold both.   He could feel

her tremble; his own pulses vibrated in touch with
hers. He took off his hat and let the heavenly
breezes, blowing straight from the Rhine, cool his
heated brow and revel among his soft, thick fair
curls. He looked down upon her drooping head,
where the glossy coil of darkest hair showed in
most striking contrast with the strip of snowy neck
beneath, and upon this spot let his famished eyes
rest. Now he was contented, happy, and at ease
as he had never in his life been before. So might
the first man and the first woman have looked,
sitting in their Garden of Eden, perfect in the
image of Him who had just created them, before
a stupid posterity obliterated and defaced what
there was of divine.

"Jettchen," he murmured softly.

She made no answer. Her chin nearly touched
her breast. The fingers of her hand lying in her
lap nervously interlaced each other. He sepa-
rated them gently and retained hold of them.

"You must not," he said, as she endeavored to
withdraw them. "I am only trying to feel your
pulse. My mother sent me here to find out what
ails you."

She looked at him in amazement. "Your mother!" she stammered.

"Is it so strange she should feel concerned
about you? She thinks you are troubled about
something. Will you not tell me what it is?"

Oh, the caressing love in his voice. The domi-
nating, magnetic touch upon her wrist. "There
is nothing — nothing the matter with me."

"You cannot impose upon the physician, or — upon the lover."

For a moment she sat transfixed, steeped from head to foot in quivering ecstasy. But not for her was this sweetest of all joys. Now she would have to show what mettle she was made of.

"Herr Doctor," she ventured timidly.

He smiled, inclining his stately head. "Not quite so formal, if you please."

"May — may I earnestly beg a favor of you?"

From beneath his shade he watched her keenly. For the matter of that, his eyes had never left her face.

"It depends," he answered, "upon the nature of your request."

"I would beg of you to go away — to go away till all is over — that is — I mean — until — until I am gone for good."

"H'm! And where wouldst thou go?"

"You — you know what is impending. He — he will be here very soon. Only a short time — then all will be over. I — I will let them hurry matters just as they wish."

"Dear child," said the doctor amiably, "thou wilt have to be a little more explicit, if I am to understand thee."

No, he would not help her. He played with her feelings as Minka would with a mouse.

She muttered brokenly, "You must know what I mean; it has been discussed openly enough. I am to be married — it will be soon now — he — he may already be on his way. It — it will soon be over. Then — you — can return here."

" Why should I go away? What does this man concern me?"

She stared at him, white to the lips. Strong shudders shook her frame. Beads of agony stood upon her brow. He flung his arm around her and strained her passionately to his breast.

"Thou shalt be tortured no more, poor, brave, darling child. Thou hast not been defenseless all this time. Have I not loved thee ever since the dawn of the morning thou stood'st over my sleeping form on the ground over yonder and badest me arise and follow thee? Like a young goddess thou stood'st in the wake of the rising sun, thy bared, milk-white arm raised to the path of light, the glow drawing closer and closer thy heavenly form in its amorous embrace. So prayed I one day to enfold thee, and to that end have I labored and struggled and toiled, denied myself all indulgences, opposed an iron determination to temptation, and kept myself free of all evil, that when the time came I might give thee an embrace as virgin as thy own. For three long years I have fed upon thy image, and have seen thee always thus, — what thou hast grown up into, — thou dearest, fairest of all fair maids. Thy sweet presence has been the polar star which guided me to the goal, — a goal I swore to myself I would reach before that other one should claim thee. For what purpose, dost thou think, have the letters flown between here and Vienna, and the least trivial circumstance been laid hold of, but to keep myself fully informed of everything concerning thee? For what my sudden return? And now, love me, — love me a little, for indeed my famished soul has hungered long and patiently enough."

He lifted her arms and put them around his neck. He had raised the shade from his eyes, and looked blissfully, silently into her own. He and she alone in the world, — let no one dare come between them. She had sat as one stunned, reason and judgment carried away by the mighty torrent of his avowal. Now she knew why he had kissed her the night before he went away. The kiss which he had just redeemed, which had waited for him all these years! Father in heaven! Could such bliss be — only to be tantalized with it! To renounce — ay, that was it. To renounce, to hunger, to go through life with a heart of lead. He had not reckoned with the consequences, but she — she knew.

"I am but a simple girl," she said, " weak, as the dear Lord has fashioned my sex. Lend me the strength of your superabundant manhood, that it may fortify me with what I have to say."

There was a grandeur in her voice, the look with which she regarded him, which inspired him with infinite pity and respect. All her arguments he knew beforehand, and how they would leave him untouched. Of what use was it to match her will against his? In the whole world there existed but one thing for him, — his love for her, her love for him. All else would have to adjust itself to this. He freed her from his embrace, and she rose and leaned against the tree, looking at him with her clear, beautiful eyes.

"If nothing divided us," she began, "I would now prostrate myself before the Giver of all things, and bless Him for the inexpressible boon of life. The angels might envy such happiness as your words for a moment gave me. Now, my most ardent wish is that I may die, that I may be wiped off the face of the earth, never to be seen or heard of any more."

He folded his arms and sat still. It would all have to come out, — the sooner the better. After that — well, he had his plans. A fierce exultation swelled his breast, — the longing for battle, in which he knew he would subdue and come off conqueror.

"That I may die," she repeated. "The torch you have set flaring high in my heart will burn and rage forever. The fire of your words has scorched me. Heaven beckons with joy divine, and I have to plunge into deepest, deepest hell."

"Where is the necessity?" he asked.

"You ask me? Ah, you know. Duty demands it — the regard for others. What! Shall I like a serpent fasten the fangs of treacherous ingratitude into your parents' hearts, and make them curse the day they rescued me from the highway? You forget what I was when I first came here. Beaten, all but stoned to death, your father took me in his arms like one of his stray sheep, and he and your mother nursed me back to life, and opened its joys, its usefulness, and possibilities to me. They rescued me from the gutter, and sheltered and fed and loved me, and brought me up in truth and honor and righteousness. All my life they have willed nothing but what was good and best for me."

"In all that," observed the doctor, "there is nothing which disqualifies you to become my wife."

She shuddered and closed her eyes. "You, the Christian, I, the Jewess?"

"Bah! What matters to either of us? Thy religion is to love me — mine to love thee. 'T is so as God intended. With the barricades, hate, superstition, prejudice has hedged around us, neither thou nor I have anything to do."

"As long as we depend upon and mingle with our fellow creatures we, too, are penned within those narrow confines. Our puny strength would soon fall exhausted before its combined force. I should be a millstone around your neck, the dead weight under which you would sink to destruction. Your career, so gloriously begun, and stretching in a vista of fame, honor, and renown before you, would be ruined forever. Those who now regard you with admiration and respect would banish you from their midst. Strong as you may be in your love and loyal to its duties, great as may be your courage to withstand and your resolve to conquer, you would inevitably go under. And I — I should have the agony of seeing you sink, my ever-restless conscience repeating the heartbreaking refrain, ' 'T is thy work; thou, thou hast done this.'"

"Is my manhood a jest?" asked he sternly.

"Am I weak enough to let myself become a by-word? Am I a puppet to allow others to mould my destiny? For what dost thou take me? For what was my strength and steadfastness given me? Is not my own sound sense and judgment to control my actions, my own honor and rectitude to be my guide? Thou arguest from thy own inexperience and limited standpoint. This spot of earth is not the whole world. Courage enough have I to wrestle with it, and wherever I go it will give me my bread. Fling away this faint-heartedness of thine. With thee by my side, let what may betide. A loving heart thou wilt ever have to cherish thee, a stout arm to protect thee, a right lusty good will to maintain thee a home in which thou and I can be alone with our happiness."

She shook her head. "Your parents, — they will never consent."

"Come, place thy hand in mine. This instant will we put it to the proof."

"Your mother's heart would break. Your father, — his stern principles of rectitude and honor, — they would revolt against the very idea of such a union."

"Because we love each other?"

"Because my religion stands between us. Like an impenetrable wall of granite, it towers between you and me. The synagogue will cast me out, it will lay its ban upon me. Nowhere shall I find any rest. Even my bones will be forbidden an abiding-place. Isolated here and hereafter shall I dwell, — never on the day of resurrection shall I

see the face of father or mother again. Nowhere
will a hand in greeting be extended to me. I
shall be banished from their midst."

"Humph! thy fears may make thee exaggerate.
Thou and I will visit thy rabbi and speedily find
out. And even if 't were so, — our love is such it
has to be battled for. Hast thou not the courage
for that? Nay, the prospect but steels my nerves
and puts my mettle on edge. As I have said, —
this spot of earth is not the whole world."

She gazed at him sadly. "The world is wide
enough; happy and miserable people dwell everywhere. But the ban of which I speak would not
be left here. Wherever I went, — to the remot-
est corner of the earth, — would it pursue me.
There would be no fleeing from it. Night and
day would it stalk like a spectre at my side, turn
the laugh of merriment to a ghastly groan, blanch
the color upon my lips, and quench the light in
my eyes. Daily, hourly, you would see me wither,
and shrink and listen in horror for the invisible
footstep beside me."

He took her in his arms, and passed his hand
over her brow.

"Priests' talk," he said contemptuously; "hell's
wiles, with which to intimidate the strong and turn
the brain of the weak. Dear, dear heart! how
canst thou conjure up such unhealthy images and
fever thy brain with such unholy things? Such
teachings emanate from the devil, not from the
Pure Source of Love. Trust to me, my own, dear,
dear one. These arms are strong enough to shelter

thee; my love shall protect thee from all evil. Only be a little strong and firm thyself. Such images as thou conjuredst up but now exist nowhere but in the disordered imagination. When thou art mine, there will be no more room for such. Give thyself into my guidance. Dost not think I am strong enough to do battle for both?"

"Oh," she uttered, "'t is not for myself that I fear. What matters! I have been a passive coward all these years, — now the end must come. Let it bring what it will, — I dare not drag you down to ruin."

"Thou canst say this with my arms enfolding thee?"

"Father in heaven," she prayed, "give me strength. Grant me the fortitude to do what is right. Imbue me with the spirit which demands this sacrifice for the welfare of those nearest and dearest to me."

"The cry of a faint heart," replied the doctor, "which would trample upon itself without benefiting others. Mark this, dearest, and mark it for all time. With me thou canst not reckon this way. If — in a mistaken idea of duty — thou contemplatest giving thyself to this man, I will pluck thee from his embrace. At the moment the word of consent is about to pass thy lips, I will step forward, and, throwing all considerations to the winds, claim thee as my own. Welcome will be the opportunity to end all this needless concealment and pain. My love is too sacred to make a flaunting thing of, and fain would I rejoice in this sweet, stolen communion for a little while longer before sordid worldly argument rears its obnoxious head. Thy love and mine, — dear, dear heart. But if thou forcest me to it, — why, then I take up the gauntlet willingly. Dost credit me with so little manhood that I would ever yield thee to another, Crœsus, king, or emperor, though he be?"

"It must be," she answered, the tears streaming down her cheeks, "or disaster will overtake us all."

"What! and take thee in his arms like this? — and kiss thy lips thus? — and lay thy head upon his bosom so? — and gird his neck with thy snowy arms?"

"I will kill myself!" she cried; "I will deface what there is of allurement in this unfortunate, unhappy face. All shall shudder who come to look upon it. Father in heaven! I dare not drag thee down to destruction."

"Thou wilt not do that, because the same bier that bears thy lifeless body hence will also contain mine. Thy life and mine are indissolubly bound to each other. Whatever thou dost to thyself, thou dost to me. Dance, sing, be happy, so wilt thou rejoice my heart; steel me for the struggle to come, that we may attain the end. Such natures as thine and mine were not made to go through life scathless. We will have to fight for our happiness, but — in the end it will come."

"Oh, no! oh, no! oh, no!" she said desolately, "such happiness as this was never given to mortals to enjoy. Too truly does my foreboding heart tell me that it can never be."

"Be brave only a little while longer," he urged; "reckon with this obnoxious suitor for all time to come. Then will I take thy hand and ask my parents for their blessing. At first they may demur, but," he threw back his head proudly, "I am a man, and shall exert a man's right to shape my own destiny. There is nothing in thee the sternest demands of honor or rectitude can object to. A king might be proud to place thee on the throne beside him. Thy religion? Bah! thou mayest bend the knee, or prostrate thyself, or worship in any manner, fashion, or form it pleases thee, — only love me, that is all I ask. In thy heart dwells the divine, thy soul is immortal. Travel thy own route for reaching the Eternal Bourne, — be sure thou takest me with thee. My soul will follow thy footsteps, devoutly grateful for such an unerring guide. Hand in hand there, as here in earth, will we step before the Father, and He will not say us nay, or refuse either thee or me his benediction."

Now of her own accord she put her arms around his neck. Admiration, love, grief, all striving so violently with one another that she could hardly speak.

"Who would not love thee?" she breathed. "Oh, if there were only more like thee! Alas, alas, the more noble and lofty thou, the more useless thy struggles! Thou wilt be derided, jeered, laughed at. Oh, my heart, my heart, my heart! Nay, let me weep, weep, till my heart breaks. Fritz, dear, *dear* Fritz, — for I will call thee so for the first, the last time, — nay, let me weep." She sank to her knees, her arms stretched to heaven, her piteous sobs convulsing her limbs, "I dare not, dare not grasp the heaven thou holdest out to me. For thee and for me there remains but one thing — renunciation."

"Never," he replied firmly. "As sure as yon sun shines in heaven and will shine again to-morrow, and for decade upon decade, long after the least speck of dust of thy bones and mine remains, surely will I never yield thee to another. Pit not thy will against mine. Useless are thy struggles, and that in the end thou wilt find."

"If my comeliness were defaced," she asked, "if I were disfigured, hideous, — surely thou wouldst not love me any more?"

"I would love thee as long as a shred remained of thee. And if — which God forbid! — anything untoward of the nature thou speakest of were to happen, the same should happen also to me, so that thou shouldst not feel shamed in looking at me. Thou must not let such unhealthy thoughts rise within thee. Strong and perfect of mind and body thou art, and so it shall be my care thou shalt remain. The great Creator of all has cast thee in his own divine mould, just to show an ungrateful posterity what his creatures from the first were intended to be. 'Tis a sacred trust, and take thou heed thou dost no blasphemy by not taking all possible care of it, and like a faithful servant guarding it with all due precaution and care."

He raised her to her feet and seated her on the stone beside him. Her head he pillowed on his shoulder, and drew her close within his sheltering arm. She was perfectly passive, for her strength was spent.

"Rest thee, Geliebte," he said so softly the angels might have whispered it. "Then we will go home."

CHAPTER XXXVIII

"Leid'l heb's Fuessel in die Hoeh' heut' geigt der Strauss," hummed the doctor, in the charming Viennese vernacular. His magnificent baritone was subdued; dreamily he watched the blue rings from his cigar mingle with, then lose themselves in the fleecy summer clouds. It was the day after his interview with Jette. He had hardly seen anything of her all day, and this made him somewhat restless. He wanted to know how she felt, for he knew that a depressing lassitude had followed the terrible mental strain of yesterday. Of what use was her fuming and fretting? She could not lay any plans without his circumventing them. Happy he wanted her to be, happy and joyous as of old, — to come to him with the dancing step which bespoke her superabundant vitality, to look at him with her half-wistful, half-roguish eyes, to see the dimples round her mouth chased away by laughter, to feast his eyes upon the harmonious picture which had tantalized him with its shadow long enough. To his mother's anxious inquiries

about the result of his interview, he gave her
cheerfully to understand that everything would
adjust itself of its own accord once the "bank
affair" was disposed of. But Jette must not be
kept in the house. It was very natural she should
feel restless, therefore what so beneficial for her
as the open?

However, she had managed very cleverly to keep
herself indoors. In the morning, at breakfast, a
pain like a dagger-thrust struck his heart when
he saw her. So wan and piteously self-torturing
he had never thought it possible a night of agony
could make her. Her voice bespoke the suffering
of her heart. She was so quiet, so subdued, so
touchingly humble in her despair. It would go
hard with her — that he knew from the first.
That she should grieve and condemn herself like
this had not entered into his calculation. He
would not stand it, he could not. Much he was
willing to concede to her, for in one thing she
was right, — it would be highly injudicious to
take his parents by storm. He owed them duty
and consideration, especially his mother, who was
now in that trying period of a woman's life where
both mind and body have to be most delicately
considered. Jette must be brought to listen to
reason and to act accordingly. In this trial she
was not alone. Some regard was due to him also,
— did she find no consolation, no compensation in
his love at all, then?

That no one should notice her distress, he rattled
on during breakfast in a manner which showed

that he was still the same roguish, boyish-hearted Fritz of old. This roused the Herr Pastor's love of fun, whose heart had never outgrown its infancy. So nonsensical and merry were they that the punctilious Frau Pastorin spilled her coffee several times, her hand shook so with laughter. For this she was fined on the spot, just as Fritz — when he was little Fritzchen — had been for any accident to the spotless table linen. Once she had to kiss the Herr Pastor on the bald spot of his head, which she did with much loving unction; another time she had to give the tips of the doctor's luxurious mustache a bolder twist, which she also did, with a hearty kiss on the tempting lips besides; a third time she was requested to count the hairs in Minka's whiskers, which she did *not* do. It was a happy, merry meal, which the four composing it had good cause to remember. Under his shade the doctor looked at Jette, and his mood became almost hilarious when he saw the smile come to her lips. And when he bent his figure in front of his mother to let her pay the penalty on his mustaches, she actually laughed, — a sound which caused his heart to dance with joy. She looked at him with a mixture of love, humility, and self-abnegation which made his eyes water; he longed to take her in his arms and kiss all her fears away.

Now, it was well on in the afternoon, and still she did not come out. Coffee had been drunk as usual in the arbor, but Babbett had brought in the tray. The Herr Pastor had been fetched

away by the peasant, whose cow was not yet recovered. He was a poor man, and the cow was
the special item in his possession. The Frau Pastorin was rummaging in her linen closet. The
doctor had just determined to bespeak his mother's
authority in sending forth the obstinate girl, when
he descried her coming out of the house, basket
and scissors in hand. She was going to cut some
flowers to grace the evening meal. Hurrah! That
suited him exactly. The garden was a good distance from the house, — one had to cross the poultry yard and outhouses first; besides, the flowering
laburnum and tall lilac bushes sheltered one completely. Now he would see and speak to her.

The strawberry bed was on the further side of
the flower garden, and she was stooping over it
when he came up. She looked so sweet in her
light blue dress, heightening the dazzling purity of
her complexion, the white neck beneath her coil
of black hair, his favorite spot of adoration,
gleaming like marble in the sun. He kissed it as
he came noiselessly behind her, put his hands to
her waist, and drew her up to him. He kissed the
small, lovely ear, rolling it playfully between his
lips, as if he meant to bite it. Her two hands he
drew up to his breast, and held them there.

" Why dost thou avoid me ? " questioned he.

The lids drooped over her eyes, so that the long
black lashes touched the white of her cheeks.
Her hands she tried to withdraw, but he kept
them firmly clasped. Well he knew the tremendous personal magnetism that streamed from his

touch to hers and set her whole body tingling. But her lips were curved in a firm resolve, her passive attitude bespoke obstinate resistance.

" Will the battle have to be fought over again ? " he asked, smiling.

" I shall do my duty," she said coldly.

" Meaning that you will accept the banker ? "

" I shall accept him," she said.

He knew he was cruel, but he felt himself goaded to it. " Do you love him ? "

Ah, the look she cast upon him, — fear, horror, aversion, disgust, mingled with the most piteous supplication. His heart cried out in pity, but not yet would he relent.

" This fair, sweet shrine, which the divinities might gladly worship, thou wilt sell for his base gold ? "

" I will sell it, so as not to bring ruin upon this house."

" And if he caress thee ? "

" I shall fall dead at his feet, or go mad and strangle him."

" Hast thou no mercy, no pity for him ? "

" None.   He is the baser of the two."

" Have I not told thee that the same fate which overtakes thee overtakes me also ? "

" You will live — live to forget me — to marry some one who will be your equal — far more worthy of you than I am."

" I have told thee that at the decisive moment I will step forward and claim thee. Dost thou think I will not do it ? "

" You may do it. But I shall give the lie to all you say, and marry the other one on the spot — that he may take me away at once."

" Thou wilt have to reckon with my father first. When I speak thou wilt have to own the truth. He will not accept the sacrifice. Thou wilt precipitate matters without gaining anything."

" But I will not own the truth. I will lie, — lie so that the fiends shall laugh, and I will laugh with them."

He was silent a moment, holding her hot fevered hands still against his breast.

" Geliebte," he inquired, in his rich, soft voice, which made her clench her teeth in curbed agonies, " hast thou no regard for my sufferings ? Is love of so little worth to thee ? "

" It is of so much worth to me," she replied, " that I shall die for it. My life I throw in the balance that you shall continue to live in honor and fame, as you are living now. A little while — and all will have forgotten me. But you — ah, how many hopes and fears are bound up in your career ! Later, when grown wise in years and renown, you will look back upon this as a foolish episode, and bless me for having remained steadfast."

" Thou hast strung thyself up to so high a pitch," he observed, " that thou art no more capable of putting forth any reason or judgment than a patient under stress of delirium. Yesterday thou wert a dove, to-day thou art a vulture, clawing thy own heart and making carrion of mine. What now passes in thy fevered brain thou wilt

never do.   Mad people have to be restrained, and
that thou surely wilt be lest thou dost eternal
harm to thyself."

Before she could answer they heard Babbett
calling, —

"Jette! Jette, where art thou?"   She came
nearer, stumbling over herself in her haste. "Those
inside there," she said with a significant smirk,
jerking her thumb towards the house, "want thee.
He for whom thou waitest has come."

CHAPTER XXXIX

THE three years which Herr Goldman had consented to wait for the consummation of his happiness had not in any wise improved him.   Neither
his temper nor his habits were calculated to hide
the passing of old Father Time.   The gold rings
in his prominent eyes looked as if they had been
sent to the wash and found wanting; unsightly
bags puffed themselves beneath.   The brittle red
hair was brushed most carefully towards the crown,
trying to conceal somewhat its very marked baldness.   His cheeks were distended, fat, and flabby,
— of a decidedly unwholesome, underdone muffin
color.   His inclination to corpulency had increased
considerably; it was plainly to be seen that the
waistline would soon be lost in abdominal proportions.   Always below the medium height, this by
no means increased the grace of his appearance.
He was most faultlessly and elegantly dressed, in

the most perfect taste, which proclaimed at once the cultivated man of the world. He had plunged at once into all necessary details, and had settled all preliminaries with the Herr Pastor before Jette made her tardy appearance. Indeed, there had been very little left to settle. During the occasional visits the Herr Pastor had consented he should pay to the parsonage matters had been discussed between them often enough, " always provided," as the Herr Pastor had stipulated, " that the girl herself should consent!" And of this consent he was so sure that he looked upon it as a mere matter of form, — a mere preliminary which should bind her to him with the putting on of the betrothal ring, speedily to be followed by the wedding.

Much to his chagrin, he had to curb his eagerness to greet Jette until the evening meal was ready to be placed upon the table. A hundred pretenses she found to help Babbett in making the necessary additions for the unexpected guest, though the old woman protested most vigorously, declaring it a scandal and a shame to treat a waiting suitor so. It was just before the big lamp on the centre table was lit. The full moon had risen and was flooding the dusky gloaming with its silvery radiance. Close behind her came the doctor, and it must be confessed that the sight of the stalwart magnificent form following close upon her heels somewhat subdued Herr Goldman's rapturous greeting, causing his jealousy to flare up sky-high.

"My son," introduced the Frau Pastorin. Like the clang of joy bells one could distinctly trace the pride and joy in the tones of her voice. "Nay, dearest, why dost thou raise the protecting shade from thy eyes? Surely thou 'lt inflame them and retard their perfect recovery."

"Only for a moment, mamma. Out of proper respect to our guest. Give thyself no uneasiness. In a day or two the obnoxious thing can be discarded for good."

For a moment the two men looked at each other, the doctor's grandeur of height and perfect symmetry of form making a mockery of the other's squat, uneven proportions. To the jealous fury of the banker it seemed like a menace which the lightning-like glance of the brown eyes challenged. The green shade dropped over the eyes again.

"Herr Dr. von Feldern," said Herr Goldman, with perfect politeness. The Frau Pastorin started and convulsively pressed the hand of her husband. It was the first time she had ever heard her son addressed by his new dignity. She could hardly contain her rapture.

Oh, yes. Herr Goldman was well informed about everything concerning the Herr Doctor. Who did not know of his fame, so wonderfully and quickly acquired? A magnificent career awaited him. The Herr Pastor and the Frau Pastorin were indeed to be congratulated upon the possession of such a son. Very seldom — in fact hardly ever — had it been known that a young man had made his way so rapidly. It

was to be presumed that the Herr Doctor could
not be spared long from his extensive practice,
that Vienna would insist upon his speedy return.

"I have but just arrived," observed the doctor
cheerfully. "You see me quite in the hands of my
dear ones, who, I very much fear, will not allow
me to depart again."

"No, indeed," said the Frau Pastorin, passing
her hand over his curls with the peculiarly lingering fond mother touch. "Of exile there has been
enough; sad and sore the time has been. There
will be no returning to Vienna, Herr Goldman.
Our beloved Rhinegau will be large enough field
for him."

Herr Goldman glanced uneasily towards Jette.
She was passing in and out, helping to arrange
the dishes on the table. Was she never coming
to speak to him? Hardly had she greeted him.
While he was talking to that great hulking, overbearing blonde ass she had quietly slipped out
again. But patience! here was the evening meal:
she would sit beside him; he would press her hand
as a mute sign of his love and adoration. Come
what would afterwards he would speak to her, and
retire for the night happy, an engaged man.

But she did not sit beside him. In the most
amiable, the most nonchalant manner possible the
doctor occupied that place. Wholly unconscious
of the vindictive anathemas simmering against
him in the banker's breast, he rattled on in the
gayest, the most unconcerned tones. He drew the
furious man beside him into discussions about life

in Vienna, challenged comparisons, exchanged re-
miniscences, related anecdotes of prominent people
they both knew, and with that irresistible smile
of his administered such stinging doses of torture
that the other could have flown at his throat
and strangled him. And all the time he knew
that seated right opposite to them she could not
avoid looking at them both.. He was not conceited, but like every one with a particle of self-
esteem, he had a proper opinion of himself. And
he smiled as he looked down at the man beside
him — with the insolence of triumph.

That evening they sat longer at table than ever
before. It seemed as if their talk never would
end. Herr Goldman had traveled more exten-
sively than the doctor, — he was at home in every
large city of the world. Once drawn into discussion and reminiscence he, too, talked as he could,·
graphically and well. It was quite late when
finally they rose from table. Fritz brought out a
case of cigars, whose brand made Herr Goldman open his eyes.

"You are a good judge, I see," he remarked,
selecting one very deliberately ; "it is seldom one
has the chance to enjoy a whiff at one like these."

"A present," he said carelessly ; "I am not very
prodigal with them, even to myself, but on an
occasion like this one can afford to be generous."

His teeth glistened between the sweep of his
mustache as he smiled amiably and assisted the
banker to a light.

"Fetch thy guitar, Jettchen," requested the pas-

tor, as with his long lean legs stretched out before
him he rapturously inhaled the aroma of his cigar.
"Sing me my favorite Tyrolean song, which thou
hast denied me so long. Since Fritz came home
thou hast given up thy habit of lulling me to sleep
with it every night."

To the doctor's delight and surprise she com-
plied. His dear, blessed old papa! As if some
strange collusion prompted him to play thus perfectly into the son's hands.

As for her — she would sing, she would dance,
she would play, she would do anything to keep
Herr Goldman from presuming upon those little
familiarities to which, under the circumstances, he
doubtless felt himself entitled. She knew that the
doctor would not hesitate to take him by the scruff
of the neck and shake the life out of him. Ex-
.planations would be precipitated — at any cost this
must be avoided.

"Ich muss von meinen Bergen scheiden," she
sung, that most pathetic, most heart-stirring
farewell of the Alpine maid to her beloved moun-
tains. With the broad blue sash of the guitar
crossing her breast, matching in color the eyes
raised above, with fevered red burning in her
cheeks, the glossy black of her hair against the
white of her brow and neck, she made a most
enchanting picture. The anguish of parting was
in her voice, and she rang out the yodel with
an unrestrained fervor which was the despairing
cry of her overladen heart. Herr Goldman hung
upon her lips entranced. Heavens! how she had

improved. If his mother heard her, — the whole world should hear her, people surely would go mad over her.

" Let who will," said the pastor when she had finished, " cater to his artificial opera airs. Give me the Lied, — our dear Volkslied, in which the throb of the nation's heart is heard. Never do I love my fatherland so passionately, or appreciate the pain or suffering of exile so acutely, as when I hear one of these simple songs."

" Sing me my favorite," begged the Frau Pastorin, " ' Heart, my heart, why so sad ? ' It never fails to bring the tears to my eyes, and makes me feel sorry for those far away from home. When thou wert in Vienna, dear Fritz, I could not bear to hear it. But now, with thee seated opposite, the sting is removed and only its pathos remains."

She hesitated a moment. Surely they asked too much of her. This anguished cry of a homesick heart, — would not her own echo it, and she break down and lose her painfully acquired self-control?

" Hand me your guitar, Jettchen," requested the doctor. " Mamma shall hear me sing it. Let me see if I cannot rival you."

She took the broad ribbon from off her neck and handed him the instrument. A timid look of gratitude she shot at him from under her lowered lashes. Because of the shade she could not see his eyes. But his mouth smiled, and the warm fingers meeting for a moment hers expressed a world of encouragement and reassurance. He touched the strings, tuning one here, another there.

He played the prelude, and by that they knew that his was a master touch. Then his voice soared forth, — that magnificent, full, sonorous baritone, making the heartstrings of his listeners vibrate to its exquisite harmony. The tone picture they saw before them: the exile's agonized longing for his mountain home and all it held sacred and dear, the questioning despair, love, sorrow, and grief, until the last where the joy of a final resolve puts all misery at rest.

"Canst sing like that — thou?" said his mother when the last lingering notes died away. "Nay, what has come over thee? Never have I heard anything like it before."

He smiled, softly thrumming the strings, "'T was a great consolation to me," he said, "in my busy life in Vienna. It brought home and all it held dear to me nearer."

"Thy heart is in thy voice," remarked the pastor, whose eyes were wet; "one can see thou understandest the true meaning of our people's Lied."

The doctor played a short prelude. Then he commenced the beautiful passionate love song, the "Serenade," by Schubert. Softly he began, subduing his powerful voice to the most entrancing appeal. The moon, shedding her beams right into the window, stood still for a moment to listen. Surely the sly old thing had heard appeals of the kind ever since the beginning of man, but never one so sweet as this. Jette's soul writhed in agony, her sufferings were almost past endurance. Noiselessly she arose and stood by the long French window, pressing her aching eyes against the glass.

"Zittere Holde nicht," sounded the sweet reassuring refrain in lingering accents. Herr Goldman stumped across the room and joined her.

"Jettchen," he said in low, intense tones, "it was originally my intention to wait with what I have to say until to-morrow. But my love overwhelms me. Long and patiently have I waited for this moment which is to crown my life with the realization of my fondest hopes. You surely anticipate what I mean?"

She bent her head. Not for her life could she have spoken.

"The Herr Pastor and the Frau Pastorin have given their most gracious consent. In a month or so from now, God willing, I shall bear you hence as my beloved, adored, idolized wife. You will let me put the betrothal ring on your finger now, — here in their presence?"

Already he poised the costly glittering thing between his fingers. Taking her hand he led her into their midst. The Herr Pastor and the Frau Pastorin looked up smiling and expectant. The doctor flung the guitar from him so fiercely that the strings broke with a dissonant crash, and rose to his feet.

"Herr Pastor and you most gracious Frau Pastorin," said the banker in happy excitement, "we call upon you both to witness our solemn betrothal as my dear, dear beloved is now about to give her consent."

"Well, Jettchen," said the Herr Pastor with kind encouragement.

Now she looked up. Like a magnet the doctor's eyes drew her gaze to his. Disdain, scorn, contempt blended like lightning in the might of his glance. Back rushed the repressed blood in a torrent to her heart. The pride of the old Castilian race, whose last representative she was, tore the fever film from her tortured brain.

" Put back the ring," she said; " I can never, never marry you."

CHAPTER XL

FOR a moment there was stillness. She had withdrawn her hand from the banker's and held both hers behind her. His mouth half open, the wide, coarse nostrils flapping like wings, he stood as if transfixed to stone. The wide satin cap ribbons hanging either side of the Frau Pastorin's breast stirred with her agitated breath. The doctor's arms were folded across his chest; his lips relaxed their fierce tension. He came a little nearer to the girl, as if by reaching out his arm he could draw her to him. The Herr Pastor, stern and erect, came forward.

" What is this ? " he demanded. " Why hast thou waited till now to tell us thou wilt not have this man ? "

" 'T is an unheard-of scandal," cried the Frau Pastorin. Her face was flaming red; never had her eyes flashed in such anger. " Surely the girl knows not what she says."

"I cannot marry him," she answered, "I cannot. All these years have I striven hard, cheated myself, tried to believe as others told me, but I could not, *could* not feel differently towards him. Cast me from your midst, upbraid me, the worst that you can do to me I deserve. Nothing will seem hard, nothing after what I have suffered."

"Thou dear Heaven!" cried the Frau Pastorin, exasperated beyond control. "Spoilt thou hast been, indulged till thou art beyond all bounds. Thou suffered! when thou wert enjoying thyself and others were planning for thy happiness."

"Now she shall speak," interpolated the pastor sternly, "and take thou heed not to interrupt her. Too long has she been muzzled, it seems."

"Every one has desired nothing but what was good and best for me," said the girl, raising her imploring eyes to his face. "Only my own foolishness has been to blame. I feared to hurt his mother," she inclined her head towards the banker, "I feared to tell the Frau Pastorin, I had not the courage to tell you. I thought when every one was so much wiser than I surely matters would come round of themselves."

"What hast thou against him?" inquired the pastor.

"He is all that is good and kind in himself. I am sorry, — sorry to have brought this upon you, — sorry that he must hear the truth. I cannot like him. He inspires me with aversion, — with horror. More welcome would be a reptile's caress than the touch of his hand. He makes my flesh creep; my blood turns cold under the look of his eyes. From the first, when I knew him, I felt this, and the years have but added to it. My own cowardice is to blame that I have not told this long ago. Forgive me, — no one ever asked me, — all took it for granted that I ought to marry him. If only I had known some one to go to — to — to say what I felt " —

She could not say any more. With a cry like that of a hyena the banker flung himself before her.

"You shall be mine!" he screamed. "What matters if you hate me? Only be mine, marry me. Beat me, scorn me, deride me. Tear me with one hand, I will kiss the other. Father on high! If any one had told me such love could be rejected! At your feet will I grovel until you no longer say me nay. Only love me, love me if 't is ever so little, and let me love you."

She tried to free her dress from his grasp, but he retained fast hold of it and kept her prisoner there.

"Have I waited all these years," he shrieked, "fed upon my own vitals, put a powerful restraint upon my feelings, fortified myself with heroic patience to await the coming of this hour, that you should scorn me? Have you held me off with every device that coyness could invent, and nourished my blood with fever dreams, to make a maniac of me at last? Relent," he supplicated; "not cruel art thou, but cast in nature's fairest mould. Mercy have thou, as I know thy heart prompts thee to. Relent; be mine, be mine."

On his knees he dragged himself after her as she tried to escape, still retaining hold of her dress. He cried, he screamed, he tore his hair.

"I cannot live without thee," he sobbed ; "the fiends in hell would have compassion did they know what I suffer. Tricked, jilted, deceived," he shrieked, clutching his head, and bringing it violently against the floor. "Is it for this I have waited — to be made drunk with the weight of your scorn at last ? "

Some one opened the door behind her. She slipped through and it closed. The doctor placed himself before it.

CHAPTER XLI

THE poor Frau Pastorin! It is to be feared that of all she really suffered the most. Never having to endure a scene of violence, not in her wildest imaginings dreaming such things could be, she was fairly beside herself with consternation to see the well-mannered, suave banker transformed into an unreasoning animal. He raved, he cursed, he accused every one present of complicity in the shipwrecking of his suit. It required all the doctor's powerful strength to restrain him from battering in the door and pursuing Jette. He vowed to kill her, to kill himself, to kill everybody. Foaming at the mouth, his eyes rolling, the long finger nails driven into the flesh, his teeth clenched, stumping the length and breadth

of the room in wildest frenzy, like an enraged animal in its cage, he was enough to make one's flesh
creep — the veritable beast stripped bare of all
manhood. It was far into the night when, his
passion exhausted, he burst into weeping and wail-
ing, succeeded by a sullen fury. He wanted to
get away from the place, — then and there, — immediately. Not one minute longer would he tarry,
— he did not care whether the postmaster slept or
not, — the rustic hind would be sufficiently indem-
nified for his loss of rest, — an " extra post " he
would have on the spot though it cost a king's
ransom. He rammed his hat over his eyes, and
with a vindictive glare stalked forth into the night,
never to be seen any more within those walls
where peace and harmony had ever walked hand
in hand. It was not long before they heard the
rumbling of wheels, the tramping of the postilion's
horses, which told that all-powerful gold had for
once served the banker in good stead. He was on
his road home, and those listening to the fainter-
growing sounds of his departure looked at each
other in relieved thankfulness.

But now the calm, the self-contained Frau Pastorin collapsed, for the first time within the recollection of anybody, as indeed there had never
before been any need. Jette, cowering on the
attic stairs, heard her hysterical sobs and tearful
exclamations, and quaked with remorse and terror.
All night she had crouched there, listening fearfully to the tempest below. Ceaselessly she re-
proached herself — it was all her fault — never

would she dare to raise her eyes to any one again. She felt herself an interloper, a thing that would have to creep in and out, shunning people's glances — she had upset the whole household. And yet through it all there ran a sense of freedom, an exaltation, which made her breathe without the crushing sense that nearer and nearer her fate was closing in around her. Cautiously she crept down the stairs, and stumbled against the doctor, who, taking flying leaps, three at a time, jostled plump against her. The landing was dark, but he caught hold of her, and gave her a fervent kiss.

"I want my medicine chest," he said breathlessly. "Mamma is all upset — no wonder — that animal — pah! Art so lost without thy shepherd hast to come in search of him, eh?" He kissed her till she was breathless. "Art a famous girl, thou," he exclaimed exultingly; "hast the true ring of the steel in thy mettle. The courage to tell the truth — that is the grandest courage of all; and that thou hast it thou hast abundantly proved but now. Art fashioned just after my own heart. Hark, thou dearest. Art no more inclined for sleep than I am, I see. Soon dawn will be breaking, the sun will be up. Then wilt thou go to feed thy doves, and I will help thee. Thou dear, brave, sweet one. Now I will go to soothe mamma. A draught I have here which will bring her round in no time. She will sleep, and awaken calm and refreshed. No, no, thou canst do nothing for her — keep out of her way just now — leave all to me. Now here is my

chest. Up thou goest to plunge thyself in cold
water — rub vigorously, and see thou puttest on
other clothing — thou wilt feel like newborn, and
never miss the loss of thy night's rest."

He was down the stairs again in flying leaps,
swinging himself over the balustrades when halfway down. Soon he appeared, his mother lying
like an infant in his arms, her hands clasped
around his neck, her convulsive sobs stilled. The
Herr Pastor followed, with a carefully shaded
candle, so that its flicker should not fall upon
Mammachen's drowsy eyes. Babbett came close
behind, lugging the Herr Doctor's medicine chest.
She had no doubt that it contained nerves and
mustard, and all those outlandish things totally
unknown in a healthy household. Therefore she
eyed it with a great deal of awe, and carried it as
gingerly as if she were afraid the nerves and
mustard might suddenly jump out and fasten themselves upon her. A little while longer — and the
house was wrapped in profound repose. The
household would sleep late that day and without
fear of undue disturbance.

Now the sun came forth, vigorously dispersing
the cold, gray dawn. It slanted across the face of
the girl, who presently stole noiselessly down the
stairs. She had done as the doctor told her,
brushed out her hair till it glittered with its own
sleekness, and now looked as fresh and as fair as
if she had just stepped from the embrace of the
young god of day himself. She carefully shut
the kitchen door, and soon the welcome aroma of

freshly made coffee rose like incense to the grateful nostrils of the doctor, plunging around in his tub. It was not long before he had a cup of the refreshing beverage in his hand, while she cut innumerable tongue sandwiches, for he was hungry enough to eat her, as he declared with rapturous glances into the eyes in which he saw his heaven. He sat on Babbett's immaculate kitchen table, swinging his long legs, gulping down the scalding hot coffee, — sugarless, but creamed plentifully, — bit off immense pieces of sandwiches, while she sat beside him, quite close, for the table was not very large; but they did not mind a little crowding, for every bite he took she had to take one, and he held his cup to her lips and she put hers in exactly the same spot his lips had touched. Occasionally his droll remarks made her laugh, when he quickly clapped his hand over her mouth, so she should not wake the sleepers, and when she choked he kissed her till she was glad to regain her breath again.

They went out to feed the pigeons. There was a bench in the shadow of the poultry yard, and there they presently sat down. A dove came and fluttered down on her shoulder. She pursed up her lips, and the pretty creature pecked at them.

"Dost thou want to make me jealous?" he asked smiling; "is that thy privileged Giselle?"

"Giselle is dead," she said; "black Peter killed her just before you came, and our Minka killed him. I have no more pets now. 'T is too painful to love them and then to lose them. Never did I see such grief as her mate showed. For days he sat on the dovecote, desolate and alone. A pretty minx of a tumbler pigeon preened her feathers and made up to him. But he would have none of her, and when she renewed the attempt again and again he at last flew away, and has not come back since. Oh, doves can scratch I can tell thee."

"As thou hast shown, eh? Thou wilt cause me abundance of heartburn, that I foresee. Thou wilt tantalize and plague me and cause me no end of trouble. One is never sure of thee from one minute to the other. Thou wilt want to set up thy will against my own, and it will take all my strength to subdue thee. Thou art angel one moment, vixen the next. But such as thou art, I love thee. No other woman in the world could ever have held me captive so long. I would not have thee different, for always will there be something left in thee to conquer."

"Fritz," she asked hesitatingly, "thy father and mother — are they very angry with me?"

"What! after the nature of the beast revealed itself as it did the night before? Never will my father be sufficiently thankful for thy escape from such a man. Neither is this all. I have told papa some things which here, in this peaceful seclusion, he never dreamt of. I can tell thee I heard enough about the banker while at the university at Bonn. Make thou thy mind easy. Many a poor girl, whom he cajoled with his vile gold, hast thou avenged. There is no man along the Rhine with a worse reputation than he. Nemesis put a fine

rod in pickle with which to scourge him when she
selected thee for the task. The only thing thou
art blamed for is that thou didst not come out
with the truth long ago. Never mind. Thou
creditest me for having put in a good word for
thee ? ''

She looked at him gratefully, and he kissed the
dear eyes lifted to his.

"Now thou shalt be happy," he said, "and
gladden our hearts with thy old-time sportiveness.
Papa is only too glad to keep thee among us. A
sore trial it would have been to him to miss the
ministry of thy hands to his comfort. Mamma
may hold thee off a little, but in the end she will
come round. Men look at these things very differently from women. She was so proud in thy
prospective greatness. In the end thou hast only
exchanged one form of yoke for another. Dost
think it will sit very heavily on thee ? "

She looked down thoughtfully. "There is a
great task before me yet, which does not seem to
enter into thy reckoning. If the rabbi gives not
his consent " —

"That shall be seen to presently; before I go to
Bonn, where I go to establish myself, thou must
find out, and set all doubts at rest. There must
be an end to all this. I shall take a house — oh,
I know of a dear, sweet nest, a little removed
from the general bustle, where thou and I can be
happy, where the prying eyes of others cannot see.
There is a garden, where thou canst have thy
flowers and lay out thy strawberry and asparagus

beds. I will build thee an arbor, over which thou canst train a vine, just like the one we have here. There, in the summer, thou wilt bring me my coffee, and place thyself beside me and put thy arms around my neck, and sweeten my cup with the first sip. Ah! dost not think we shall be happy? "

He drew her blushing face to his, and blissfully kissed her lips.

" Tell me," he questioned presently, " if thou hadst not looked at me wouldst thou have let that man put the ring on thy finger? "

" Oh," she ejaculated with passion, " mayst thou never know the extent of suffering I went through the night before. I wrestled with my inclination so fearfully my mind almost gave way. I wanted to do my duty — God knows I was sincere enough. There seemed but one way out of this labyrinth — to sacrifice myself. At that moment my faculties were numbed; I seemed to have died and some one else to have taken my place. Thy glance restored me to myself; what I read there tore the veil from my eyes. Thy love I could have surrendered, but — thy contempt I would not have."

" Dost thou love me? " he whispered. It was the motif of every one of these delicious stolen interviews. He knew it sufficiently well, but like an insatiable gourmand he could never get enough. She put her cheek against his, and murmured softly as the cooing of a dove between his lips; " I love thee."

Thus it always was and always will be. Hope unfurls her radiant banner, and we confidently follow as long as it flutters in sight.

CHAPTER XLII

" THE owl has built her nest in the eaves of our roof," announced Babbett one morning at breakfast. Babbett had adopted a good many of the Rhineland peasant-folk superstitions, and held signs and omens in religious awe. Where the owl built her nest tradition had it death was sure to invade the household. The Frau Pastorin, like a stanch Pomeranian, had a healthy contempt for these little weaknesses.

" Well," she inquired sarcastically, " wouldst rather it was the stork?" The doctor laughed, and the Herr Pastor, looking archly at her, smiled. She had quite recovered her former good humor, though she was still very distant and dignified with Jette. She had kicked her good fortune like a football, she said, and would surely live to repent it. What did she expect would become of her? Here she was in the ripe bloom of her youth — the only dower she was possessed of. If she did not marry now, good-by to all prospects of a settlement in life. Now she would have to wait — wait till some poor man asked her; eventually she would be glad to marry any one. She certainly could not afford the luxury of becoming an old maid. For that one needed money; surely one had to live.

The good Frau Pastorin! She lamented, she prophesied all sorts of terrible things. She declared Jette's good looks would be the undoing of her. Such girls, if allowed to pick and choose, generally ended by doing the worst for themselves. And it was for this she had brought her up. It was in her blood — her foolish mother had done the same thing. She did not want any gratitude — Heaven forbid! She only wanted the girl to allow herself to be guided a little by those whose common sense she lacked so lamentably herself. In fact Jette was in disgrace, and she surely let her feel it.

A week had gone by since the banker's last visit which had resulted so disastrously to himself. The doctor had discarded his shade; he declared his eyes perfectly cured. This went a great way to console the Frau Pastorin, who rejoiced exceedingly. In a few days he would go to Bonn to make the necessary arrangements for establishing himself. On his return she made up her mind to speak to him. Surely now he would want a wife to keep house for him. Why did not Thekla come back? For the last year she had lived with her father in Athens. What interest was there delving after the antiquities of dead and gone days, when a brand-new joy awaited one? Oh, only let him wait! matters should be settled now for good and all.

It was a cheerful sunny morning when Jette started for the little town where the synagogue was situated in which she had worshiped since

she came to the parsonage. Under the pretense
of buying a few necessities for herself and the
household, she had readily obtained permission
from the Frau Pastorin to go. The doctor was to
leave in a day or two, and he had insisted upon
some certainty before doing so. He would have
preferred to accompany her, but she vehemently
disclaimed against the imprudence of such a step.
She knew the rabbi, and stood in great awe of him.
The doctor was hopeful and sanguine, a state of
mind she by no means shared. He watched her
graceful, erect figure as, with the dancing, gliding
step, so peculiar to her, she was about to disappear round the bend in the road. For a minute
she stopped, turned her bright face towards him,
and blew him a kiss with her arch, happy smile.
Then she was gone, and the sunlight went with
her.

How beautiful she was! Who would not adore
her, the innocent light-hearted girl! What royal
dignity there was in the poise of her head; with
what majesty she carried herself! There was a
lightness, an elegance, about her movements which
her occasional visits to Cologne had not alone im-
parted. The ancient lineage from which she
sprung showed plainly in the slight aristocratic
hauteur of her manner, mingled with the most
gracious cordiality. She was a treasure beyond
compare, a pearl without price. There was no
other like her, and so the whole world should own.
Every one would envy him his good fortune; people should feel themselves honored by coming into

contact with her. But to very few would he
accord the privilege — he wanted her for himself
alone, to love, to idolize, to cherish. Ah, they would
be happy : the angels in heaven should envy them.
Who talked about paradise ? surely this world
was paradise enough. There were a few difficulties in the way, of course ; his manhood would be
worth very little were he not strong enough to
wrestle with them. In the end they would be overcome, and then — forward ! march ! straight to the
goal.

Thus mused the doctor, as with his book upside
down he sat under the old sycamore-tree awaiting
her return. He was happy in anticipating his
future happiness. Who shall grudge it him ? Is
not the greatest good in life gained this way ? The
birds sang, the pure bracing air sent renewed blood
with a joyous tingle through the veins. Nature
smiled, and her gracious mood was infectious.
The dreamy smile on the lover's lips had a portion
of heaven in it. He crossed his arms across his
chest and closed his eyes. But he still dreamed
on.

It was not long before Minka came along. The
great tabby came in search of her young mistress.
She prowled around the doctor, then stretched her
full length at his feet. So the two watched and
waited. The morning wore on. Soon the mid-day
meal would be ready, though to-day it had been
set an hour later. The doctor had said he was
going to make some botanical researches, and could
not be back till then.

The great cat rose and rubbed herself against the doctor's legs. She purred vigorously, and by that he knew some one was coming. His dreamy content vanished, he started to his feet. He had hardly done so when Jette was upon him.

But not as she had left him. The happy, joyous expression had fled from her face, her eyes were set and glassy in their despair. His heart fell. He knew before she spoke what had happened. Then a great anger rose within him. Let priests rave as they might — interpret the Divine will according to their own perverted intelligence — nothing should come between these two whom plainly God had intended for each other. He would have drawn her to him; but she repulsed him. He knew why she did it, and it increased his wrath to fever heat.

"Sit thee down," he said, "and rest thyself. Thou hast walked too fast, dearest. See, thou art all overheated."

"'T was not half fast enough for the fever of my mind," she exclaimed; "my feet were like wings, though my heart is turned to stone in my bosom. Fritz, dear Fritz! it can never, never be."

She wrung her hands, as if the fingers would crack. Her hot dry eyes looked at him in the most heartrending despair. He set his teeth, and the frown she knew so well — the resolute, obstinate frown, when he set his determined will against that of another — appeared upon his face.

" Let me see if my love will not prove stronger
than the wiles of priestcraft. Out with it. What
did he say ? "

" Just what I foreboded — what I told thee
from the first. And more. Oh ! if thou couldst
have heard him. It seems — it seems that this unfortunate story — thou knowest about the banker
— has reached him, and he put his own construc-
tion upon it, long before I spoke. Then his anger
knew no bounds. He said I was a renegade, an
apostate — I dare not repeat to thee all. Oh,"
she cried with an impassioned gesture, " the bare
recollection withers me."

" Fling off this yoke, wash thyself clean of these
ragged remnants of a mediæval age. See how
gloriously the sun shines ! Would God have made
it so, that a race of slaves should flourish in its
benignant rays ? "

" Thy father taught me to respect my religion ;
more scrupulous was he in exacting its requirements than if I had grown up in the midst of its
adherents. I reverence, I worship it. Wouldst
thou have me fling his own teachings in his face ?
Then, indeed, the world were turned upside down,
and I lost in it."

" Thou art enlightened enough to see as I do.
If there is aught in thy religion which cannot
reconcile itself with thy love, then indeed the spirit
of the Almighty is not in it. Above all things
did he want that we should love one another. If
there is crime in that, be the consequences on my
head — not on thine. Be thyself — strong in the

might of thy own heart. Wilt thou not find compensation in my love for thee?"

"Dearest, best beloved," she sobbed, "I cannot drag thee down to ruin. The world will scorn thee for marrying the banned Jewess. I will be thy handmaid — thy slave — do with me as thou wilt — but I cannot, cannot marry thee."

So this whole miserable business would have to be gone over again. He clenched his hands, his brow darkened.

"I will not have thee mar thy fair cheeks with these bitter drops," he said fiercely; "they sear the heart and leave it scarred. Heavy indeed is the task thou settest me — the stanchest heart might well break under it. A way there must be found out of this — the quickest dispatch cannot be quick enough to end this wear and tear of suspense. I thought to take a light heart with me, that hope might guide my endeavors. The day after to-morrow I depart, and fear not but while I am gone there shall be found a final settlement to this question. Now sit thee down and compose thyself. I care not how soon my parents will know of this — indeed they shall be approached very soon — but mamma is not quite strong yet; she would be upset all over again."

He kissed the tears from her face, and breathing upon his handkerchief, gently dabbed her eyes with it to eradicate the telltale traces. But his brow was moody and stern — he did not smile again

CHAPTER XLIII

"THERE is sickness at the Wildhof," said the Frau Pastorin. "Hans's wife is down with gastric fever — I must go and see her. Pack thou a basket with wine and jellies, Babbett. Right after dinner we will start."

"May I not go with you?" asked Jette timidly.

"No," said the Frau Pastorin curtly; "I prefer Babbett to come along. Thou canst prepare the evening meal, so it will be ready when we come back."

Babbett grumbled at the long walk, for her poor old legs were not as supple as they used to be, and she would very much rather Jette had gone. But Jette was not out of disgrace yet, and the Frau Pastorin lost no opportunity in letting her feel it. So she stayed behind, and watched them sadly as they went down the hill towards the Wildhof. The doctor had gone, and the void lay heavy on her heart. He was the sum and substance of her happiness; that she knew now. Without his strong arm to guide her she would drop by the wayside. What terrible destiny was that, which had flung her in his very path, just to show her how perfect life could be, and then to mock her by withholding the cup, placed so temptingly to her lips. Dark and dreary the vista of her days stretched, like an arid waste before her, with never an oasis in sight. But he, he would

not submit to it. Her heart quaked as she ac-
knowledged to herself that against his strong
aggressive will she could not hold out forever;
either she would perish or — further she dared
not think.

She gave the Herr Pastor his coffee when he
woke up from his nap, and brought him his long-
stemmed Fatherland pipe. The large china bowl
she cleaned out carefully, and placed the pretty
chamois tobacco-bag she had embroidered for him
within his easy reach. Everything she did was
gracious and sweet, " just like herself," the Herr
Pastor thought.   He took a fond pleasure in
watching her hands twinkle like white asters in
and out among the china cups. When she inclined her head a little to one side, looking up at
him with her eyes of pansy blue, and asked the customary question " More cream? " he beamed upon
her so brightly that the tears rose to her eyes. It
was as if the doctor looked at her, the same keen,
penetrating, but velvety soft brown eyes — those
dear eyes she loved so well. Dear, good old man!
never had he had any but kind, cheerful words for
her; his admonitions had been benedictions. And
she was deceiving him — sorrow and tribulation
was she about to bring to his whitening hairs.
What would he say? Would he not curse the
day he had carried her in his arms to his home —
that home she had already profaned with her
deceit?

It was already quite dark when at length the
Frau Pastorin and Babbett were descried in the

distance, wearily trudging along. Jette flew to
meet them, took the empty basket from Babbett,
and offered her sturdy young shoulder to the Frau
Pastorin to lean upon. The latter ungraciously
availed herself of it — she seemed thoroughly tired
out. But as soon as the Herr Pastor came up,
whose step was not quite as agile as the young
girl's, she took her hand off her shoulder and
slipped it through his arm.

" Those at the Wildhof should not have allowed
thee to walk back," he said; " 't was far too much
for thee to trudge both ways."

" There is work enough at the Wildhof," she
replied, " without my adding to it. The mistress
is far worse than the nature of the illness would
warrant. Two of the children are down since last
night. Hans is in terror the illness might spread
throughout the household. I did what I could for
them, but that was not much. 'T would be best
if he got one of the Sisters from the convent at
Neustadt to properly care for them. He promised
he would do it, if they did not mend soon."

" I must go over to-morrow," observed the pastor anxiously; "indeed I had no idea the sickness
would spread. Of course they must have proper
care: without it they cannot get better. Hans is
not a poor man; he can very well afford to have
his family properly looked after. I will rub it
into him, never fear."

" May I go?" begged Jette. " I know the ways
of the Wildhof well; I could be of some use until
somebody comes."

" Thou 'lt do nothing of the kind," said the Herr Pastor with decision ; " the young take infection far more easily than older people. I only hope that mamma and our good Babbett have taken no harm."

" Nonsense," said the Frau Pastorin ; " never since my infant days have I had an illness, neither has Babbett as far as I know. What sayest thou, Babbett ; we are far too well seasoned to begin in our old age, eh ? "

She laughed, and sank gratefully into her large easy-chair when they reached the sitting-room. Jette would have removed her bonnet and silk scarf, but she repulsed her, and let the Herr Pastor do it.

" Now I want nothing but something to drink," she said, " and then I will go to bed. Thou canst look after things to-night, Henriette ; let Babbett rest herself. Thou dear Heaven ! A few years since I could have walked twice the distance and gone to a ball afterwards. Surely I must be growing old."

Slowly she went up the stairs, affectionately leaning upon her husband. Five, six days went by — then a special messenger was hastily dispatched to Bonn. The Frau Pastorin and Babbett had taken the fever.

CHAPTER XLIV

Now it was that Jette in some measure repaid
the love and care that had been lavished upon her.
Alert, vigilant, ever on the watch, her noiseless
footfall went to and fro between the sick-beds.
It was not long before the pastor was stricken.
The doctor pronounced it an especially virulent
form of typhoid, and inveighed against the stupid-
ity of the local physician, who, under the guise of
gastric fever, had allowed the sickness to spread.
Soon over the whole village the dark angel of
death stalked abroad. Day and night the tall
erect form of the doctor could be seen going from
one house to another. People kissed his hands
and dropped many a tear upon them, for he carried consolation and comfort wherever he went.
All the time he could snatch from his own beloved
ones he devoted to others, for he knew he left
them in good hands. For three weeks, night and
day, neither he nor the girl who watched at home
had time to change their clothing. And with it
all, she was concerned for his comfort, always had
the nourishment ready with which it was necessary
to keep up his strength. His efforts to get some
sort of help for her proved unavailing. Scarcely
a household was there that was not stricken, and
the Sisters at the convent had their hands full
among the poor. Every morning and night he
anxiously scanned his faithful nurse, but she had
the whole capital of her young untried strength

to draw upon, and she did it unsparingly. The healthy, vigorous blood in her veins withstood the fierce onslaught of the dread disease, and as if daunted by her fearless courage it reluctantly passed her by. Reluctantly, it seems; for one morning, when all were out of danger and on a fair road to recovery, the doctor, after drawing her into the light and anxiously looking at her as usual, peremptorily ordered her off to bed.

"Go thou," he said, "this instant. Sleep; do not be in haste to rise. Strip off thy clothing and instantly to bed. Sleep the whole day. I will take thy place and not stir hence until thou comest back."

But she demurred. "Thou art in worse need of rest than I," she said; "go thou first. To-morrow"—

"Wilt thou do as I tell thee?" he commanded. "What will become of our dear ones if thou also succumbest? What will become of me with the additional burden of thee flung upon my hands?"

This convinced her, and she went. Faint and dizzy she felt, her throat was parched and hot. She stopped for a moment on the landing and looked out upon the Frau Pastorin's flower-garden. Desolate and neglected it looked, the trim, neatly kept beds overrun with rank weeds. Scarcely a flower could be seen, and those which did rear a drooping head looked miserable and forlorn. This sight she could not bear. Swiftly, with her noise-less footfall, she ran down the stairs, opened the kitchen door, and slipped out. The sun was hot, though it was already September. She snatched the kerchief from her shoulders, flung it over her head, and commenced to work as if for a wager. She never heeded how the time went, but with the heat and the haste the perspiration streamed down her body, drenching every particle of her clothing as if she were dipped in the brook. And as soon as one bed was cleared she fetched water from the pump and sprinkled her beloved rescued, first gently, then generously, until they laughed in the sun, invigorated and refreshed. Her haste was so great that her breath came in quick gasps, and ever faster she worked until the afternoon sun looked in at the west window. Then she staggered to her feet, — her limbs were stiff from crouching down so long, but the work was done. Proudly, as never victorious general surveyed a vanquished battlefield, did she look down at the heaps of uprooted weeds at her feet, at the fair smiling garden, and she laughed with content. Then she remembered the doctor, — what would he say if he found out how she had obeyed him? Hot, perspiring, begrimed, she yet felt happy; the lassitude which made her limbs feel like lead had given way to a springy elasticity, her throat felt dusty, but no longer parched. She would go and rub herself well down, make herself clean and sweet with much needed fresh clothing, and above all eat something, for she felt an appetite as ferocious as the traditional plough-boy's. Upstairs on the landing she came face to face with the doctor.

"Father in heaven!" he ejaculated, and could

say no more. He stared at her, — her grimy, perspiring face, her disheveled hair. " What hast thou done? " he said.

She drew him to the window, and pointed to the garden. A low, happy laugh came from her lips.

" Does it not look beautiful? Now thy mother's eyes will not be offended when she sits up and looks out of the window. Dost see the heap of weeds? I wanted to cart them away, but I feared it would take too long. I am so hungry I could gnaw the banisters."

" Hast been down there all day? " he asked, "and hast got thyself in this state from overwork? Thou hast not a dry thread on thee. Hasten, hasten, all thou canst to put dry clothing on thee. If thou art not down again very soon I will come up to thee."

But he smiled, and there was a look of ineffable happiness on his face when afterwards he said to her, " 'T was the wisest thing thou couldst have done. The fever was about to grip thee, but the plentiful perspiration carried the poison away from thee. Thank God for the lucky impulse. But no more must thou disobey me. Matters may not turn out so luckily next time."

CHAPTER XLV

THE Herr Pastor was now quite convalescent, and Babbett commenced to go a little about the house again. It was Jette's task to nourish the fever-drained veins with all sorts of strengthening dainties, which had to be doled out very carefully. The Frau Pastorin's recovery was not so very rapid, as her craving for food was insatiable, and in spite of the utmost vigilance she often contrived to abstract little portions from Babbett's or the Herr Pastor's plate, which considerably retarded her recovery. The doctor enjoined upon Jette the absolute necessity of carrying the key to the pantry and the meat-safe continually about her person, as a relapse into her former condition might prove fatal to his mother. He implored her to restrain herself for a little, just a little while longer, until it was safe to indulge in a generous diet again. The gentle old pastor and poor old Babbett were tractable enough. The former was well aware that the chief danger of a typhoid-recovered patient lay in overeating. And as for Babbett, she looked upon the doctor as an inspired being, whose word was no more to be doubted than that of the gospel itself. But the Frau Pastorin was as irritable and irrational a patient as ever tried the patience of doctor and nurse. To her son she listened in rebellious silence, but all the vials of her wrath she emptied upon Jette. She called her a deceitful, double-dealing, under-handed traitress, who aimed at taking the upper hand in everything. What, was she not mistress in her own house! Immediately, this instant, let the keys be given up to her. She demanded to see Babbett, and when the old woman hobbled up, commanded her to take charge of the pantry as usual, and bring her mistress something, anything, no matter what, to eat. When the maid declared it was against the Herr Doctor's orders, she became almost ferocious in being balked in her desire for food. She cried, she implored, she upbraided Jette for wanting to starve her, so that she could become mistress of the parsonage. It was very hard to remain steadfast under these trying circumstances, especially as she had to battle alone, the doctor having been obliged to attend a very important consultation in Bonn. She herself had urged him to go. The two other convalescents gave her no trouble, and as for his mother, she felt herself strong enough to bear her reproaches, providing she made fair progress towards recovery.

The little sleep Jette could indulge in at night was always deep and sound, as her duties were very trying and harassing. She still occupied the couch in the Frau Pastorin's room. Till the doctor's return she would not leave her alone at night. The large, old-fashioned mahogany bedstead, with its fantastic carving, and piled high with the swelling feather bed, stood in the middle of the airy, well ventilated room. On a little table near by a rushlight burnt dimly, shrouding the corners in ghostly gloom. That the keys of the pantry and storeroom should be in safe keeping both day and night, Jette wore them fastened to a ribbon around her neck. One night she thought she felt a fumbling at her nightgown, but as it was only the drowsy feeling of half-consciousness, she still slept on. Of a sudden she sat up and listened. She looked towards the bed. The swelling down cover was just as she had arranged it around the invalid, before retiring herself. Minka came with tail erect and tiptoed towards the door. With a rush Jette flung off the bedclothes. The intelligent animal had never once left the sick-room, and whenever Jette had been obliged to leave it for a moment, she had always scratched at the door and mewed as soon as any of the invalids stirred. Now it was slightly open — she leaped towards the bed — it was empty. Her hand went up to her neck — the ribbon was there, but the keys were gone.

The girl seized the light and bounded down the stairs. The kitchen door was wide open, but the door of the pantry was shut. She tried the handle — it was locked. Through the chinks streamed the faint flicker of a candle — low murmurings mixed with laughter came from within.

"Open," she said; "if you believe there is a God above you, open. You shall have all you want — only open for the sake of your dear ones."

"Aha," laughed the Frau Pastorin; "art over-ready, now I have outwitted thee. Certainly I will open, — in my own good time. If thou couldst only see how I am feasting. Art a generous provider, thou. Aha, aha! not until, like the vampire, I have glutted and glutted again, will I come forth, though the night wind blows chilly, and I was in such haste to get down I would not stop to throw anything over me."

The girl flung herself against the door. It was

stout and durable, and would not yield. She dared not rouse the rest of the household : in the chill night air they would get their deaths. By the time she summoned help from without the mischief would be done — as probably it already was now. Again and again she hurled herself against the door; her shoulder bled, her body was bruised from head to foot. She begged, she prayed, she implored.

"Alas," she said, "have you no regard for your son? Think of the terrible work you are preparing for him anew. Now all will have to be fought over again, worse, far worse, than before. If you want to live," she cried in anguish, "open the door. You have flung yourself into your grave, and you do not know it."

"Not because thou biddest me will I open," said the Frau Pastorin, "but because I am glutted full."

She turned the key and threw back the door. There she stood in her long chemise and night-jacket. It had been necessary to shave off her plentiful fair hair, and she looked grotesque and horrible in the extreme, with her frilled nightcap askew on her bare skull. She shivered so her teeth rattled in her head. But she looked at the girl in mingled triumph and gratified malice.

"That was a royal meal," she said; "now thou canst do what thou likest. I feel as if I had satisfied my appetite for all time to come."

Jette's sobs were so heartrending she could hardly hurry the unfortunate woman up the stairs.

The doctor had left ample directions with her in case of anything unforeseen happening. But anything like this had of course never entered into his calculation. Hurriedly and swiftly the girl did what her own good sense and the means at hand prompted her to do. Then she flung a warm wadded gown over herself, thrust her bare feet into slippers, locked the door from the outside, and sped down the village street to rouse the postmaster. A special mounted messenger was to start for Bonn immediately, without once drawing rein until he had put the note she now hastily scribbled into Herr Dr. von Feldern's own hand. Then she flew back to the house and up to the sick-room. The Frau Pastorin lay exactly as she had left her. Only now she was burning hot, and her tongue heavy with the mutterings of delirium.

Late the following night an "extra post," the postilion's horses covered with foam, dashed up to the parsonage door. The doctor came not alone; he brought Professor von B——, the most noted medical expert along the Rhine and lecturer at the Bonn University, with him. They immediately ascended to the sick-room. One glance they gave at the patient, then their eyes met. The same look was in both. The Frau Pastorin was past all help: no skill on earth could save her.

More as a matter of form and in deference to his distinguished colleague, the eminent professor examined the patient, looked at the medicines, asked some questions as to what brought on this dangerous relapse, looked professionally important, and gravely retired with the doctor into the adjoining room, where they conferred long in low, hushed tones. Then they went downstairs together, the eminent professor stepped into the waiting post-chaise, sympathetically pressed his distinguished colleague's hand, and turned his face homeward, leaving sorrow and grief behind him.

The news that the Frau Pastorin was hardly likely to survive the night had to be broken to the Herr Pastor. There was no one but the son to do it. When the father looked upon his ashen face and trembling lips, there was no need of telling. The fiat had gone forth: the loving, lovable, cherished companion who had sweetened life's journey for him for the last twenty-eight years was about to leave him solitary and alone. He bowed his whitened head, but not quite yet in submission. The recent severe illness had left him weak.

He knelt beside the bed, there where the candle's faint light lit up the beloved face in the strongest relief. The son sat at the other side, holding the dear, dear hand which had ever lovingly caressed him, watching the flickering pulse, his ear anxiously strained to catch her breathing. Babbett knelt at the foot of the bed, and incessantly prayed under her breath. Jette, her face rigid in despair, leaned against the head of the couch, her fingers mechanically interlacing each other. She was in an agony of remorse and self-reproach — yet she was perfectly blameless for what had happened. She had never witnessed a death-bed — she trembled with awe as nearer and nearer approached the Great

Unknown. Minka crouched at the feet of her dying mistress and would not be driven away. Her great eyes gleamed, her fur stood on end.

All night long they watched. Towards morning the Frau Pastorin, who had lain all the time in a stupor, suddenly spoke.

"My poor Jette," she said, "thou canst not toil up the mountain alone. Give me thy hand, I will help thee."

Her voice was perfectly strong, but it had a strange sound, as if spoken in the far distance. Babbett gave a terrified start and looked towards the girl.

"She is calling thee," she said in a low, trembling whisper. "The end of the woe is not yet."

Jette was so intensely moved she hardly could stand. For the first time in her life the dying woman called her by the name she was generally known by. It was startling, just as her spirit hovered already on the border-land! Whether it similarly affected the rest in that grief-stricken hour is hard to tell. But the doctor stretched' out his hand and clasped her hand; and so she stood beside him till the end.

When the first faint gray of dawn streaked the darkened sky, it came. A bright sunbeam, just darting into life, caught up her spirit and winged it up to her God.

CHAPTER XLVI

THE same cause which had resulted in the Frau
Pastorin's death kept the fever raging in the village. The convalescent patients were imprudent,
or their attendants did not restrain them sufficiently in their craving for food. There were con-
tinual relapses, which almost always ended fatally.
It was felt at the parsonage that, unless matters
were taken hold of with a strong hand, this awful
state of affairs might be prolonged indefinitely.
The white-haired pastor, leaning on his staff, went
forth to exhort, to admonish, to comfort his people. No consideration for himself deterred him.
The beloved partner of his life was gone; his
own sun had set. But what remained of vitality
and strength he was glad to expend in the welfare of others. It was a welcome opportunity to
smother his own grief. The doctor sacrificed his
own interests at Bonn in his determined efforts to
stamp out the dread disease in his native place.
Only one there was for whose safety he trembled.
But she seemed to bear a charmed life. She went
from one fever-stricken house to another, indefatigable in her exhaustless young strength to second his efforts. Long years after, when the history of her life had passed into a reminiscence,
hoary-headed grandfathers told the story of her
angelic devotion to the little prattlers on their
knees, ever in whispers, throwing many an awestruck glance behind them, as, indeed, they had

good reason to do. And so by the grace of God, who surely had imbued these three earnest souls with a portion of His own divine spirit, the menacing spectre, stalking abroad, was finally exorcised and laid.

Lieschen, sweet little Lieschen, was one of the last to be stricken. The ugly, useless lump of flesh calling itself her mother was beside herself with terror. Strangely enough, sloth and sloven though she was, the fever till now had passed her household by. Now she trembled with terror for her own life, and could not be induced to go near the child. It was Jette who hung over the little crib, kept the covering over the restless limbs, and did grim battle with the fell destroyer, hovering for many days dangerously near. The great hulking lout of a father sat always at the other side of the bed, his dry, grief-stricken eyes fastened upon the sufferer's face. He was as grateful as a dog if allowed to do her the least service; his lumbering step was hushed, the touch of his clumsy hand as gentle as that of love. Never devotee watched the lips of his oracle as eagerly as Lieschen's father those of the doctor. He came often, for between himself and the devoted nurse there was a fixed determination to save the life of the sweet darling, provided human skill could do it. Everybody predicted that now surely the child would die. And as on so many former, though far less perilous occasions, the little one put the discomfited prophets to rout by pulling through gloriously. Well, they said, it was surely unheard of. Now, indeed, a

tragic end was in store for her. It would have
been better had she peaceably gone then.

When the child was quite well and out of
danger, Gret came back. She made a great outcry about her poor blessed darling, volubly took
charge of her herself, and with a great deal of
effrontery and impudent brag, claimed the credit
of her recovery. Doctor and nurse smiled quietly
at each other, and gave all further necessary directions to the father. Between his long anxious
watch and the uproar of his wife's return, he
was too bewildered to upbraid her. However, they
could depend upon his dog-like devotion to pre-
vent harm to his recovered daughter.

Therefore as from chaos order is evolved, so
matters fell into their usual routine again. With
the old year the fever fled and was heard of no
more. In some houses there was mourning, in
others rejoicing. 'T is the unalterable trend of
fate, and will be so to the last. At the parsonage
a great quiet reigned. The poignancy of the first
grief had been swallowed up in the anxiety for the
common weal ; now that this was ended, lassitude
weighed down the spirits of its inmates. The void
in their hearts was in keeping with that in the
house. With trembling lips the Herr Pastor looked
at the empty chair beside his own. Sometimes
he would pass his hand over the arms, stretching
themselves into empty space, with a loving, lingering touch, as if she were there, and smiled back at
him with her clear, truthful eyes. Babbett slunk
about with lagging steps. The mistress whom she

had romped with in childhood, accompanied to the
altar, and left home to serve, lay at rest in the
little churchyard over yonder, where the hill dipped
gently towards the horizon. The faithful old peasant woman could not rally from the shock.   Her
strength would not come back.   Sadly she went
about the house, glad that younger, more vigorous
hands relieved her of most of its duties.

The doctor went back to his busy life at Bonn.
Often he wrote to the lonely white-haired father
at home, whose sole prop and comfort he now was.
As often as he could he came.   Hurried, flying
visits they necessarily were, but upon the loved
ones at home they acted like an exhilarating tonic.
The life and stirring buoyancy of the outer world
he brought with him; his manner, though still subdued, inspired them with hope and courage.   The
dreary winter passed, and a most glorious spring,
with floods of sunshine and the happy song of
birds, rejoiced sorrowing hearts once more.   Dear
mother Nature kissed the brow of her sorrowing
children, and chased away what there was of grief
and troubled thought with her loving maternal
touch.   Now one could live out of doors again;
field, orchard, and garden resounded to the merry
crunch of the plough, and the cheerful tingle of the
cow-bell was heard once more.   The Herr Pastor
armed himself with spade and shovel, and stole
forth to the grave of his dear one, and made of it
a bed of glorious fragrance.   Nowhere did roses,
mignonette, and violets bloom in more luxurious
sweetness.   Jette, seeing him thus occupied, let

him alone. He was jealous of the least interference; no one should touch anything on that beloved resting-place but himself. "No one," he declared. "But when I lie beside her and share her last long sleep, then thou mayest come and plant a rosebush on my grave. I shall know thy footfall and rejoice that it is thy hands which tend me as lovingly in death as they have done in life. Surely a kind fate brought thee to my door, that thou mightest be the comfort of my old age. What now should I do without thee?"

The tears were in her eyes as she took the staff from his weary hands and knelt down to unbutton his gaiters. Formerly he would not allow her to do it, but insisted she should call Babbett.

"Babbett is old," she protested; "her back is stiff and her hands tremble. Grief-stricken and work-worn she is, and now she shall rest. What comes hard to her is most loving servitude to me. Let me have the privilege, and say no more about it."

"How like the dear mamma thou art," he remarked, smiling. "In all thy manners and ways dost thou remind me of her. Most peremptory in her loving solicitude, she was always careful for the comfort of others, herself a delight to the eye, with a gift to impart, with a touch here and a touch there, creating the order and neatness which is the soul of a household and brings harmony to the weary mind and rest to the tired limbs."

He took his coffee from her hand, and gulped it slowly with dreamy contentment.

"Everything," he said, "is as it always was, — everything. Only she is gone."

So it was all the time. Never could he forget her. Not once was she ever absent from his mind.

"Thou art treading exactly in her footsteps," he continued. "It would rejoice her to see how good and useful thou hast become. But thou must not do overmuch. Of late I have fancied thou art not as light-hearted as thou hast a right to be. Thy cheek is not as blooming as at thy age it should be. Be merry, my child. Sing, laugh, as is thy birthright. 'T was always music in my ears, and like the praise of the lark 't will be a welcome sound now. The roses bloom for thee now, and thou must haste and pluck them before they fade."

But it was not grief for the death of the Frau Pastorin alone which kept Jette quiet and subdued. Despair lay heavy on her heart. The future held no more brightness for her; she seemed to be groping about in the dark, without any prospect of reaching the light. The end of the summer had come; September, with its fulfillment of golden promise, was at the door. A few weeks would see the end of the first year of mourning. During all this time the doctor had not spoken one word of love to her, yet his eyes, hanging upon her every movement with a lover's rapture, told her plainly enough that his heart was hers, unalterably and forever.

At the end of the month he came on one of his short flying visits. Dr. von Feldern was a very

busy man now, with a large, growing practice which
the reputation preceding him had very materially
assisted to build up. Besides this, people liked
him exceedingly; which was not to be wondered
at, as the first requisite of a physician is plenty of
personal magnetism, a manner thoroughly sure of
its subject, and these Dr. von Feldern possessed
in a very marked degree. Then he was so full of
pulsing, buoyant life; there was a grandeur in his
superabundant vitality and strength, so that the
first thought of a patient, no matter how depressed
with illness, on seeing him was, "Surely in the
presence of so much life I cannot die." The clasp
of his hand on a patient's wrist sent a stream of
renewed vitality through his perished veins, comforting him with the assurance that he would re-
cover, and this, no one will deny, is a first and
very important step towards convalescence.

The doctor had the faculty of inspiring every
one with complete confidence in himself. Arguments, however plausibly built up beforehand, fell
to pieces before his vigorous, aggressive onslaught.
One glance of his keen eye demolished more mental calculations than one could build up in a year.
Against his strength and sound common sense there
was no appeal. What the mind yet cherished of
rebellion, the heart was unable to support. His
irresistible charm of manner, his bright, joyous
spirit, fascinated and subdued all.

Jette often thought sadly how enviable indeed
her lot would be did no impediment stand in the
way to unite her life with his. The world over,

there were very few men like him — in her estimation none. Like a giant, he towered high
above a puny race, great alike in his strength and
his humility. Not a bit was he vain or conceited,
a child was not more perfect in its simplicity.
The adulation showered upon him he took as a
matter of course, never caring whence it came so
long as he was successful in what he undertook to
do. With military precision he marched to the
post of duty, allowing no difficulties to stand in
the way. There was something to be done—and
he did it.

On a balmy, soft September morning, when summer joys still lingered in the air, he strolled out
into the garden, which had been his mother's, to
seek her. Most religiously was it kept in order ;
the rosebushes glowed in luxurious splendor, the
rosemary and jasmine she had so loved were
trained high against the south paling. Everything she had ever touched or cared for was most
assiduously cherished, in pious memory. From
early morning to sundown, the girl busied herself
in keeping everything exactly as the inmates of
the parsonage were accustomed to from their earli-
est recollections. He came upon her where she
stood close to the bed of pansies, where every
variety grew in fragrant profusion.

" Stiefmütterchen," he said, breaking one of the
velvety darkest. He held it up to her eyes, but
she dropped them with a vivid blush.

" Just as if Herr von Czechy had said it," she
laughed.

" Herr von Czechy, indeed ! what has he to do with thine eyes ? They belong to me. Whoever else makes comparisons commits high treason, and that they shall find quickly enough."

" Thou didst not always think so," she remarked slyly. " I might pass my days in banishment at the Wildhof yet hadst thou not accidentally " —

He caught her round the neck and smothered the saucy mouth with kisses. Indeed, continually he kissed, and kissed again, until forced to stop for sheer want of breath.

" There," he exclaimed, " now have I broken my long fast at last. Oh, thou dear, sweet angelic one, thou ! And that thou mayest further forbear to say one single word on this tabooed subject, know whenever thou doest so the same punishment awaits thee."

She pouted so adorably that again he would have kissed her. But she quickly placed her hand over his mouth, which he kept there, putting the finger tips between his lips and playfully biting them.

" I will give thee something better to chew than these," she said. She stooped over the strawberry bed, pulling him down with her. There among the fading leaves, bare now of all fruit, reposed two gigantic berries, glistening in their tempting lusciousness.

" Immense ! " he said with emphasis. He carefully detached them, placed one between his lips, and stooped towards her to take it. She stood on tiptoe, taking one half, leaving him the other half.

"Greedy thou," he said, "thou tookest nearly all. Hardly did I have a taste."

"That is because thou gavest me the largest portion." She put the remaining berry between her lips, while he bent his stately head, taking in one comprehensive kiss both the alluring baits so temptingly held out to him.

"Now thou canst complain no more," she observed, "for surely I have made up to thee. Scarcely anything but the stalk remained in my mouth. 'Tis odd, though, I should have discovered them, — just as if they hid themselves there purposely for thee and me."

"And we gathered them," he replied with a look full of smiling bliss, "and shared them between us, as indeed everything from now on should be shared between thee and me."

He took her hand and drew off the small black circlet she still wore on her finger. "Now," he said, "thou shalt yield this to me. Many a time have I felt jealous in seeing thee wear it. Were it not that I knew thou didst so in all innocence of feeling, I should have taken it from thee long ago."

"The ring is very dear to me, both for the sake of him who gave it and the dear memories it contains. To no one else in the world would I have yielded it. Now thou must wear it, and never, never part with it."

She placed it on the little finger of his left hand, which it exactly fitted. Odd and striking it looked there. She passed her hand caressingly over it and kissed it once or twice.

"Now it is hallowed," he said, "and as such shall never come into contact with anything profane. See now what I have for thee."

He pressed the spring of a little morocco case. Inside lay a plain gold band, with a beautiful large pearl, set boldly in the middle. From its satin-lined bed it glistened at her like a big tear, trembling as if about to fall. She drew in her breath and looked at him in alternate surprise and dismay.

"For me?" she asked.

"Certainly for thee. Dost think in all the world there lives one for whom I would buy gewgaws? 'T is the sacred symbol of that which united our hearts long ago, to be replaced by one which shall unite us in all eternity."

He put it upon her finger, took her in his arms, and kissed her.

"It cannot be," she answered. She drew the ring from her finger, fastened it on her satin waist ribbon, and put it around her neck.

"Canst thou wound me thus?" he asked in stern reproach.

"Thus will I wear it, hidden close to my heart. Dearest beloved one! Better were it for thee to forget me, and choose some one who is better suited to thee."

"Have done with this," he ejaculated with fierce scorn. "Thou knowest not how childish is thy talk. Now once for all shalt thou decide, — either thou lovest me, or thou dost not."

She gave a startled cry. Then she wound her

arms about his neck and kissed him passionately.

"Ah," she exclaimed, breathing between his lips, "confess thou saidst it to try me. Thou thyself dost not know how I love thee. Never, never would one heart-beat be the less for thee. Thou art my heaven, my prayers breathe but of thee, my first thought on arising, the last one when I go to sleep. For thee I would suffer the world's scorn, the jeers of the multitude. To all would I be deaf, hearing nothing but the sound of thy beloved voice, blind, seeing only the glance of thy dear, dear eyes."

"Then," replied he with kindling glance, "let us go to my father. He will not deny us his blessing. Marry me, be mine now."

"I cannot marry thee," she said, wringing her hands. "I will do anything thou wishest, but I cannot forego my religion or be banned forever."

"Thou wilt deprive me of my manhood; do not try my fortitude too far. Saint I am not; there is a limit to my forbearance. Human nature is but faulty at its best. What in God's name dost thou think will become of either thee or me?"

She fell down at his feet. "Forgive me," she sobbed, "I cannot — cannot do otherwise. Oh, if the fear of being cast out did not stand between us. It haunts me day and night. Nowhere can I find rest, — nowhere. It saps at my life, ever does it wrestle to the same tune. It burns in my brain, and sometimes I think it will turn it afire."

He raised her and strained her to him in silent despair. Against anything tangible he could fight sturdily enough and take up the odds gladly. This spectre unmanned and dismayed him.

CHAPTER XLVII

"THOU dost not appear as well as usual, Liebchen," remarked the pastor kindly to Jette one afternoon. The early winter twilight cast its frolicking shadows into the corners of the sitting-room, where a great fire roared in the porcelain stove. The cold weather had set in early this year, following close upon the heels of a most glorious but brief autumn. The pastor sat again at his chess table, puzzling out his problems as of old. His pipe, with its great china bowl, was between his lips. A deep meditative frown intensified the lines between the eyebrows, as his hand hovered over the chessmen.

Jette sat in the south window, where her place had always been, opposite the Frau Pastorin, ever since the time that good soul had taught her the sampler stitch and how to sew. The Frau Pastorin's chair, with its cushions of faded chintz, stood exactly in the same position. Her little work-table, with the old-fashioned sandal-wood work-box, stood in its old place. Only now it was closed; the deft fingers which had ever searched for reels of sewing thread and scissors would never use it more. Her large mending-basket

stood on the floor close beside her chair, the things
she had last touched neatly folded up, just as she
had left them.   Her monthly roses, jasmine and
rosemary bushes, bloomed as brightly as ever.
The silver sand on the snow-white floor glistened,
the room was bright, cosy, and warm.   Everywhere
was the evidence of a prudent, industrious, vigorous hand, ever busy for the comfort and welfare
of the household.

The linen band Jette had been stitching had
dropped unheeded into her lap.   It was too dark
to work, but the lamp had not yet been lit.   The
Herr Pastor liked the twilight, when the bright
fire threw its fitful shadows into the corners, and
he could hug himself in the comfort within from
the dreariness without.

There was something in Jette's attitude, the
ever busy hands listlessly stretched before her,
which compelled the Herr Pastor's attention and
set him to thinking deeply.   He was startled to
see the impression his words made upon her.   She
almost jumped from her chair, her eyes wide with
fright, her whole attitude, as she thrust herself far
over the seat, most expressive of terror.

"Nay, I did not mean to startle thee," he said
half soothingly, half reprovingly; "surely there
was nothing in what I said to make thee act so.
It seems to me thou art pining for something, for
lately thou art strangely quiet and sedate.   Wilt
thou not tell me what ails thee?"

"Nothing—nothing ails me," she replied hurriedly; "indeed you are mistaken."

"Ah, well," he said softly. "'T were better thou hadst some one of thy own sex, young like thyself, to go to at times and talk to. Often have I regretted the want of a suitable companion for thee. Youth seeks youth, as is but natural. I do not know of anything that could lie heavy on thy heart. Since the dear mamma is gone thou hast no one to admonish or advise thee."

He was silent for a moment as he watched her in mute perplexity. The gathering shadows prevented him from seeing her face. But he heard her quick, hurried breathing.

"Jettchen," he queried hesitatingly, "hast thou ever regretted thou didst not marry the banker?"

"Never," she answered emphatically; "come what may, never can I regret it. He was hateful, abhorrent to me. More plainly do I see every day that he would have made my life unbearable. I loved his mother, but I shrank from him."

"It is a great relief to me to hear thee say that. I am glad thou didst not marry him, for he was no fit man for a girl like thee. There are other things besides money necessary for a wife's happiness. I am only sorry thou didst not tell me the truth earlier. Thou mightest have had a desirable wooer in the mean time, who would have suited thee, and carried thee off to a home of thy own by now."

"Are you sorry to have me here?" she asked with strange wistfulness.

"Now thou hast made me angry! Thou knowest very well what thou art to me and good old

Babbett. Especially at the time when — when the dear mamma went — what should we have done without thee?"

"Oh," she muttered in a stifled voice, "if I could only take out my heart and show you what passes within there now. What have I done in return for all the love and kindness heaped upon me?" She wrung her hands under her black silk apron, but he did not see it.

"Like a dutiful, loving daughter hast thou been," he answered with emotion. "A thousandfold hast thou repaid what little we ever did for thee. And to see thee grow up in maidenly beauty and purity — dost thou think that is no pleasure for an old man like me?" She uttered a suppressed moan, as he continued, "But in the comfort thou preparest for me thy own welfare must not be forgotten. Thou art now in the full heyday of thy lovely youth and must get a home of thy own. Never thou fear, we will get a suitable husband for thee." He rose and cordially tapped her on the shoulder. She shrank, as if she felt herself withering under his touch.

"Oh no, oh no," she said; "let me stay here and care for you. I ask no better lot in life."

"Thou must not worry about me; Fritz will marry, and I shall do very well. Besides, Babbett seems to be growing strong again. What little there is to do for us two old people she will be able to manage."

"Alas," she replied, "nowhere — nowhere seems there to be a place for me."

"How sayest thou that?" he uttered. He stood still, looking at her through the enshrouding gloom. "What strange words are these? How comest thou to that tone of voice?" He was silent for a moment, then he said so softly it brought the tears in a rush to her eyes, "Thou hast something on thy mind, girl! Canst thou not trust me? Speak to me as if I were thy confessor and none but the Almighty One and I heard thee!"

In the darkness he could see that she struggled with herself. Then she murmured, "Sitting here in the dark has depressed me. 'T is then one's thoughts turn to gloomy things. I will go out for a moment into the fresh air, then bring in the lamp."

He detained her. "Remember," he said, "all evil comes from deceit. It brings woe unutterable to the unsuspecting innocent, who more often than not go under, unable to extricate themselves from the snare others spread for their unwary feet."

With bowed head she passed out. But she did not speak.

CHAPTER XLVIII

At the end of the week the doctor came. The interval between this and his last visit had been longer than usual. Therefore his father's heart rejoiced exceedingly to see him again, for these visits, necessarily brief and few and far between, were to him like a glimpse of his own happy youth. The doctor looked strong and well as usual, but there was a restless activity about his

movements which would hardly allow him to be
still for two minutes at a time.   He arrived about
the same hour as he always did, late in the evening.
The household crowded to the gate, of course, as
soon as they heard the guard's horn merrily tooting
" Die Post im Walde."   All knew that Fritz had
come, and the Herr Pastor had his head in at the
post-chaise window before it had fairly stopped.
Everybody's eyes sparkled, the father kissed and
hugged his big boy, and had to stand on tiptoe to
do it.   There were merry greetings and hand-
shakings all round.   The traveler was hurried
into the warm sitting-room, where he threw off
his fur cloak, and greeted everybody again in his
boyish, hearty fashion.   A bright red spot burned
in either of Jette's cheeks, as she quickly went to
and fro, caring for the dear arrival's comfort.   An
ardent, meaning look he gave her, as she placed
the steaming hot dishes before him, a look which
sent a tremor through her limbs and made the
pupil of her eye large with fear.   The pastor sat
opposite him, hugging his lean knees with delight.
His joy and happiness as he watched his boy eat
fairly transfigured his plain, homely features.

    " Thou dost not seem to have brought thy usual
appetite with thee," he complained rather disconso-
lately ; " is not everything prepared to thy liking ? "

    " Everything is as excellent as the fondest care
combined with skill could make it," replied the doctor heartily.   " I was provided with an excellent
lunch on the way, which probably took the edge
off my hunger."

He got up and walked about restlessly, taking up an object here, another one there, intently examining it as if he saw it for the first time, yet in reality seeing nothing. His eyes flashed with concentrated brilliancy, a dark red flame in his cheeks. Never in his life had he looked so handsome; even his father was struck by it.

"Now sit thee down," he observed, "here where I can see thee. There is thy pipe just where thou leftest it. Jettchen is always careful to clean out the bowl and put it back in its accustomed place. And now tell me of what goes on outside, — thy world, dear boy, in which I am most interested."

"One moment, dear papa, and I'm at your service." He followed Jette into the passage outside, and with a gesture full of love and passionate devotion took her in his arms.

"Do thou go to rest, dearest," he said, as he fondly smoothed the hair back from her brow. "To-night all shall be told."

"Thou art about to plant the dagger in his heart," she sighed in a broken voice, "and he will bleed to death."

"Nay, thou art forever seeing phantoms. Trust me, all will turn out well."

"Oh, if the night were passed," she groaned. "I quake in trembling and fear."

"Nay, 't is not thus thou must fortify me; be strong with me, dearest. Now everything shall be made clear between us. No longer will we dwell apart, thou here, I there, leaving all that puts heart in a man's work behind me. Thou must

come with me, — thou, the light and spirit of my
life, my dear, dear wife, — to go hand in hand
with me forever."

Her head was hidden in his breast, low sobs
came from her lips. He kissed her again and
again. As he watched her go up the stairs, the
pastor opened the sitting-room door.

"Boy," he called, — "boy, where art thou?
what detains thee?" He made a step out into
the passage and saw Jette as she vanished round
the first landing. She had just sent a last glance
out of her troubled eyes to the doctor, standing
below, who, with one hand on the banisters, the
other gracefully held on his hip, returned it with
one of loving assurance. The pastor saw the smile
upon his lips and the look in his eyes, and a vague
feeling of uneasiness tightened about his heart.

"Hast been talking to Jettchen?" he asked.
In the dimly lighted passage he looked at him
keenly. "Perhaps she has confided to thee what
ails her."

The doctor led the way back to the sitting-room.
The opening was just what he wanted. "What
should ail her?" he inquired.

"She is not her usual self," said the pastor;
"the girl frets, I think. At odd times I have seen
her look so forlorn, so sad, it sent all kinds of
strange thoughts through my brain. Perhaps she
worries about the future — she ought not to waste
the best part of her life in this solitude. A husband must be found for her. When spring comes
again and one can more easily move about from

one place to another, I must set myself to the task in earnest."

" Give thyself no further concern on that score," answered the doctor; "a husband has been found for her long ago."

Not the words, but the tone in which he spoke them made the pastor rise from his chair. He trembled so he had to steady himself by a corner of the table. Articulating slowly he said unsteadily, —

" Thou seemest to be wonderfully well informed. Perhaps thou wilt be kind enough to tell me who he is ? "

Their eyes met. The Frau Pastorin had always said that for tale-bearing she had never seen anything like it. Both were alike in that respect. If either of them ever tried to conceal anything one had only to look into his eyes to see it legibly written there. What the pastor now saw in the glance meeting his own made him reel as if he were about to fall.

" It cannot be," he faltered; "surely — surely thou dost not mean " —

" Sit down, papa," begged the doctor. He put his arm round the father's shoulder and gently replaced him in his chair.

" Thou must listen to what I have to tell thee," he said, "without exciting thyself. Long and heavy has it lain on my heart, and now the load must off for evermore. Neither she nor I can live like this any longer."

" But this is fearful," exclaimed the old pastor

piteously; "thou — she — boy, thou knowest not
what thou sayest." He gazed around him vacantly,
then said with sudden vehemence, " Hast thou told
her of thy love ? "

" She knows it, since the day I came back from
Vienna."

" For years," cried the pastor, — " for years
this deceit has gone on ? Here — while thy mother was alive — before our very faces ? Hadst thou
no manhood and she no shame — and yet — yet —
since thou camest back from Vienna, sayest thou ?
How then is it possible " —

" Dost thou remember when in the dawn of the
morning she found Hans and me asleep in the
orchard out yonder, and she awoke us and brought
us here ? that was also the dawn of my love, papa.
Ever she grew dearer to me, day by day; it was
a passion against which there was no arguing or
appeal. I thought that perhaps absence and a
busy life would cure it, but, strong as the breath
of life I drew, it shadowed me wherever I went,
— at once the sweet and the torment of my existence. I could not forget her ; struggle as I might
ever and ever the feeling came back to me a thousandfold stronger than before. Then I knew that
fate had overtaken me ; I ceased to battle with
what was stronger than I. I labored — thou and
the world know how — that I might win her and
bear her off to my home, where she should be my
own, my beloved, dearly cherished wife. Ah ! "
he cried passionately, thrusting his hands out before him, " never was battle harder to fight, never

was dream more difficult of realization.   What
we have suffered — she and I — surely needs some
compensation."

Under the rapid flow of his son's speech, the
pastor sat as one stunned.   Picture after picture
unrolled itself before his mind — probabilities he
dared not contemplate, and yet — he must know
all.

"And all this time," he ejaculated, — "all this
time thou never saidst a word, but hugged thy
guilty secret — thou and she."

"In that I have erred," answered the doctor
humbly; "I acknowledge it to my shame and
sorrow.   If the great calamity — thou knowest,
mamma's death — had not overtaken us, all should
have been told long ago."

"God in heaven!" said the old man helplessly,
"what is to be the end of this?   Thou canst not
marry her — and she — I suppose thou wilt tell me
that she returns thy love?"

"She loves me as I love her, and she will no
more deny her love than I will."

"She must go away from here," exclaimed the
pastor, springing to his feet; "no longer can this
horrible thing continue.   This, then, is the reason
she is so sad and depressed all the time" —

"Stay, papa," interrupted the doctor, "thou
saidst horrible — is it such a fearful thing to love
one another?"

"Canst thou not see," uttered his father, agitated almost beyond control, "that a marriage
between you two is impossible?   Aside from all

other considerations, thou wouldst ruin thy career and ostracize thyself from society for all time to come."

" Because she is poor ? "

" Thou fool ! because she is a Jewess, and being such cannot wed with thee, the Christian."

The doctor walked up and down the room in silence. Then he said, " Is it on that score thou refusest thy consent ? "

" Aye, on that score, and on that alone. And if this is not enough for thee, there are worse difficulties in the way. The synagogue will cast her out from among her people should she wed with thee."

" 'T is nothing new ; we have known it a long time, — ever since I first told her of my love."

" And yet she listened to thee ? Father in heaven ! Where does this deceit begin and where does it end ? Is she then forsworn, ready to cast off what she has been taught to hold as nearest and sacred — what even the most degraded cling to if all else is forsaken ? "

" We will reckon with that afterwards. Do thou first give thy consent. Papa, dear papa ! do not abandon us to misery. Listen, I beseech thee ! do not forever make two lives miserable. Do thou give thy consent to our union. Then I shall be strong to battle with the rest."

" Cease," said the pastor harshly ; " 't is not seemly thou shouldst degrade thy manhood still further than thou hast already done. Never will I give my consent to such an unnatural union.

Thou knowest me, and that what I say I adhere to. Forsworn and deceitful have you been both, and 't is only fair you should suffer for it. Now stern duty beckons with unrelenting finger, and it shall be my care to see that she is obeyed. You must part, and that instantly."

"Man forsakes me," replied the doctor, "but God always remains. To the father I have appealed in vain — now man must speak to man." He drew a deep breath, flung back his head, and clasped his hands behind him. Then he said very low, so that his voice was hardly that above a whisper, "I shall cleave to her as God himself commanded husband should cleave to wife."

CHAPTER XLIX

THE two men stood opposite each other, the pastor as if turned to stone. He flung his hands from before him as if he saw some horrible spectre. Then he said in tones fearful to hear, —

"Thou Fritz, thou!" He stopped, then uttered with difficulty; "Thou liest; thou art not so abandoned as that." He came and knelt in front of him. "Where, then, is manhood and manhood's vaunted boast, — honor? Surely they rove abroad, rioting in drunken frenzy at their own worthlessness! Thou the crown and glory of my whitening hairs, the trusty staff of these trembling limbs! Yesterday more blessed than a king, to-day more sorely abased than a beggar!"

He staggered to his feet and reeled about the room as if drunk. He flung out his arms and cried out in tones of terrible grandeur, —

"Heap the weight of thy misdoing upon this hoary head, that it may be trailed deep, deep in the dust! Sear this furrowed brow with the hot iron rankling in my soul, that all may read the shame writ thereupon! Now is the world a howling chaos, for all its highways and signposts are swept away. The light has forsaken mine eyes; blind shall I be and blind shall I remain forever, groping I know not where, seeking in vain for a hand to guide me. Thou hast wrested the staff from my hand, broken it in pieces, and flung it in sheer wantonness of spirit at my aged and trembling feet!"

He was silent a moment. His arms hung helplessly at his side, his head sunk upon his breast. He walked to his wife's empty chair and steadied himself by its arms.

"One brings children into the world," he said, "and counts upon them as a safe investment to support one's feeble old age, and then wakes up to find one's self bankrupt — thus!"

He threw out his hands towards his son and fell prone upon the floor.

CHAPTER L

Days went by before the stricken man regained consciousness. It was a stroke of paralysis, and for some time it looked as if he would pass away. Nothing but the most assiduous care could ever have brought him round again. Time and his own indefatigable spirit might do wonders, but he would never be the same vigorous, hale, hearty man again ; that was plain to every one.

As his senses slowly came back to him, who shall say what thoughts struggled for supremacy out of the warring confusion of his heart and brain? To no one but the Divine is it given to read what passes in the human breast. No one but the Divine can inspire what there is of pity, sympathy, and understanding for human suffering and human woe. No one but the Divine can infuse that spark from his own mighty spirit which makes human nature view itself as it really is — with all its failings and all its foibles, think upon it, — weak, erring, incomplete. And as it is given to no man to be anything but human, so no man has the right to condemn his erring brother to shame and torture by flinging him deeper into the pit into which his weakness of will or errors of judgment have thrown him. Lives there one in all the world who can come forward preening an unsullied plumage, lifting high his crest to proclaim with haughty assurance that he alone of all is guiltless? If so, then let him step forth, that all may fall down and worship him.

The march of our much vaunted enlightenment, lumbering on its ponderous way, is like that of an unlicked schoolboy on his way to school, stopping for a wrangle here, a bullying contention there. One longs to knock some sense into his unfledged carcass, or to accelerate his speed by a timely and vigorous shove. There is too much religion upon the lips, too little spirituality in the heart. Creed wars with creed, splits itself into factions, denominations, — God knows what. One calls itself this, the other one that; and in their struggle for supremacy give the direct lie to that which they claim alone animates them, — the Divine. Each is like a fakir at the fair, — denouncing his competitor's wares while claiming perfection for his own.

The pastor, lying upon his couch of pain near the undraped window, blinked his dazzled eyes in the brightening sun, and felt that it was good to be warmed by its rays once more. As he watched the radiant beams mounting higher and higher in the heavens, there were illumined for him many things which had hitherto been enshrouded in darkness. At last he understood in its grand, full significance, " Let there be light." He looked back down the road of his earthly journey, and now near the end, saw all he had been blind to on the way. No, not blind ; his vision had only been obscured. Now the film was removed he could see all the roses, as well as the thorns, he had missed on the way. He saw his son as he really was, shorn of the crown of glory he had woven around his head, — only human, that was all ; human in his folly, his pride, his love, his strength, his errors, and his judgment, — in all those attri-

butes, some more, some less, which go to make
up the sum and substance of our natures. He
saw him with all his imperfections, but also his
virtues thick upon him. The highway of life is
thorny and rough, sometimes our vision is dimmed
that we cannot see, — what wonder that many lose
their foothold, stumble, and fall. He was his son,
flesh of his flesh, blood of his blood, — aye, that
was it! It was the father who looked at him, —
the father!

The father who has never watched beside the
sick-bed of a beloved child; who has never heark-
ened to its cry of distress in the still hours of the
night; who has never moistened the fever-parched
lips, or gazed into the wandering eyes, seeking for
the truant consciousness; who has never strained
the cherished little form to his agonized breast,
beseeching Him on high to take all of his worldly
goods, but to spare him this one little blossom;
who has never done fierce battle with the gaunt
destroyer, and fought the bitter fight inch by inch,
until the enemy was routed — he has never had his
foot on the step of the sanctuary or probed in its
depths the might of fatherly love.

Looking at the bronzed man before him, he
lived over again the hour of peril and travail.
The boy was six years old when he was stricken
with scarlet fever. He was saved, — but the struggle had been fearful. Night after night he had sat
at his bedside, soothing the pain-racked form, cooling the burning throat, and beguiling the tedium
of convalescence with stories of Struwelpeter and

Ruebezahl. Death had hovered very nigh then, so nigh that the Heavenly Father had approached very near to the earthly one.

Our Father, which art in heaven! Our Father! — the Father who enfolds all in his pitying embrace; who looks down on every one alike, reading what is in the human heart, seeing its pitfalls and its errors; whom all must face some day with no pleader but their own conscience, dependent upon his mercy and clemency; before whom soon he must take his stand, — he — what was he — that he should set himself up as judge above his fellows? Would he not soon have to plead for that clemency he had a little while since refused his son?

"Fritz," he said softly.

The doctor's eyelids had drooped over his tired eyes. No hands but his had been allowed to touch the stricken father. Day and night had he sat beside him, giving the medicine, watchful of his every breath. His face was worn and haggard; what he had suffered was plainly written there.

"Fritz, dear child," called the pastor.

The doctor opened his eyes with a look of wonder, as if he were dreaming. When he saw what was in the pastor's face, he was beside him with one bound.

"Papa, dear papa." His voice was almost a sob. He took the thin white hands in his own, and lovingly pressed them to his cheeks and lips.

"Lie still!" he said; "not yet must thou exert thyself in speech. Thou hast been ill; thou knowest it, eh?"

" 'T is over," answered the pastor.   " Give thyself no concern.   My wandering senses have returned, — my mind has seen while my eyes were
shut.   If thou hast anything ready with which to
nourish me, let me have it ; not yet can my weak
body keep pace with my stronger spirit, and what
I have to say must be told without delay."

The doctor hurried into the passage and called
to Babbett, who soon appeared, bearing a basin of
strong broth and a glass of wine.   She was followed by Minka, who jumped upon the pastor's
lap and affectionately stroked her long whiskers
against his face.

" Thou truant," he said, passing his hand over
her coat; " where hast thou been all the time ?
Formerly thou wert content to stay beside me;
now thou payest only stately visits, few and far
between."

" Thank Heaven you are better, master ! " in-
spirated Babbett.   She looked more upright and
stronger now since she found there was need of
her services.   The tears were in her eyes as she
noticed how the pastor had aged during these few
days' illness.   But he looked at her with his kind
smile, and took the napkin she was about to fasten
under his chin in his own trembling hands.

" I will not be coddled," he said.   " I am quite
strong, and will soon be downstairs again.   Is
everything well as usual ? "

" Quite well," replied the old woman cheerfully.
She knew that his anxiety was for the lonely,
heart-broken girl downstairs, to whom it would be

renewed life to hear he had inquired for her. She
went down, leaving Minka with her master, who
would not leave him.

The doctor sat on a low stool in front of his
father's couch, holding the tray on his knees, rejoicing at every spoonful he swallowed. At first
he had attempted to feed him, but the pastor had
resented it with playful indignation.

"See," he challenged, holding out his hand
which, in spite of his immense will power, trembled
incessantly, "how strong I am. I need only to
nourish myself for a few days, then all will be as
before. Give me the wine, boy. Nay, thou mayest
hold it to my lips till the first drops are sipped.
'T is not because my hand trembles, but the good
soul, Babbett, filled the glass over full. Ah, that
is good! that puts new life into one. Thou must
have paid a great price for this port, my son, for
every drop seems to renew into vigor the old blood
in my heart."

When he had drained the last drop of wine and
swallowed all the broth he lay back, strengthened
and refreshed. A bright spot burned in either
thin cheek, a steady fire glowed in his sunken
eyes.

"Now I can speak," he said. "Stand over
yonder, Fritz, — there right in the light where I
can see thee."

The doctor went and leaned against the window-
frame, where the sunbeams turned his curls into
gold and lit up with the same glory the depths of
his dark brown eyes. For a moment the father

looked at him steadily, with a tremor of the lip and a moisture in the eye.

" Thou art all that is fair and comely to the eye," he observed, " just as thy mother of blessed memory was. Long did I murmur when she was taken away ; but now I see that it was best, as everything the Lord does in his infinite wisdom and mercy."

The doctor made a gesture as if afraid his father was about to excite himself. But the pastor was quite composed and calm.

" I do not say it to reproach thee," he continued. " Fools upbraid, wise men act. And as thy behavior has been such as to call forth immediate action, I can only tell thee what is in my mind according to the light vouchsafed me. Thou must go away, — at once. 'T is not seemly thou shouldst continue in the house thy mother sanctified with her presence, — not you and *she* together. Nay, hear me in silence until I have finished. Thou must marry her — now, — that is plain enough. First comes duty, — to the rest you must both adjust yourselves. 'T will not be easy, depend upon it."

The doctor threw himself beside his father's couch. " I knew thee," he exclaimed. " All the devotion of my life shall testify to the burden of gratitude I owe thee. Now thy consent is gained I do not fear the rest."

The pastor shook his head. " The most difficult remains. Tell me — was she ever willing to marry thee ? "

"No," said the doctor, "else " — He hesitated. His head was lowered upon his breast.

"Else had this never happened," concluded the pastor. "'T is I myself who insisted upon the rigorous fulfillment of all the requirements of her religion. 'T is the most sacred duty of the individual to cherish the belief of his ancestors. Of all misdoings of human kind, none stink worse in the nostril than apostasy. Being born a Jewess, not all the might of her love can undo the fact, and I rejoice that in this, at least, she showed herself stanch and true."

"Papa," entreated the son, — "papa," he pleaded, "do thou not be hard upon her. Before God she is blameless " —

"Thou art a man," said the pastor steadily, "and must bear thy man's measure."

"If I were less of a man, would it concern me near so much? Would that I could absorb her part of the burden into my very marrow, that once being there it should knit itself into the bone and absolve her forever."

"Speech must rest idle now; a remedy must be found for what is done. Now you will have to wait awhile until I am strong enough to have speech with her rabbi. He must if possible be induced to give his consent, that her scruples may be allayed."

He stopped a moment, then asked softly, "Hast thou thought of any plan in case — in case this fails ? "

The doctor's color came and went. Then he

said quickly and ever more quickly and passionately, " She must not be disgraced. There is a land — far across the sea — where neither she nor I are known — where liberty of thought and action prevails — where life may be begun anew and made hallowed and sweet by our own efforts. 'T would be a hard wrench, I know " —

" Thou wouldst leave me ! " cried the pastor. Neither his body nor his faculties were as strong as he led others to believe. He trembled like a child about to be left alone in the dark. The tears ran down his furrowed cheeks. " Thou wouldst leave me," he repeated in tones pitiful to hear, " to die desolate and alone, with strange hands to close my eyes in death ! Oh, no, thou couldst not do this. Wait but a little while — it will not be for long " —

" Papa ! " cried the doctor. He fell on his knees beside him and took the dear, honored white head between his hands. " What am I," he said, " compared to thy heroic unselfishness ? Thou dear, good, purest of all pure souls ! come what may, never will I leave thy tottering old footsteps to grope their way alone. We are young, — the woman I love and I, — and shame to us both if we do not shoulder the burden of our responsibility. Now thou shalt see of what mettle we are both made. Let there be no more talk of this. Hard as the conditions are, we must comply with them. I will go away, as thou commandest. I will not return until thou givest me leave to. Only — only be kind to her " —

"This is her home, doubly so now, by every right on earth and in heaven. Be thou not uneasy, my son. Soon will these tangled skeins be unraveled. Count thou upon my discretion — all must be settled satisfactorily before things get whispered abroad."

The son embraced him in mute fervor. "I hardly like to leave thee yet," he said anxiously; "thou hast spent thyself, and must rest."

"I shall rest when thou art gone; thou knowest I am in good hands. Do thou delay no longer. Go back to thy duties at Bonn — soon shalt thou hear from me." He smiled and looked lovingly into his eyes. "Be of good heart. Now kiss me and say good-by."

The doctor leaned over and kissed him. There was reverence mingled with love in the caress he gave, as well there might be.

"Thou stanch friend," he said, "dear, most loyal sorely tried one; who never from the time thou guidedst my first tottering footsteps hast ever failed me; thou shalt yet hug the comforting assurance to thy heart that in thy eyes I have redeemed myself, God helping me, of course." He bent the knee, and the old pastor raised his trembling hands over the bowed head and blessed him. For a moment both were silent; then the son arose, softly pressed his lips to the old father's brow, and left him. At the door he stopped and half turned round.

"Thou wilt ever remember," he reminded him, "what a terribly aching heart awaits thy message,

— not so much for my own relief, but what might happen to her."

He went to his room, ordered his few belongings, — for his visits being necessarily brief, he was not overburdened with luggage, — and while Babbett was gone to order the special post-chaise, he went in search of Jette.

She was in the sitting-room. Always had it been the centre of the family life, the meeting place where each had met the other on common ground, where everything of interest had been discussed, and the events of the day were talked over. Its dreary loneliness struck a chill to the already overburdened heart of the doctor. He came behind her softly, and leaning over the back of her chair kissed her.

"Thou must not sit about so forlorn," he reproved, "else thou wilt take all heart out of me."

She flushed red as she always did whenever he looked at her or came near her. The soft pink bloom no longer graced her cheek, but more beautiful than ever she looked, with the blue of her eye dark with its load of pain, and the clear pallor of her face transparent against the background of black hair. She clasped her hands upon his breast and looked at him beseechingly.

"He is better," she said; "Babbett has told me — he is quite cheerful, like his old self again. Will he allow me to go near him — can he bear the sight of me?"

"Thou art a foolish child," answered the doctor, "given to all sorts of unwholesome fancies when

I 'm away from thee." He put his arm around her and drew her up to him. " Thou must promise me not to fret," he whispered, " otherwise my heart will be heavy indeed. Be cheerful, dearest. The dark days are past — dawn is breaking. A little while yet — then we will be united, nevermore to part."

" It would be too heavenly. I cannot realize it. When one is inured to suffering the transition to joy is not easy."

" Joy follows upon the footsteps of grief, as surely as the sun smiles from the clouds. Papa is better ; soon he will be about again. Then he will set himself the task to grapple with this matter — that thy religious scruples may be set at rest."

" And if he does not succeed ? "

" Then we go away from here to another land, where we may all dwell in peace and happiness together. Thou, and I, and he."

" Thy father will not go; his home is in thy mother's grave. 'T would be like tearing the fibres from his heart to take him away from it."

" He will go with us, never fear. We will give him time to grow used to the idea. We will come back and fetch him — after a year or so — when matters have quite adjusted themselves — and you and I have grown old in our new happiness."

" I am happy," she replied, " when thou art near me. With thee I would go barefooted all over the world, following thee through the burning desert'or the ice-clad plains, proud if I could minister to thee, contented with a look, a word, a smile. If I cannot be thy wife, I will be thy handmaiden, happy to be of use to thee — for there is no other man like thee, no one worthy to compare with thee. Thou hast given me the love of a *man;* what greater honor is there for woman? Thou hast my heart entirely, — my soul I cannot give thee. It belongs to God, and as He gave it to me in trust, so will I have to reckon with Him one day. And as all there is of divine in me comes from Him, so do I throw myself upon his mercy, sure that He knows what is in my heart and will judge accordingly."

"As thou art," he said, "thou suitest me — thou hast taken hold of every fibre of my being. Never, since the world stood, has woman entwined herself around the heart of man as thou hast around mine. 'T is not thy beauty alone — thou art gifted with a fatal charm. Whoever looks into these eyes feels all there is of love within him drawn forth unresistingly and lost within their depths. Never did I think it possible love could possess one so. Thou art mine as I am thine — nothing earthly can ever part us. We were created for each other — thou and I."

He kissed her as she kissed him, long and fervently. They were about to part — he with hope burning bright, as is the manner of man accustomed to plunge in and overcome strife; she with heart depressed, as is the manner of woman left behind to watch and weep. Her heart was in her kisses, as it was in her eyes as she said, —

" If happiness were no more in store for me; if

I had to die to-morrow foregoing all that life holds
dear; still should I be satisfied to go. I have
lived — for I have had the glory of being loved
by thee."

"Thou must not droop thy head now," he remarked, "or go about dejected. Promise me till
I return thou wilt be cheerful. When next I come
there will be no more parting, — nevermore in
this world. If thou art sad I shall feel it and all
heart will go out of my work. Buoy me up with
thy hopefulness — so shall I be strong to battle
for us both."

It had grown dark. The post-chaise stood waiting at the door. There would be a bright moon
presently — the doctor preferred to journey by
night. He threw his fur-lined traveling-cloak
around him; no king could have looked more royal,
with the rich sable, covering his tall stately form.
He flung back a corner and she crept under it, with
his arm clasping her to him close. He peered
through the slight aperture, while she peered upward into his eyes.

"Come with me," he said; "it is dark, no one
will see us. I would like to take thee with me;
God only knows how strongly I wish it."

He lifted her over the doorsill and almost carried
her down to the gate.

"Run in," he urged, when he had taken his
seat in the chaise; "thou hast no covering over
thy head, thou wilt catch thy death of cold."

His eyes were still on her face; like phosphorus
they gleamed in the dark, revealing what there

was of pain, of anguish, of sorrow there. She did
not heed his admonition, but stood where he had
left her, tall, motionless, rigid, both hands raised
in farewell. Now the moon rose in the radiant
east, full glorious, bathing the motionless figure at
the gate in a halo of white transparent light. He
had turned for a last adieu, and seeing her thus
peremptorily bade the postilions to stop. Before
they had fairly obeyed him, he had leapt from the
post-chaise, run back, and clasped her as if he
would never let her go.

"How can I leave thee," he uttered, "when
thou lookest so. Like a ghost thou stoodest there,
bidding me an eternal farewell. Oh, be careful —
be careful of thyself. Write to me every day,
dost thou hear? — every hour of the day. Tell
me everything, omit not the merest trifle. Quick
as the breath of life will I fly to thee shouldst
thou need me. Go in — I pray thee obey me. I
cannot go while thou standest here — come, let me
take thee in myself."

Another moment, and from her seat at the
window the rumble of wheels told her that he was
gone.

CHAPTER LI

No one is solitary in merriment. His own joyous mood keeps him company. The whole world
is kin. A merry smile, a bright glance, kindles
a responsive spark. Everything is in sympathy.
But let a great heartbreak come; let it creep

up unawares or foreshadowed by passing events, then it is the human soul finds it best to stand alone. It is its foretaste of eternity. The vast Infinite, enfolding one like the loving arms of maternity, stimulates and consoles. What was scorned in happiness becomes a desirable possibility in sorrow. The erring soul, struggling upward toward the light, must do so unaided and alone.

To the girl up at the parsonage time crept along on leaden wings. She had need of all her heroic resolves, to sustain her during this time of watching and waiting. The pastor did not mend as rapidly as he thought he would. The winter passed, spring was near at hand before he went about the house again. Often his eye was vacant, his mien abstracted. Rumor reared its snaky crest, bared its grinning fangs, and scattered its venom abroad. It burst out in foul invective, it lifted the finger of scorn as the hapless girl passed by. Gret, lifting little Lieschen up in her arms, taught the baby lips to utter ribald gibes, to point the finger of derision, to denounce most fiercely, where she had most fondly worshiped. Poor trembling, suffering Lieschen! She could not understand why she should despise to-day what she had been taught to respect yesterday. Jette, looking with her stricken eyes into those of the terrified baby's, saw that the little heart was broken, and in seeing thus felt her own break. She crept back to the house, and left it no more.

It was not long before these rumors reached

Babbett. She came in one morning before the noon hour, all in a white heat, and all unheeding of the pastor's presence walked straight up to Jette.

" Is it true," she asked fiercely, " what people are saying of thee ? "

" Saying of me ? " repeated the girl with ashen lips.

" It *is* true then," said the old woman; " God help thee, thou unfortunate jade."

She looked at her in silence. More of sorrow than of anger there was in that look.

" I knew how it would be," she exclaimed; " I knew it all the time. Such girls as thou never come to any good. Thou wert too finicking by far. This did not suit thee — the other was not to thy liking — now thou hast stirred up a nice broth for thyself. If thou hadst only married the banker. Thou dear Heaven! How hast thou kicked thy good fortune out of sight. But there was no one to knock any sense into thee — if only they had seen in the cards what I saw they would have sung a different tune. Thank Heaven, the mistress did not live to see this. And now I suppose the rest will happen also; oh, I know what I know. Thou poor, poor thing, one could cry over and pity thee. 'T was this, I suppose, which made the mistress of blessed memory call out in her last moments, wanting to help thee, as was ever her wont, sweet, blessed saint that she is. And now I suppose she is helping the angels fit on their halos properly."

Up rose the pastor, straight and upright, from his chair.

"Bring me my staff," he commanded in his strong, resonant voice. "I may be late to-night. Let no one worry on my account."

CHAPTER LII

THE sun stood high in the western horizon when the pastor reached the rabbi's door. Neustadt was a market town, of some little pretension, close upon the Nassau frontier. The house in which the rabbi lived was tall and dingy, and the time being close upon Passover, it presented anything but an inviting appearance. The windows were bare and undraped; everything that was movable had been taken down to undergo the annual purifying process. Furniture was piled together; all was in that state of disheartening confusion in which the feminine soul delights in the happy springtime, and which is enough to make the stoutest male heart quail.

The rabbi himself opened the door in response to the pastor's knock. He was a small weazened man, with a caved-in chest and the student's stoop in his narrow shoulders. His skin was swarthy as a Moor's, which the scant gray hair, falling upon his shoulders and covered by a black skull cap, accentuated. A long patriarchal beard framed in his chin and fell in a tangled mass upon his breast. His narrow forehead, deeply seamed with wrinkles, rose boldly above eyebrows drawn so close together as almost to overshadow his one eye, for the lid of the other was drawn over an empty socket. It was an ecce homo face, full of suffering, pain, and weariness. He stared when he saw the pastor, for they knew each other very well, but courteously invited him to enter. As, with a shuffling gait, he walked on before, he made profuse apologies for the disorder of the house.

"The confusion of my mind is such," remarked the visitor, "that I have no eye for outward things. Pray do not humiliate me with excuses which must discourage me with the thought that the time for my visit was ill chosen."

The rabbi led the way to his study, a small room at the back of the house, where no noises penetrated and where at all times he was safe from unwelcome intrusion. The pastor sank into a large leather armchair near the window, while his host left him for a moment alone. He returned bearing a tray with some glasses and a bottle of wine, which he first carefully dusted, and then, with a great deal of precaution, opened.

"Old vintage," he observed, as he filled the glass and handed it to his guest. He filled one for himself, and they gravely clinked their glasses against each other. Then they both said "Prosit," and drank, at first slowly, — the rabbi with a wink of the eye, and a subdued smack of enjoyment; the pastor mechanically, as if it were necessary to fortify his waning strength.

"Pardon me, reverend sir," began the rabbi; "you do not seem to be in your usual robust health."

"Since we last met afflictions of all sorts have overtaken me. It has turned the silver of my hair into snow and my heart into everlasting mourning."

"I know, I know," answered the rabbi with a look of deep sympathy. "I have heard of the calamity which scourged your village, and deprived you of a dear and cherished wife. These are afflictions sent by the Lord, and all that we can do is to submit ourselves to His will."

"What God does is well done," replied the other with grandeur. "Happy am I, thrice happy, that she was removed before that which has brought me here overtook my house and brought perpetual mourning to my heart."

The rabbi's eye gleamed. "Has it reference to the maid?" he asked.

"It is in reference to her that I come. Perhaps you have heard"—

"Rumors have been flying about lately, which have not at all surprised me. Matters generally turn out this way when a maid is willful and wayward-hearted."

The pastor rose from his chair. "Unheard of! intolerable!" he cried. "Oh, that I had not been oblivious to this, sunk in the selfishness of my own grief. This could not have happened then."

"Why reproach yourself? matters will take their course. I do not see how you could have prevented it."

"If she had been a lawful wedded wife would her name be bandied about?"

"Oh," exclaimed the rabbi, "lies the land that way?" His bushy brows drew themselves together. A look of fierce resistance came into his face.

"She must marry; no longer can it be delayed. Honor, justice, every right, human and divine, demands it."

"'T is their own affair; what have I to do with it?"

"The girl's religious scruples stand in the way," said the pastor.

The rabbi laughed with taunting bitterness, "Oh, she has scruples! had she any when she committed herself?"

"Rabbi," said the pastor with emotion, "leave that to the One on high to judge."

"I do not presume to judge. Who am I that I should? Only it seems to me that a maid who has shown herself to be as misguided as she evidently appears to be deserves very little commiseration."

"You make my task thrice difficult," said the pastor.

"She knew well what was in store for her," pursued the rabbi, "after the shameful manner in which she treated the man who so highly honored her above her deserts. He was of her own religion, pious, God-fearing, blest abundantly with this world's goods, the prop and pillar of the community. And he stooped down from his great

height to her, a beggar maid, when he might have
chosen among the mighty of the land. Without
a murmur he waited for her, yea, as patiently as
ever did Jacob for Rachel." He laughed bitterly.
"God save the mark! what is she now!"

"All that you can say I know," the pastor answered, "and more. Circumstances there may
have been, of which outsiders know nothing, which
put another face upon this matter. The errand
which brings me here is this : has she your consent
in marrying my son?"

"What have I to do with it! 'T is the consent
of the synagogue that she wants — and that she
will never obtain — to marry the Christian. I
made this clear enough to her when she came and
plead with me over a year ago. 'T is not for want
of warning that she closed the trap upon herself:
now let her see how she gets out of it."

"Oh, no," observed the pastor mildly, "that
cannot be thy creed. God is merciful, and 't is
thy office to practice what He commands."

"Exactly. The Jewess cannot wed with the
Christian. If she does, she dies to her people ;
they know her no more. I admire, but I cannot
imitate thee."

"Thou art more priest than man, and 't was
to the man I came to appeal."

"I have yet to learn," said the rabbi, "that the
two are incompatible."

"If one overrules the other, yes. 'T was the
manhood within me which scorned to take advantage of a poor, defenseless child flung for protec-

tion at my door. Had I not in my own self-conceit been weaponed against future contingencies, I would not stand before thee now suing for clemency in vain. Man is most weak where he thinks himself most strong — bethink thee, thy judgment may be fallible."

" What! Shall it be said that for one wanton maid concessions shall be made which may tumble the whole edifice about our ears, and bring on endless destruction ! Fools there are enough already digging at the foundation, so that only the merest shell remains. What she has sown she must reap ; 't is the inexorable result of all our actions."

" Beware," said the pastor, " lest in trying my manhood too far I spit upon thine. Wanton she is not and never has been. I will choke the foul lie in any one's throat who dare proclaim it. 'T is not for thee to add affliction to the already afflicted. Leave that to the rabble, who lack enlightenment to know better."

" Ay," sneered the rabbi, " 't is for the sons of such true believers as thou to despoil the flower of our race. Let her take comfort. In that she is not alone."

" If I have offended thee," begged the other, who bitterly rued his violence, " visit thy wrath upon my head alone. The maid is very dear to me." His voice vibrated like reeds in the wind. " Be merciful, rabbi. Neither thy days or mine are much longer in this land of travail. Bethink thee of the terrible responsibility thou takest upon thyself if thou refusest."

"Merciful!" cried the rabbi furiously; "let me conjure up a picture in thy mind." His eyes shot forth sparks of fire, the drawn eyelid over the empty socket quivered. "In the streets of Warsaw, at high noon, there stands a beautiful young woman, stripped bare to the waist. She is tied to a post, and clasps a young boy to her breast. The soldiers are scourging her body till the lash cuts to the bone, tearing great strips of flesh with it. Suddenly they wrest the child from her, fling him to the ground and deliberately gouge his eye out. They jerk him to his feet, and, disfigured and bleeding as he is, thrust the child into the mother's face. She goes stark staring mad, and dies in the most frightful convulsions. Now why, thou wilt ask, was this done? Because she was a Jewess and would not disclose her husband's hiding-place, whom they were seeking for no worse crime than that he was a Jew. So they killed the mother, and tortured the child."

"God in heaven!" uttered the pastor. He moaned, and ran up and down the room like mad. The whole frightful tragedy he saw enacted before him; the horror of it made his heart burst. The rabbi's voice sounded to him as a far-away chant of the Miserere as he continued, —

"The child escaped, and was sent by compassionate people to his father, who had fled to Paris. But the horrors of that day remained fixed in his memory forever. It will stay by him at the judgment seat, where thou, pastor, and I one day must stand — for it was *my* mother whom they did to death, it was I whom they dismembered — and it will guide my accusing finger to point out, not the butcher hirelings who do but as they are bidden, but those who are the fomenters and instigators of such deeds."

" There is nothing more base," said the pastor, "than human nature when shorn of the divine. There is nothing more grand or noble with it instilled. 'T is given to man himself to sink below the depth of the most ferocious brute, or to rise to the grandeur of a god. But man will not see this till, like the pestilence, he has destroyed what was noblest and best within him. Then will come purification. Let thou and I take time by the forelock, and, casting all there is of rancor out of the heart, act in unison for the welfare of others. Nay, hear me. I came not to argue with thee. Far was it from my purpose to conjure up the frightful memories thou hast evoked. For this I would ask pardon of thee. Alas! what can I say! truly thou hast cause for rancor. But temper justice with mercy; bethink thee, thou wilt have need of it thyself one day."

" I have said my say, I can do no more. Fain would I console thee, for thou art an upright and true man. But for the maid I have no other message than what she has already heard herself, what I said to thee from the first. Let her marry the Christian if she will. However, she will be cast out from among her people : they will know her no more."

" I have done," exclaimed the pastor; " here

below we meet no more. 'Tis an ill creed thou preachest in preparation of the life to come, where all are thought to be equal." His voice rose and gradually swelled like the deep tones of an organ, filling the little room with its grand rhythm. "Years hence, when both thou and I are as if we had never been, the edifice thou tryest so hard to preserve will have crumbled into dust. For nothing on earth can prevail unless it be founded on the solid rock of brotherly love."

He went, and softly closed the door behind him.

CHAPTER LIII

His old-time vigor seemed all at once to have returned to the pastor. He went about with an alert step, his eye was keen and bright. It was so sudden that everybody saw and marveled at it. There was an air of haughty command in his carriage: he squared his shoulders and held his head high, looking every one steadily in the face on his way through the village. Before the grandeur of his mien base effrontery slunk away abashed — who dared lift up a voice or cast a look of derision in presence of so much majesty?

He wrote a letter to his son, brief and to the point: "Thou must order thy affairs," he said, " in as short a time and with as much dispatch as thy eagerness will dictate. I have failed in my mission, and were it not that it will deprive me of the comfort of having you both near me I should not be sorry for it. Thou must take her away, — at once. God will take care of the rest."

This he sealed and sent by special messenger. A few days after, when the reply came, he said to her, " Go out into the warm spring sunshine. No longer must thou be sad. He is coming to go away with thee across the trackless ocean. Thou must be strong; for the journey is long and rough."

For the first time since his son's confession he looked at her in the old way, and laid his hand upon her head. She was grateful, so humbly grateful, the sobs threatened to choke her. She prostrated herself before him as she prayed, —

" My father, my more than father, say you forgive me for all the sorrow I have brought upon your honored head."

" I do forgive thee, as I hope to be forgiven myself one day."

Ever after he was glad that he had looked at and spoken to her kindly. He saw her go down the garden path, followed by Minka. The great cat never left her now, just as if she had a presentiment that her young mistress was about to leave her forever. When she reached the little gate leading into the road, Babbett ran out of her kitchen and came flying after her.

" Art thou going out? Nay, I would rather thou wouldst not."

"The Herr Pastor wishes it," returned Jette. She spoke humbly, as if she could never be grateful enough for the kind consideration shown her.

" Nonsense," said the old woman crossly ; " thou
canst get all the air and sunshine thou needest in
walking around the garden here."

" I want to go to the orchard, and my own garden
I took care of all these years. It may be the last
time I shall see them. We are to go away, — he
and I, you know, — perhaps already on the morrow."

"So soon?" ejaculated the old woman. A pallor
came over her tight, winter-apple-like cheek ; she
drew her breath in troubled gasps. " Wait," she
exclaimed almost fiercely ; " if thou *must* go out
now, I will go with thee. I will put all my preparations for the evening meal under way, so it will
not take long to do when we come back."

" Oh, no," protested the girl. " I pray thee do
not put thyself out for me. Thou dear old goose!
one would think I was about to start on a long
journey instead of a little walk almost within
sight of the house. Besides," — she turned red,
hesitated, then went on quickly, — " he will be
here to-night. Thou wilt have enough to do in
preparing something nice for him. Perhaps I
may meet the post-chaise on my way back. Thou
knowest the chaussée runs right by our garden
fence. Then I will come back with him, and help
thee."

For the first time Babbett saw her smile again
in her old bright fashion. It moved the old woman
strangely, as she said reluctantly enough : —

" Oh, well, if that is the case, — if thou goest to
meet him — However, do not wait for him. 'T is

short time enough thou wilt yet be here, — and he will have thee all his life long."

She gazed after her as she went off followed by Minka, who with her stealthy footstep sometimes trotted on before, then came back, looking at the girl with her great phosphorescent eyes. And the pastor from his easy-chair in the south window saw them, too. He noticed that her step had regained some of its former elasticity, her head no longer drooped as if overweighted with its burden of sorrow. Just where the bend in the road dipped towards the valley she stopped, turned round, and with a bright smile waved her hand to Babbett, who still stood watching at the gate. And that was the last he saw of her.

CHAPTER LIV

With a lighter heart then had lain in her bosom for many a day, Jette descended into the valley. The afternoon was moving on apace; a vaporous haze rested on the early budding trees, gladly responding to the blandishments of the sun. She met an old crone, the two front fangs of her otherwise toothless mouth showing between her withered lips. With her baleful, bleared eyes, she looked the incarnation of the wicked old fairy who used to frighten the fancy of our infant days. Her back was bent as she supported herself on a strong staff; in the other hand she carried a basket of eggs. Jette recognized her as a fre-

quent visitor to the village, a mischievous, wicked
old gossip, who matched Gret in the length and
foulness of her tongue. The crone stood still,
and from beneath her bent back let her baleful
glance travel over the girl in a triumphant, malicious sneer.

"Aha, my little doll," she jeered, "that's what
we come to when we carry our heads so high, eh ?
Now thou art no better than a cast-off garment
which nobody would stoop to for the picking up."

The girl was about to pass on without deigning
look or answer when a rushing little noise behind
her made her stop. It was Lieschen, with her
face grimed, and a shockingly dirty pinafore, her
flaxen hair streaming far behind her.

"At last I have caught you," she panted, clutching tight hold of the girl's dress. "Always when
you passed I wanted to run to you, but little
mother would n't let me. I saw you from the road
while mother was at a neighbor's, and I gave her
the slip, and have run all the way."

Jette stooped and took the little thing, all dirty
as she was, up in her arms, looking fondly at her.

"Let go the child!" said the crone roughly;
"such as thou have no business with her any
more." She tottered towards them, and pulled the
child by its dress, but the little thing kicked out
her legs so vigorously that one of them struck the
old hag squarely in the chest, causing her to reel
backward.

"Thou venomous little imp!" she screamed.
"Wait; if I don't tell thy mother. Such a wal-

loping shalt thou have as will make thy ugly limbs stiff for many a day to come."

The child clung in a frightened manner to Jette, who carried her away some distance, till quite near the garden fence.

"Now thou must run back home ; run as quick as thou canst. I am glad that I have seen thee again, dear, dear little Lieschen. Here, give me another kiss, — for the last time. No, not that road must thou take ; that leads away from home. But, this one, — yes, that is right. Now let me see thee use thy little legs."

She watched the child with moist eyes, glad her active little limbs would out-distance the hobbling hag's. But when she opened the wicket gate to turn into the orchard, she did not see that the child turned round, stopped, then slyly crept back, that she stood for some moments trying to climb the palings, and that finally she went on again, wandering down the chaussée instead of choosing the road home.

The encounter with the old hag had chased the brightness from the girl's face. With lagging steps she went on, stopping for a moment to look around her. Her dress caught in a thorn-bush ; she tried to disentangle it, but the thorns were long and sharp ; they pierced her hands, and made the blood gush forth freely. She took out her handkerchief, but it was soon stained through, — wherever she touched herself the blood trickled over. The wind flung back her mantle ; she drew it together again, shivering, for it blew chill and

cold. As she did so her white fichu beneath became stained with the crimson drops, but she did
not know it. She still held her handkerchief in
her hand, and went on till she came to the cherry-
tree where the doctor had hung Hans's coat, which
he had made her climb up to redeem. The smile
came back to her face as she recalled the scene.
He had loved her then, when she would sooner
have thought the skies would drop before such a
miracle could take place. And now she was going
away with him to be his wife, — old tree, do you
hear? his wife! You never would have thought
that, old tree, would you? — you, upon whose
trusty branches his sturdy little limbs had clam-
bered when he was not much more than a baby,
and he gathered your ripe red fruit with both
hands, and gayly threw it down to the anxious old
Babbett below. How often he had told her this,
and of other little pranks the old tree had been
silent witness to. Also it had been witness of his
wooing, for there, right opposite, was the old sycamore-tree, overshadowing the stone upon which
he had seated himself beside her when first he
drew her to his breast. Old tree, if you could
speak! You who have seen the blissful ecstasy
of my breast, and its deepest sorrow! Fate steals
along with swift noiseless footstep, while we never
know it is so close upon our heels. What will it
bring me in the coming years? — you shake your
branches, old tree, and don't know. You will be
there, straight upright at your post, when my hands
may not gather your gracious bounty any more, —

many, many years yet, after I am laid low. However, something I must have of you, old tree, to take away with me, — some tangible memento which shall recall you to me, something which at times I may look at, — who knows! perhaps weep over, — something that shall be as a shrine at which to renew old scenes and memories. But now you stand stiff and unapproachable, because the sun has not warmed your sap yet, like in the gracious summer time when you droop your branches, with their tempting load, like an alluring coquette waiting to be embraced. High up there, but tantalizingly beyond my reach, there is a small twig, a pretty, symmetrical thing. That I will have, old tree, and it will not hurt thee, for it is so small thou 'lt never miss it.

She looked around her for a stout stick, long enough to reach the coveted branch. But there was none in sight, for in her painful neatness everything of the kind had always been picked up and carefully put out of the way. She walked over to the sycamore-tree, whose hanging boughs she could easily reach, and though it hurt her to despoil it, she tried to break off a long branch. It crackled and bent in her grasp, but it would not break. She took hold of it securely; it swayed hither and thither; finally it hung limp by a bit of bark. It was wrenched off; it had not broken.

There, where the thorns had pierced her flesh, the blood broke out afresh again. She wrapped her stained handkerchief around it, grasped hold of her stick, and commenced to aim at the coveted branch. A commotion, at first faint, was heard coming up the road behind her. So intent was she upon bringing down her prize that she paid no attention to it. Nearer and nearer it came, — women's voices, shrill with anger, men's deeper notes, gruff and stern. The stick was lowered in her tight clutch; with head slightly turned and breath fluttering between half opened lips, she listened. Minka came and placed herself close beside her, watching with gleaming eyes from whence the sound came.

The sun was about to go down. A chill mist arose from the distant river, glooming the landscape in a vaporous haze. The birds had ceased singing, a sudden pall seemed to spread itself far and near. Now she saw men and women, an angry, excited mob, not many — perhaps a dozen in all. They were the riffraff of the village, the idle, the lazy, the dissolute. Gret and her husband were well in advance — they were running, the rest trailing behind, supporting the old crone in the rear. When they reached the inclosure they saw the girl under the bare and leafless tree, the stick still grasped in her hand. A shout went up from them all; helter-skelter they leapt the palings, flinging the old crone across as if she were a bag of potatoes. Gret was the first to reach the tree; with venomous ire she shook her fist in the girl's face.

"Lieschen!" she shrieked. "Where is my child, my sweet little one? Jade, what hast thou done with her?"

"I!" stammered the girl. She was deadly white; her teeth chattered in her head.

"Aye, thou, thou, thou!" screeched Gret, her voice rising in shriller inflections, as she tried to grasp hold of her arm.

"Have a care," cried some one, "the cat will spring upon thee and claw thee to pieces."

The burly lout, Gret's husband, caught her by the arm and dragged her back. In truth the cat looked dangerous. With her fur on end, so that she looked almost twice her natural size, her lips drawn back in a ferocious snarl, showing the gleaming teeth between, her eyes dazzling with electric flashes, she crouched back ready to spring. So formidable did she look that even the most hulking bully carefully backed out of her reach.

"The jade is a witch," croaked the old hag, "and that beast is the devil's own imp, given to her as an ally. Surely, no one ever saw cat act thus before."

"Aye, she is a witch. A witch of a surety, — a witch," was tossed from one ignorant mouth to another.

"Else had she not bamboozled the pastor so," cried Gret. "Thou wanton, thou madest the good Frau Pastorin die so that thou couldst have thy own godless way in everything up at the house, thou jade, thou."

"Let us know what has become of Lieschen," broke in her husband, "then thou mayest say whatever is on thy evil tongue, and may it fly away with thee to the devil."

" I know nothing of Lieschen," said the girl.
Her temples were throbbing ; her wits, usually so
alert, had entirely forsaken her.   A scene arose in
her mind's eye — was it not there, outside on the
highway, where years ago they had all but stoned
her to death ?   Gret had been there too — they
were children then, now they had grown up in
strength and ferociousness.   Now the whole thing
would be acted over again — she knew it — only
this time there would be no awakening, only in
the dim shadow land where her hunted soul would
be at rest.   Already the film of death was over
her eyes; stark and rigid she stood as if turned to
stone.

" Dost thou mean to say," spluttered the old
hag, " that thou didst not draw the child to thee,
and took her up in thy arms, and cozened her and
wheedled her, and walked away to the woods with
her ? "

" 'T is true I took the child in my arms," replied
the girl, " and comforted her because she ran after
me and would not let me go."

" Aha ! " shrieked Gret.   " What didst thou lie
for then, and deny thou knewest anything of her ?
What hast thou done with her ? Speak quick ! or
I will tear thy eyes out."

" I told her to go home. She went the wrong
way, but I called her back, and watched her run as
fast as she could towards home."

" How comes it, then," demanded her father,
" that nothing has been seen of her all the afternoon ? To every house in the village have we

been, everybody has been questioned, no one has seen her since she was with thee."

" She took her away," mumbled the old crone, pointing at Jette; " she carried her into the woods — I saw her. I wanted to snatch the child away from her, but she would not let me, and called me foul and abusive names."

" Why didst thou not come sooner and tell?" asked a hulking fellow.

" Because she is a witch, I tell thee," whimpered the old hag; " she put a murrain upon me so that I stumbled and fell, breaking my basket of eggs under me. Had I been lusty as thou, thou ox, I should not have been so long gathering myself together again."

The wind blew a strand of hair across the girl's face. As she raised her hand to brush it out of her eyes her mantle opened, disclosing the blood-stained fichu beneath. Gret's eyes fairly started out of her head, and she raised her hand to point an accusing finger at it.

" She has killed her!" she shrieked; " she has murdered my baby. Oh, my darling, my little one, these eyes will never, never see thee any more."

" What is this?" said the father, aghast; " blood, girl, upon thy clothing! and thy hand — see — it is stained all over."

She stared down as if bereft of her senses. A shudder convulsed her from head to foot; she flung the stick from her as if it branded her skin. Her handkerchief fluttered down to the ground close to

where the man stood. A cry, which swelled to a
roar, went up simultaneously, as all dived down to
pick up this indisputable evidence of her guilt.
Gret shrieked and wrung her hands, and was only
with difficulty restrained from flying at the throat
of the girl.

"Girl," said the father sternly, "now thou
shalt confess. See! the stick is still wet and slippery — whose blood is this?"

"Mine," she cried; "the thorns pierced my
hand, — see, it bleeds still. Are you all mad,
bereft of all reason? Why should I hurt the little
innocent? — did I not nurse her through the fever,
and love her as if she were my own? and now you
accuse me of killing her!"

"'T is true," they all said. They looked at
each other. The time when she had gone among
them, fearless of the scourge which had devastated
their homes, came back to them.

But it infuriated Gret the more. Like a red
rag to a mad bull was all mention of that time to
her when she had fled in cowardly fear, leaving
her sick child to the mercy of strangers.

"Thou wanton, thou!" she screeched; "thou
take care of my child!   Only too glad wert thou
of the opportunity to meet thy paramour, who has
now left thee, as thou deservest. Tell me, what
thou hast done with the little one, or I will tear
the words from thy lying tongue."

"'T is useless to harass me further," said the
girl; "as Heaven hears me, I know nothing further of the child than what I have told you."

"Go into the woods," croaked the old hag; "I warrant ye, ye'll find the little body there. She has killed her, and gathered the blood that she may sprinkle it over the altar in her synagogue, for it is near Passover time."

At this, in all her fright, the girl could not help laughing, for it sounded too grotesque to her. Infuriated beyond all bounds, Gret sprang at her, dealing her a sounding blow on the cheek. Then a fearful thing happened. Before she had fairly withdrawn her hand Minka was upon her, tearing, spitting, clawing, wherever she could find a place.

The most frightful shrieks rent the air; not one of those present ever forgot the woman's cries of agony. They broke down the trees in their frantic efforts to arm themselves with something to beat off the savage animal. Jette cried and implored them to let her alone to manage the cat. She was knocked down, trampled upon — savage fists beat her till she could neither see nor hear any more.

"Die Post im Walde!" rang out clear and shrill. A post-chaise came whirling down the road as fast as the four horses, reeking with foam, could bear it. In front of one of the postilions a little child sat, her long fair hair streaming far behind her.

"Lieschen!" cried all with one accord. They looked at each other; they slunk away. Presently there would be a fearful reckoning for them.

The father remained. His wife lay maimed and

senseless on the ground, her eyes torn out of her head. But he had his little daughter back, his Lieschen. He motioned the postilions to stop, and the child sprang joyfully into his arms. The door of the post-chaise was flung back, the doctor stepped out.

" A little runaway," he said genially; " we picked her up on the road and brought her back." He looked into the man's face, saw the ashen pallor there, his torn, disordered clothing, and the terrified manner in which he occasionally turned his head toward the inclosure. A peculiar, heartrending sound struck upon his ear.

"Gracious Heaven," he cried, ".what is that?" He looked over the paling, and with one bound vaulted over. There lay Minka, her head literally battered in, a ferocious grin upon her dead face. Quite close to her was Gret, a frightful object to look upon. It was she whom the doctor had heard moan. And there prone upon her face he saw *her*.

Upon the bed in which the Frau Pastorin had died they laid her. The pastor knelt beside her, his white head bowed in his hands. Babbett held the cushions against the battered form, whose head was pillowed on her lover's breast. Her breaking eyes were looking into his breaking heart. For him the sun would rise nevermore, — nevermore. She made an almost imperceptible gesture, but he understood. He put her arms around his neck — those arms which had been his all of earthly bliss.

Her smile, which already saw heaven open, shed a reflecting halo over his face. With a sigh which received her soul on its expiring breath she laid her lips upon his. As she had given him her all, so she gave him her last. Her toil up the mountain was done.